Jane Casey

The Missing

EBURY
PRESS

Published in 2010 by Ebury Press, an imprint of Ebury Publishing
A Random House Group Company

The Random House Group Limited Reg. No. 954009

Addresses for companies within the Random House Group can be found at
www.randomhouse.co.uk

A CIP catalogue record for this book is available from the British Library

Typeset in Adobe Caslon by Palimpsest Book Production Limited,
Grangemouth, Stirlingshire

ISBN 9780091935993

To buy books by your favourite authors and register for offers visit
www.randomhouse.co.uk

Penguin Random House is committed to a sustainable future for
our business, our readers and our planet. This book is made from
Forest Stewardship Council® certified paper.

Printed and bound in Great Britain by Clays Ltd, St Ives plc

For my mother and father, with love

Those houses, that are haunted, are most still
Till the devil be up.

Webster, *The Duchess of Malfi*

Some of it, I remember very well. Other parts aren't so clear. Over the years, I've shaded in the bits I can't quite recall until I'm not sure which details are real and which I've made up. But this is how I think it started.

I think this is what happened.

This is the best I can do.

1992

I am lying on a scratchy tartan picnic rug in the garden, pretending to read. It's mid-afternoon and the sun is hot on the top of my head and my back, scorching the soles of my feet. My school is closed today for teacher training and I have been outside for hours. The rug is covered with bits of grass that I have ripped up from the lawn; they tickle where they touch my bare skin. My head is heavy, my eyelids drooping. The words on the page march around like ants, no matter how hard I try to keep them in neat lines, and I give in, pushing the book to one side and burying my head in my arms.

Parched grass crackles under the rug, brown and dying from weeks of hot weather. Bees hum in the summer roses, and not far away a lawn-mower drones. The radio is on in the kitchen, a woman's voice rising and falling in measured cadences, interrupted occasionally by a burst of music. The words are indistinct, blurring into one another. A regular thunk-thud-thud is my brother playing tennis against the side of the house. Racket, wall, ground. Thunk-thud-thud. I have already asked if I can play with him. He'd rather play alone than with me; that's how it goes when you're four years younger and a girl.

I peek through my arms at a ladybird climbing up a blade of grass. I like ladybirds; I have just done a project on them in school. I hold my finger out so the ladybird can walk onto it, but it lifts up its wings and flies away. A tickle on my calf is a fat black fly; they seem to be everywhere this year, and they have been landing on me all afternoon. I bury my head deeper in the cradle of my arms, shutting my eyes. The rug smells of warm wool and sweet summer days. The sun is hot and the bees are murmuring a lullaby.

Minutes or hours later, I hear feet crossing the lawn, crushing the dry, brittle grass at every step. Charlie.

'Tell Mum I'll be back soon.'

The feet move away again.

I don't look up. I don't ask where he's going. I'm more asleep than awake. I might even be dreaming already.

When I open my eyes, I know that something has happened, but not what. I don't know how long I have slept. The sun is still high in the sky, the lawnmower still thrums, the radio burbles, but something is missing. It takes me a moment to realise that the ball isn't bouncing any more. The racket is on the ground, and my brother is gone.

Chapter 1

I didn't go out looking for her; I just couldn't stand to stay at home. I'd left school as soon as the last class ended, avoiding the staffroom and going straight to the car park, where my tired little Renault started at the first time of asking. It was the first thing that had gone right all day.

I usually didn't leave straight after school. I had got into the habit of staying behind in my quiet classroom. Sometimes I worked on lesson plans or marked homework. Often I would just sit and gaze out of the window. The silence would press against my ears as if I was fathoms below sea level. There was nothing to make me resurface; I had no children to rush home to, no husband to see. All that was waiting for me at home was grief, in every sense of the word.

But today was different. Today I had had enough. It was a warm day in early May and the afternoon sun heated the air inside my car beyond comfort. I rolled my window down, but in nose-to-tail rush-hour traffic I barely got up enough speed to ruffle my hair. I wasn't used to fighting through the school traffic and my arms ached from gripping the steering wheel too hard. I put the radio on and snapped it off again after a few seconds. It wasn't far from the school to my house; the journey usually took fifteen minutes. That afternoon, I sat in the car and fumed for almost fifty.

The house was quiet when I got back. Too quiet. I stood in the cool, dim hall and listened, feeling the hairs on my arms lift from the drop in temperature. My top was clammy under the arms and along my spine and I shivered a little, chilled. The sitting-room door was open, exactly as I had left it that morning. The only sound from the kitchen was the two-note drip from the kitchen tap, falling into the cereal bowl I had left in the sink after breakfast. I would have laid money that no one had been in there since I went to work. Which meant . . .

With little enthusiasm, I started up the stairs, slinging my bag on the newel post as I passed it. 'I'm back.'

That got a response of sorts – a scuffling sound from the bedroom at the end of the hall. Charlie's room. The door was closed and I hesitated on the landing, unsure whether to knock or not. At the precise second I'd decided to make my escape, the handle turned. It was too late to reach my bedroom before the door opened, so I stood and waited with resignation. The first words would tell me everything I needed to know about how her day had been.

'What do you want?'

Belligerence, barely contained.

Pretty much normal.

'Hi, Mum,' I said. 'Everything OK?'

The door, which had only opened a crack, swung back further. I could see Charlie's bed, the bed sheets ruffled slightly from where Mum had been sitting. She was still in her dressing gown and slippers, clinging on to the handle and swaying slightly, like a cobra. She frowned deeply, trying to focus.

'What are you doing?'

'Nothing.' I suddenly felt very tired. 'I've just come home from work, that's all. I was just saying hello.'

'I didn't think you'd be back for a while.' She looked puzzled and faintly suspicious. 'What time is it?'

As if that mattered to her. 'I'm a bit earlier than usual,' I said, without explaining why. There was no point. She wouldn't care. She didn't care about much.

Except Charlie. Charlie boy. Charlie was her darling, all right. His room was pristine. Not a thing had changed in sixteen years. Not a toy soldier had moved, not a poster had been allowed to peel off the walls. A stack of folded clothes waited to be put away in the chest of drawers. The clock on the bedside table was still ticking. His books were arranged neatly on shelves above the bed: schoolbooks, comics, thick hardback guides to planes of the Second World War. Boy books. It was all just as it had been when he disappeared, as if he could walk back in and pick up where he left off. I missed him – every day I missed him – but I hated that room.

Mum was fidgeting now, running the belt of her dressing gown through her fingers. 'I was just tidying up,' she said. I refrained from asking what exactly had needed tidying in the room that never changed. The air in there was stale, stagnant. I caught an acrid waft of unwashed flesh and partially metabolised alcohol and felt a spasm of revulsion. All I wanted was to get away, get out of the house and go as far away as possible.

'Sorry. I didn't mean to bother you.' I backed down the hall towards my room. 'I'm just going to go out for a run.'

'A run,' Mum repeated, her eyes narrowing. 'Well, don't let me keep you.'

I was wrong-footed by her change of tone. 'I – I thought I was disturbing you.'

'Oh no, please yourself. You always do.'

I shouldn't have responded. I shouldn't have let myself get drawn in. Usually, I knew better than to think I could win.

'What's that supposed to mean?'

'I think you know.' With the help of the door handle, she pulled herself up to her full height, half an inch shorter than me – in other words, not tall. 'You come and go as you please. It's always whatever suits you, isn't it, Sarah?'

I would have had to count to a million to keep my temper. Nonetheless, I bit back what I really wanted to say, which was: *shut up, you selfish bitch. I'm only here because of my misguided sense of loyalty. I'm only here because Dad wouldn't want you to be left alone, and for no other reason, because you burned through whatever love I had for you a long time ago, you ungrateful, self-pitying cow.*

What I actually said was: 'I didn't think you'd mind.'

'Think? You didn't think at all. You never do.'

Her hauteur was spoiled slightly by a stumble as she stalked past me, heading for her bedroom. In the doorway she paused. 'When you come back, don't disturb me. I'm going to bed early.'

As if I wanted to go near her in the first place. But I nodded as if I understood, turning the movement into a slow, sarcastic shake of my head once the door had slammed behind her. I shut myself in my own room with a sense of release. She was unbelievable, as I informed the picture of my father that stood on my bedside table. 'You owe me,' I muttered. 'Really, properly owe me.'

He smiled on, unmoved, and after a second or two I stirred myself into action, digging under the bed for my trainers.

It was the greatest of pleasures to strip off my creased, damp clothes and pull on running shorts and vest, to tie my thick curls out of the way and feel the cool air on my neck. After a moment's hesitation I put on a lightweight jacket, conscious of the evening chill, even though the day had been warm. I grabbed my water bottle and my phone and headed out, sniffing the air appreciatively as I stood on the front doorstep, shaking the stiffness out of my legs. It had just gone five and the sun was still bright, the light warm and golden. The blackbirds were calling to one another across the gardens as I set off down the road, not too fast at first, feeling my breathing quicken before it settled into a rhythm that matched my stride. I lived in a small cul-de-sac on the Wilmington Estate, a development built to accommodate Londoners pursuing the suburban dream in the 1930s. Curzon Close was a neglected little backwater of twenty houses, inhabited by those residents who'd lived there for years, like me and Mum, and the newcomers, refugees from London house prices. One of the new arrivals was out in her front garden and I smiled at her shyly as I jogged by. No response. I shouldn't have been surprised. We didn't, on the whole, have much to do with the neighbours, even the ones who'd been there as long as we had, or even longer. Especially the ones who'd been there as long as we had, maybe. The ones who might remember. The ones who might know.

I picked up speed as I reached the main road, trying to outrun my own thoughts. I had been sideswiped all day by long-suppressed memories that rose to the surface of my mind, greasy bubbles in a stagnant pond. It was strange; I hadn't felt the least twinge of foreboding when there was a knock on my classroom door at five minutes to twelve. I had been alone, getting myself organised for my Year 8 class, and opened the door to find Elaine Pennington, the fierce and intensely frightening head teacher of Edgeworth School for Girls, and, behind her, tall and glowering, a man. A parent, in fact. Jenny Shepherd's father, I realised after a second. He had looked grim, desolate, and straightaway I had known that there was a problem.

I couldn't help replaying the scene in my head, as I had been all day. Elaine hadn't wasted any time on introductions.

'Do you have your Year 8 group next lesson?'

After working for her for nearly a year, I was still thoroughly intimidated by Elaine. Her presence was enough to glue my tongue to the roof of my mouth with fear. 'Er – yes,' I'd managed eventually. 'Who were you looking for?'

'All of them.' It was Mr Shepherd who had spoken, cutting across whatever Elaine was starting to say. 'I need to ask them if they know where my daughter is.'

They had come in then, both of them, Mr Shepherd pacing back and forth restlessly. I had met him in November at my first round of parent-teacher meetings, when he had been loudly cheerful, cracking jokes that made his pretty, glamorous wife roll her eyes good-naturedly. Jenny had Mrs Shepherd's fine-boned build and long-lashed eyes, but she'd inherited her father's smile. Today that smile had not been in evidence in my classroom, his anxiety vibrating in the air around him, lines scoring his forehead above dark, intense eyes. He towered over me, but his physical strength was undermined by his evident distress. He fetched up by one of the windows and leaned against the sill as if his legs wouldn't support him any longer, looking at us hopelessly, hands dangling by his sides, waiting.

'I suppose I should fill you in, Sarah, so you know what's going on. Mr Shepherd came to see me this morning to ask for our help in finding his daughter, Jennifer. She went out over the weekend – on Saturday, wasn't it?'

Shepherd nodded. 'Saturday evening. Around six.'

I tallied it up and bit my lip. Saturday evening, and it was now nearly midday on Monday. Almost two days. Not long – or a lifetime too long, depending on your perspective.

'He and Mrs Shepherd waited, but there was no sign of her by nightfall, and no answer from her mobile phone. They went out looking for her along the route they thought she had taken, but didn't find any sign of her. On their return, Mrs Shepherd called the police, but they weren't particularly helpful.'

'They said she'd come back in her own time.' His voice was low, gravelly, filled with pain. 'They said that girls that age don't have any idea of time. They told us to keep calling her mobile, and if she didn't pick up, to call all of her friends and ask their parents if they'd seen her. They said that she'd have to be missing for longer before they would do anything. They said a kid goes missing in the UK every five minutes – can you believe that? – and they can't commit resources until they're concerned the child is at risk. They said a twelve-year-old wasn't particularly vulnerable, that she'd probably turn up and say sorry for worrying us. As if she'd go out and not come back and not tell us where she was if everything was OK. They didn't know my daughter.' He looked at me. 'You know her, don't you? You know she'd never just go off without telling us.'

'I can't imagine that she'd do that,' I said carefully, thinking of what I knew of Jenny Shepherd. Twelve years old, pretty, academically diligent, always ready with a smile. There was no hint of rebellion in her, none of the anger that I saw in some of the older girls, who seemed to take vindictive pleasure in worrying their parents. My throat had closed up with worry for her, with the dreadful familiarity of what he was saying – *two days missing* – and I had to clear it to speak. 'Did you manage to convince them to take it seriously?'

He laughed, without humour. 'Oh yes. They took me seriously once the dog turned up.'

'The dog?'

'She was out walking the dog on Saturday evening. She has a little Westie – a West Highland terrier – and it's one of her jobs to walk him twice a day, unless there's a very good reason why she can't. That was one of the conditions she had to agree to before we got the dog. She had to take responsibility for it.' He sagged against the windowsill, suddenly stricken. 'And she did. She's so good with that animal. She never minds going out in bad weather or early in the morning. Totally devoted. So I knew, as soon as I saw the bloody dog, I knew that something had happened to her.' He choked a little, blinking away tears. 'I should never have let her go out on her own, but I thought she was safe . . .'

He buried his face in his hands and Elaine and I waited for him to recover his composure, not wanting to intrude on his private grief. I didn't know what Elaine was thinking, but I found it pretty unbearable. After a moment, the bell for the end of class cut through the silent room and he jumped, brought back to himself.

'So the dog just turned up at your house?' I prompted once the bell had vibrated itself to silence.

He looked baffled for a second. 'Oh – yes. It was around eleven o'clock. We opened the door and there he was.'

'Did he still have his lead on?' I could tell that both of them thought I had taken leave of my senses, but I wanted to know if Jenny had let the dog off the lead and then lost sight of it. She might have stayed out late looking for it, and could have had an accident. On the other hand, she might have lost hold of the lead – perhaps if someone had made her let go of it. No dog lover would choose to let a dog run around unsupervised with a trailing lead; it would be too easy for it to get tangled up in something and hurt itself.

'I don't remember,' he said eventually, rubbing his forehead in bewilderment.

Elaine took over the story. 'Michael – Mr Shepherd

– went to the police station in person and asked them to investigate, and they finally got started on filling out the correct forms around midnight.'

'By which time she'd been gone for six hours,' Shepherd interjected.

'That's ridiculous. Don't they know how important it is to find missing children quickly?' I couldn't believe they had been so slow; I couldn't believe they had waited to take his statement. 'The first twenty-four hours are critical, absolutely key, and they threw away a quarter of them.'

'I didn't realise you were so knowledgeable, Sarah,' Elaine said, smiling thinly, and I read the expression on her face all too easily. *Shut up and listen, you stupid girl.*

'The police helicopter went up around two,' Michael Shepherd went on. 'They used their infrared camera to search the woods where she usually walked Archie. They said she'd glow, even in undergrowth, from her body heat, and they'd see her. But they didn't find anything.'

So either she wasn't there or her body was no longer emitting heat. You didn't have to be an expert to work out where this was going.

'They keep saying it takes time to trace a runaway. I told them, she's not a runaway. When they didn't find her in the woods, they started looking at CCTV from the stations around here, to see if she went to London. She wouldn't do that; she found it scary, any time we went there with her. She wouldn't let go of my hand the whole time when we went Christmas shopping last year. The crowds were so dense, and she was afraid she'd get lost.'

He looked from me to Elaine and back again, helplessly. 'She's out there somewhere and they haven't found her, and she's all alone.'

My heart twisted with sympathy for him and his wife and for what they were going through, but my mind was still turning over what he had said and there was a question I had to ask. 'Why hasn't there been an appeal? Shouldn't they be asking people if they've seen her?'

'They wanted to wait. They told us that it was best to have a look themselves first, before they had to deal with false sightings and members of the public starting their own search, getting in the way. We wanted to go out looking ourselves, but they told us to wait at home in case she came back. At this stage, I just don't think she's going to walk through the door under her own steam.' He ran his hands through his hair, digging his fingers into his scalp. 'Yesterday, they searched along the river, by the railway line near our house, the reservoir up near the A3 and the woods, and they still haven't found her.'

I wondered if he could miss the awful significance of the places they were focusing on. Whatever her parents thought, the police seemed to have made up their minds that what they were searching for was a body.

Without noticing, I'd reached the edge of the woods. I put on a turn of speed and slipped in between two oaks, following a sketchy path that forked almost immediately. On the right side, I saw a chocolate-brown Labrador barrelling towards me, towing a slender, elderly woman in pristine slacks and full make-up. It didn't look like the kind of dog that spooked easily, but even so, I turned to the left path, running away from where people might be. The path I took looked more challenging. It led towards the middle of the woods, where the tracks were narrow and steep and tended to peter out unexpectedly in a welter of brambles and unkempt bushes. The paths nearer the road were the dog walkers' favourites, well worn and wide. A wide, even path wouldn't distract me from the dark beat of tension that had been thudding monotonously in my head all day with heavy, unforgiving force. I headed uphill, thinking about Jenny's father.

The quiet of the classroom was disturbed again, this time by scuffling outside the door, footsteps clattering up the corridor, and voices. Jenny's classmates, 8A. There was a ripple of laughter and Michael Shepherd flinched.

I let them in, telling them to hurry to their seats. Their eyes were round with curiosity at the sight of the head teacher and a parent; this was far better than discussing *Jane Eyre*. Michael Shepherd squared his shoulders as if preparing for a round in the boxing ring and faced his daughter's contemporaries. The role of victim didn't suit him. The desire to do something had driven him to the school. He wouldn't wait around for the police; he would do what he thought was right and deal with the consequences later.

Once they were all waiting in their places, silently attentive, Elaine began to speak.

'Some of you will know Mr Shepherd, I'm sure, but for those of you who don't, this is Jennifer's father. I want you all to listen very carefully to what he has to say. If you can help him in any way, I am sure you will do so.'

Rows of heads nodded obediently. Michael Shepherd moved to stand beside Elaine at her invitation. He looked around the room, seeming slightly confused.

'You all look so different in your uniforms,' he said eventually. 'I know I've met some of you before, but I can't quite . . .'

A ripple of amusement went through the class, and I hid a smile. I'd had the same experience myself in reverse, seeing some of my students in town at the weekend. They looked so much older and more sophisticated out of uniform. It was unsettling.

He had spotted a couple of girls he recognised. 'Hi, Anna. Rachel.'

They blushed and mumbled hello, simultaneously delighted and appalled to be singled out.

'I know this is going to sound silly,' he began, trying to smile, 'but we've lost our daughter. We haven't seen her for a couple of days now, and I was wondering if any of you had heard from her or if you had any idea where she is.' He waited for a beat, but no one said anything. 'I know it's a lot to ask – I do understand that Jenny may have her own reasons for not coming home. But her mother is very worried, as am I, and we just want to know that she's OK. If you haven't seen her, I'd like to know whether anyone has spoken to her or had any contact with her since Saturday evening – a text or an email or whatever.'

There was a muted chorus of 'no' from around the room.

'OK, well, I'd like to ask you to check when you last

heard from Jenny, and what she said. Does anyone know if she had any plans to go somewhere over the weekend? She won't get in trouble – we just need to know that she's safe.'

The girls stared at him in silence. He had earned their sympathy, but no useful response. Elaine stepped in.

'I want you all to think very carefully about what Mr Shepherd has asked you, and if you remember anything – anything at all – that you think we should know, I'd like you to tell us. You can talk to me in complete confidence, or Miss Finch, or you can ask your parents to call me if you feel more comfortable talking to them.' Her face darkened. 'I know you are all too sensible to keep quiet because of some misplaced sense of loyalty to Jennifer.' She turned to me. 'Miss Finch, we'll leave you to get on with your class.'

I could tell that Michael Shepherd was unhappy about leaving the classroom without finding out anything from his daughter's classmates, though he had little choice but to follow Elaine as she swept out. He nodded to me as he went, and I smiled, trying to think of something to say, but he was gone before anything remotely suitable occurred to me. He walked with his head down, like a bull being led into an abattoir, all that power and determination draining away, leaving only despair.

In the woods, the traffic noise fell away as if a soundproof curtain had dropped behind me. The birds sang and a breeze sighed through the treetops with a sound like rushing water. The rhythmic thud of my feet on the dark, firm ground punctuated the rasping of my breath and every now and then a singing note was the whiplash of a thin, reaching branch that had snagged on my sleeve for an instant. Tall, ancient trees with knotted trunks spread a canopy of bitingly green new leaves overhead. The sunlight slid through their shade in slanting beams and pinpricks of light, dizzying brilliance that glanced off a surface and was gone the next instant. I felt, briefly, almost happy.

I kicked myself up a long, steep hill, toes digging for purchase in the leaf mould, my heart thumping as my muscles burned. The ground was as dark and rich as chocolate cake; it had just enough give in it. I had run on iron-hard, ankle-killing parched earth the previous summer, and slithered through slick mud on icy days midwinter, black splashes streaking up the backs of my legs like tar. These conditions were perfect. No excuses. I fought all the way to the top, to the pay-off downhill slope on the other side, and it felt as if I was flying.

After a while, of course, the euphoria wore off. My legs started to complain at the exertion, my thigh muscles aching. I could run through that sort of niggling discomfort, but my knees were also protesting and that was more serious. I winced as a careless step on the uneven surface jarred my left knee, sending a jolt of pain up the outside of my thigh. Checking my watch, I was surprised to see that half an hour had slid by since I left the house; I had done about three and a half miles. It was far enough to count as a decent run by the time I got home.

I made a wide loop and doubled back on myself, running parallel to the route I'd taken on the way out. There was something disheartening about running over the same ground on the way back; I hated to do it. The new route took me along a spine of higher ground that ran between two steep-sided depressions. The surface here was crumbly and knotted with roots. I slowed right down, wary of twisting an ankle, eyes glued to the ground in front of me. Even so, I came to grief, skidding on a smooth root that angled sharply downwards. With a muffled squawk I pitched forward, hands outstretched, and ended up sprawling in the dirt. I stayed in that position for a second, my breath rasping, the woods around me suddenly hushed. Slowly, painfully, I peeled my hands off the ground and sat back on my heels to inspect the damage. No broken bones, no blood. *Good.* I brushed the worst of the dirt off my hands and knees. Bruises, maybe a slight graze on the heel of my right hand. Nothing too remarkable. I stood up, holding on to a convenient tree trunk for support, grimacing as I stretched out my legs, glad that no one had seen me fall. I bent forward and stretched out my hamstrings, then walked around in a tight circle, gathering the motivation to carry on. I was about to set off again when I stopped, frowning. Something nagged at me, something strange that I'd half seen out of the corner of my eye, something out of context. Even then, it didn't occur to me to worry, even though I'd been thinking of the missing girl all day.

I stood on tiptoe and looked properly, peering through the gathering shadows. Down in the hollow to my left there was a gap in the leaf canopy where an old tree had fallen, and a shaft of sunlight illuminated that patch of undergrowth like a stage set. The hollow was entirely filled with bluebells that crowded around the fallen tree. The flowers' hazy bluish purple mirrored the clear evening sky above. All around, silvery-white birches lined the clearing, their bark streaked with definite black lines, their leaves the sour-apple green of new growth. The sunlight picked out the tiny bodies of flies and gnats, turning them to gold as they whirled in endless circles above the petals.

That wasn't what had caught my attention, though. I frowned, hands on hips, scanning the clearing. Something was off. What was it? Trees, flowers, sunshine, so pretty – so what?

There. Something white among the bluebells. Something pale behind the tree trunk. I edged down the bank carefully, trying to get closer, straining to see. Bluebell stems crunched under my trainers, the glossy leaves squeaking as I inched forward, closer now, able to see . . .

A hand.

The breath rushed out of my lungs as if I had been punched. I think I knew right away what I was looking at, I knew what I had found, but something made me keep moving forward, something made me creep around the old tree trunk, stepping carefully over the splintered end that was brittle and hollow with rot. Along with the shock came a feeling of inevitability, a feeling that I had been moving towards this moment since I'd heard that Jenny was missing. As I crouched down beside the trunk, my heart was pounding faster than it had when I had run up the steepest hill earlier.

Jenny was lying in the lee of the fallen tree, almost

underneath it, one hand placed carefully on the middle of her narrow chest, legs decorously together. She wore jeans, black Converse shoes and a fleece that had been pale pink, but was grey around the cuffs. The hand that I had seen was the left hand, flung out at an angle. It lay among the flowers as if it had been dropped there.

Up close, the pallor of her skin had a bluish tinge and the nails were the grey-purple of an old bruise. I didn't have to touch her to know that she was far beyond help, but I reached out and ran the back of one finger along her cheek and the chill of her lifeless flesh made me shudder. I made myself look at her face, at her features, wanting to confirm what I knew to be true, knowing I would never forget what I saw. An ashy face, framed with tangled dirty blonde hair, matted and lank. Her eyes were closed, her lashes a dark fan on colourless cheeks. Her mouth was grey and bloodless; it had fallen open, pulled down by her slack jaw. Her lips stretched thinly over teeth that seemed more prominent than they had in life. Unmistakably, there were signs of violence on her face and neck: faint shadows of bruises that dappled her cheek and smudged across her fragile collarbones. A thin dark line showed on her lower lip where a narrow smear of blood had dried to black.

She lay where she had been dumped, where someone had arranged her body once they were finished with her as they had wanted her to be found. The pose was a grotesque parody of how an undertaker might display a corpse, a travesty of dignity. It couldn't take away from the reality of what had been done to her. Abused, injured, abandoned, dead. Just twelve years old. All of that limitless potential brought to nothing, just an empty husk in a quiet wood.

I had been looking at Jenny's body with a detachment that bordered on the clinical, examining every detail without really taking in what I was seeing. Now it was as if a dam burst in my brain and the full horror broke over me like a wave. Everything I had feared for Jenny had come to pass, and it was worse than I could ever have imagined. The blood roared in my ears and the ground tilted under my feet. I squeezed my water bottle tightly with both hands, the cool ridged plastic reassuringly familiar. I was drenched in sweat, but ice-cold and shivering. Waves of nausea swept over me and I shuddered, pushing my head between my knees. It was hard to think, I couldn't move and the forest spun out of control around me. For a moment, I looked and saw myself at that age – the same hair, the same shape of face, but I hadn't died, I was the one who had lived . . .

I don't know how long it would have taken for me to recover if I hadn't been brought back to myself abruptly. Somewhere behind me, not close, a dog whined once, urgently, then stopped dead as if cut off, and awareness roared back to me like an express train.

What if I wasn't alone?

I stood up and looked around the little clearing, eyes wide, alert to any sudden movements near me. I was standing beside a body that had been left there by someone – presumably whoever had murdered her. And murderers sometimes went back to a body, I had read. I swallowed nervously, a knot of fear tight in my throat. The breeze swept through the trees again, drowning out all other sounds, and I jumped as a bird whirred out of its hiding place somewhere on my right and rocketed through the branches to the open air. What had disturbed it? Should I call for help? Who would hear me in the middle of the woods, where I had gone to be alone? Stupid, stupid Sarah . . .

Before I panicked completely, cold common sense clamped down on the rising hysteria. Stupid Sarah indeed, with her mobile phone in her pocket, just waiting to be used. I dragged it out, almost sobbing with relief, then panicked again when the screen lit up to show only one bar of reception. Not enough. I scrambled back up the steep bank, holding the phone tightly. It was hard to climb up the sharp gradient and I scrabbled to get purchase with my free hand as grass and roots pulled away from the soft earth, *please please please* running through my head. Two more bars appeared as soon as I reached the top of the ridge. I stood with my back to a solid, sturdy old tree and stabbed 999 into the phone, feeling slightly unreal as I did so, my heart beating so hard that the thin material of my vest top was shaking.

'Emergency, which service?' asked a slightly nasal female voice.

'Police,' I gasped, still out of breath from the clamber up the bank and the shock I was feeling. It was as if a tight band was wrapped around my chest, constricting my ribs. Somehow, I didn't seem to be able to get a deep enough breath.

'Putting you through, thank you.' She sounded bored; it almost made me laugh.

There was a click. A different voice. 'Hello, you're through to the police.'

I swallowed. 'Yes, I – I've found a body.'

The operator sounded completely unsurprised. 'A body. Right. Whereabouts are you at the moment?'

I did my best to describe the location, getting flustered as the operator pushed me for more details. It wasn't exactly easy to pinpoint where I was without convenient road signs or buildings to act as points of reference, and I got completely confused when she asked if I was to the east of the main road, first saying yes, then contradicting myself. My head felt fuzzy, as if there was static interfering with my thoughts. The woman on the other end of the line was patient with me, warm even, which made me feel even worse about how useless I was being.

'It's all right, you're doing fine. Can you tell me your name, please?'

'Sarah Finch.'

'And you're still with the body,' the operator checked.

'I'm nearby,' I said, wanting to be accurate. 'I – I know her. Her name is Jenny Shepherd. She's been reported missing – I saw her father this morning. She—' I broke off, struggling not to cry.

'Is there any sign of life? Can you check if the person is breathing for me?'

'She's cold to the touch – I'm sure she's dead.' *Cover her face. Mine eyes dazzle. She died young.*

The woods spiralled around me again, and as my eyes filled with tears I reached back to touch the tree trunk behind me. It was solidly real and reassuring.

The operator was talking. 'OK, Sarah, the police will be with you shortly. Just stay put and keep your mobile phone switched on. They may ring you to get further directions.'

'I can go nearer to the road,' I offered, suddenly oppressed by the stillness, horribly aware of what was hidden behind the tree down in the gully.

'Just stay where you are,' the operator said firmly. 'They'll find you.'

When she had hung up, I sagged to the ground, still clutching my phone, my lifeline. The breeze had picked up and I was cold in spite of my jacket, chilled to the bone, and utterly exhausted. But it was all right. They were coming. They would be there soon. All I had to do was wait.

1992

Three hours missing

I run into the kitchen as soon as I hear Mum
calling. Being indoors feels weird at first – dark
and cool, like being underwater. The tiles are
cold under my bare feet. I slide into a chair at
the kitchen table where two places are laid: one
for me, one for Charlie. Mum has poured two
glasses of milk and I take a big gulp from the
one in front of me. The sweet coldness slides
down my throat and into my stomach, spreading
a chill through my body that makes me wriggle.
I put the glass down carefully, without making
a sound.

'Did you wash your hands?'

She hasn't even turned around from the
cooker. I look at my palms. Too dirty to lie. With
a sigh, I get off my chair and go to the kitchen
sink. I let the water run over my fingers for a
minute, making a cup of my hands and filling
it to overflowing. Because I feel lazy and Mum
isn't watching, I don't use soap, even though

my hands are tacky with grime and sweat. The water drums on the sink, drowning out my mother's voice. It's only when I turn off the tap that I hear her.

'I said, where's your brother?'

Telling the truth feels like a betrayal. 'I haven't seen him.'

'Since when?' She doesn't wait for an answer, walking to the back door to look out. 'Honestly, he should know better than to turn up late for his tea. Don't you turn into a teenage rebel when you're Charlie's age.'

'He's not a teenager.'

'Not yet, but he acts like one sometimes. Wait until your father hears about this.'

I kick the chair leg. Mum says a word I know I'm not supposed to hear, something I store away, even though I know I definitely shouldn't repeat it – at least, not in front of her. She goes back to the cooker, scooping up oven chips with fast, angry movements. Some of them skid off the tray and fall on the floor and she throws the spoon down with a clatter. When it comes, my plate is overloaded with food. Two eggs glistening with oil stare up at me, a pile of chips beside them, balanced like a game of spillikins. Carefully, I draw out one chip from the bottom of the pile and press the sharp end of it into a round, quivering egg. Yellow oozes out onto the plate, mingling with the ketchup I squiggle over everything. I expect to be told off for playing with my food, but Mum leaves me to eat alone and I hear her at the front of the house, calling Charlie. I plough through the stack of chips, the sound of chewing too loud in the quiet kitchen. I eat until my stomach aches, until my jaw is tired. When Mum comes back, I think she'll be annoyed with me for leaving food on my plate, but she tips the leftovers into the bin and doesn't say anything.

I am still sitting at the table, dazed with food, when Mum goes into the hall to phone my father. Anxiety gives an edge to her voice, an edge that makes me nervous, even though I'm not the one in trouble.

The hands of the kitchen clock slide around the face and there's still no sign of Charlie and I'm scared. And almost in spite of myself, without really knowing why, I start to cry.

Chapter 2

It took Surrey's finest quite a while to reach me, in the end.

I sat with my back to the tree and watched the sky fade in colour as the sun slid down towards the horizon. The shadows lengthened and joined up around me. It was getting dark under the trees and cold. I wrapped my arms around my knees, holding them close, trying to hug myself warm. I checked my watch every minute or so, for no real reason. The operator hadn't been very specific about how long it would take the police to get there. It didn't matter, really. It wasn't as if I had somewhere better to go.

I didn't really believe that Jenny's killer would come back to that quiet spot in the woods, but my heart still pounded at every sudden noise and half-seen movement. Tiny sounds all around me suggested invisible animals going about their business, unmoved by my presence, but every rustle in the dry leaves had me twitching with nerves. I could only see a few yards in any direction as the trees grew so close together in that part of the woods, and it was hard to shake the tingle at the back of my neck that said *you're being watched* . . .

All in all, it was a great relief to hear voices in the distance, along with the rattle and cough of police radios.

I stood up, wincing as I straightened stiffening limbs, and shouted, 'Over here!' I waved my arms over my head, lighting up the screen on my mobile phone to try to attract their attention. I could see them now, two of them, moving through the trees with purpose, high-visibility jackets gleaming in the fading light. Both were male, one stocky and middle-aged, the other younger, leaner. The stocky one was in the lead and, it quickly became apparent, in charge.

'Are you Sarah Finch?' he asked, stumbling a little as he approached me. I nodded. He stopped, bracing his hands on his knees, and coughed alarmingly. 'Long way in from the road,' he explained at last in a strangulated voice, then hawked up something unspeakable and spat it to his left. 'Not used to all this exercise.'

He had taken out a handkerchief and was wiping sweat from his quivering cheeks, which were latticed with broken veins. 'I'm PC Anson and this is PC McAvoy,' he said, indicating his colleague. PC McAvoy smiled at me tentatively. He was really very young, on closer inspection. They were oddly mismatched, and I wondered, irrelevantly, what they found to talk about.

Anson had got his breath back. 'Right, so where's this body you've found, then? We've got to check before the rest of the crew turns up. Not that we think you're a nutter with nothing better to do than call 999 for kicks.' He paused for a moment. 'You'd be surprised how many of them there are, though.'

I stared at him, unimpressed, then pointed down into the hollow. 'She's down there.'

'Down that slope? Bugger it. Hop down and check it out, Mattie, would you?'

Clearly Anson resented having to do anything that involved physical exertion. McAvoy hurried to the edge of the gully and peered over.

'What am I looking for?' His voice was taut with suppressed excitement.

I stepped forward to join him. 'The body is behind the tree. The easiest way to get down is probably to your left.' I pointed to the rudimentary path I had made in my flight up the hill.

But he had already gone over the edge. Branches cracked under his feet as he ran down the slope, gathering speed as he went. I winced, anticipating a crash at the bottom. Anson rolled his eyes in a long-suffering manner. 'Enthusiasm of youth,' he said. 'He'll learn. Faster isn't always better, is it?'

The crudeness in his tone made my skin crawl.

McAvoy had made it down the hill and was peering nervously over the fallen tree. 'There's something here all right,' he shouted, his voice cracking a little on the 'something'.

'Get a closer look, Mattie, and then get back up here,' Anson boomed. He had one hand on his radio, ready to report back. I watched McAvoy sidestep the tree's tangled roots, and bend to look at what lay behind it. Even at that distance I could see the blood draining from his face. He turned away sharply, his shoulders heaving.

'For God's sake,' Anson said in disgust. 'That's a crime

scene, Mattie. I don't want to have to explain a dirty great puddle of vomit in the middle of it, thanks.'

McAvoy walked away a couple of paces, not answering. After a moment or two he turned to start back up the slope, carefully not looking in the direction of Jenny's body. 'It's a young girl. You can call it in,' he said, scrambling over the top, eyes trained on the ground. Shamefaced was not the word for how he looked. I could understand why; I doubted that Anson would be quick to forget his display of weakness. But to my surprise, the older policeman didn't comment beyond sending McAvoy to wait by their car, to guide the other police to the scene.

'I'm not walking back all that way. Hop to it, son.'

The expression on Anson's face was kindly as he watched McAvoy hurry off. 'Give him time, he'll get used to that sort of thing,' he said, almost to himself. 'He's a good lad.'

'I don't blame him for being upset.'

Anson looked at me without warmth. 'You'll have to wait, I'm afraid. CID will want to talk to you. They'd have my guts for garters if I let you swan off.'

I shrugged, then went back to sit down where I had waited before, settling against the familiar tree trunk in as comfortable position as I could, which was pretty far from being comfortable. I didn't feel like making conversation with Anson and after a moment or two he moved away, turning his back to me, hands jammed in his pockets. He was whistling quietly under his breath, the same tune over and over. It took me a second to think of the words that fitted it.

'If you go down to the woods today, you're sure of a big surprise . . .'

It was a nice touch.

PC McAvoy did his job well. Within the hour they were there, lots of them: police in uniform, men and women in disposable white paper suits with hoods, officers in blue overalls, one or two in casual clothes or suits. Most of them arrived carrying equipment: bags, boxes, canvas screens, arc lights, a stretcher complete with body bag, a generator that coughed into life and pumped a brackish mechanical smell into the air. Some paused beside me to ask questions: how had I spotted the body? What had I touched? Had I seen anyone else while I was out running? Had I noticed anything out of the ordinary? I answered almost without thinking; I told them where I had walked and stood and what I had touched, and my shivers turned to shudders of fatigue. Anson and McAvoy had disappeared, sent back to their regular duties, replaced by people whose job it was to investigate murder, who were now combing the woodland area. What a strange job they did, I couldn't help thinking. They were calmly professional, as organised and methodical as if they were in an office, shuffling paper. No one looked hurried or upset or anything but focused on the job they had to do. McAvoy was the only one who had reacted to the horror of what lay in the little clearing and I was grateful for it. I would almost have doubted the strength of my own feeling otherwise. Then again, they didn't know Jenny. I had seen her alive, vital, laughing at a joke in the back row of my class, earnestly holding her arm in the air when she had a question. I would see the gap in the ranks of her classmates, the absent face in the school photograph. They would see a file, a sheaf of photographs, evidence in bags. To them, she was a job – nothing more.

Someone had found a rough blanket and wrapped it around my shoulders. I gripped the edges of it now, holding it so tightly that my knuckles shone white. It had a strangely musty smell but I didn't care; it was warm. I watched the police moving around, their faces ghostly in the harsh grey-white light cast by the arc lights, which were now mounted on stands all around the clearing. It felt odd to be looking down on the people below, all knowing the part they had to play, moving to a rhythm I couldn't quite hear. I was very tired and I wanted more than anything to go home.

A female police officer in plain clothes detached herself from a group of people that had gathered near to the spot where Jenny's body still lay. She climbed up the slope, heading straight for me.

'DC Valerie Wade,' she said, holding out a hand. 'Call me Valerie.'

'I'm Sarah.' I worked an arm free from the heavy blanket to shake hands.

She smiled at me, blue eyes shining in the cold glare from the lights. She was round faced and slightly plump, with light brown hair. I thought she was older than me, but not much.

'I suppose it all looks very confusing.'

'Everyone looks so busy,' I said lamely.

'I can tell you what they're doing, if you like. You see those people in the white suits – they're the SOCOs. Scene of crime officers, that means. They find the clues – like on TV, you know, *CSI.*' She was speaking in a slightly sing-song voice, as if explaining their role to a child. 'And that man over there, crouching down near –'

She stopped short, and I turned, surprised at the look on her face until I realised that she was trying to avoid any reference to Jenny's body. As if I could forget it was there.

'That man, crouching down, he's the pathologist. And those two behind him are detectives, like me.'

She was pointing at two men who weren't in uniform either, one in his fifties, the other thirty-ish. The older man had hair that shaded from iron-grey to white. He stooped as he watched the pathologist at work, his shoulders rounded, his hands buried in the pockets of his wrinkled suit trousers. He seemed hollowed out by exhaustion and the look on his face was grim. He was the single still point in the flurry of activity around the crime scene. The younger detective was tall, broad-shouldered, on the thin side, with light brown hair. Energy ran through him like an electric current.

'The one with grey hair is Chief Inspector Vickers,' call-me-Valerie said reverently. 'And the other is Detective Sergeant Blake.' The change in tone between the first part of the sentence and the second was comic; she'd dropped the reverence in favour of slightly clipped disapproval, and when I glanced at her I noticed that colour had risen in her cheeks. That old story, I diagnosed: she liked him, he didn't know she existed, and even saying his name ruffled her feathers. Poor Valerie.

The pathologist looked up and gestured to a couple of the policemen who were standing nearby. They picked up the canvas screens that had been left to one side and lifted them carefully into position, hiding the next part from my view. I turned away, trying not to think about what might be happening down in the hollow. Jenny, I reminded myself, was long gone. What was left behind couldn't feel what was happening to her, couldn't care about any indignity. But I cared on her behalf.

I would have given anything at all to turn back the previous hours, to choose a different route through the woods. And yet . . . I knew very well that it could be worse to live in hope. Finding Jenny's body meant that her parents would at least know something of what had happened to their daughter. At least they would be certain that she was beyond pain, beyond fear.

I cleared my throat. 'Valerie, do you think I could head off soon? It's just that I've been here for quite a while and I'd like to get home.'

Valerie looked alarmed. 'Oh no, we'd like you to wait until the chief inspector gets a chance to speak to you. We like to talk to whoever finds a body as soon as we possibly can. And even more so this time, because you know the victim.' She leaned forward. 'Actually, I wouldn't mind finding out a bit about her, and about the parents. I'm going to be the family liaison officer. It's always good to know what I'm going to be dealing with beforehand, if at all possible.'

She would be good at that, I thought vaguely. She had

shoulders that were made for crying on, plump and cushioned. I realised she was looking at me expectantly, and I hadn't replied. All of a sudden, I didn't feel inclined to talk to her any more – I was too cold, underdressed, dirty and upset. I busied myself by taking the elastic off my ponytail and shaking my hair free. 'Do you mind if I don't talk about it now?'

'Not at all,' she said warmly, after a beat. That was probably her training kicking in: *never show your frustration with a witness. Bond with them.* She laid a hand on my arm. 'You really want to get home, don't you? But it shouldn't be much longer.' Her eyes slid over my shoulder and she brightened. 'Here they are now.'

DCI Vickers came straight over to us, his chest heaving from the climb up the bank. 'Sorry for keeping you hanging around, Miss . . .'

'Finch,' Valerie supplied.

Up close, the bags under the chief inspector's eyes spoke of too many late nights, as did the vertical trenches carved in his cheeks. His eyes were red-rimmed and threaded with veins, but the irises were a clear blue and I felt they missed nothing. He had a slightly hangdog air, the opposite of charisma, and I liked him immediately.

'Miss Finch,' he said, and shook my hand. 'I think DS Blake and I should have a chat with you before we do anything else.' His eyes swept over the blanket I was clutching around me, up to my face where I was trying to hide the fact that my teeth were chattering. 'Let's go somewhere warmer, though. I think we'd be better off at the station, if you don't mind coming back there with us.'

'Not at all,' I said, mesmerised by the chief inspector's gentle manner.

'Do you want me to drive, guv?' DS Blake asked and I turned my attention to him, noting that he was very good-looking, with a lean face and a sensitive mouth. I could tell that his offer was all about getting a head start on finding out more about Jenny. Valerie Wade crashed in desperately with: 'No point in you wasting your time doing taxi duty, Andy. I can drive her.'

'Good idea,' Vickers said, slightly absent-mindedly. 'I'm going to have a team conference at the station, so stick with me, Andy. I'd like to talk things over with you on the way.' He turned back to Valerie. 'Get Miss Finch settled in my office, and get her a cup of tea, won't you.'

Valerie herded me through the woods and into the front seat of her car in short order. I found it slightly surreal to be in a strange car – a police car, no less – driving through the familiar streets of my home town. The radio burped incomprehensibly every few seconds, and although Valerie didn't miss a beat in her attempts at small talk, I knew that she was really focused on the static-filled chatter that I couldn't interpret. The street-lights had come on and I watched the play of light and dark over the car's bonnet as Valerie drove, adhering to the rules of the road as rigorously as if I had been a driving examiner. I was in a bit of a daze by the time she pulled up outside the police station. She led me through the public area with the reception desk and, with a flourish, punched a code into a keypad to unlock a heavy door. It was painted a dull shade of green and had three or four really handsome dents in it, as if someone very frustrated had tried to kick it in.

I followed Valerie down a narrow corridor into an overheated and untidy office and sat in the chair she told me to use, beside a desk that was covered in files. The chair was a utilitarian number with rough orange fabric on the seat. It had a greyish tinge from years of use, and at some stage someone had picked a hole in the seat cover. Little crumbs of yellow foam spilled out through the frayed fabric and attached themselves to my running shorts. I brushed at them half-heartedly, then gave up.

As ordered, Valerie produced a cup of tea, strong and dark, in a mug with *Fun Run '03* on the side, then bustled off, leaving me to contemplate the posters that someone had stuck up around the little office. Florence's skyline from the Belvedere, overlooking the city. A stagnant green canal lined with gorgeously decaying buildings – *Venezia* written in hysterical italics across the bottom. Someone liked Italy, but not enough to stick the Venice poster up properly. One corner curled upwards where the Blu-tac had lost its stick, and it had been by no means straight to begin with.

There was only a mouthful or two of tea left in my mug when the door swung open and DS Blake strode in.

'Sorry for the wait. We had a few things to finish up at the scene.'

He sounded abrupt, distracted. I could tell that his mind was moving at a million miles an hour and felt even more lethargic in comparison. He leaned on a radiator behind the desk, gazing into the middle distance, and didn't say anything else. After a minute or two, I felt that he had forgotten I was there.

The door banged again as Vickers came in, carrying a cardboard folder. He threw himself into the chair opposite me and leaned on the desk for a second, one hand to his head. I could practically see the effort that was going into gathering his strength.

'So, they tell me that in addition to finding the body, you know our victim,' Vickers said at last, pinching the bridge of his nose with his eyes closed.

'Er, yes. Not well. I mean, I teach her.' All that time to think, to compose myself, and there I was, getting flustered by the first question. I took a deep breath and let it out slowly, as unobtrusively as possible. My heart was racing. Ridiculous. 'I'm her English teacher. I see – *saw* – her four times a week.'

'And that's at the posh girls' school on the hill, is it, just off the Kingston road? Edgeworth School? Costs a fair bit, doesn't it?'

'I suppose it does.'

Vickers was looking at a piece of paper from the file. 'The family home isn't in a particularly posh area. Morley Drive.'

My eyebrows shot up. 'My house is just a couple of streets away from there. I had no idea she lived so close to me.'

'So would it surprise you that they sent Jenny to such an expensive school?'

'I got the impression that the Shepherds were happy to spend their money on school fees. They wanted what was best for Jenny. They pushed her to achieve. She was a bright girl. She could have done anything with her life.' I blinked rapidly, annoyed by the tears that were thickening my voice. While I waited for Vickers to think up another question, I concentrated on picking at the chair innards. It gave me something to do. I now saw how the hole had developed. If Vickers minded me making it worse, he didn't say anything about it.

'Did you know she was missing?'

'Michael Shepherd came to the school this morning to see if he could find out anything from Jenny's classmates,' I explained. 'He didn't think the police –'

'– were taking him seriously,' Vickers finished off as I ground to a halt. He flapped a hand in my direction as if to reassure me that he didn't mind. 'Did he find out anything useful?'

'He was just . . . desperate. I think he'd have tried anything to find his daughter.' I looked up at Vickers, almost afraid to ask. 'Do they know yet? The Shepherds?'

'Not yet. Soon.' He looked even more exhausted at the thought. 'Andy and I are going to tell them ourselves.'

'It's hard on you,' I offered.

'Part of the job.' But Vickers didn't sound as if it was routine, and Blake was frowning at his feet when I looked at him.

Vickers flicked open the file and closed it again. 'So you didn't have a relationship beyond teacher and student, you said. Nothing personal there. You weren't really in touch with her outside of class.'

I shook my head. 'I mean, I kept an eye on her. That's

part of my job, to see if the girls are happy, if they're dealing with any problems. She seemed perfectly OK.'

'No hint of trouble?' Blake asked. 'Nothing that gave you cause for concern? Drugs, boyfriends, bad behaviour in class, truancy – anything like that?'

'Absolutely not. She was completely normal. Look, don't try and make Jenny into something she wasn't. She was a twelve-year-old girl. A child. She was ... she was innocent.'

'You reckon?' Blake folded his arms, cynicism in every line of his body.

I glared at him. 'Yes. There's no scandal there, OK? You're barking up the wrong tree.' I turned to Vickers. 'Look, shouldn't you be out looking for whoever did this? Checking CCTV or what the local paedophiles have been up to? There's a child killer out there, and I don't see what Jenny's attendance record has to do with it. It was probably a stranger – some creep in a car who offered her a lift or something.'

Before Vickers could speak, Blake answered, his tone sarcastic. 'Thanks for the advice, Miss Finch. We do have officers following up a number of lines of enquiry. But it might surprise you to know that, statistically, most murders are committed by people who know their victims. In fact, very often the murderers are family members.'

He didn't mean any harm. He didn't mean to sound condescending. He didn't know it was absolutely the wrong thing to say to me.

'As if the Shepherds don't have enough to worry about, now you're suggesting they're suspects? I hope you've got a better opening line than "statistically speaking, you probably did it", or I doubt you'll find it easy to gain their trust.'

'Well, actually——' Blake began, then broke off as Vickers reached out and patted his sleeve.

'Leave it now, Andy,' he murmured. Then he smiled at me. 'We have to consider all the angles, Miss Finch, even the ones that nice people like you don't like to think about. That's what they pay us for.'

'They pay you to lock criminals up,' I snapped, still rattled. 'And since I am not a criminal, maybe you could let me go home.'

'Of course,' Vickers said, and he hit Blake with a pale-blue stare. 'Take Miss Finch home, Andy. You can meet me at the Shepherds' house. Just wait outside until I get there.'

'There's no need,' I said hastily, jumping up. That earned *me* a cold stare from the stonewashed blue eyes. Vickers kept it well hidden, but he had a serious edge under the rumpled grey exterior.

'You won't miss much at the conference, Andy,' he said mildly. 'You know what I'm thinking anyway.'

Blake hooked his car keys out of his pocket and looked at me without enthusiasm. 'Ready to go?'

I headed for the door, not bothering to reply.

'Miss Finch?' came from behind me. Vickers. The senior policeman was leaning across his desk, forehead crinkling with sincerity. 'Miss Finch, I just want to reassure you before you go that violent crime is very rare. Most people never come into contact with it at all. Please, don't feel threatened by your experiences today. It really doesn't mean that you aren't safe.'

I felt he had delivered this little speech more than a few times before. I smiled a silent thank you. I didn't have the heart to tell him that I was all too familiar with violent crime already, one way or another.

Blake's car was a silver-grey Ford Focus that was parked at the far end of the police station car park. I collapsed into the passenger seat. The dashboard clock read 9.34 and I blinked at it, exhausted. I felt like it was the middle of the night.

The detective was digging around in the boot. While he couldn't see me, I had a good look at my surroundings. The car was exceptionally tidy, with none of the rubbish that accumulated in mine – no papers, no empty water bottles, no shopping bags or parking dockets. The inside was as clean as if it had just been valeted. Somewhat guiltily, I checked the mat at my feet to discover that the muddy soles of my trainers had left two dark imprints on the previously spotless pile. I put my feet down carefully, fitting them into the outlines I had already made. No point in making things worse. Besides, that way the mud would be completely invisible until I got out of the car.

There were only two clues to the life of the car's owner: the radio handset that lay on the dashboard and a laminated card that read 'Police Vehicle' in the storage space beside the handbrake. There was nothing personal at all. It didn't take an enormous leap of intuition to work out that DS Blake lived for his job.

I would have known that he was annoyed about having to drive me home even if he hadn't muttered something to me and ducked back into Vickers' office just after we'd left it. I'd heard 'Sir, couldn't Valerie—' before the door closed. I could fill in the rest of the sentence for myself. The answer had evidently been no; he was stuck with me, and I with him, for the duration of my journey home. And if I was uncomfortable about it and he was angry, that was nothing to the reaction I'd seen on the face of a pretty uniformed officer we'd passed on the way to the car park. Blake received a winning smile from her; I'd walked past a wall of disapproval mixed with envy. More than ever, I had the impression that what Blake did and who he was with was big news in that particular police station.

At last he sat into the driver's seat.

'Do you know where you're going?' I asked diffidently.

'Yep.'

Oh great. This was going to be fun.

'Look, I'm really sorry you're having to do this. I did try to tell DCI Vickers—'

Blake cut me off. 'Don't worry. I was there, remember? What the boss wants, the boss gets. And I do know the Wilmington Estate fairly well; I think I can find it OK.'

Not exactly gracious, but then what did I expect? I folded my arms across my chest. It was ridiculous, I told myself, to feel like crying because someone I didn't know – someone whose opinion I had no reason to value – had snapped at me.

Blake slammed the car into reverse and tore out of the parking space, revving the engine impatiently at the exit from the car park while he waited for a gap in the traffic. As he changed gear, his elbow brushed against my sleeve. I shifted a little, moving away from him. He glanced at me absent-mindedly, then looked again.

'Are you OK?'

Instead of answering, I sniffled. He looked appalled.

'God – I didn't mean – look, don't get upset . . .'

I tried to pull myself together. 'It's not your fault. Probably just post-traumatic stress or something. It's just been a really long, bad day. I don't know how you manage – dealing with stuff like this all the time.'

'It's not all the time. This sort of case doesn't come along that often. I'm nine years in and this is one of the worst I've had to work on.' He shot a look at me. 'But this is my job, remember? Even though it's upsetting that Jennifer Shepherd's dead, I have to be unemotional about it, as far as that's possible. I'm paid to consider the evidence, and the best way to do that is to keep a clear head.'

I sighed. 'I couldn't do your job.'

'Well, I couldn't do yours. I can't think of anything worse than standing in front of a classroom of kids, trying to keep them in line.'

'Oh, I feel like that a lot of the time, believe me.' *Like every day*.

'So why did you decide to become a teacher?'

I blinked at him, startled. Because I'm an idiot and I didn't know how hard it was going to be. Because it seemed like the best option at the time and I hadn't realised I was temperamentally unsuited to it. Because I hadn't realised how cruel and unforgiving teenagers could be to people who were supposedly in positions of authority, even if they completely lacked the ability to impose discipline, let alone teach. The last two years had been hell on earth.

Blake was still waiting for a reply. 'Oh . . . it was just something to do, really. I liked English and I studied it at university. Then, well, some of my friends went into teaching, and I just did the same.' I laughed, though it sounded brittle and forced to my ear. 'It's OK, you know. You get long holidays.'

He looked sceptical. 'That can't be the only reason you like it. There must be more to it than that. You really care about your students – I could see that from the way you reacted when we talked about Jenny.'

The truth was that I had only really started to care about her once she had gone missing. I hadn't cared when she was alive – not enough to know that she lived around the corner from my house. I didn't answer him; I just sat and watched the road paying out like an endless ribbon in the wing mirror. I couldn't say that I loved my job. I didn't even like it. I couldn't stand to do it for ever, going over the same old poems and plays, the lines worn smooth by constant repetition. I didn't want to spend a lifetime standing at the blackboard, teasing out the answers I wanted from sullen teenagers, watching them grow up and move on while I stayed in the same place, marking time.

The car pulled in to the kerb and stopped. Blake looked at me. 'Curzon Close. Which house?'

He had stopped near the entrance to the cul-de-sac, engine running.

'This is fine,' I said hurriedly, preparing to get out of

the car. In fact, it was perfect. There was a high hedge beside us that would shield me from any curtain twitchers.

'I might as well drive you to the door.'

'No, really.' I scrabbled for the door handle.

'Look, there's no rush. The boss won't be finished with his conference for a while. Now, which number is your house?'

'Fourteen, but please, don't go any further. It's not far; I can walk. I just don't want – I don't want anyone to see me being dropped off by you.'

He shrugged, then turned the engine off, leaving the keys dangling in the ignition. 'Up to you. What is it – jealous boyfriend?'

If only. 'It's just that my mum might hear the car. I live with her, and she – well, she doesn't like the police very much, and I don't want to upset her. And the whole thing with finding Jenny this evening – I just don't want to talk about it any more. I don't want to have to explain where I've been. So if I can just go back on my own and let myself in quietly, she'll never know anything about it.'

I risked a look in his direction to see if he understood. He was frowning. 'You live with your mother?'

Thanks for listening. 'Yes,' I said stiffly.

'How come?'

'It suits me to.' He could make of that what he liked. 'What about you?'

'Me?' Blake looked surprised, but he did reply. 'I live on my own. No girlfriend.'

Great. Now he would think I had been fishing. Most women would. There was no denying that he was attractive.

In other circumstances, I might even have been glad to know that he was single.

'I meant, where do you live?'

'I have a flat in the old printing works by the river.'

'Very nice,' I said. The printing works was a recent, impressively swanky development on the way out of town, towards Walton.

'Yeah, it is. Not that I'm ever there. My dad wasn't crazy about me becoming a copper, but he helped out with buying the flat.' He yawned uninhibitedly, showing off white, even teeth. 'Sorry. Too many late nights.'

'I should go,' I said, realising that there was no reason to stay in the car. 'Thanks for the lift.'

'Any time.' I took that to be an automatic response until he reached out and put a hand on my arm. 'Seriously. Call me if you need me.' He held out a business card. 'Mobile's on the back.'

I took it, thanked him again and got out. I pushed the card into the pocket of my jacket, unaccountably embarrassed, and walked towards the house quickly. The cool night air was like iced water on my cheeks. Behind me the lights of Blake's car flicked on and my shadow stretched in front of me, then wheeled away to the left as he turned in the generous width of the cul-de-sac. I listened as his engine sang out, fading into the distance as he drove away. Flicking the edge of the card with my thumbnail as I walked, I hurried the last few yards to the house and let myself in. The hallway was quiet and dark, with everything just as I had left it. I stood for a second and listened to the silence. It had been a long, strange and stressful evening. It was no wonder that I felt unsettled. But there seemed to be no reason why I should have that jarring feeling, that sense that something was somehow out of place. And why, I wondered, looking around the deserted street before I closed the door, did I still feel like someone was out there, watching me?

1992

Six hours missing

I don't look at the clock on the mantelpiece, but I know it's late, long past my bedtime. I should be delighted; I have a long-running campaign to be allowed to stay up later, but I am tired. I'm leaning against the back of the sofa and my feet don't touch the floor. My legs are sticking out in front of me, my calves squashed flat on the edge of the seat. The material that covers the sofa is fluffy and soft, but it prickles against my skin.

I yawn, then look at my hands lying in my lap, curved around one another, brown against the blue cotton of my skirt. If I look up, I will see my mother pacing back and forth, her sandals making tiny dents in the living-room carpet. The shape to my right is my father, leaning back in an armchair as if he is relaxed. There are black lines of dirt under all of my fingernails. A fresh scratch wavers across the back of my left hand and the skin around it has

turned pink. I don't remember when it happened.
It doesn't hurt at all.

'It's not funny any more, Sarah. This is ridiculous. Forget whatever Charlie told you to say – I
want the truth.'

I drag my eyes up from my lap and look at
Mum. She has dark marks under her eyes, as
if someone had dipped their thumbs in ink and
jabbed them into her face.

'You're not in trouble,' my father says softly.
'Just tell us.'

'Tell us where Charlie is.' Mum's voice is tight.
She is tired too. 'You'd better start talking, young
lady. Don't make it worse for yourself and your
brother.'

I don't say anything. I have already said that
I don't know, that Charlie said he would be
back soon and nothing more. This is the first
time I have ever told the truth and not been
believed. I have been crying on and off all
evening, wishing Charlie would come home,
wishing they would leave me alone. Now I have
settled into silence.

I concentrate on folding the hem of my cotton
skirt into pleats like an accordion – wide pleats
at first, then narrow pleats, then I smooth them
out and start again. The material slides back
over my knees. They stick up, the skin stretched
thinly over the bone of my kneecaps. Sometimes
I like to draw faces on them or pretend that

they are mountains, but today they are just knees.

'Come on, Sarah, for God's sake. Just tell us.' Mum is crying again, and my father stands up. He wraps his arms around her and whispers in her ear, softly, so that I can't hear what he's saying. I don't care. They are both looking at me, I can tell, the way they have been looking at me all evening, since Mum realised that Charlie was gone. There is a part of me – a very small part – that is almost enjoying it.

On my right knee, there is a blue-white scar the size and shape of an apple pip. I fell and landed on a piece of glass when I was little. Mum and Dad were watching Charlie play football, and they didn't notice what had happened to me until the blood from my knee had turned my sock bright red. I got in trouble for dirtying my new summer shoes, but it wasn't my fault. They hadn't been paying attention.

Not like now.

Chapter 3

If ever there was a day for calling in sick, that Tuesday was it. I sat in my car and checked my appearance in the rear-view mirror, noting the greenish pallor and heavy shadows under my eyes, the result of seriously disturbed sleep. I had slept badly, waking every hour or so to stare into the dark with wide eyes. The events of the previous evening seemed so unreal when the alarm woke me up that I had actually gone to the cupboard in my room to check the pocket of my jacket, and didn't know whether to be relieved or disappointed when my fingers touched the little rectangle of card with DS Blake's contact details on it. And I had watched the morning news as I choked down some cereal, seeing the Shepherds, as yet unidentified by the media, as they went in the pale dawn to see where their daughter's body had lain. Mrs Shepherd's hair was all over the place, straggling in strawberry-blonde rats' tails rather than the sleek bob I remembered. As they reached the edge of the woods, Michael Shepherd looked back over his shoulder, straight into the camera, with red-rimmed, haunted eyes. I put my cereal bowl down, suddenly nauseated.

In the rear-view mirror, my eyes were red too. I definitely looked sick. But staying at home was even less appealing than going to work. Last night Mum had been asleep when I had come home, and hadn't surfaced while I was getting up. But it couldn't last. If I stayed, I'd have to see her sometime. Speak to her, even.

I started the car and put it into reverse, but then sat, immobile, gripping the steering wheel until my knuckles bleached white. I couldn't go to school, but I had to, and in the end I said aloud, 'Fuck it. Fuck everything,' and let the handbrake off, letting the car roll down towards the road. The next second I jammed on the brakes, as a motorbike roared past me with a loud, indignant blast on the horn. I hadn't even seen him. I hadn't even looked. My heart pounded and I felt weak as I pulled out on to the main road, checking obsessively that I wasn't endangering anyone else. *Get a grip . . . come on, don't fall apart . . .*

What made it worse – what made it absolutely bloody intolerable – was that I knew exactly who the motorcyclist was: Danny Keane, who had been Charlie's best friend. I couldn't remember a time when he hadn't lived across the road from us. He might as well have lived on the moon. We were well beyond the point where I could start up a friendly conversation with him; I avoided him deliberately, and he knew it, and it was a long time since he'd smiled or nodded in my direction or indicated in any way that he knew of my existence. It wasn't his fault that I associated him with some of the worst moments of my life, that I wasn't able to break the connection in my head between Danny Keane and despair. I usually left early and got home late; our paths rarely crossed, but I still knew him, and he would remember me. Knocking him off his bike would have been a pretty bad way to start making friends again.

The roads were busy and traffic was slow, much slower than usual. Cars were queuing at all the junctions, backing up the side roads, and I wondered what was going on. Human nature at work, it turned out. All along the main road, skirting the woods, the verges were rutted and scarred where the wheels of the news vans had bitten into the soft earth. Their roof-mounted satellite dishes were beaming the Shepherds' misfortune all over the world. Each van had its little group of attendants, a cameraman, soundman and reporter. It was the other side of what I had been watching on my television at breakfast. It was also Surrey's latest tourist attraction. The drivers slowed down to a crawl. It was better than a car crash; there was a chance of seeing genuine celebrities in the shape of one or two of the better-known reporters. There was even the possibility that a panning cameraman might catch a slow-moving motorist on film for a second or two. Fame at last. No wonder the traffic was virtually at a standstill. I drove as close to the car in front as I dared, edging forwards without looking too closely at the temporary news village that had mushroomed on the verge.

At the school gates, I noted an increase in the numbers of parents who were gathering there, talking earnestly to one another, but I ignored them, sweeping past without slowing down. Even a cursory glance in their direction told me that the only topic for discussion was the body, and I didn't want to hear their speculation about what had happened and who it was and was it true . . . I could see from a mile off that the rumour mills were in over-drive.

And so were the professional gossips. In the staff car park, I pulled into a space by the wall. As I switched off the engine, there was a sudden rat-tat-tat on my window that practically sent me into orbit. I whipped around, ready to snarl at whoever had crept up on me, assuming it would be a colleague. But the face peering in at me through the window didn't belong to any of the other teachers. I frowned, trying to place the woman who was standing there. She was middle-aged, with a puffy face that was coated in a slick of tan foundation. Her pale pink lipstick made her teeth look yellow, and she wore a drab brown coat that did nothing for her figure or her colouring. Although she was smiling, her eyes were cold. They scanned the interior of the car, including me, missing nothing. With great reluctance, I rolled down the window.

'Can I help you?'

'Carol Shapley, chief reporter from the *Elmview Examiner*,' she said, and leaned into the car, practically touching me. 'Are you a teacher here?'

I looked pointedly at the sign on the wall that said 'Teachers' Car Park' in letters about a foot high, roughly ten feet from where I was parked. 'Were you looking for someone in particular?'

'Not as such,' she said, and smiled even wider. 'I'm reporting on this murder that's happened, one of your students, and I've got some information that I'd like you to confirm.'

She spoke quickly, reeling off her little speech with

great fluency, giving the impression that she knew everything there was to know about it already. My alarm bells were ringing so loudly, I was surprised she couldn't hear them. I remembered seeing her before at various school performances, fundraisers and local events, barrelling around self-importantly. The *Elmview Examiner* was the most local of local papers; parochial was not the word. And calling herself the chief reporter was a bit rich. As far as I knew, she was the only reporter.

'I'm sorry, but I don't think I can help,' I said sweetly, and started to roll up the window again, in spite of the fact that she was leaning on the edge of it. For a second, I could see her struggling with the urge to insist on speaking to me, but she backed off a foot or two. Not far enough.

I gathered my things together and opened the car door to find that she had left me just enough room to get out.

'I only have a couple of questions.'

I straightened to my full height and discovered she had a couple of inches on me; not for the first time I regretted that I wasn't tall enough to look down my nose at anyone. But I didn't need a height advantage when I had the moral high ground.

'Look, I've got to go in and speak to my students. I'm afraid I don't have time to talk at the moment.' I summoned up a smile from somewhere. 'I know you're just doing your job, but I have a job to do too.'

'Oh, I do understand. Can I ask you your name?' She waved an A4 sheet at me. 'I've got a list, you see. It's always nice to put a face to a name.'

I couldn't see a way to avoid telling her. 'Sarah Finch.'

'Finch . . .' She ran her pen down the list and put a tick by my name. 'Thanks, Sarah. Maybe we can have a chat some other time.'

Or maybe not.

I started to walk towards the school, but of course she wasn't finished. 'I've heard from sources in the police that the body was found by one of the teachers from this school. That wasn't you, was it?'

I stopped and turned, mind racing. Obviously I didn't want her to know that it had been me, but I wasn't sure I could get away with an out-and-out lie. 'God, how awful,' I said in the end.

'Yeah, dreadful,' the journalist said, looking anything but bothered.

I gave Carol another meaningless little smile and half-shrug, then headed for the staffroom, aware of her eyes on me as I crossed the car park. I had to hope that Carol would categorise me as bland, unquotable, totally uninteresting, because if she started to dig, there was every chance that she might put it all together. And not just about Jenny. If she was looking for an angle for a follow-up piece on what was undoubtedly going to be the story of the year, she might think to compare the circumstances of Jenny's death with other local murders and mysteries. Charlie's disappearance was an obvious one to drag up out of the archives. Not for the first time, I was glad I had changed my surname and that none of my colleagues knew anything about Charlie. It wouldn't be so easy for Carol to make the connection. And after all, why should she? The only thing the two cases had in common was me.

Even though the staffroom was as crowded as I'd ever seen it, the assembled teachers and staff were almost silent. It seemed every employee of Edgeworth School was there. Everyone was on time today. I looked at the drawn, worried faces that surrounded me and felt unutterably wretched. We were all involved in this now; there was no way to opt out.

Elaine Pennington stood at one end of the room, DCI Vickers beside her. Next to him there was a young woman with a clipboard and immaculate make-up, who had introduced herself as the police press officer. The head teacher had been talking for some time now about Jenny, cooperation with the police and answering parents' questions. She was making a brave attempt to seem as decisive and in control as normal, but the piece of paper she was using as a prompt sheet vibrated in her hands. One side of her narrow face looked frozen, palsied, with a twitch that tugged at her eyelid intermittently. I hoped she was planning to stay away from the media until she'd clawed back some of her composure. Her voice was uncharacteristically reedy, and as she spoke her eyes slid about the room. I forced myself to pay attention to what she was saying.

'So in consultation with the police, bearing in mind the disruption that is likely to affect all of us in the coming days, I have decided to suspend classes for the time being.'

A ripple of disturbance ran through the assembled teachers. Elaine's neck became mottled with pink patches, the traditional sign that she was about to lose her temper.

Stephen Smith, a sweet-natured man and one of the longest-serving teachers at the school, raised his hand.

'Elaine, don't you think the girls might need the routine of classes and work to keep their minds off what has happened?'

'I did consider that, Stephen, thank you. But I am led to believe that the next couple of days are going to be a write-off from the point of view of concentration. Already it is impossible to work with all the noise and disruption that is going on.'

As one, we turned to look out of the window, to where the news crews were setting up, their vans parked along the school wall. They had started to move on from the woods. The media would need a new backdrop for the lunchtime news and it looked like the school was it.

'I don't know if any of you have been in the school office this morning, but it has been chaotic to say the least. Janet has been fielding calls from worried parents since she arrived. They are concerned about their children's safety, even though no one has suggested that the school is in any way involved in this terrible tragedy.' Elaine's voice broke a little over the last few words. I wondered, perhaps unfairly, if her grief was for the school's reputation rather than Jenny.

'We have a duty to guarantee the safety of the girls, and I don't feel comfortable about making that sort of promise to the parents. It's not that I think they are at risk of being attacked. I'm simply aware that the press are going to be very intrusive, and that sort of publicity can attract the wrong sort of attention. I don't want them to be exposed to that sort of atmosphere.'

Which was fair enough.

Elaine darted a look at Vickers, who looked even more desiccated than he had the night before. His eyes were hooded and I found it hard to guess what he was thinking. 'Also, Detective Chief Inspector Vickers has asked if he can use some of the school facilities, so I want us to be able to give him free access to the school.'

'Very kind,' Vickers said. He straightened a little, straining to pitch his voice so that everyone could hear. 'Our main incident room is at Elmview Police Station, but we'll be doing some interviews here. We're interested in talking to Jennifer's friends and classmates, and we don't like to conduct interviews of that sort in a police station. We prefer to keep them in familiar surroundings. We'll also be using the school hall for a press conference later on today as it's got all the facilities we'll need.'

I couldn't understand what Elaine was thinking. If I had been her, I would have wanted to keep the school as far away from the investigation as possible. From the way she kept looking to DCI Vickers for guidance, he seemed to have conquered her completely. It was all very inconvenient, particularly given the fact that I wanted to stay out of the investigation, off the radar, out of the loop.

'So can we all go home or what?' Geoff Turnbull spoke from the back of the room, as unruffled as if this sort of thing was routine, predictably crass. I didn't bother to turn around to look at him, though I could picture him lounging there, all blue eyes and biceps and carefully groomed black hair. He was one of the PE teachers at Edgeworth, and I liked him not at all.

Elaine bristled. 'No, Geoff. I would like the teachers to make themselves available to the police and the girls, even though no actual teaching will take place. Given that we are going to have a lot of students hanging around, waiting to be picked up by their parents, it's more important than ever that you should be here. We will divide the girls up into groups and supervise them until their parents or guardians arrive to collect them. I'm afraid I will be asking you to stay on after the end of the school day also. I'm going to need your support today, so I would ask you all to bear with me.'

Jules Martin said, 'How long is this going to take? When are we going to get back to normal? Some of the girls are preparing for exams at the moment and I don't want their work to be disrupted.'

I shot a cynical look at her and got a bland smile in response. If I had a friend in the staffroom, it was Jules, and she was about as dedicated as I was. Her concern was laudable, and almost definitely faked.

'I'm very much aware of the exam students,' Elaine said. 'For them, this will be a study week. Janet will help by sending out revision plans for the relevant classes, which I expect all of you to supply to the school office by lunchtime today. As for how long this will take . . .' She turned to Vickers.

'I can't give you an estimate at the moment. Based on

my experience of previous investigations, the media interest will die down over the next few days unless there are significant developments. We'll do our best to minimise the disturbance and hopefully everything will run as normal here next week. We should have finished our interviews by then anyway. I've got a big team here, so we should get through everyone quite quickly.'

Elaine checked her watch. 'OK, everyone. I'd like you all to go to your form rooms and take the register, then send the girls to the school hall. I'll tell them what's going on. I think it's important to involve them in this and keep them informed.'

'But what will we say if they ask us questions?' Stephen asked, looking troubled.

'Think of something,' Elaine said through gritted teeth, clearly teetering on the edge of her last nerve.

The staffroom emptied in record time. I slid out past DCI Vickers, making eye contact for a split second. He nodded discreetly – almost imperceptibly – in return, to my relief. The last thing I wanted was for everyone else to work out that I'd met DCI Vickers before, and recently. The identity of the person who'd discovered Jenny's body had been the main topic of conversation when I got to the staffroom. If nothing else, Carol Shapley was thorough – she had interrogated pretty much everyone before they got through the door.

The assembly hall was almost full. I had managed to find a chair near the front, by the wall, facing in so I could scan the entire room. The girls, who had never been known to be completely quiet in their lives, were just as silent as the teachers had been earlier. Not a flicker interrupted the rapt attention they were paying to the stage where Elaine was speaking, again flanked by the chief inspector and the press officer. In the intervening hour or so, Elaine had ironed out a few of the kinks in her presentation. She ripped through her speech without a twitch.

The assembly hall was much emptier than it should have been; I guessed, looking along the rows of girls, that around half had been kept home from school or had gone home already. That tallied with what I'd found in my own greatly diminished class on taking the roll. Word had got around already that it was an Edgeworth girl who had died. Now they just wanted to hear the details.

'This will be a difficult time for all of us,' Elaine intoned, 'but I expect you to behave with dignity and decorum. Please respect the Shepherds' privacy. If you should happen to be approached by the media, don't comment on Jenny, the school or anything to do with the investigation. I do not want to see an Edgeworth student speaking to any journalists. Anyone who does will be suspended. Or worse.'

Some of the older girls looked more devastated by the media ban than the news about Jenny. Their heartfelt sobbing had not so much as smudged their impeccably applied make-up, I noted.

'The school secretary is contacting your parents as I speak,' Elaine continued. 'We are asking them to collect you or make other arrangements for you to be looked after for the next few hours. The school will be closed for the rest of the week.'

DCI Vickers looked a bit shocked at the fizz of excitement that spread through the assembly hall. I wasn't. The girls, like all teenagers, were self-centred and unthinkingly brutal on occasion. They may have been genuinely upset about Jenny, but they were also working the angles for themselves. An unexpected week off, for whatever reason, was not to be sniffed at.

Elaine held up her hands and silence fell again. 'This is Detective Chief Inspector Vickers. He is leading the investigation into this very sad death and he has a couple of things he would like to say to you.' Another ripple ran through the hall. I wondered if Vickers had ever been the focus of so much overexcited female attention before. His ears, I was amused to see, were delicately shading to dark pink before my eyes. He stepped forward and leaned in to the microphone. Looking rumpled, pale, slightly shabby, his edge was well disguised.

'Thank you, Ms Pennington.' He had leaned too close to the microphone and the 'p' of Pennington popped from the overamplification. 'I'd like to appeal to any of you who have any information regarding Jenny Shepherd to come forward and speak to me or one of my team.' He nodded to the back of the hall. Like everyone else, I looked around and I jumped when I noticed Andrew Blake leaning against the door frame, two uniformed police officers beside him. Valerie was presumably tied up with the Shepherds.

'Alternatively, you can speak to one of your teachers if

you find that easier,' Vickers said. Every head in the hall turned back to face him, as synchronised as the crowd at a tennis match. 'They'll be able to help. Don't think that what you know isn't worth telling us. We'll decide if it's useful or not. What we're looking for is information about Jenny – in particular her friends in and outside school, and anything strange that you might have heard from her or about her, anything out of the ordinary. Was there anything worrying her? Was she in any kind of trouble? Was she involved in any disagreements with other students or anyone else? Was there anything going on that she was keeping a secret from grown-ups? If anything, anything at all occurs to you, please don't keep it to yourself. But I would say one thing: try not to gossip among yourselves before you talk to us. It's all too easy to talk something up until you're not sure you can distinguish between what you know and what you've heard.' He looked around the room again. 'I know there will be a great temptation to speak to the media about this. They are very good at getting information out of people – better than the police, sometimes. But you can't trust them, and you really shouldn't talk to them, as your headmistress says. If you have something to say, talk to us.'

The girls nodded, hypnotised. For a man who was about a thousand points down on the glamour scale from Inspector Morse, Vickers had done pretty well.

What he hadn't done, of course, was answer the questions they had really wanted to ask. So for the rest of the day, in between supervising study groups and developing emergency revision plans for the exam students, I tried to deal with the speculation that was raging through the school.

'Miss, did she have her head cut off? Someone said her head was, like, gone?'

'I heard that she was stabbed hundreds and hundreds of times, yeah? And all her guts were hanging out, and you could see her bones and everything.'

'Miss, was she tortured? I heard she was all burned and cut.'

'Was she raped, Miss?'

'How did she die, Miss?'

'Who killed her, Miss?'

I was as repressive as I knew how to be. 'Get on with your work, girls. You've got plenty to do. The police will find out who did it.'

I actually felt sorry for them. Despite their bravado, the girls were scared. As an introduction to mortality, it was a tough one. What teenager doesn't think she'll live for ever? To have one of their own snuffed out so violently was a shock, and they needed to talk about it. I got it. But it made for a tiring sort of day.

I was still at the school at half past five, as Elaine had predicted. The last of the girls in my care had just been collected by her father, a fat-necked man in an expensive suit, driving a Jaguar. He had taken the opportunity to tell me what a waste of his time it had been to make him collect his daughter, and that as usual the school had completely overreacted. I wondered what exactly was usual about the murder of one of his daughter's contemporaries, but I managed not to say anything as the girl climbed into the car, mute and round-eyed with misery. I could practically hear her begging me not to make things worse by arguing with him, so I smiled serenely.

'We're just doing our best to make sure the girls are safe. That's the most important thing, I'm sure you agree.'

'It's a bit late now to worry about keeping the girls safe. Horse and stable-door stuff, this. And you get yourselves a nice little holiday into the bargain by closing the school for the rest of the week. No consideration for the parents, who have to sort out childcare for the next four days.' His face, which was already flushed, went a shade darker. 'You can tell your headmistress that I am deducting a week from this term's fees. That should make her reconsider her priorities.'

'I'll pass that on,' I said, then stepped back smartly as he revved the engine and sped away, tyres spitting gravel. It hadn't been worth pointing out to him that the Shepherds would give everything they had to be in his position, but I had thought it.

As I turned to go back into the school, someone called my name and I looked around. *Oh no.* Geoff Turnbull was jogging across the car park, heading straight for me. Running away would have been undignified. Besides, he was quick on his feet. I'd have to tough it out.

'I haven't seen you all day.' He stopped altogether too close to where I was standing and ran a hand down my arm caringly. 'This is horrendous, isn't it? How are you coping?'

To my utter horror, the question made my eyes fill

with tears. It was totally involuntary, the product of exhaustion and stress. 'I'm OK.'

'Hey,' he said, shaking my arm gently. 'You don't have to pretend with me, you know. Let it out.'

I didn't want to let it out, especially not in front of him. Geoff was the staffroom flirt and he'd been pursuing me since I started working at Edgeworth. The only reason he was still interested was because I wasn't. As I tried to think of a nice way of getting rid of him, I found myself being pulled into his arms for what was supposed to be a reassuring hug. Geoff manoeuvred himself so that his entire body was in contact with mine, pressing himself against me. My skin crawled. I patted his back feebly, hoping he would let go, while mentally debating the relative merits of the swift-knee-to-the-groin approach versus taking one of his grabby hands and bending the fingers back. Too polite to do either, I gazed dully over his shoulder – straight into the eyes of Andrew Blake, who was crossing the car park himself, heading for the school hall.

'Geoff,' I said, beginning to wriggle. 'Geoff, get off me. That's enough.'

He loosened his hold on me so he could look down at my face. He was still looking intensely sincere, an expression I felt he had been practising in the mirror. 'Poor little Jenny. It's no wonder you're upset about her. Did you hear, they're saying it was one of us who found her? I wonder who that could have been. Who goes jogging around here?'

He knew very well that I ran to keep fit; he'd offered

to run with me more than once. I shrugged, managing not to react, and took a step back to put a few important inches of air between us. 'It's really dreadful. But seriously, I'm coping. I just had a moment of being upset.'

'It's nothing to be ashamed of.' He reached down and took my hand. 'It's just a sign of what a caring person you are.'

Oh, please.

'Maybe we should sit down and talk about this over a drink. You deserve it. You've done your duty. Let's get out of here.'

I thought fast as I worked my hand free. 'Sorry, Geoff. I'm going to the press conference. I just want to keep in touch with the investigation. You know.'

Without waiting for a reply, I started towards the school, heading for the door Blake had gone through. The press conference should have started already, I thought, checking my watch. I hadn't been planning to go, but anything was better than being interrogated by Geoff in some tacky bar, sipping a warm Coke and watching his every move.

I slipped through the door at the back of the school hall, closing it behind me. The room was absolutely packed – journalists at the front, photographers along the aisles and cameramen at the back of the room. Some of the other teachers were there, standing to one side. I found myself a spot beside Stephen Smith, who nodded at me wordlessly. He looked exhausted and upset. Once again, I felt the slow burn of rage at whoever had done this.

At the front of the room, DCI Vickers was sitting at

the centre of a long table. Jenny's parents were to one side of him and I spotted Valerie Wade not too far away, standing beside Blake. On the other side of Vickers was the press officer who was running the press conference, and beside her was Elaine. I guessed that she had insisted on representing the school, in case there were any questions that might reflect badly on us. She looked terribly nervous. So, it had to be said, did Vickers, who was shuffling his papers and patting his pockets while the press officer introduced him.

'Right,' he said. 'I'm just going to announce the preliminary results of the autopsy, which we've had performed today, and then pass you over to the Shepherds, who would like to make an appeal for information. We've been informed by the pathologist that Jennifer Shepherd drowned some time yesterday.'

Drowned?

At his words, every journalist in the room stuck a hand in the air. Vickers, who had no sense of the theatrical, was looking through his papers again. My eyes were locked on the Shepherds, who clung to one another. Mrs Shepherd was weeping silently, while her husband looked like he had aged ten years over the course of the past thirty-six hours.

The press officer selected one of the waving journalists to ask the question everyone was thinking. 'How did she drown? Is there any chance that this was an accident after all?'

Vickers shook his head. 'No. There are suspicious circumstances to do with this death, and we are quite sure that we are not dealing with an accident. These are preliminary results from the autopsy, but the pathologist is quite definite about the cause of death.'

I flashed back to the woods, to Jenny lying fully clothed in a hollow, nowhere near a source of water. I hadn't even seen a puddle nearby. Wherever she'd drowned, it hadn't been where I'd found her body.

Vickers was still speaking and I stood on my tiptoes, straining to hear what he was saying. 'We aren't yet sure where Jenny died, or the circumstances, and for that reason her father, Michael Shepherd, has agreed to make an appeal for information, in case anyone out there can tell us where Jenny was between Saturday evening around six and Sunday night.'

'Sunday night,' another of the journalists repeated. 'So that was when she died, you believe?'

Vickers shook his head slowly. 'We're not sure of that at this stage. We're waiting for further information from the pathologist, but that's the margin of time we're interested in at present.

'We want to know where Jenny was during that time, and who she might have been with. We want to know if anyone saw her. We want to know if anyone is acting suspiciously, or has been behaving in a strange manner since the weekend. We want any information that might lead us to her murderer, no matter how insignificant it might seem.'

Just as Vickers said the word 'murderer', Diane Shepherd gave a sob. Instantly camera flashes exploded around the room. Her husband glanced at her, then spread a piece of paper in front of him, flattening it out with his hands. Even from the back of the hall, I could see the tremor in his fingers. At a nod from the press officer, he began to speak, faltering a little, but seeming to be very much in control.

'Our little girl, Jenny, was just twelve years old. She's – she was a beautiful little girl, always smiling, always laughing. She's been taken from us too soon. This is our worst nightmare, as it would be for any parent. Please, if you have any information about this crime, anything at all, please tell the police. Nothing will bring her back, but at least we can try to get justice for her. Thank you.'

He swallowed convulsively as he finished, then turned to wrap his arms around his wife, who was now crying hysterically. Valerie ran forward and whispered in Michael Shepherd's ear. He nodded and got to his feet, supporting his wife. The pair followed Valerie to the side door that led out of the hall. As the door closed behind them, a confused babble of questions rose from the assembled reporters.

'Is this the work of a paedophile?' one shouted above the others and Vickers leaned back in his chair, gathering his strength before replying.

'We don't yet know . . .' I heard as I opened the door at the back of the hall and slipped out. I couldn't stand to hear any more speculation. The journalists were just doing what they had to do, but the atmosphere in the room made me feel uncomfortable. I was heartsick for the Shepherds and tired to my very bones. The rest of the press conference would be too much to bear.

Lost in thought, I didn't realise that the Shepherds were walking towards me, guided by Valerie, until they had almost passed by. I was standing beside the main door to the car park, where their car was waiting.

'Mr Shepherd,' I said impulsively, 'I'm so sorry for your loss.'

He turned and looked at me, his eyes coal-black with hostility, and I shrank back against the wall. Valerie ushered him on with a pert little nod in my direction and I watched them go, open-mouthed. Then I realised – of course. He knew exactly who had discovered the body; he would have been told. I was the one who had taken away the desperate hope that she might be found alive and well. I could understand why he might be upset with me, even though it was far from fair.

I swallowed, fighting for composure. I could cope, I told myself, with a bit of misdirected loathing, even though it stung.

'Are you OK?'

I looked up to see Andrew Blake leaning over me, concern on his face.

'I'm all right. I just don't understand why those poor people couldn't be allowed some privacy. Was there really any reason to drag them out in front of the press like that?'

'We've got to take advantage of the media interest at this stage, before they start criticising us for not finding the killer. The parents make good TV. We'll be at the top of all the news bulletins.'

'Practical as ever,' I observed.

'So what? It's not like we can get on with doing anything useful at the moment. My boss is stuck in there, trying to cope with that pack of sharks. Every time I try to get out and do some actual policing, I get hassled by them. Not to mention the fact that they're conducting their own investigation. They're doing more interviews than we are. I've heard back from the guys who are doing door-to-door – the tabloids have got there first. They're stepping all over this, getting in the way, and they'll be the first to tell us that we've cocked it up when they're the ones who are causing the problems.' His voice had risen. He ran his hands through his hair and paced back and forth a couple of times before turning to face me again. 'Sorry. I shouldn't shout at you. It's not your fault.'

'I'm used to it,' I said lightly. 'Don't worry about it.' He looked quizzically at me, but I shook my head. I wasn't going to elaborate.

'It just frustrates me. The first few days of the investigation are the most important, and what are we titting about with? Play-acting for the media instead of actual investigating. And if we wanted to get press attention for something they could actually help with, we could whistle for it.' He sighed. 'But we still need to do it, just in case something comes of it. And if we didn't give them information and access to the family, they'd be ten times worse.'

'You don't think the Shepherds' appeal is going to be useful?'

'It never is, in my experience. What sort of killer is going to come forward just because he sees the parents looking upset? If you've got the balls to murder a kid, don't tell me that a few tears on camera are going to remind you that you've got a conscience.'

'But maybe the family of the murderer – his wife, his mother . . .'

Blake was shaking his head. 'Come on. Look at what they've got to lose. Most people wouldn't give a shit if it meant they had to hand over a family member to the cops.'

'Really?' I couldn't believe it. 'They'd rather live with a murderer?'

'Think about it,' Blake said, ticking off the points on his fingers. 'Total upheaval – your whole family gets turned upside-down. Loss of income – could be the chief earner who gets nicked, and that's you and your family living on benefits. You get bricks through your windows, graffiti, people whispering about you when you go down to the shops. The neighbours hate you, so there's no more chatting over the fence. And that's before you consider that your potential witnesses who are supposed to point the finger at the killer are more than likely related to him. Would you turn in someone you loved?'

'But Jenny was murdered! She was a twelve-year-old girl who hadn't done anything wrong. How could anyone feel any loyalty to someone who was responsible for that death?'

He shook his head. 'Loyalty is a strong emotion. It's hard to go against it and do the right thing. You can understand why someone might prefer to look the other way.'

I thought back to the journalists' questions. While Blake was in such a forthcoming mood, there was something I needed to know. 'The autopsy . . . Did they . . . was she . . . assaulted?'

He hesitated for a second. 'Not as such.'

'What does that mean?'

'Not recently,' he said slowly, and his mouth narrowed to a grim line as my eyes widened.

'So you could tell – there were signs –'

'We could tell that she was four months pregnant. That made things easy.' His voice was low, clipped, matter-of-fact. I couldn't even pretend that I had misheard.

'But she was a *child*,' I managed to say eventually. There wasn't enough air in my lungs; I couldn't take a deep enough breath.

'Almost thirteen.' He was frowning. 'I shouldn't have told you that – any of it. You're the only one who knows, outside the police. If it goes any further, I'll know you leaked it.'

'There's no need to threaten me. I won't say anything.' I couldn't imagine telling anyone what Blake had just told me. What it implied was too terrible to contemplate.

'I wasn't trying to threaten you. I just – I could get in serious trouble for talking out of turn, OK?'

'So why did you tell me in the first place?' I said, nettled.

He shrugged. 'I suppose I didn't want to lie to you.'

I didn't say anything in response – I couldn't. But my face burned. I barely knew the detective, but he had a definite talent for wrong-footing me.

He looked down at me compassionately. 'Why don't you get out of here? No reason why you should have to hang around, is there?'

I shook my head and he turned to go back into the school hall. With his hand on the door-handle, he paused for a second, steeling himself. Then he pulled open the door and was gone.

1992

Eight hours missing

My cheek is buried in one of the cushions that sit along the back of the sofa. As I breathe in and out, the silky fabric draws towards my mouth a little and then falls back again. I watch it through my eyelashes. In. Out. In. Out.

I have been asleep for a while – not long. My neck is stiff from the awkward way I am lying, and I am cold. I want to go to bed. I think about why I have woken up. I hear voices: my parents and two strangers, one male and one female. I stay absolutely still and keep my breathing regular while I listen to them. I don't want to be asked any more questions. I am in trouble and I hate Charlie for it.

'Any problems at school, do you know? Bullying? Not doing his homework?'

My mother answers, her voice faint and distant. 'Charlie's a good boy. He likes school.'

'We often find there's been a row at home when a child goes missing – a falling-out with parents or siblings, something of that sort. Anything like that happen here?' A gentler enquiry this time, the woman speaking with a soft voice.

'Certainly not,' my father replies. He sounds tense and angry.

'Well – there were a few rows. He was growing up. Rebelling a bit. But nothing serious.'

After Mum stops speaking, there's a silence. My nose tickles. I think about lifting my hand and rubbing it, digging the itch out of it, but that would give me away. I start to count instead. By the time I get to thirty, the itch is nothing more than a tingle.

'So you think that this young lady knows where he is, do you?' A shock runs through me; I almost jump. 'Do you want to wake her up so we can talk to her?'

Someone touches my bare leg, just below the knee, and shakes it gently. When I open my eyes, I expect to see my mother, but it is my father who is standing beside me. Mum is sitting on the other side of the room, sideways on an upright chair, her eyes on the floor. Her arm is hooked over the back of the chair and she is biting her thumbnail the way she does when she's nervous or angry or both.

'Come on, wake up,' my father says. 'The police are here.'

I rub my eyes and squint at the two strangers.

They are in uniform, white shirtsleeves rolled up, wrinkled dark trousers that are limp from hours of wear on what has been a hot day. The woman smiles at me. 'All right?'

I nod.

'What's your name, sweetheart?'

'Sarah,' I say, my voice low and a little bit husky from long silence and shyness.

'Your parents tell us that your brother's gone missing, and that you haven't been able to tell them where he is. Is that right, Sarah?'

I nod again.

The policewoman's voice is pitched higher now that she is talking to me. Royal blue mascara has streaked into the creases around her eyes. The blue lines bunch together tightly when the policewoman smiles at me, leaning forward. 'Do you think that you could tell me where he is?'

I shake my head solemnly. *I would if I could,* I think, but I don't say it out loud. A glance leaps between the policewoman and her colleague. For a second, his cold stare is reflected in her eyes, but she turns back to me with another smile. 'Why don't you show me your brother's bedroom, then.'

I look to my mother for guidance. 'Go on,' she says, looking away from me. 'Hurry up.'

I get up and walk slowly out of the room, turning towards the stairs, followed by the policewoman. I have never met her before, but I know already that she prides herself on being good with children, that when the door closes behind us she will lean down, make eye contact and ask me again if I know where my brother has gone. I walk up the stairs slowly, holding on to the handrail, hoping that when we get to Charlie's room, I'll open the door and he'll be there.

Chapter 4

As I walked through the front door, the phone was ringing. I hurried to pick it up, knowing that Mum wouldn't bother. My jaw was tight as I lifted the receiver; the last thing I wanted was to talk to anyone else that day, but I couldn't ignore the insistent shrill of the phone the way Mum could. It was bound to be a sales call anyway.

'Hello?'

'Sarah?' The voice on the other end was warm, full of concern. 'Are you all right, dear?'

'I'm OK, Aunt Lucy,' I said, and the tension in my body eased as I sat down on the bottom step of the stairs. Aunt Lucy was Mum's older sister. There were only three years between them, but she had always mothered Mum. In all the pictures of them as children, she is pushing Mum's pram or dragging her around by the hand. Without complaint, without regard for herself, Aunt Lucy had been there to support Mum when Charlie disappeared. Out of all her friends she was the only person that Mum hadn't managed to push away. If I didn't have any other reason to love Aunt Lucy, it would be enough that she was as loyal as ever to her sister, no matter how difficult she had become. Aunt Lucy never gave up.

'I thought of you as soon as I heard about that poor girl. How is your mother?'

I leaned around to check that the kitchen was empty. 'I haven't seen her yet. I didn't see her this morning. I don't even know if she knows what's happened.'

'Best not to upset her if she doesn't.' Aunt Lucy sounded worried. 'I don't know how she's going to react. I couldn't believe it when I saw the news. Where she was found – it's very close to where you live, isn't it?'

'Yes,' I said, and in spite of myself, my eyes were starting to water. I cleared my throat. 'Jenny went to Edgeworth School. She was one of my students, Aunt Lucy.' *Oh, and I found the body, by the way.* I couldn't bring myself to say the words out loud.

She gasped. 'I didn't realise you knew her. How dreadful. That's just going to make it worse for your mum, you know.'

I held the phone so tightly that the plastic of the receiver creaked in protest, discarding the first three things it occurred to me to say in response on the grounds that they would be too hurtful to my poor, well-meaning aunt. It wasn't Aunt Lucy's fault. We all spent our time worrying about how Mum was going to react to things, drawn into her emotional orbit by the enormous gravitational pull of her self-pity. I wanted to punish Aunt Lucy for thinking only of Mum, instead of the Shepherds or Jenny's friends or even me. But I didn't. In the end, I managed to keep most of the irritation out of my voice when I replied, the words a little stiff. 'Obviously I won't say anything to her that would upset her. I wouldn't dream of mentioning the connection.'

There was a tiny pause before Aunt Lucy spoke again,

and I felt like a heel. She knew me well enough to have noticed that I was annoyed, even if she didn't know why. It wasn't what she deserved.

'How is your mother these days?'

'About the same.'

A little hiss of sympathy and concern came down the wire and I smiled to myself, picturing Aunt Lucy sitting on the edge of her bed, a shorter version of Mum but with her hair and make-up immaculate; I thought she might sleep in her mascara. She always called from the bedroom to avoid disturbing Uncle Harry. He liked his quiet. I sometimes wondered if that was the reason they hadn't had children, or if they just hadn't been able to. I had never dared to ask. It had meant that she had been free to be a wonderful aunt to me – even, sometimes, a mother.

'It's not easy for you, is it?' my lovely aunt said now, and as usual, I felt instantly consoled.

'I don't really see much of her, to be honest. I keep my distance.'

'Have you given any more thought to moving out?'

I rolled my eyes. *What a great suggestion, Aunt L. Thanks for thinking of it.* 'I don't think this is the best time to bring it up, given everything that's going on.'

Aunt Lucy snorted. 'If you keep waiting for the right time, you'll never leave. There'll always be some good reason why you can't. But really, the only thing that's keeping you there is *you*.'

Good old Aunt Lucy, on a mission to rescue the last known survivor of the family catastrophe. She was the one who had encouraged me to use Mum's maiden name instead of Barnes, to shield me from casual curiosity and speculation; she had produced stacks of university prospectuses during my last year in school and oversaw my applications. She had done everything in her power to keep me from going back home, degree and teaching qualification completed, to live with Mum. But it was my responsibility, whatever Aunt Lucy said.

A noise from behind me made me jump and I turned around. My mother, at the top of the stairs. Listening. 'Mum,' I exclaimed, running through my side of the conversation as far as I could recall it, checking for any possible offence.

'You've got to let it go, Sarah. Forget about her,' Aunt Lucy chirped, not quite up to speed on what was going on at my end of the line. 'I love your mother very much, but she's a grown woman and she has to live with the decisions she's made. You have your own life to lead; you can't let her have that too. And it's bad for her to live there in a . . . a . . . *museum*. I've told her she should move up here, make a new life for herself. I'd look after her, you know. She'd be back on her feet in no time.'

'Er, no, Aunt Lucy –' I began, eyes trained on Mum. She was barefoot, wearing her nightie and an ancient, moth-perforated cardigan.

'Lucy!' Mum wobbled down the stairs towards me, hand out for the phone. 'I wanted to talk to her.' Her eyes weren't quite focused, wavering from side to side, and I guessed that she was already a few drinks down, but she seemed fairly in control. I gave up the phone and stood up, murmuring something about getting dinner ready. As I headed for the kitchen, I heard her say: 'Oh, Luce. Did you see the news? I just don't know if I can bear it.'

I closed the kitchen door behind me, very softly, and stood in the middle of the room. My hands had balled themselves into fists and I forced myself to uncurl my fingers, one by one. I waited while the good-daughter part of my brain talked the bad daughter out of kicking the kitchen to pieces. It would have been too much to expect that Mum might think first of Jenny, or her parents. Of course, like everything else, this was all about her.

I ended up making beans on toast for dinner. There wasn't much in the fridge. I'd have to go shopping, I had been forced to conclude, throwing out a sheaf of rubbery, yellowed celery and a bag of tomatoes that had liquefied in the crisper, but I couldn't face it just then. Baked beans would do. Fortunately, perhaps, neither of us was particularly hungry. I picked at them, rock-hard in cloudy, congealing sauce, speckled with black where I had allowed them to burn to the bottom of the pan. I had been a bit distracted while I was cooking, understandably enough. Mum didn't even pretend to eat. She just sat there, staring into space, until I decided dinner was over and picked up her untouched plate. 'Go and watch some TV, Mum. I'll wash up.'

She shuffled off into the sitting room. Before I turned on the tap, I heard the TV explode into life in the middle of an inane ad. It didn't really matter to her what programme was on. It was just something to do while she took on board her daily calorific requirements in liquid form.

Washing up was a cheap form of therapy; I worked on the gungy saucepan until every trace of tomato sauce had come off, thinking about nothing in particular. I felt edgy, for no real reason. From the kitchen window, the garden was beginning to lose definition, merging into the darkness. It was a pearly evening, shaded in blue and purple, still and serene. Impossible to imagine that twenty-four hours earlier, I had been at the centre of a storm of activity, the police listening to what little I knew as if I and I alone held the secret to cracking the case. Impossible to come to terms with the fact that we had all arrived in the woods too late, that finding Jenny's killer was a poor second-best to finding her alive. I dried my hands on a tea towel and sighed; I was feeling, I realised, depressed. Whether that was because I was on the sidelines – where I had wanted to be, after all – or because of deferred emotional fallout from the previous day, I couldn't tell. And what did I want, anyway? Another opportunity to spar with DS Blake? Another moment in the limelight? The inside track on the case? I needed to get over myself and get on with my life, however dull a prospect that was.

My eyes were blurring with tiredness and I turned off the light, dragging myself towards the sitting room, and the evening news that was just starting. I sat down beside Mum on the sofa, deliberately sitting back against the cushions so she couldn't see my face without turning her head. I wanted to be able to watch it in peace, without worrying about what she thought.

The titles rolled over a picture of Jenny, a school photograph that had been taken a couple of months earlier.

Tie neatly knotted, as it never was in life, and hair pulled back in a tidy ponytail. A tight smile; the photographer had been annoying, I recalled – testy, treating the girls as if they were idiots. No one had liked him. I gazed at the image on screen, trying to reconcile it with what Blake had told me. *We could tell that she was four months pregnant* . . . but the face on screen was that of a child. And I knew that was the real Jenny, didn't I? I had seen her almost every weekday since she arrived at the school; I had spoken to her hundreds of times. This wasn't one of those cases where the picture released to the press lags behind the reality of a victim who had turned to drugs or rebellion before meeting their unlucky end. She had really looked like the sweet, good-natured child in the photograph. I had thought her innocent, untroubled, straightforward. How could I have been so wrong?

The grave, sober-suited anchorman gave a brief summary of what had been made public about Jenny's death. The report opened with footage from the press conference: Vickers first, then the Shepherds themselves. The harsh lights from the cameras picked out the dark circles under their eyes, the lines bracketing Michael Shepherd's mouth. I hoped it would prompt someone to contact the police, whatever Blake had said. The scene switched to show the reporter outside, the school behind her. I recognised her from the press conference; she had been sitting near the front. I had thought that she was attractive, with arched dark eyebrows, defined cheekbones and a wide mouth. Her red shirt and glossy black hair looked good on camera, too, vivid under the lights. Her voice was carefully modulated, classless, neutrally accented. I forced myself to listen to what she was saying.

'So we now know the identity of the victim, Jennifer Shepherd, and we know how she died – but if the police know anything else, they aren't telling us. There are questions about where she drowned and how she ended up in the woods not far from here, and of course the biggest question of all: who killed her?'

More pre-recorded footage appeared, this time showing the Shepherds walking into the school building, Valerie acting like a sturdy little icebreaker to make a path for them through the crowd. The reporter's voiceover continued: 'For the parents and Jenny's family, a shattering ordeal. For her fellow students,' and here the image changed to show a group of girls standing together, sobbing, 'an alarming reminder that the world is a violent place. And for all who knew Jenny, a terrible loss.' As she said the last three words, the scene changed again. I stared, open-mouthed, as I recognised Geoff Turnbull, his arms wrapped around a young woman with curly fair hair hanging down her back, a small, slender woman who looked distraught. Me. Every muscle in my body went into a spasm of pure embarrassment. Of all the shots they could have included, of all the emotive images they might have used, they had to choose that one. I remembered what I had been thinking; I had been frantic to escape. 'Unbelievable,' I mouthed silently, shaking my head. Mum gazed woodenly at the screen.

'Louisa Shaw in Surrey, thank you,' the anchorman said, swivelling to face another camera as a picture of a running tap flipped onto the screen behind him.

I waited for Mum to mention the fact that her daughter had just been on the news, but she was still staring vacantly at the screen, to all intents and purposes absorbed in a story about water charges. Maybe she hadn't recognised me. Well, at least it saved me from explaining. I felt tired beyond belief. I had had enough of the day, the week, everything. 'I'm going to head up to bed, Mum.'

'Sleep well,' she said automatically, not registering the fact that it was barely dark outside and I was about two hours ahead of schedule. I left her staring at the screen. If I had had to bet, I would have guessed that the only thing in her mind was Charlie.

The bulb in the light fitting over the bathroom sink had burned out. The ceiling light cast a greyish glare that made my skin look dead, tinged my lips with blue, shadowed my eyes so they looked dull and dark. I gazed at myself in the bathroom mirror, reminded of Jenny. For an instant I saw her as she had been in real life, then as she was when I found her in the woods. Something was missing from the second image – whatever made her who she was. It had gone. *Put out the light and then put out the light.* Shakespeare had got that right, with his poor, baffled, murderous Moor. *When I have plucked thy rose, I cannot give it vital growth again. It needs must wither . . .* I switched off the bathroom light and found my way into bed in the semi-darkness of my room, crawling between the covers with a sigh. I stared up at the ceiling, waiting for sleep. I should have felt anger, or sorrow, or some sort of resolve. But what I mostly felt was numb.

* * *

In the morning, I went to school with no great pleasure. I had to be there; Elaine had made it clear that the teachers were to show up, even if the students didn't. I expected that more than one of my colleagues would have seen the news, and my skin prickled with the anticipation of embarrassment. But as it happened, when I got to the school gates, the first people I recognised were girls from Jenny's class, three of them – Anna Philips, Corinne Summers and Rachel Boyd. They were dressed casually in jeans and hoodies. As I drove in, they were hugging one another self-consciously in front of the numerous camera crews and reporters that still besieged the school. But there was something sincere about their display of emotion, something real – they were blotchy and pink from crying, not groomed and camera-ready. I pulled in to the first available space and hopped out of the car, heading back to do my duty as a bodyguard or counsellor or friend, whatever they required.

They had been laying flowers, I realised once I got closer. An impromptu shrine had sprung up all along the school railings, with cards, teddy bears – balloons, even – and posters that featured pictures cut out of the newspapers. Jenny's face appeared time after time in blurry, poorly reproduced newsprint. And of course there were bunches of flowers, gaudy in brightly coloured wrapping paper. Candles flickered wanly in the bright sunlight. While I waited for the girls to finish their little vigil I walked up and down along the railings, reading some of the cards and posters. *A little angel taken too soon. We won't forget you, Jennifer. Although I never knew you, I will always remember you . . .* The collection spoke of a desperate need for people to involve themselves in the tragedy, to show how much it had affected them. It was spectacularly futile.

I didn't have to worry about getting the trio to talk to me; they came straight up to me as soon as they noticed I was there. And that was the difference between children and teenagers, I reflected. Another year and they would have walked the other way, just to avoid having to talk to a teacher. These girls were unsophisticated, trusting. Easy prey. Jenny had been the same way.

'How are you doing?' I asked sympathetically, leading them over to a bench that was safely out of bounds to the media, well inside the school grounds.

Corinne, who was a beanpole, dark-skinned and slender, gave me a one-sided smile. 'We're OK. It's just really hard to believe.'

'Have the police spoken to you yet?' I asked. Three heads shook in unison.

'When they talk to you,' I began, choosing my words carefully, 'if they need to talk to you, you might find that they ask you about Jenny's life.'

Three heads nodded.

'They might ask you about people that Jenny knew – friends.'

More nodding.

'Maybe about people who her parents didn't know about,' I suggested.

Wide eyes at that from Corinne and Anna, whose little round face and sturdy body reminded me irresistibly of a hamster. Rachel's blue eyes dropped to the ground and stayed there. *Interesting.*

'You see, if Jenny had any secret friends, it might help the police to find whoever killed her,' I said, watching to see if there was any reaction from Rachel. She had a naturally downturned mouth that gave her a sulky look in repose; usually this was misleading, but today maybe not. She didn't move a muscle, and her eyes were still locked on the grass at our feet.

Anna cleared her throat. She was looking even more upset than she had been earlier. 'Jenny was friends with us, Miss, but we don't know anything about who killed her, I promise . . .'

I hurried to reassure her. 'No one thinks that you're involved, Anna. Just, if she mentioned anyone strange, anyone who might have asked her to do something, or asked to meet up with her, you'd remember that, wouldn't you? Someone outside school? Maybe a boyfriend?'

Corinne shook her head. 'She definitely didn't have a boyfriend. No way.'

'Are you sure?' I pressed. 'No one at all? Rachel?'

At that, she dragged her eyes back up and looked right at me, with a gaze so direct and guileless that I knew before she even spoke that she was about to lie. 'No. No one.'

'And would you know if she was having problems at home? Was anything bothering her?'

Three nos. I gave a tiny sigh. This was useless. 'OK,' I said brightly. 'Well, if anything occurs to you, don't be afraid to talk to someone. You won't get in trouble.'

A chorus of yeses, thank yous and goodbyes and the three girls leaped to their feet. I watched them walk away and disappear around the side of the school. I'd done my best, but it was hard not to feel disheartened. I should tell someone about Rachel, tell Vickers or someone that I thought she had something to say that might be important. But who would listen to me? And how could I be sure I was right?

I sat on the bench for a few minutes more, turning it over in my mind. There was nothing I could do, I decided in the end. I'd just have to wait for her to come to me. And having concluded that, I looked up to see a small figure coming across the car park. Rachel, unencumbered by her friends. She had allowed the neutral mask to drop, and her rounded, still-childish face was troubled as she approached me.

'Miss Finch, I'm not sure, but – well . . . ' She looked back over her shoulder. 'I didn't want to say anything in front of the others, because Jenny told me not to tell anyone.'

I sat up, trying to look calm. 'What is it, Rachel?'

The girl was looking increasingly distressed. 'You know how you said if she knew anyone? Someone out of school? Well, she showed me once, she had a picture of herself with – with her boyfriend.'

'Her *boyfriend*? Are you sure?' I was sounding far too excited; Rachel looked at me with doubt in her eyes and I realised how close she was to bolting, secrets untold. I took a deep breath and said, very gently, 'Who was he?'

'I don't know. He was someone she saw after school.'

'Every day?'

Rachel shook her head. 'No. She had a friend – a boy

she knew. She used to go around to see him a couple of times a week.'

'And it was him in the picture?'

'No!' Rachel was beginning to get frustrated with me. 'He was just a friend. It was his older brother who she liked.'

'OK,' I said calmly. 'And what was the brother's name?'

She shrugged. 'She never said.'

'Well, what was Jenny's friend's name?'

'She never told me that either. I don't know anything else about them except – except . . . '

I waited.

'Her boyfriend – the person in the picture was – he was *old*, Miss Finch. Grown-up. It was only the side of his face that I saw, because he was kissing her, but he was definitely a grown-up.'

'Grown-up like a parent, or grown-up like me?' There was no point in asking her to be more specific; we all looked ancient to twelve-year-olds, but I felt she wouldn't be likely to confuse early twenties with mid-thirties and older.

'Grown-up like you,' she said. 'Miss, do you really think that he . . . do you think he might know who killed Jenny?'

The adult boyfriend of a twelve-year-old child, a girl who just happened to be murdered and dumped in a lonely patch of woodland? I imagine so, I thought, but what I actually said was, 'Maybe. But don't worry. You've done the right thing by telling me about it. And I'm sure the police will have found her friend already.'

I spoke without really thinking, concentrating on my

own train of thought. So it was really that simple – a misconceived crush leading to an unsuitable relationship that had ended in a crisis pregnancy and a clumsy, violent solution. All of the pieces were fitting into place. The police probably had him in custody already. I'd get them to speak to Rachel and she'd confirm what they knew already and it would all be over, pretty much. Justice would be done, Jenny would be avenged, the Shepherds and everyone else would grieve, but essentially everything would go back to normal. And I would have done something to help. Made a difference, even though it was too late to save Jenny.

I noticed that Rachel was balancing on the outside edge of her feet in an ecstasy of agitation; I was missing something here, something important. 'Don't worry,' I repeated. 'They'll know who it is and where to find him. Jenny's parents will tell them.'

When she spoke, her voice was high and tight with tears. 'That's the thing. She never told her parents where she was going. She always told them she was at my house, and they always believed her. I don't know who her boyfriend was, and I lied for her, and now she's dead.'

Just under an hour later I arrived in Elaine's office with Rachel and her mother in tow, to find DCI Vickers staring moodily out of the window. I guessed he wasn't really seeing the beech trees outside. The overall impression he gave was of a man in the depths of despair. It certainly didn't look as if the investigation was proceeding satisfactorily, as his press officer had suggested on the news that morning. On the other hand, this was the third or fourth time I'd seen him, and every time he had looked dispirited to the point of collapse, so it was probably best not to read too much into it.

'Hello,' I said quietly, tapping softly on the open door, and he turned, his hangdog expression lifting slightly. A split-second later, he clocked Rachel, who was standing a little bit behind me, still red-nosed and woebegone, drawing the sleeves of her sweatshirt down over her hands compulsively. He looked back at me expectantly, fatigue swept aside by the razor-sharp acuity I had noticed before.

'This is Rachel, one of Jenny's friends,' I said. 'She's just been telling me a couple of things about Jenny's life out of school that I thought you would find interesting.' I didn't want to overplay it. I had been deliberately low-key with Mrs Boyd on the phone when I asked her to come up to the school, not wanting her to think that her daughter was the star witness in case she got into an overprotective flap. I hoped Vickers was reading between the lines.

He smiled at her and all of the lines on his face creased into curves. 'Rachel, is it? Thank you for coming to talk to me, Rachel. Is this your mum? Very good. We'll just get ourselves into the little meeting room, and then we'll have a chat, all right?'

Without seeming to hurry, he had moved the two of them into a room that had been set up for interviews with armchairs and a coffee table. One of his female police officers appeared out of nowhere and sat to one side, notebook at the ready. I hesitated in the hallway, wondering if I should try to explain to Vickers that I had met Rachel by chance – that I hadn't meant to interfere.

The inspector crossed the room, intending to close the door, but stopped when he saw me standing there. He leaned out and muttered in a voice pitched too low for those inside the room to overhear, 'Thanks, Sarah. You've been very helpful. I won't keep you hanging around any longer.'

And with that, he closed the door. I stood there for a couple of moments, looking at the blank, uninformative wood, nonplussed. I had the distinct feeling that I had been dismissed.

1992

Three days missing

'We want you to do another TV spot.'

The big policeman is sitting at the kitchen table. His shirt is dark under the arms and there are two damp half-moons on his chest. It's hot in the kitchen and hot outside, but no one else is sweating. Every now and then, the policeman wipes his face, mopping the drops of liquid that roll down from his hairline to his jaw. He whispers to himself as he wipes the sweat away – *oh God, oh Christ* – so I am watching him intently, watching the beads of water prickle on the surface of his skin, swelling and joining up until they are heavy enough to slide downwards, like rain on a windowpane.

'Another one?' Dad says, and his face is grey. 'What's the problem? Wasn't one enough?'

The policeman spreads his hands out, helpless. 'It did what it was supposed to do, but –'

'It wasted everyone's time. I told you there was no point to all that "please come home, you're not in trouble" crap. As if Charlie wouldn't be here if he could be. As if he'd stay away if he had the choice.'

'I agree, it didn't get us anywhere.'

'So what point is there in doing it again?'

'We're changing the focus of the publicity. We now want to appeal to someone who might be with Charlie. We're now concerned that he may be being held captive.'

Dad folds his arms. 'Oh, so you've finally decided that someone's taken him, have you?'

'It's our view that it's a definite possibility, yes.' Mop mop mop. 'Oh Christ . . . ' he whispers, then looks around the table with piteous eyes. 'We've got to listen to the psychologist's opinion. She knows how they operate. Paedophiles, I mean. She says we need to make them aware that Charlie is a real person, part of a family. Most of them would see a child like Charlie as a commodity, according to her, so we have to get through to them that he's more than that.'

Mum makes a tiny sound under her breath. Her eyes are closed and she is swaying in her seat. I edge around the table to stand next to her, leaning into her. She feels slight – fragile almost, as if I might break her. I butt up against her like a little goat, but she doesn't respond.

'What do you want us to do?' Dad asks.

'We want you to speak about Charlie on camera. We want to put him in a family context, maybe by looking at family photographs that include him. We want to release some new images of him to the media, and also get a film crew in here to get some footage of you as a family. All three of you.'

I jump, a thrill of excitement running through me at the thought of being on TV. A big smile that I can't stop spreads across my face. I hope the girls in my class will see me.

'I don't want her to be involved.'

I don't realise what Mum means straightaway. Then everyone around the table looks at me.

'I know you want to protect your daughter from the publicity, but this is really, really important, Mrs Barnes,' the policeman says, his face serious.

Mum's mouth is a thin line. 'I don't think it's right for her to be on TV.'

She doesn't want me to be on TV because she knows how much I want it. She doesn't want anything good to happen to me because I don't deserve it. My knees are shaking so badly I can hardly stand up. 'But Mum—' I start to say.

Dad interrupts. 'Laura, we have to do this.'

She doesn't answer him, just shakes her head, looking down into her lap where her hands are knotted together, working all the time. Her face is shuttered, blank.

Dad tries again. 'We have to do this. For Charlie.'

That's what he's been saying all the time. Eat something, for Charlie. Talk to the police, for Charlie. Get some rest, for Charlie. It's the one thing she can't refuse.

The TV crew set up their equipment in the garden. They tell us where to sit and what to do. I sit between my parents, the ruffles of my favourite dress foaming up between us. We are pretending to look through a photograph album – pictures of Charlie as a baby, then as a toddler with a red tricycle that I recognise. I played with it too. It's still in the garden shed, though the paint is chipped and worn now.

I'm waiting for the first picture of me, with Charlie leaning over the edge of the cot to look at me. I know exactly what page it's on. I've looked at it many times, trying to recognise my own features in the little round red-faced bundle wrapped up in a blanket, one fat hand poking out. Mum turns the pages slowly, too slowly, stopping to sigh every now and then. When I look up, her face is twisted with grief.

From behind the camera comes, 'Now, Sarah, put your hand on your mother's arm.'

I obey, patting her arm gently. Her skin is cold to the touch, even though we are sitting in the full heat of the afternoon sun. She pulls her arm away as if I've burned her. For the first time, I understand that I will never be able to comfort her. I will never be able to make her happy. I will never be enough.

The tears come then, without warning. I sit and sob my heart out, crying as if I'll never stop. On the evening news, it looks as if I'm crying for Charlie. Only I know that I'm crying for me.

Chapter 5

It was after one o'clock when Andrew Blake came to the school office, where Elaine had put me to work in the absence of any actual teaching duties. My colleagues were lurking in the staffroom, catching up on paperwork. That had been my plan too. I'd been unlucky to run into Elaine, and unluckier still that I hadn't been able to think of an excuse to get out of helping, but I didn't really mind. Opening post and answering the telephone all morning hadn't been exactly taxing. In fact, the only downside was the presence of Janet, the school secretary. A skeletal woman in her early fifties, Janet had been teetering on the brink of a nervous breakdown the entire time I had been working at Edgeworth School. She was useless at her job in normal circumstances; the current situation had made it completely impossible for her to do anything but talk about her medical problems, past and present, and cry. From the moment I walked into the office and saw her inflamed eyelids and reddened nose I had known that there was no point in actually listening to her. I managed to tune her out quite successfully, retreating into my own world while mechanically going through a pile of junk mail and phone messages. Sorting things out was therapeutic. Janet's monologue flowed on in the background, as unstoppable as a river. If you didn't listen to the words, it was almost soothing.

When the door opened and Blake poked his head into the room, it took me a second to come back to reality. Janet was saying, 'So I knew straightaway, of course, that it was a prolapse, because it had happened before . . . Can I help you?'

He beamed at her, charm at full wattage. 'Not at the moment, love. It's Miss Finch I've come to see.'

I stood up and smoothed the creases out of my dress with my hands, playing for time. Why did he want to speak to me? It had to be something to do with Rachel. I went towards the door, my mind a whirl of half-remembered things I had intended to say to Vickers earlier.

'Are you going to be long?' came from behind me. Janet's voice was sharp-edged with irritation. 'Because one of us should really be here over lunchtime, you know. Given how busy it is.'

I stopped, confused, and looked from her to Blake and back again.

'I hope you don't mind,' Blake said gently, but without the least hint that negotiation was possible. 'We won't be very long.'

Janet sniffed. 'Fine. I'll take my lunch later. I haven't really got much appetite these days, anyway.'

With my back to her, I pulled a face at Blake, who half-laughed, half-coughed his way down the corridor, out of Janet's field of vision. As soon as the door was safely shut behind me, he said, 'What was *that*?'

'What, Janet? She's special, isn't she?'

'You can say that again. She's about as cheerful as those

women who used to knit at the foot of the guillotine. How did you get trapped in there?'

'No students to teach and I was in the wrong place at the wrong time. It's better than doing nothing, but thanks for rescuing me anyway.' I hesitated for a second. 'What was it that you wanted to talk to me about?'

Blake looked immensely serious and I waited, cringing a little, to hear what he wanted. 'I was wondering if you were hungry. Because if you *were* heartless enough to want to eat something at a time like this, I would be very happy to offer you one of these sandwiches –,' and he held up a paper bag '– at the location of your choice. It's a nice day. Is there anywhere we can go that's out of doors?'

I blinked, surprised, before feeling a sudden lift in my mood. It *was* a nice day. There was no reason to martyr myself by spending lunchtime in the stuffy school office, or worse, the staffroom, where I would have to listen to Stephen Smith's dentures clack as he ate. It made no sense, especially when there was a much more appealing option available. Would I regret turning Blake down? In a word, yes.

'I don't know,' I said, mirroring Blake's serious demeanour. 'What kind of sandwiches did you get?'

'One ham and salad, one cheese and tomato.'

I considered. 'Can I have the cheese one?'

'Absolutely.'

'In that case, follow me.' I led the way to the door that opened into the car park. 'Somewhere quiet outdoors, is that the brief?'

Blake put on a turn of speed to get to the door first

and held it open for me. 'Somewhere away from that lot, ideally.' He nodded towards the milling reporters by the school gate.

'No problem.' I set off along the side of the school building, past the hockey pitch, to the small, high-walled school garden. It was where the girls were encouraged to try out their green fingers, with varying degrees of success. The vegetable patch was a sorry sight, full of blasted lettuces that had lost the competition with flourishing weeds, but the walls were mantled with honeysuckle that scented the air, and two large apple trees scattered fractured shade across the grass. The garden had the virtue of not being overlooked, which meant that in normal conditions it was the number one choice for those girls who indulged in illicit smoking at lunchtime. Currently, though, it was deserted.

'Perfect,' Blake said from over my shoulder, looking in through the gate. He was standing close behind me, and I was intensely aware of him. It took me a second to remember what I had been doing. I unlatched the gate and stepped down onto the grass, and he followed.

'You can't beat a private school, can you?'

'I suppose not.' I looked at him dubiously; he was wearing a fairly sharp suit. 'Do you want to sit on a bench or lie on the grass?'

He crouched and pressed his hands onto the lawn for a moment. 'Bone dry. Grass it is.'

He took off his jacket and tie and rolled up his shirt-sleeves before lying down on his back. I watched, amused, as he pressed the heels of his hands into his eye sockets. 'Tired?'

'Just a bit,' Blake said, and his voice was blurry with sleep.

He had chosen to lie in the sun, but there was a patch of shade nearby. I curled up in it and began to explore the contents of the bag he had brought. As the silence stretched out I began to feel self-conscious.

'So how are things going?' I said eventually.

He jerked back to wakefulness and blinked, looking at me as if I was a complete stranger. 'Sorry – did I drop off?'

I bit into my sandwich instead of answering. Blake sat up, leaning on one elbow, and rooted in the bag. 'I don't know if I'm hungry or tired these days. We've been flat out since Monday.'

'And are you making progress?'

Through a mouthful of bread, he said, 'Sort of. You raking up the friend was a help. How did that happen?'

I shrugged. 'I just bumped into Rachel. She was dying to tell someone about it, and she knows me, so . . . '

He nodded. 'They probably trust you because you're young. You're more like them than most of the other teachers around here.'

'You'd be surprised. I might look young to you, but I don't think they see me as one of them. I'm very definitely a grown-up as far as they're concerned.' I sighed. 'This whole thing with Jenny – I just didn't see it. Not at all.'

'Don't blame yourself. No one knew. Even her parents were in the dark. How could you have picked up on it?'

I put my sandwich back down and wrapped my arms around my knees. 'I should have, though. I keep thinking about it. She used to hang back and talk to me after class sometimes, about nothing in particular. Just . . . chat. I never really thought much of it, but she might have been waiting for a chance to talk about what was going on. And I used to tell her to hurry up so she would get to her next class on time.' I put my forehead down on my knees, hiding my face from him, afraid to see the judgement in his eyes. But the certainty in his voice when he spoke made me look up.

'Bollocks. If she'd wanted to talk to you, she would have found a way. Look, I'm not trying to change the way you feel about her, but the girl was plain devious. We ripped her bedroom apart – carted away tons of stuff for forensic examination – but we haven't found anything useful. The only person she seems to have talked to is this Rachel, and even then she hasn't told her much. Can you think of anyone else she might have confided in?'

'No,' I said regretfully. 'To be honest, I think Jenny only talked to Rachel about it because she needed someone to cover for her, not because she wanted someone to talk to about her boyfriend.'

'How did Rachel cover for her?' Blake asked, interested.

'She was the only one in the class who lived reasonably close to Jenny – about a ten-minute bike ride. According to Rachel, Jenny was allowed to cycle over to her house so they could do homework together. But of course, she didn't go to Rachel's house; she went somewhere else – to see this friend of hers and his brother.'

'And the parents never suspected a thing?'

'That's the beauty of mobile phones. Diane Shepherd would call or text Jenny when she wanted her to come home. She never rang the Boyds, so there was no danger of her finding out that Jenny wasn't there. But Jenny had Rachel primed to cover for her in case Mrs Shepherd ever spoke to her at the school.'

'That's clever. She had everyone dancing to her tune, didn't she?'

'I suppose.' The idea was so much at odds with my impression of Jenny that it made me uncomfortable. 'Maybe it was the boyfriend's plan, though.'

'Mmm,' Blake said neutrally. 'Maybe.'

He didn't say anything else and neither did I. A wood pigeon crooned in the trees, filling the silence. He was looking down at the grass, thinking, and I took advantage of that to stare at him. The bright sunshine gleamed in the hairs on his arms and his eyelashes, which fanned down on to his cheeks. I had never seen longer eyelashes on a man, and they were the only remotely feminine thing about him. His shirt was carelessly tucked in and a triangle of skin was visible above his belt, taut and brown, with a trail of dark hair leading my mind to places it shouldn't go. He was as still as a photograph. The only movement was the second hand of his watch. I hugged my knees and felt something unfamiliar bubbling up inside me, something that after a second, with some surprise, I recognised as happiness.

Blake looked up at me and I felt my stomach flip over. 'Are you going to finish your sandwich or what?'

The second half of the sandwich was still wrapped in greaseproof paper from the deli. 'I'm not that hungry, I'm afraid.'

'I'll eat it if you don't want it.'

I passed it over. He wolfed it down in about three bites, then lay down again, one arm thrown over his face to shield his eyes from the sun. 'So, how's your mum?'

'Mum?' Until that moment, I had completely forgotten that I'd mentioned her to Blake. I tried to recall what I might have said, settling on a vague, 'Oh – she's much the same.'

'Did you tell her where you were on Monday night? Spending time with evil policemen?'

I laughed. 'No, I didn't have to say anything about it. She was asleep when I got back.'

'Why does she hate the police?' He lifted his arm away from his face for a second and squinted at me. 'It's been bothering me since you said it.'

'People do.' I turned my head away. 'We had a few dealings with them and they weren't all that helpful, let's put it that way.'

'What sort of thing?'

I wavered for a second, tempted to tell him about Charlie, but it was too long a story, and besides, he couldn't really be that interested. I told myself he was just asking questions as a good policeman should.

'Ancient history. You know how it is. Surrey Police priorities didn't match up with hers. She felt a bit let down. If she wasn't the sort to hold a grudge, I'm sure she'd be over it by now.'

'Is it just the two of you living there? No dad?'

'Dad died,' I said, and I don't think my voice changed, but he sat up.

'When did that happen?'

'When I was fourteen. Ten years ago. God, it doesn't seem that long.'

'How did he die?'

I had got used to saying what happened without getting emotional. 'Car accident. It was after they'd split up. He'd moved out. He was driving up from Bristol to see me and – well, it was just a stupid accident.'

Not suicide, either. Whatever people had thought.

'That must have been tough.'

'Mm,' I said, not looking at him. 'It made things pretty difficult at home. Mum wasn't in great shape after the divorce, which was why I'd stayed with her. When Dad died . . .' I swallowed. 'She had to go into hospital for a while. She just couldn't manage.'

It had been far worse than that. She had been psychotic with grief – out of her mind, dangerously so. She had been sectioned, for her own safety and for mine, and Aunt Lucy had come like an angel and spirited me away to Manchester for a few months. I had written to Mum every day, and never heard a word in return.

'When she got out of hospital, she was still a bit of a wreck, to be honest. And she's never really recovered. There's just the two of us, so I look after her. It's sort of the least I can do.'

'What happened to your dad –' he put his hand out and touched my ankle '– it wasn't your fault, you know.'

'Did I say it was?' My voice was sharp; I had spent years listening to Mum tell me that I was responsible. 'I know it was just bad luck. It shouldn't have happened, but it did.

And you wouldn't have thought that Mum would care, considering they'd split up two years earlier. But she was devastated.'

'Maybe she still loved him. How did they break up?'

'Dad left. But she made him go.' I shook my head. 'I heard the way she used to talk to him. I heard the things she used to say about him. She *hated* him.'

'Did she take off her wedding ring?'

'What?'

'Did she stop wearing it – after the divorce?'

'No. Actually, she still wears it.'

Blake shrugged. 'Then she still loves him.'

I considered it for a second, reluctant to give Mum credit for anything. But maybe he had a point. And for the first time in years, I actually felt genuinely sorry for my mother, who hadn't wanted her life to work out the way it had, who couldn't deal with the crappy things that had happened to her, who just wanted the world to go away.

Blake had rolled on to his back again and closed his eyes. My ankle tingled where his hand had rested. Without thinking, without even really meaning to say it out loud, I blurted out, 'Why don't you have a girlfriend?'

He twisted his head to look at me and grinned. 'I work terrible hours, remember? They don't stick around.'

'Oh, right.' More likely that he went through them at a rate – he couldn't be short of willing candidates. I had more self-respect than that, though. I wouldn't be joining the queue. 'Speaking of work, I'd better get back. Janet will be furious.'

I expected him to laugh, but he didn't. He frowned, then sat up. 'Sarah . . . about this case. Promise me that you'll be careful. Promise me that you'll keep out of the investigation.'

I felt my face go blank. 'What do you mean?'

'Look, you're a nice person. You take responsibility for things, even when maybe you shouldn't. But this – this isn't something you want to be involved with.'

'I don't know what you're talking about.' I began to fold the sandwich wrappers for the sake of having something to do.

'Listen, it's not that you haven't helped us. You've been great. But you've been a bit too close to this case from the start. I like you, Sarah, and I don't want to see you get hurt.'

I was half annoyed, half occupied with trying to work out what he meant when he said he liked me. *Liked* me, or just liked me? I pushed that question out of my head and made myself focus. 'How would I get hurt?'

'Lots of ways.' Blake stood up then, towering over me. The sun was behind him and he was silhouetted against the bright sky. I couldn't see the expression on his face. 'Someone always gets the blame, sooner or later, in a case like this. It hasn't started yet, but if we don't get any results soon, people are going to start asking questions, wondering who should have spotted what was going on. Believe me, you don't want to be in the frame when they come looking.'

'I hardly think that's likely.'

'I've seen it happen,' Blake said. 'Just go back to work,

Sarah. Don't try to do our job for us, and don't put yourself in harm's way.'

I looked up at him dumbly. Suddenly awkward, he checked his watch. 'I'd better go. Thanks for having lunch with me.'

I watched him walk away across the lawn, his head down. My throat was aching as if I might cry, but it was anger I felt. *He* had come to find *me*, after all. I had just been trying to help the Shepherds when I spoke to Rachel. Surely there was no harm in wanting to do what I could?

As there was no one to hear my unanswerable arguments, I ran out of steam eventually and got up to go. By the time I had finished collecting the rubbish, there was no trace at all of us having been there, except for some flattened grass.

It had been a mistake to think that my new sympathy for my mother would survive an actual face-to-face encounter with her. I hadn't been at home for two minutes before the pity withered and died.

I had got home sticky, hot and tired, to be greeted by the smell of stale air and musty fabric that was the signature scent of home. It was a long way from freshly baked bread or roasting coffee. On the sofa, Mum was leafing through a large, leather-effect scrapbook that I recognised immediately.

The scrapbooks had been Granny's idea. She had spent the weeks and months after Charlie's disappearance working her way through stacks of newspapers, cutting out any reference to him that she could find. There was a perverse kind of pride in it, as if this was Charlie's outstanding achievement – something to commemorate, like sporting prowess or academic excellence. Why she thought they would help, I had never understood. Mum had inherited them when Granny died: three heavy albums that crackled as the glue-stiffened pages turned. I had seen them many times but never actually looked through them. For one thing, I didn't want to, and for another, Mum guarded them with her life. She kept them hidden away in a safe place, which I suspected was under her bed, but I had never bothered to look. Recent events seemed to have prompted her to dig them out for a wallow, for old times' sake.

'I'm back,' I said unnecessarily, passing through the sitting room to the kitchen, where I took a tumbler out of the cupboard and filled it at the kitchen tap. The water was tepid and faintly metallic, but I was parched and drank the whole glass in one go. I refilled it and came back to stand beside the sofa. Mum looked up for a second, then returned to the page in front of her. I craned my neck, trying to read the headline upside-down. With a thud that was loud enough to make me jump, she snapped the book shut and glared at me.

'What do you want?'

I shrugged. 'Nothing. I was just looking.' I sat down on the arm of the sofa tentatively. 'Are you reading about Charlie?'

Something like an electric shock ran through me as the syllables left my mouth. I never said his name, never. Especially not to Mum. *There are two things*, an old teacher of mine had once told the class, *that cannot be taken back: the sped arrow and the spoken word.* I waited, cringing slightly, for the reaction.

After a second and quite calmly, Mum said, 'I'm just looking through these.' She patted the album that was on her knee.

'Can I see?' Without waiting for a reply, I reached over to pick up one of the other scrapbooks from the coffee table. We could look at them together. It might help us to come to a better understanding of each other. I was beginning to think that I didn't know her at all. Maybe that was the problem.

The scrapbook was a little too far away to reach comfortably. I managed to hook one finger under the spine and pulled it, trying to draw it nearer to me. It had stuck to the book underneath it and I yanked at it to break the seal that had formed. With a crack, the plastic binding ripped in a horrible jagged tear that wavered across the base of the spine for about two inches. The paper lining showed through the tear, stark white against the chocolate-brown of the cover. I froze.

Mum leaned forward and picked up the scrapbook, running her fingers over the damage, not saying a word.

'I – I'm sorry,' I started to say, but she turned her face up to me, her eyes blazing.

'This is typical of you. Typical. You just want to destroy everything that matters to me, don't you?'

'It was an accident. The books are old. They weren't that expensive anyway. The plastic must have perished.'

'Oh, they mean very little to you, I can tell that. But they matter to me, Sarah.' Her voice got louder, higher. 'Look at it. It's ruined.'

Ruined was a bit much. 'We can tape it up,' I said, hating that I was in the wrong.

'No, *we* can't. You aren't to touch these again.' She gathered them into her arms, glaring. 'You are a destructive, careless girl. You always have been. Especially where your brother is concerned.'

'What's that supposed to mean?'

'I shouldn't have to explain it to you,' Mum said, standing up with some difficulty, still cradling the books. 'You've always resented him. Always.'

'That's absolutely untrue. I—'

'I don't care, Sarah!' Her words cracked like a whip, and I actually flinched. 'You are a very great disappointment to me. My only consolation is that your father isn't alive to see how you've turned out. He would be devastated if he knew.'

'If he knew what?' I stood up too, and I was shaking. 'If he knew that I lived here to babysit you, instead of having a life of my own? If he knew the opportunities I'd passed up rather than leave you on your own?'

'I never asked you to come back here,' Mum spat. 'This has nothing to do with me, and everything to do with you not taking responsibility for your own life. It's much easier to stay here and resent me for the way you live than to make your own way in the world. But you can't blame me. I didn't even want you here. I'd rather be alone.'

'Oh, because you managed so well when I was at university. You wouldn't last a week,' I said coldly. 'Unless you actually want to die. I can see how I would be inconvenient to have around the place if you were trying to drink yourself to death.'

'How *dare* you!'

'How dare *you*? You really shouldn't be encouraging me to leave. I might take you up on it, you know.'

'I would never be that lucky,' Mum said flatly.

I looked at her for a long minute. 'You really hate me, don't you?'

'I don't hate you. I just don't need you.'

Two lies for the price of one. But she knew, and I knew, that it didn't make any difference. She could say what she liked. I couldn't leave, and neither could she.

I walked past her without saying another word and went upstairs to my bedroom, slamming the door behind me with violence. Standing with my back to the door, I looked around the room – really looked at it, for once. It was depressing to see how little it had changed since my childhood. The room was small, dominated by the double bed I had bought with my first pay cheque, feeling like a grown-up at last. I had revised for countless exams at the little desk that was jammed awkwardly into the bay window, sitting for hours with my feet braced on the radiator. Beside my bed, there was a bookcase crammed with the books I had read at university and before – the classics, for the most part, their spines threaded with white from reading and rereading. Apart from my chest of drawers and the tiny bedside table, there was nothing else in the room. There was nothing that reflected my own taste. There was nothing I wouldn't have been happy to walk out and never see again, with the exception of my father's photograph.

A fly was buzzing somewhere in the room. I walked over to open the window, then stood by the desk, opening and closing the drawers aimlessly, looking for nothing in particular. The drawers were stuffed with bank statements, receipts and old postcards that I'd never bothered to throw out, from university friends. *Fell asleep on the beach and burned my back! Greece is lovely – can't wait to come back here!* Or *Alain is a sweetie and such a good skier . . . Wish you had come with us!* I wasn't on the postcard or Christmas-card list for anyone any more. It was hard to keep in touch when the answer to 'What's new with you?' was always 'Nothing'.

The fly zipped past me and out through the open window. Was it true what Mum had said? Was I blaming her for my own mistakes? A feeling was building inside me, one I hadn't had for a long time, a kind of recklessness born of frustration and fatigue and just being fed up. I didn't, on the whole, allow myself to be emotional often, and the strength of what I was feeling surprised me.

The floorboards creaked on the landing and I stiffened, waiting until I heard Mum's bedroom door close. She had gone to ground as well. It was our tacitly accepted practice to stay out of each other's way for a few days after a row. Nothing was ever resolved, or forgotten, but time passed. Time passed and there was no end in sight.

I sat down on the edge of my bed and thought about everything and nothing, about Charlie and Jenny and Dad and the rest, and reached no conclusion at all except that something had to happen, and soon. I wondered what it was I really wanted. I watched the clouds and let ideas drift through my mind until I settled on one thing that I longed for, something that, once I'd thought of it, I couldn't put out of my mind, something that was within my reach, if I hadn't misread the signs. I went and found my phone, checked the number I needed, and sent a short message without stopping for long enough to let myself second-guess what I was planning. And the reply, when it came, was simple: yes.

The light was draining from the sky when I let myself out of my room and slipped into the bathroom, stripping off my clothes and turning the shower on full. I stepped under it while it was still running cold and tilted my head back, letting the water rush through my hair for a minute or two. I moved slowly, deliberately, meticulous in washing my hair until it squeaked, the water running over me as my skin tingled. When I was finished, I wrapped my hair in a towel and worked moisturiser into every inch of my body until my skin gleamed like satin.

Back in my bedroom, I put on barely-there black chiffon underwear that I had bought in Paris what seemed like a lifetime ago, at the insistence of one of my friends, and had never worn. There had been no reason to. There had been no one to see that kind of thing since Ben. But I didn't allow myself to think about Ben. And now was definitely not the time to start.

At the back of a drawer, I found a fitted black top with a plunging neckline and pulled it on, along with my favourite jeans, which were ancient, soft as suede. Flat sandals

on my feet and a wide bangle on one arm were the last
details. It was the right balance between looking good and
trying too hard, I judged, looking at myself in the mirror
critically before starting to work on my hair. After drying
it, I pulled it all back into a low knot at the base of my
head and clipped it. A few soft tendrils spiralled on either
side of my face. I left them as they were. There was colour
in my cheeks from the heat of the hairdryer, but there was
heat within me too, a self-sustaining slow burn of determination and desire.

I took my time with my make-up, emphasising my eyes
with dark liner and mascara so they looked huge, and
dabbing just a little gloss on my lips. In the mirror my
eyes were steady but wary. I looked different, even to myself.
I looked like someone I hadn't been for a long time. I
looked like the person I should have been all along, not
the pale shadow I'd become.

It was after ten by the time I was finished. Grabbing
my bag, I hurried downstairs, not bothering to be quiet,
and slammed the front door, some childish part of me
hoping that Mum had heard, that she was wondering
where I was going at that hour, and why.

I was dry-mouthed with nerves as I parked, refusing to
listen to the little voice in my head that said I was making
a fool of myself, that he would back off. He'd have to,
some part of me knew. What I was planning was a bad
idea in so many ways. I got out of the car and walked into
the building decisively, taking the lift to the top floor as
if I had every right to be there. I walked up to his door.
Faint music was just audible from where I stood. I knocked

gently and closed my eyes for a second. My heart was fluttering in my chest like a trapped bird.

When Blake opened the door, our eyes met and it was as physical a jolt to me as if I'd parried a blow. He was barefoot, in jeans and a T-shirt, and his hair was slightly ruffled, as if he'd been lying down. He looked at me impassively for a moment that seemed to stretch for hours, then smiled and stood back.

'Come in.'

'Thanks.'

I stepped past him into the hallway, dropping my bag on the floor before going any further. To my right was the main room, an open-plan living room and kitchen, lit softly by a couple of lamps. Uncurtained floor-to-ceiling windows opened onto a balcony that ran the length of the room. In daytime, it would make the most of the river view. The room was indefinably masculine, functional. There were no pictures on the cream-painted walls and it was minimally furnished: a vast brown sofa, a dining table and chairs, an intimidating music system and shelves of records and CDs. There were books, too, and I wandered towards them, skimming the spines for titles I knew. They were all nonfiction – history, biographies, even politics. I smiled to myself; Blake was a man who appreciated facts. It was no wonder he enjoyed his job. The kitchen was spotless; I wondered if he'd ever cooked anything in it.

'The bedrooms and bathroom are on the other side,' he said from the hall, where he was watching me. Whatever he was thinking was masked by his usual self-possession. It was as effective as a steel shutter at locking me out.

'Very nice.' I walked back through the room towards him. 'Your parents were generous.'

'Can't fault my dad for that,' he said with a grin. 'He never held back when it came to money. Emotional support you could whistle for, but there was always plenty of cash.'

'Lucky for you.'

'If you say so.' He looked around, as if seeing the flat for the first time. 'Anyway, this is it. My inheritance. More of an investment than a home.'

It did look impersonal, like a stage set or a hotel suite. Somewhere Blake was prepared to leave at a moment's notice, I guessed.

'It's very tidy.'

He shrugged. 'I like to keep things neat. And I'm never here to make it untidy.'

'Lucky that you were in this evening, then,' I said lightly. 'I was expecting you to say you weren't free when I texted you.'

'Vickers gave me the night off. He told me there was no point in being there if I was too tired to think.'

'You do look tired.'

'Thanks very much.' He moved a couple of paces forward, into the living room. 'Did you just come over to check the place out or can I get you a drink?'

I shook my head. 'I didn't come here to drink.'

'I see. So it's the conversation that brought you here.'

'I wouldn't say that either.'

We were standing a few feet apart by then. I moved closer to him, until he was within touching distance. The air between us seemed to crackle. I took another step towards him, so close that I could feel the heat of his skin through the thin cotton of his T-shirt, and waited, my eyes locked on his, for him to move. Slowly, deliberately, he trailed his fingertips down from the hollow at the base of my throat to the deep V of my top, feather-light contact that made me shiver with desire. I leaned into him, sliding my hands up his chest, and turned my face up to him for a kiss that started out as tentative, then grew deeper, passionate. He slid a hand around to the back of my head and freed my hair from the clip to let it fall down my back. He twined his fingers through it, holding a handful at the base of my neck, so that I couldn't move away, even if I had wanted to. I pressed myself against him, sighing as he kissed my neck, his other hand exploring, the taste of him in my mouth, his heart thudding against mine.

I don't know what it was that made him stop. Without warning, he grabbed hold of my upper arms and held me away from him. I felt dazed, as if I had been roused from a deep sleep. He was breathing hard and at first he couldn't meet my eyes.

'What's wrong?'

'Sarah . . . I shouldn't be doing this.'

'Why not?'

He looked straight at me, obviously angry. 'Don't be obtuse. You know why. It's unprofessional.'

'It has nothing to do with being professional. It's personal.'

'It's just—' He broke off, struggling to find the words. 'I just can't.'

I waited for a second to see if he was going to go on,

then stepped back. 'OK. I get it. You could have told me not to come over.'

I kept my tone light, not confrontational, but he folded his arms and glared at me as if I'd attacked him. 'I don't always make the best decisions. Especially where you're concerned, it seems. You're a witness in the biggest case of my career. I can't do this, no matter how much I might want to. I could lose my job.'

I dredged up a crooked smile. 'It's nice to know you want to, anyway.'

'Don't do that. Don't be so humble.' His tone was sharp. 'I've wanted you from the first time I saw you. You don't have a clue how men look at you, do you?'

He reached out and ran a finger down the side of my face, tracing the line of my cheek, and I closed my eyes for a moment. I felt tears sting the back of my throat and swallowed hard; I would not cry in front of Andy Blake. I had more pride than that.

I turned away from him and walked over to the window, pushing the hair back from my face. My cheeks felt hot. For a second, I stared at my face floating against the dark background, blurry and indistinct. Then I leaned against the glass, cupping my hands around my eyes, and peered out at the buildings opposite and the lights reflected in the river. 'It *is* a great view,' I said in an absurdly conversational tone, as if nothing had interrupted our discussion of the flat.

'Fuck the view,' Blake said violently, and crossed the room in a couple of strides, pulling me around to face him. He looked down at me with something like despair. Then his mouth was on mine again and I gave myself up to him willingly, wrapping myself around him when he lifted me up and carried me to his bedroom, helping him to take off my clothes and his. The world was reduced to his skin against mine, his hands, his mouth, and as I arched my back and cried out, I had no thoughts in my head, not a one, and it was bliss. And afterwards, he held me tightly, and I didn't even know that I was crying until he wiped my tears away.

1992

Two weeks missing

I know that I'm in trouble as soon as they tell me we are going to the police station. Every time Mum and Dad have been there since Charlie disappeared, they have left me with Aunt Lucy. I sit in the back of the car, behind my mother, and I think about saying that my stomach hurts. It's not a lie. But I doubt that it would be enough to make Mum and Dad change their minds. There is something in their faces that makes me think that I am not going to get out of this, and at that thought, my stomach hurts more.

Someone is waiting for us at the station. When we walk in, my father holding my hand, a small woman with short hair rushes over.

'Thank you for coming in, Laura, Alan. And this must be Sarah. We're going to have a little chat, Sarah – would you like that?'

If I was braver, I would say no, but my father's hand tightens on mine and I squeak something that sounds like yes.

'Good girl. Would you like to come with me?'

My father pulls my hand forward so the woman can take hold of it, and she starts to walk away, drawing me behind her, heading for a plain white door. I look back over my shoulder to where Mum and Dad are standing, not touching, watching me. Dad's face is worried. Mum has a dead look, as if I mean nothing to her. Suddenly, I am afraid that they are going to leave, and I try to twist my hand out of the woman's grasp, leaning away from her, back towards my parents, crying, 'Mum, I don't want to go.'

Dad starts forward a pace and then stops. Mum doesn't move an inch.

'Now, don't be silly,' the woman says briskly. 'I just want to have a talk with you in a special room. Your parents are going to be watching you on a little television. Come on.'

I give in, following her through the door and down a corridor, to a small room with an armchair and a very old, sagging sofa. There are toys in a heap in the corner – dolls, teddy bears, an Action Man with felt hair whose arms are thrown up over his head.

The woman says, 'Why don't you go and choose a doll to look after while we're talking?'

I go over and stand by the pile, looking at the tangle of legs and arms. I don't really want to touch any of them. In the end, I pick the one on top of the pile, a floppy doll with a smiling face and bright red wool hair, wearing a frilled dress with a flowery pattern. Her face is painted on, and the paint has gone grey around her mouth and cheeks.

I come back and sit down on the sofa, holding the doll stiffly. The woman sits in the armchair and watches me. She isn't wearing make-up and her mouth is colourless, her lips almost invisible until she smiles. But she smiles often.

'I haven't introduced myself, have I? I'm a police officer, a detective constable. My name is DC Helen Cooper, but you can just call me Helen. I've got you to come here today to have a little talk with me about your brother, because we haven't found him yet, have we? I just wanted to go through it with you one more time, in case you'd remembered anything since the police first talked to you.'

I want to tell her that I haven't remembered anything, that I've tried, but she doesn't give me a chance to speak.

'This is a special room with cameras to record what you and I say to each other. There's one there, up in the corner –' and she points with her biro at a white, boxy camera mounted near the ceiling '– and one over there on a stand. And what we're saying is being recorded, so other people can listen to what you have to say. Don't worry about them, though, just talk to me normally, because we're just having a little conversation, aren't we? So there's nothing to be scared about.'

I start to comb out the doll's yarn hair with my fingers. It is stuck together in places with something that might be hardened snot.

'Do you like school, Sarah?'

I nod without looking up.

'What's your favourite subject?'

'English,' I whisper.

She smiles widely. 'I used to like English too. I like stories, don't you? But do you know the difference between a story that someone has made up and something that really happened?'

'Yes.'

'What do we call it if someone pretends something happened, but it really didn't?'

'A lie.'

'That's right, good girl. Just say that I went out of the room and I left these papers here, and another police officer came in and ripped them up – if I came back and said, "Who ripped up my papers?" and the police officer said, "Sarah did," what would that be?'

'A lie,' I say again.

'But if the other police officer said, "I ripped them up," what would that be?'

'The truth.'

'That's right. And we're only interested in the truth in this conversation, aren't we? We only want to hear what really happened, don't we?'

But they don't. They don't want to hear that I don't know anything. They don't want to believe that I fell asleep, that I didn't ask Charlie where he was going. Everyone wants me to tell the truth, but they want a better version of it than the one I can tell them, and there's nothing I can do about it.

The questions are all the same: what I saw, what I heard, what Charlie said, when he left, whether anyone else was there. I answer automatically, without stopping to think much about what I'm saying.

Then, all of a sudden, Helen leans forward and asks, 'Are you trying to hide anything, Sarah? Are you trying to protect someone?'

I look up, feeling cold. What does she mean?

'If someone told you to tell us something that wasn't true, you can tell me.' Her voice is quiet, gentle. 'You're safe here. You won't get in trouble.'

I stare at her without saying anything. I can't answer.

'Sometimes people ask us to keep secrets, don't they, Sarah? Maybe someone you love has asked you to keep something secret. Has your mummy asked you not to say something to us?'

I shake my head.

'What about your daddy? Has he asked you to pretend that something happened when it didn't, or that something didn't happen when it did?'

I shake my head again, still staring at her. Her eyes don't blink, I notice. She's watching me intently.

After a minute or two, she sits back. 'OK. Let's start again, shall we?'

I answer Helen's questions as best I can while I plait the red wool into two neat braids. Every time I finish, I undo the plaits so that I can start again, to get it right, to make it perfect. By the time Helen gives up, I almost like the rag doll and her faded, gentle face. I'm sorry to leave her in the stuffy little room, and I lay her down on top of the pile of toys while Helen stands by the door, clicking the top of her pen impatiently, her smile long gone.

Chapter 6

Later, quite a long time later, Blake slept. He was as self-contained in sleep as he was in everyday life, his face serious, composed. I sat up, leaning on one elbow, and watched him for a while. I didn't feel like sleeping yet. Nor did I want to wake up in the morning and feel, in the cold light of day, like I wasn't welcome. Better to leave before he thought I should go.

I flipped back the duvet and eased myself out of bed, careful not to disturb him, then hunted for my clothes in the half-light of the bedroom. My legs weren't quite steady; I felt giddy, slightly drunk. I found my jeans and my pants together where I had slid them off – or had he? I couldn't quite recall – but my bra was nowhere to be found. I searched the carpet, running my hands over it in a widening arc, finding nothing on the soft smooth pile but a butterfly earring back that didn't belong to me. I smiled wryly to myself; no point in thinking that this was the first time Blake had entertained female company in his bedroom. I left the butterfly where it was and crept out into the hall, where my top was lying in a crumpled heap. Still no sign of my bra. I would have to go without. The thin silk fabric of my top was cool to the touch, and sent a light chill racing over my overheated skin as I pulled it down over my torso. I winced a little as I bent to pick up my bag from the floor; I was beginning to feel slightly sore in certain places. He had been gentle at first, and then had forgotten himself enough to be less so, which I had taken as a compliment. I couldn't help playing it back in my mind, especially since I didn't expect it to be anything more than a one-off. How could it be anything more? He'd been right; I should have been off limits. There wouldn't be a next time.

I caught sight of myself in the hall mirror on my way to the front door and didn't know myself: eyeliner had smudged under my eyes and my hair was all over the place. I ran my fingers through it, shaking out the curls. There was nothing I could do with it, except to be glad that it was unlikely anyone would see me on my way home at that hour – after one o'clock, I noted with a mild sense of surprise, wondering where I had lost the time, knowing full well that it had been in Andy Blake's arms, on the first or maybe the second time.

I drew the front door close behind me, not daring to shut it properly in case the sound woke him, gambling that he was unlikely to be burgled. I walked down the stairs, too wound up to wait for the lift. I could still feel him on me, in me as I unlocked my car. I sat there for a second before starting the engine, looking at my hands on the steering wheel as if I'd never seen them before. I should have spoken to him before I left – sneaking out guaranteed that it would be awkward when I saw him next. But I couldn't deal with reality now. I couldn't deal with seeing regret on his face when he woke up. It was no one else's business, what we had done. As long as he kept it to himself, I would do the same. And no one need ever know.

When I turned off the main road into the Wilmington Estate, I decided on a whim not to go straight home. There was something I had been avoiding that I felt I should do, and there would never be a better time to do it unobserved. I drove past the entrance to my road, carrying on up the central road that curved through the estate. The houses on either side of the road looked deserted in the harsh orange streetlights. Nothing moved, and for a moment I felt as if I was the only one alive on the whole estate, in all of Elmview. I turned right, then right again, following a half-remembered route to a small open space surrounded by houses, where the far-sighted 1930s planners had left a place for children to play. My parents had once taken us to a fireworks display there; we had had sparklers, and I had cried at the noise of the rockets. Near there, as far as I knew, was Morley Drive. I had to hunt around a bit, going the wrong way a couple of times, but I had the general direction right and eventually I spotted it. I drove down the narrow road, scanning both sides until I saw the police car parked on the pavement. It would have to be outside Jenny's house, I reasoned, as I started to look for a space. I found one a few car-lengths away from the police car on the opposite side of the road and pulled in.

The red-brick house was familiar to me from the news; it seemed strange to see it in real life. The curtains were all closed, blankly uninformative, and I wondered if the Shepherds were living there or if they had fled to neutral territory, away from the media. The house looked immaculate in the orange glare of the streetlights, neatly painted, the hedge trimmed, a cherry tree in the front garden still dappled with blossom. But as I looked closer I could see a large hand-tied bouquet standing in the porch with another bunch of flowers laid beside it. The grass straggled over the kerbstones that lined the driveway, as if mowing the lawn had been put off a couple of times. When would that be a priority for the Shepherds again, if ever? Who could be bothered to care about the appearance of their house when they had lost the most important thing in it?

I sat in the car and just looked at the house. I didn't know what I had hoped to see. I had just wanted to be there, to see for myself how close to me Jenny had lived out the short span of her days, to pay my respects, to take a sounding of the Shepherds' grief and know it as I knew my own. The small signs of neglect that I could see from where I sat were like blemishes on an overripe pear, tokens of rot that ran to the core. There had been no outward sign of the corruption that ran through the Shepherds' daughter, but it had been there all the same, and when the press got wind of it, if they hadn't already, the Shepherds would lose Jenny all over again. I shivered at the thought, at the tabloid editor's dream and middle-class mother's nightmare that was the pretty child with a double life. Poor Jenny, with her innocent face and her grown-up problems. She had been an only child. Did that make it less likely that the Shepherds would one day recover? Would it matter to them that they had each other? Maybe if they found out what had happened to her, and who was responsible, it would help. It was the not knowing that had corroded my family. My parents had come apart instead of drawing together, and I had fallen into the gap between them.

A thought was beginning to form somewhere at the back of my mind – an idea. I had spent so long not thinking about Charlie, not allowing him to be a part of my life. I had tried to forget about him, and it made it all the harder to live with his loss. I needed to confront what had happened to him. No one else was going to do it. The police were not likely to be helpful about a case that had run out of leads sixteen years before. I couldn't expect anyone else to care. But I cared, I admitted to myself. Jenny's death was resonating in my own life. I needed to find some answers, or at the very least know that I had tried. I had wanted to help the Shepherds when really I needed to help myself. And no one would tell me I couldn't, I thought, my cheeks warm at the recollection of Blake's warning earlier in the day. It was well worth doing a bit of research. OK, so I probably wouldn't solve the case, but I should really understand what had happened to my brother. The bare facts were familiar enough, but undoubtedly there was a lot of nuance that I was too young to understand at the time. Not to mention the fact that a lot of water had flowed under various bridges since 1992. It couldn't hurt to see if any connections could be made between Charlie's disappearance and other crimes that had occurred locally since then. I might see something that everyone else had missed.

It felt good to make that decision; for the second time

that night, it felt as if I was taking control. I had seen enough in Morley Drive. It was time to go home. I took one last look at the Shepherds' house, then turned the key in the ignition. With a wet cough, the engine failed to catch. I swore quietly and tried again, and then again, horribly self-conscious about the noise I was making. The car rattled unhelpfully a couple of times and then fell silent. Nothing. I smacked the steering wheel in frustration, and even though it had zero effect on the car and hurt me quite a bit, I felt slightly better. It wasn't the first time my car had let me down, but the timing was horrendous. I couldn't think of calling the AA at that hour of the night. It would cause a fuss in the quiet street, and draw attention to me, attention that I profoundly did not want. However, I wasn't far from home. I could walk. At least it hadn't happened at Blake's. I imagined myself returning to his flat five minutes after stealing away, to ask if I could have a lift home. Embarrassing would not have been the word.

The night air was like cold fingers running up my bare arms. I hadn't thought to bring a jacket. I locked the car, even though there was nothing of value in it and it was unlikely to be stolen, unless someone wanted it badly enough to tow it away. They were welcome to it, I thought sourly, dropping the keys into my bag, but I didn't mean it really. I loved my car, unreliable and shabby though it was. I found some comfort in the thought that there was a police car nearby, that someone would be keeping an eye on it until the following morning, when I could get it back on the road. I wouldn't even allow myself to consider the possibility that what I had just heard from it was a last-gasp death rattle. I needed it to work. Until it did, I was effectively grounded.

My footsteps sounded unnaturally loud on the pavement as I walked quickly back along the road, wondering if there was any sound as lonely as someone walking on their own in the small hours of the morning. A faint bloom of condensation blurred my reflection in the car windows as I passed and I folded my arms across my chest, hugging myself for warmth. When I breathed out, my breath misted in front of me for a split second. The ice-white moon shone in chill perfection, high and remote. The clear night had let the warmth of the day seep away. My bag swung against my hip rhythmically as I walked; I was jangling as loudly as a caravan of fully laden camels in the desert. I expected at any minute that someone would pull open their curtains to glare at me as I passed.

It seemed to take a long time to get back to the main road. I crossed over, checking both ways automatically, even though I would have heard anything coming a mile off. The road stretched away into the distance; it was a good ten-minute walk to Curzon Close from where I was. I started walking on the grass strip that bordered the road rather than the pavement, muffling my footsteps deliberately. The dew saturated the bottom of my jeans and my feet slipped wetly in my sandals. A playing field was dark and deserted on my right and I swallowed, assuring myself that I was not afraid. The goose bumps, dry mouth and damp palms were caused by something else entirely.

Nearly there. Nearly home.

As I walked into Curzon Close, something crunched under my feet. Broken glass lay scattered all over the ground, a cluster of orange sparkles showing where the streetlight glinted on the mazy remains of a wine bottle. The air was heavy with the sweet musky smell of cheap wine. I slowed down, trying to avoid the worst of the glass, conscious that my toes were unprotected in my sandals. The night was still, with no breeze to disperse the smell – the bottle could have fallen hours before. There was no one behind me, no one lurking in the shadows, no reason for the hairs on the back of my neck to be standing on end. On the other hand, there was no harm in checking. I stopped and half turned to look behind me, pretending to be casual about it, ready to run if I had to, and saw nothing at all that would make my heart pound in my chest. I shook my head, annoyed with myself, and rummaged in my bag for my keys. As I walked up the path to the front door, I was aware of nothing but relief. I know I didn't hear a sound, and only half saw the shape detaching itself from the overgrown bushes as I passed. Without being properly conscious of what was happening, acting on pure instinct, I ducked, twisting away so the blow that was aimed at the back of my head landed across my shoulder. It connected with shattering force and I fell hard, landing on one knee. The pain ran up into my hip like fire.

I don't think I lost consciousness, but I was quite a long way from alert in the minutes after he struck me. I was floating, lost in a sea of agony, too shocked to put anything like a coherent thought together, and when hands grabbed me under the arms and hauled me to my feet, I didn't try to resist. I lolled against the warm bulk behind me, as limp as a rag doll. My left arm hung down by my side, useless, and I couldn't feel it. With strange detachment I wondered why that might be, while at the same time I knew that there was something much more important to worry about. Slowly, painfully, the distant alarm bells I could hear came closer and louder, until they were jangling in my mind, drowning everything else out. *I'm in danger*, I thought. *I should do something about that.*

While the bit of my mind that was still functioning properly tried to raise some sort of response from the rest of me, I was dimly aware that my attacker was moving. He – and I knew it was a man from his strength and his smell, a mixture of cigarettes and engine oil and hot, acrid excitement – dragged me into the shelter of the bushes, out of sight of anyone who might be passing. Panic flared then and I opened my mouth to scream, but he pounced like a cat, one fist jammed into my throat, pressing on my larynx. I couldn't cry out. I couldn't even breathe. White lights whirled and exploded behind my eyelids and I felt my knees start to buckle. If he hadn't been holding me up, I would certainly have fallen.

After what seemed like centuries the pressure on my throat slackened and his hand dropped away. I pulled air into my lungs in huge, ragged gasps. When I could speak again, I croaked, 'What . . . do you . . . want?'

I wasn't really expecting an answer, and I didn't get one. I felt rather than heard him laugh, hot breath against the side of my face, ruffling my hair. He ran a fingertip down my cheek and the stitching on his glove scraped against my skin. He held me by the jaw, forcing my head back so the tendons in my neck strained as he slid his other hand up my torso, to my chest, and cupped my left breast, squeezing gently at first, then hard enough to force a small noise from me that was half pain, half fear. I felt him start, surprised; he must have discovered that I was wearing nothing under my flimsy top. His hand went to his face and he dragged off his glove with his teeth; I barely had time to register it before he ran his hand under my top and began to fondle me again, his fingers damp on my skin. Tears sprang into my eyes. I couldn't believe this was happening to me, in my own driveway, not six feet from the front door. I could try to fight back, but at that moment, I couldn't see how. If I had been facing him . . . if my left arm wasn't incapacitated . . . if I wasn't trying to tackle someone far heavier and stronger than me . . . I might have had a chance.

'Please,' I said, and couldn't think what to say next. *Please don't kill me. Please don't rape me. Please don't hurt me.* He would if he wanted to. It was as simple as that.

With a tiny sigh, he slackened his grip on me. For a moment, I thought he was going to turn me around to face him as he put his hands on my shoulders. Then he was forcing me down, pushing me onto my knees. The weight on my right knee was agony and I was almost glad when he shoved me hard between the shoulder blades so that I fell onto my hands, my face inches from the earth. He stepped forwards and put his hand on the back of my head, pressing me into the ground. I inhaled tiny crumbs of soil and gagged, struggling upwards, beginning to panic again, but he forced my head back down.

'Stay,' came from behind me, as if I were a dog. His voice was no more than a whisper, unidentifiable, terrifying. I had no plan to disobey. I felt rather than heard him move away, with just a small scuffing sound as he paused to pick something up. My watch ticked under my cheek: ten seconds, twenty, a full minute, and I couldn't hear him any more. I stayed where I was, shivering, until I was as sure as I could be that he was gone, but pushing myself up and looking around me was still the bravest thing I'd ever done. Relief coursed through me, followed almost immediately by the sharp thud of dismay: my attacker had gone, but so had my bag.

It seemed stupid to worry about a handbag when I had been afraid for my life only minutes before, but the discovery that it was gone made me angry – beyond angry: furious. My whole life was in that bag, not just replaceable things like bankcards and credit cards. There were photographs of my parents and my brother, my little diary and a notebook that I scribbled lists in. It had been stuffed with business cards, scraps of paper with phone numbers and addresses and other useful information that was now gone for good. Keys for both house and car: gone. There wasn't even anything especially valuable in my bag; my phone was ancient and battered and essentially worthless. I could have told him if he'd asked. I would have given him the cash and the cards and wished him well. There had been no need for violence, none at all. And yet I couldn't shake the feeling that he had enjoyed touching me – hurting me – and that the bag had been something of an afterthought. My face burned with shame at the memory of his hands on me; I felt filthy.

Slowly, painfully, I dragged myself to my feet. The horizon seesawed crazily and I shut my eyes, holding on to branches so that I didn't pitch forward again. I knew that if I waited, things would improve, but I couldn't wait. What if he came back? I forced myself to let go of the bushes and make for the wall of the house, and I got there with a sort of drunken stagger. Not elegant, but effective enough. I stood, clinging on to the brickwork, feeling feeble, and wondered if there was any chance at all that Mum was up. The living-room window was beside me, and there was a gap in the curtains; bluish light leaked out, suggesting that the TV was on. I edged along the wall and peered in. Mum was stretched out on the sofa, her face grey-blue in the flickering light from the TV. She was dead to the world. An empty glass stood on the coffee table in front of the sofa. I rapped on the window gently, knowing that she wouldn't respond, hoping I might be wrong. Not a twitch.

I stood there for a moment, trying to think what to do, then turned very slowly to look behind me. I had been looking for my front-door key, hadn't I? And I had found it just as I walked in through the gate, just before the shadows had come to malignant life. I crouched down and worked my way along the path, peering at the ground, and was rewarded by a metallic gleam under the bushes, where the front-door key had fallen out of my hand. A foot, mine or his, had trodden it into the dirt, and it was only the shiny fob on the keyring that was visible. I brushed the earth off it, feeling, in a small way at least, triumphant. He hadn't got *that*, whatever else he'd managed to steal from me.

I hauled myself back to the front door and slid the key into the lock. My knee was really hurting now. I almost fell as I limped into the hall and shut the front door behind me, locking and bolting it before I did anything else. From the living room came the shrill music of late-night television; I couldn't stand to leave it on, no matter how much pain I was in. I hobbled in and switched it off. In the silence that followed, Mum's breathing sounded harsh. I looked down at her vacant face, her slack mouth and the glint of whitish eyeball where her left eye wasn't properly closed, and I felt nothing: not hatred, not love, not pity. Nothing. Without affection, because it was there, I pulled a blanket off the back of the sofa and spread it over her. She didn't stir.

The feeling was starting to come back to my left arm. I flexed my fingers gingerly and touched my hand to my shoulder a couple of times. Nothing was broken, I thought, though I couldn't lift my arm higher than my shoulder, and it hurt so much that I was reluctant to try it again after the first time. I limped through to the kitchen and gulped down a glass of water. My throat ached. My knee throbbed. I found two dusty ibuprofen tablets in a drawer and swallowed them. It was about as much use as throwing an eggcup of water on a bonfire.

Crisis management next: I rang the card-cancelling services and my mobile phone operator. They made it so easy. Everything could be replaced in a couple of days. My phone would be upgraded; they'd send the new one out in the post. All done in about ten minutes, in the middle of the night, via call centres in India. No questions asked. Apart from the personal items I had lost, the only real problem was my car. The spare keys were in Manchester, with Aunt Lucy, kept safe from Mum because twice she'd taken my car in the middle of the night, when she'd been in no condition to drive. I couldn't take the risk of having another set of keys in the house. I would have to ring Aunt Lucy in the morning and get her to post them to me. In the meantime, my car would have to stay where it was. At least it was legally parked. Getting a sheaf of parking tickets would have been the last straw.

I refilled my glass and sat down gingerly at the kitchen table. As I sipped the tepid water, I considered the following: if I called the police, there would be questions about where I had been, and what I was doing walking through the neighbourhood at that hour of the morning. Blake wouldn't thank me if it came out that I had been with him. I would be mortally embarrassed to have to explain what I had been doing in the Shepherds' street. So no police. And besides, they weren't likely to find whoever had done the mugging. As far as I knew, they never managed to arrest anyone for crimes like that unless they actually caught them in the act.

Also, it was important not to overreact. So someone had stolen my bag. Big deal. He had probably wanted to sell the contents and buy drugs. Even in the suburbs, that wasn't unusual. It was a casual crime. Nothing to worry about. A one-off. I could read more into it if I liked, but that wouldn't get me anywhere. OK, so he had been outside my house. But that was just bad luck, wasn't it? He couldn't have been waiting for me specifically. I had blundered into his path and he had taken advantage of it. I would not, I decided, allow myself to worry about it. I would pick myself up and get on with it.

With that in mind, it was time to get going. I felt in desperate need of a long shower and a decent night's sleep. Before I tackled the stairs, I paused in the hall, reluctantly, to inspect the damage. I flicked on the overhead light, which seemed very bright and unnecessarily harsh, and went over to the mirror that hung by the door. Steeling myself, I looked at my reflection for a long, awestruck moment: the dirt in my hair and on my face, the make-up that was streaking my cheeks, the mark on my cheekbone where he had pressed my face into the ground without pity.

Then I switched off the light and went to bed.

1992

Four weeks missing

I am standing beside Mum, looking at tins of
chopped tomatoes. They stretch away into the
distance, different brands, different types of
tomato. I don't know which one to choose and
neither, it seems, does Mum. She is just
standing, looking at the labels. It's the first time
we have been to the supermarket since Charlie
disappeared. We had a routine for the supermarket. Charlie pushed the trolley, Mum decided
what to buy and I put it in the trolley. Afterwards,
we had a bun and a drink in the little café opposite the supermarket. Mum had coffee. I don't
like the taste, but I love the smell, and I loved
sitting in the café, watching all the people going
into the supermarket and coming out again.

Today, the routine isn't working. I am putting
things in the trolley, then running around to
push it, but Mum doesn't seem to notice. She
has walked past things we always buy, and picked
up stuff that we wouldn't usually eat – frozen

pizzas, pre-cooked chicken in a foil-lined paper bag spotted with dark smears of grease, a net of limes, shrink-wrapped frankfurters that look like sweaty fingers. I'm afraid to say anything. She has been quiet today – sort of dreamy, lost in her own world. I prefer it to the snappish moods that make me scared to speak to her.

I stand beside her and hold on to the fabric of her skirt, just lightly, so that she doesn't feel it, and I pretend that things are normal. Charlie is just around the corner. He'll come back soon with boxes of cereal, and Mum will tell him off for getting the kind covered with chocolate, and we'll go to the café and have drinks and laugh at stupid jokes and watch the people come and go.

A large lady pushes her trolley into the aisle, at the other end. The trolley looks heavy and the lady's face is red. She stops short when she sees us standing there, stops and stares. I stare back, wondering what she wants. Mum is still gazing at the tins, not aware of the woman's eyes on her or the look on her face. The lady pulls her trolley back a little, and leans around the corner, saying something that I can't hear to someone I can't yet see. There's a pause, and then another woman appears, small and thin, also with a trolley. She stands beside the fat one, and they look funny, little and large, both of them with the exact same expression on their faces. Surprise, curiosity and disapproval. The two of them together are blocking the whole aisle with their trolleys, and I wonder how we are going to get past them. They are whispering to one another, still looking at us. I know that they have recognised us, I hear the words 'poor little boy' and 'their own fault', and Mum must have heard them too because her head snaps up, just as if she's woken up. She looks down the aisle at them for a moment, and I glance up at her face. Her lips are tight. She looks angry.

'Come on,' she says to me, and grabs hold of the trolley, spinning it around smartly so we can escape the way we came. Her heels stab the floor, tap tap tap, and I hurry after her, into the next aisle where we don't stop for anything, and the one after that where Mum barely hesitates as she scoops up a jar of instant coffee and drops it into the trolley without looking. I'm glad that we've left the women behind, but I can tell that Mum is furious. I trail along after her, running now and then to keep up. The bright colours of the packaging on the shelves are a blur as we hurry up and down the last few aisles, through the cleaning products and cosmetics, ending up slightly out of breath at a checkout.

The woman on the checkout smiles a hello without really seeing us and starts to drag our things over the scanner, pushing them to the end where the plastic bags are hanging. Mum jabs me in the back. 'Go and pack.'

I would prefer to unload the shopping trolley. I like to arrange the things on the conveyor belt in groups, fitting everything in so that there are no gaps. Mum is throwing the food we've chosen onto the belt carelessly. The bananas hang over the edge and the jars roll around noisily every time it lurches forward. I pull a plastic bag off the stand and start to fill it. I hate Mum, I really do. Packing is no fun. I deliberately put heavy tins in on top of the fresh fruit and squash too many things into the fragile plastic bag so that it stretches and tears a little. When I look up, Mum has gone, leaving the empty trolley at an angle at the top of the conveyor belt. For a moment I feel pure terror.

The checkout lady swipes another jar across the scanner with a beep. 'Don't worry. She's just gone to get something else.' She eyes the bag I am holding and reaches up to the stand. 'Want a new one?'

I nod then watch, disgusted, as she licks her fingers and rubs the top of the bag to open it. I don't want to touch it as her spit is all over it, but I can't think of a way to get out of using it. I fill it up, and another one, and still Mum doesn't come back. The checkout lady is looking at me now, frowning a little. My cheeks are burning. If Mum doesn't come back, I can't pay for the shopping. I can't carry it home.

All at once she is there, her arms full of bottles. She stands them up at the end of the conveyor belt: three glass bottles filled with clear liquid, each with a silver cap and a blue label that is turned away from me. The woman scans them quickly and Mum puts them into a bag herself, pushing me out of the way. She pays, handing over her card. When the checkout lady reads the name, she looks up, her mouth a little O of surprise. I look straight back, daring her to say anything, while Mum waits to sign the receipt.

We march out of the supermarket and I help to pack the car. Mum drives home in silence. When we get back, she goes to the boot and takes out a single bag. It clinks musically. Bottles.

'I'll help to carry the bags in.'

'Just go into the house, please.'

She unlocks the door and pushes me inside, in front of her. She goes straight through to the kitchen and gets a glass from the cupboard. I watch from the doorway as she sits down at the table and breaks the seal on the first bottle out of the bag. It looks like water as she tilts it into the glass. She drinks it in one long swallow, then sits with her eyes closed and her face scrunched up for a second. Then she pours another glass and does the same. And again.

The rest of the shopping stays in the boot, and I stay in the doorway. I watch and I wait as for the first time ever my mother drinks in front of me, and drinks, and drinks, as if there's no one watching, as if I'm not even there.

Chapter 7

I tried very, very hard to clear my mind when I turned out the light and settled down to sleep, but along with the darkness came the memories, splintered images from the past few days. A dead branch on the forest floor, a pale hand in the grass beside it. A curling poster of a green canal. Blake lying on the grass, eyes closed. Glass splintered on tarmac. A man reaching out of the shadows, violence on his mind. I stuck on the last one, unable to shake it. I had no face to put to him, no idea at all who had attacked me. I should just forget about it. But I couldn't.

I couldn't help thinking about what I had noticed, trying, in spite of myself, to work out if I'd known him, or would know him again. He was taller than me, like most men. The best I could do was to put him between five foot six and six foot. He had a slim build, but he was strong. Dark shoes – probably trainers; he had been almost silent as he moved away. Dark trousers. A jacket that was made of some sort of rainproof material. Leather gloves. Nothing specific, nothing that would make him stand out. I could walk past him in the street and I'd never recognise him.

The only other distinctive feature I could remember was the combination of smells: cigarettes and engine oil. Not exactly unique to one individual. He could have picked up the engine oil anywhere; it was easy enough to find a greasy patch on the road where a car had been parked. If he had walked through one of those, the smell could have lingered quite strongly. I had done it myself.

The feeling that tormented me above all others was not fear, but irritation with myself that I hadn't been paying attention, that I had dropped my guard. If he had wanted to rape or murder me, what would have stopped him? Not me; I hadn't even been able to struggle. Maybe if I had seen him, I could have run away, or screamed loudly enough to wake the neighbours. It was futile to dwell on the ifs and the maybes, but I did it anyway, my arm throbbing sullenly all the while. The luminous hands inched around the face of my bedside clock and methodically, monotonously, I plodded again and again through the who and the why of what had happened and got no nearer to an answer.

I slipped into a heavy, dreamless sleep near dawn, and woke up long after my usual getting-up time with gritty eyes, a sore throat and a face that felt as if it had been snipped off with pinking shears and stapled back on in a fairly approximate way. I had, I discovered as I walked to the bathroom, a limp. My knee was stiff and protested when I bent it. It was pulpy with swelling and bruised, but wasn't as extravagantly lurid as my shoulder. I still couldn't lift my arm above my shoulder and both were vibrant with colour, shading from purple to bluey-black at the most tender point. The bruising extended down my arm to about halfway between my shoulder and elbow, like a longshoreman's tattoo, and it was exquisitely painful.

My face in the mirror was grim. I felt exhausted; I was too shattered to think of going to school.

I padded unevenly downstairs to the phone and called the school office, expecting Janet, and got Elaine. I had to stumble through my excuse, hoping that it didn't sound too much like a lie, knowing that Elaine was a tough audience and wouldn't believe it in any event. I sold the *terrible, blinding headache, I really don't think I can make it in today* line like my life depended on it. She harrumphed. Something told me that I wasn't the only one calling in sick. I upped the pathetic quaver in my voice as I elaborated on the nausea I had also been experiencing, and got a grudging assent out of her.

'But I will need you to come to St Michael's tonight. There's going to be a prayer service in memory of Jenny Shepherd, and I want all the teachers to attend.'

'What time does it start?'

'Six o'clock. I do hope that your headache will have gone by then.'

Choosing to ignore the sarcasm in her voice, I promised to be there and hung up, wondering how on earth I was going to make myself presentable in a mere ten hours. More sleep seemed like the best option. I wrote a note for Mum, explaining that I hadn't had to go to work and could I not be disturbed, please, and tiptoed into the living room. She was still there, curled up on the sofa, and didn't stir. The room was sour with night-breath and alcohol, dark and hot. I left the note in a prominent place and slid out again.

The stairs seemed longer and steeper than usual and

I dragged myself up, holding on to the banister. My limbs ached and every joint complained. I felt as if I had acquired a bad case of the flu along with my bruises, and the only thing that gave me the strength to get back to my bedroom was the prospect of peace, cool sheets and solitude for the next few hours. I clambered back into bed. Falling asleep was as easy – and as sudden – as falling off a cliff.

It was the rain that woke me in the end. The weather broke mid-afternoon, the first fragile warmth of summer subdued by a soggy low pressure that swept in from the Atlantic, pushing a clutch of heavy showers before it. I had left my window ajar and opened my eyes to dark spots on the pink carpet and a dappling of water across my desk from fat raindrops that had landed on the windowsill and exploded like tiny grenades. I got up, fuzzy-headed from sleep, and reached out with my left hand to shut the window. My arm thrilled with electric pain and I gasped, wondering how I could have forgotten. I switched hands and drew the window down, leaving an inch-wide gap so the pure, rain-washed air could flow in. The rain rattled like drumbeats on the roof and hung in an almost solid sheet in front of the houses across the road, turning them into faded, softened approximations of themselves, water-colours painted with dirty water. I watched idly for a few minutes as the rainwater leaped off the road surface and ran in rivers down the pavement. There was something fascinating about the heavy rain, hypnotic. Especially if you didn't have to go out in it.

It came as something of a shock to remember that I

did have to go out, and moreover that I had to walk. I was far too frightened of Elaine to be a no-show at the prayer service. I checked my watch, wincing at the discovery that it was half past four. My only hope was to ring Jules. I had her telephone number; it was in last year's diary. She had written it herself, with big looping writing that took up two lines at a time. I hopped back downstairs to the phone, hoping grimly that the guy who had nicked my bag was enjoying the use of my Nokia. It would have been so much more convenient if he'd left me my phone. And my keys. And my wallet. But then it wouldn't have been much of a mugging.

'Hello?'

'Jules, it's me, Sarah.'

'Sarah! I didn't recognise the number. God, I nearly didn't bother to answer it. How are you?'

'I'm OK,' I said quickly. 'Listen, I'm having car trouble. Could you possibly pick me up on your way to St Michael's for the prayer service?'

'The what?' Jules sounded vague. 'Oh, that. Sorry, sweetie, I'm not going.'

'I thought we had to go.'

'Not my kind of thing. I told Elaine I had a family commitment that I couldn't get out of.'

'Right,' I said, wishing I'd thought of something similar. 'Good for you.'

'Elaine was fee-urious. Not that I care. She can't fire me for not being there. I'm really sorry, though. Are you going to be able to manage?'

It wasn't far, really – just a couple of miles. Without the

bruised knee, I wouldn't have thought twice about walking. I laughed. 'Of course. I was being lazy because of the rain.'

'I've just had my hair done,' Jules said in a small voice. 'By the time I get to the pub, it's going to be totally ruined.'

'Is that where the family commitment is, then?' I asked, grinning as Jules said something extremely rude in return before hanging up.

As I put the phone down, my smile faded. It was all very well laughing, but there was no one else I could ask. If I wanted to get there, I'd have to walk, and in my present state I wasn't altogether sure I would make it.

By a miracle, I got there on time, and as it turned out I was quite grateful for the bad weather. There were cameras massed on the far side of the road from the church, filming people as they filed in, but under my umbrella I was safely anonymous. The umbrella shielded my face from anyone who might just spot the bruising high on my cheekbone, even though I had coated it in layers of foundation.

Leaving my umbrella to drip in a stand in the porch along with a forest of others, I crept into the church and looked around. I hadn't been inside it for a long time. The foundations of St Michael's went back hundreds of years, but the church wore its history lightly. Along the walls, antique brasses and monuments to long-forgotten parishioners fought for space with posters about Christian charity and poverty in the developing world. A lurid stained-glass window had been added some time in the seventies, incongruous against the old grey stone that surrounded it. Part of the left side-aisle had been glassed in at some point to corral noisy children and their suffering parents during services. But the old box pews were satisfyingly unaltered and my footsteps sounded muffled on the worn stone floor, polished over the centuries by the feet of the faithful, as I limped into the side-aisle on the right in search of an unobtrusive place to sit. It wasn't going to be easy. There was still a quarter of an hour to go before the service was due to start, but the pews were almost full.

I recognised parents from the school and Jenny's classmates in the congregation, but scuttled past before they noticed me, quick in spite of my new hop-and-step style of walking. I had prepared a story in case anyone asked why I was limping, but I didn't want to expose it or myself to too much scrutiny. The rain had dulled the light outside to the point that it seemed more like a winter evening than early summer, and the church wasn't well lit. It was a gift. I slipped into a pew near the front, beside a pair of old ladies who were deep in conversation. They shuffled along to make room for me, but otherwise didn't acknowledge my presence at all. Perfect.

Looking around, I saw a little group of my colleagues sitting together in the middle of the nave, talking among themselves. They looked tired and unhappy, more because they were there on duty than because they were grief-stricken, I felt. From where I sat, I could see them looking at their watches, foreheads wrinkled with indignation.

Elaine herself was sitting in the front row of the church beside the deputy head, who had dug out a tie for the occasion. Elaine had had her hair done and was wearing lipstick; she was definitely thinking of this as an opportunity to impress. The little old lady next to me was holding an order of service, a single piece of A4 paper; I had missed out on picking one up on my way into the church. I wondered if poor Janet had had to do all of the copying and folding herself. By dint of squinting, I could just about read it. Elaine was doing a reading and the school choir was performing.

On the way into the church I had seen a polite notice asking the media to respect the community's privacy, discouraging them from attending the service. At least one of them had ignored the notice, although I had to acknowledge that she had the excuse of being part of the community too. Carol Shapley was sitting two rows from the front of the church, right behind the pew that had been reserved for the Shepherds themselves. She had her arms around two teenage children, presumably her own, and looked totally harmless, but I could see that she was taking in every detail of the church and congregation. Her head swivelled on her neck like an owl's. She would miss nothing, that woman, and the local paper would get an exclusive.

A low rumble of conversation came from the back of the church. I craned my neck to see what was going on and realised that the police had arrived, along with the Shepherds. DCI Vickers led the procession up the aisle, as unlikely a bride as you ever saw. He filed into the pew in front of the journalist, who caught his eye as he did so. She dropped her head and a flush swept up her face.

I didn't think that he had spoken to her; perhaps he hadn't needed to.

The Shepherds weren't far behind, walking in the company of the vicar. Diane Shepherd didn't seem to know where she was, looking around her with a little half-smile frozen on her face. Her husband walked heavily, his head down. He had lost a lot of weight in the days since Jenny disappeared and his clothes hung on his frame. The collar of his shirt was loose, but he was smartly dressed; this was a man for whom appearance mattered, and even in his grief he was conscious of dressing appropriately. Valerie walked behind them, her self-important strut only slightly muted by the circumstances. And at the back of the church, Blake. Of course he was there. He took up a position by the door, flanked by a couple of colleagues. Their backs were to the wall, hands clasped in front of them in the classic footballer's pose. They looked remote, as if what was going on had nothing to do with them, but their eyes swept over the congregation. I wondered what they were looking for, and at that moment Blake caught my eye. He raised one eyebrow a millimetre and I whipped around to face the front of the church, embarrassed at being caught staring, as the young vicar launched into his opening prayer. It evolved into a bit of a sermon, which apparently came as a surprise to him as well as everyone else. His Adam's apple shuttled up and down his neck in between phrases that led nowhere. Fatally off the point, he plunged about, getting more and more lost.

'For without God, where can there be comfort?

But with God, what can there be but comfort, the comfort that is of God and from God. That comfort that . . . who is the one true God. And Jennifer is with God, in the sanctity of heaven, one of his children as we all are . . . and for her family, that must console. That must console, because . . . '

He shuffled papers, looking in them for the answer and, finding neither a conclusion to his train of thought nor a new one to follow, gave up and rather lamely introduced the school choir. They launched into a hymn, a loud and enthusiastic rendition of 'Be Thou My Vision'. I gazed sightlessly at the hymnal in front of me, not reading the words, wondering if Jenny had prayed before she died, and if her prayers had been heard.

To say that my attention wandered during the service would be an understatement. Elaine's voice rang out, the words of a suitable bit of Ecclesiastes delivered in meas-ured cadences, and I drifted, contemplating the fine vaulted ceiling above my head and the gothic arch that led to the transept. Thoughts slid into my mind and I let them float there, not really focusing.

But someone was focusing on me. As I rose to my feet along with the rest of the congregation to sing 'The Lord Is My Shepherd', I looked around idly and found myself looking straight at Geoff, who was staring back. As soon as he made eye contact with me, he raised his hand, cupping it around an invisible glass, and tilted it – the universal sign for 'do you fancy a drink?' I frowned dis-couragingly and bent my head to the hymnal as though I had never read the words of the psalm before.

When the last notes from the organ had died away, the vicar bent down and wrestled the microphone from its stand. It issued short barks of static and feedback as the stony-faced congregation watched him struggle. He launched into another endless, rambling prayer delivered off the cuff, apparently without any forethought, and I found my attention wandering again.

'I'll now invite the rest of Jennifer's class to come up onto the altar to sing the final hymn,' he intoned breathily at last and waited while girls came from all over the church, looking self-conscious and hanging back so as not to arrive on the altar first. Some of them had shot up to their adult height already, looking years older than their classmates in their outfits and demeanour – all straightened hair and emo-eyeliner. But there were those who held on to childish prettiness and fragility, as Jenny had done, small-framed girls with babyish faces. They all shared the same expression: frozen confusion.

'If you'd all just hold hands . . . ' the vicar suggested and Jenny's classmates linked hands obediently. The school choir mistress stepped delicately in front of the altar and gave a nod to the organist. A long-held note resolved itself into the opening bars of 'Amazing Grace'. The girls were word perfect. They had learned it for a school concert a couple of months earlier. I wondered what their parents were feeling, watching them. Sick with fear at the thought that it might have been their daughter who was missing from the line-up? Secretly giving thanks that it wasn't? Who could blame them for that?

While the singing was still going on, Vickers and Valerie

marched the Shepherds out before anyone else in the congregation had a chance to stir. I found myself wondering who, exactly, the service had been intended to help. The Shepherds looked just as stunned and heartsick going out as they had when they came in.

A tug at my sleeve turned out to be the little old ladies wanting to escape, and I got up so the three of us could slide away. It was a fine plan, but two things served to sabotage it. One, my knee gave way almost as soon as I tried to walk on it and I ended up leaning against a pillar, waiting for the world to stop whirling. Two, Geoff had been waiting for his opportunity, and while I was standing there, he swooped.

'Hey you,' he murmured, coming much too close. I felt like the weakest animal in the herd, defenceless and vulnerable; it was as if he could sense it. He wrapped his arms around me for a too-enthusiastic hug. The pressure on my arm sent shooting pains from my shoulder up to my neck and I gasped. Geoff looked down, assessing me. 'Was it a bit much for you? All the emotion?'

'I'm OK,' I gritted, peeling myself off the pillar and starting to make for the door. Every other punter in the congregation had had the same thought by now, though, so I was forced to stand and wait while the crowd trickled through the double doors agonisingly slowly, like cattle at a mart. Geoff followed, of course, and stood behind me, so close that I could feel his breath on my neck. I edged forwards into a non-existent gap, pushing through the crowd to put some distance between us.

'I think what you need is a drink,' he said into my ear,

shuffling forwards too. Net gain to me: nil. 'Come on. We'll find somewhere nice.'

'No thanks. I'm going to go home.' My knee was aching and I felt sick. Even if I had wanted to go out for a drink – even in the exceptionally unlikely circumstances that I might have considered going out for that drink with Geoff – I really, truly didn't feel up to it. The next minute, I nearly jumped out of my skin as two heavy hands landed on my shoulders and started kneading them. It was as if he was irresistibly attracted to the place that would cause me the most pain and I ducked free of him before whipping around, one hand protectively guarding my shoulder in case he tried again. 'Geoff, for God's sake!'

'You're so tense,' he whispered. 'Calm down.'

'Stop mauling me!'

He held his hands up. 'OK, you win. What's the problem? Have you done something to your back?'

'It's nothing,' I said, noticing that we were attracting strange looks from others in the crowd. 'Forget it.'

We were at the doorway by now. Heavy raindrops splashing on the path beyond the porch reminded me to retrieve my umbrella. I manoeuvred across to where I had left it, to discover that the umbrella stand was empty. Someone had taken it already. I stood there, looking stupidly at where it should have been, until a man shouldered past me with a tut of irritation.

'No umbrella?' Geoff sounded sympathetic. 'How far away is your car?'

'At home,' I said, without thinking. It was going to be a long walk back, given my ever-stiffer leg and the thundery rain that showed no sign of slackening off. The puddles that had been collecting on the pavements earlier would be lakes by now.

'You can't walk in this,' Geoff said firmly, taking my arm and drawing me out of the way. 'Let me drive you.'

I was just about to say no when I saw Blake coming towards us, a look of concern on his face. Of all the ways I would have chosen to meet him again, this was absolutely not one of them.

'You're limping,' he said without preamble. 'What happened?'

'I caught my heel and fell downstairs.'

A sceptical look came over his face. Before he could say anything else, Geoff said, 'I really think we should get a move on, Sarah.' He sounded bossy and possessive and Blake glared at him.

'What did you say your name was?'

'I didn't. Geoff Turnbull.' He stuck out his hand and Blake shook it briefly, introducing himself with his full rank, and without enthusiasm.

'I didn't meet you at the school.'

'One of your collegues interviewed me. Nice girl.' Geoff sounded relaxed, but one of his feet was tapping and I realised he was tense under his surface calm.

Formalities over, the two of them stared at one another with undisguised hostility. Deadlock.

I turned to Geoff. 'You know, if it's not too much trouble, I'd be really grateful for a lift. Where did you say you were parked?'

'Round the corner, but you wait here. I don't want you

getting drenched. I'll fetch the car.' He shot off down the path.

Blake looked after him. 'You're going home with him? Why don't you wait? I can drive you.'

'I don't think that's a good idea.' I meant for his sake, in case anyone guessed there was something going on between us, but he looked hurt for a second. Then his face went blank, unreadable, the mask back in place.

'Oh, I didn't realise. Are you fucking him too?'

'For God's sake,' I hissed, grabbing him by the arm and moving away from where the last of the congregation were leaving. 'Keep your voice down. This isn't the time or place.'

'When would suit you? I noticed you didn't hang around last night.'

'I can't have this conversation now,' I said flatly. 'And you of all people should be trying to stay away from me in public. I can't think that your boss would be pleased to know what we did.'

Blake frowned. 'That's my problem.'

'Yes, it is, so I suggest you worry about that and let me leave with my colleague without making a fuss.' I turned to go, then swung back. 'Er – that's all he is, by the way. Just a colleague.'

'Pretty friendly for a colleague. Isn't he the one you were hugging at the school the other day? I knew I recognised him from somewhere.'

'*He* was hugging *me*,' I said, annoyed. 'But I'm not – I mean, I don't – I mean, you're different.' I could feel the heat radiate from my face as I blushed, wondering what the hell I'd said.

The corner of Blake's mouth twitched. Before he could respond, a car horn beeped and I peered through the rain to see a VW Golf had drawn up at the churchyard gate.

'There he is. I've got to go.' I hobbled away from Blake, hoping that he wouldn't bother to ask again about my limp.

Always the gentleman, Geoff leaned across to pop the passenger door open and I slid into the car. For the second time in three days I was aware of how small a space there is between the passenger and driver in the average car. Blake – even though he would have interrogated me about what had happened to my leg, even though I didn't want anyone to know what we had done the night before – might just have been a better option. Geoff turned to look at me, giving me the benefit of his brilliant blue eyes. 'OK?'

'Fine. Turn left at the lights and I'll guide you from there,' I said shortly, determined to keep conversation to a minimum. Naturally, Geoff had other ideas.

'How come you never want to spend any time with me, Sarah?' This was accompanied by a mournful look.

'I don't know what you're talking about. Left again here.'

Geoff turned the wheel smoothly. 'I was beginning to think that you didn't like me.'

'Not at all,' I said, aiming for politeness. 'You're – er – very nice. A very nice colleague.'

'I was hoping I could be a bit more than a colleague.'

I dug my nails into the palms of my hands. *Dear God, please no.* If he tried to make a pass at me, I would die. Just die. The irony was that it was all because I didn't want him to like me that he was so single-minded in his pursuit of me. There were women who suffered torments because he didn't speak to them, and others who glowed for days after earning one of his smiles. Why couldn't he go after one of them?

He flicked another look at me. 'I turn right up here, yeah?'

I nodded, surprised. *And how exactly do you know where to go, Geoff?*

As if he'd heard me, he said easily, 'I remember you said once that you lived on the Wilmington Estate. You haven't moved, have you?'

'No.' I was racking my brains, trying to think when I might have let that slip in front of him. As if he wanted to change the subject, he rattled on, making small talk about the other teachers. I made noncommittal noises in response, miles away. And then I looked down to see something that brought me back to the present in a hurry. I bent down and hooked the object out from under my seat. I'd only needed to see a corner of the familiar white and red livery to recognise a pack of Marlboro cigarettes.

'Geoff, what are you doing with these?'

He glanced over. 'You aren't going to give me a hard time, are you? I sometimes have one, when I need a break.'

'But you're a PE teacher,' I said.

'Yeah, but I'm not a monk. So I drink a fair bit, smoke now and then – so what? You don't need to be an athlete to teach sport at a girls' school, I promise you.' He looked over at me again. 'Elaine doesn't know – I'd like to keep it that way.'

'Of course.' My mind was whirling. I hadn't thought that Geoff might have been the one that attacked me, perhaps because I had been sure the mugger was a smoker. But now . . .

The old gag ran through my mind: *just because I'm paranoid, it doesn't mean they aren't out to get me.*

'You'll have to direct me from here,' he said, making the turn into the estate and slowing to a crawl.

I had a powerful urge to get out of the car. 'I can walk from here. Why don't you just drop me off?'

'Absolutely not. It's no trouble. Now where am I going?' He nudged the accelerator a little, speeding up so that it was too dangerous to think of opening the door. Geoff was in control and he was loving it.

I told him the name of my road and how to get to it, defeated. When he pulled up in front of the house he looked at it, assessing it.

'Not a bad place, but it needs a bit of TLC, I reckon.'

He was right. There were weeds sprouting in the guttering. Paint peeled off the windowsills and front door in curls, like dead skin.

'I love a bit of DIY,' Geoff said, flexing his hands so the muscles in his super-tanned forearms rippled. 'Shirt off, up a ladder, painting windows in the sunshine – can't beat it. I'd be happy to do yours, if you like.'

'That's really kind,' I said, undoing my seatbelt. 'But please, don't think of it. I wouldn't want you to go to the trouble.'

'No trouble – I'd enjoy it,' he said quickly. I was being too nice. Time to make myself clear.

'Look, Geoff, I don't really care about how the house looks, OK? Just forget about it.'

He shrugged. 'Sure.' Then, as I fumbled for the door

handle, his hand shot across and held it. His arm pressed against me, pushing me back against the seat. 'Sarah,' he said throatily. 'Wait.'

'Get off me!' My throat and chest had tightened and I was struggling to breathe. 'Geoff, let go!'

'I just want to talk,' he whispered, undoing his seatbelt. 'Sarah . . .'

He took his hand off the door handle so he could clamp both hands to my face and draw it closer to his. He was far, far stronger than me. I realised with detachment that he was going to kiss me and there was nothing I could do about it. His mouth came down on mine and I pressed my lips together primly, repulsed by the sucking lips and probing, wet tongue that was trying to pry them apart. I reached past him to find the horn and hit it with as much force as I could muster. It was shatteringly loud, the sound waves vibrating through the car.

'Jesus,' he howled, leaping back. 'What the fuck did you do that for?'

'Leave me alone, Geoff,' I said levelly. 'I mean it. I'm not interested in you.' *Don't leave him on bad terms*, a voice inside my head commanded. *You don't want any staffroom drama, do you?* 'Listen, I'm just not in a position to take this any further at the moment. I'm not in the market for a relationship.'

'Well, you only had to say that.'

I suppressed the urge to roll my eyes. He looked out through the windscreen and sighed. 'Look, can I at least try to convince you that I could make a good friend, if nothing else?'

I squirmed. 'Geoff, you don't have to—'

'I want to,' he said.

And it's all about you, isn't it? It was my turn to sigh. 'Whatever you like.' I picked up my bag. 'Look, Geoff, I'm knackered. Thanks for the lift. No hard feelings?'

'No hard feelings.'

As I got out of the car, I looked up at the house across the road, Danny Keane's house. Something had attracted my attention. Movement. The classic suburban curtain twitch. I turned and began to limp up the drive, going as fast as I could.

As if Geoff hadn't provided enough interest to the neighbours already, he rolled down his window and called after me, 'You're something special, Sarah, you know. I'll see you soon.'

I didn't dare turn around. I was inside, locking and bolting the door when he finally drove away with a valedictory toot on the horn. I leaned against the door and made a noise born of pure frustration. Now he knew exactly where I lived, always assuming that he hadn't already. Either he or I had slipped up. It was my fault if I had mentioned the Wilmington Estate in his hearing, but if he had found out by some other means, he had just blown it. I wasn't at all sure that I believed his *you'll-have-to-direct-me-from-here* line. He was the sort of person who wouldn't give up until he knew everything there was to know. *He knew the house*, I thought. He had seen it before. Maybe he had been watching me. I shivered, suddenly cold, my damp clothing clinging to me. I had always thought Geoff was creepy but essentially harmless – what if I had been wrong?

What if he had known exactly where to touch me to get a reaction? What if he was responsible for the bruises? What if he knew that I didn't have car keys and would need a lift home?

I swallowed, trying to calm down. *Colleague, not threat*, I assured myself. *Interest is not obsession. Friendliness is not stalking.* Even if he had mugged me, he couldn't have known I wouldn't have a spare set of car keys. He couldn't have been sure I wouldn't have got a lift from someone else.

I needed to stop worrying about Geoff, because I certainly hadn't managed to get rid of him. Somehow I had found myself promising to get to know him better. Somehow I had brought him right to my door. It might have been the paranoia again, but I had a feeling that had been his plan all along.

1992

Six weeks missing

I push the door to Charlie's room and it swings open. I stand on the landing, listening, holding my three Barbie dolls by their legs. Mum is downstairs, watching television. It's a cold, wet day, too cold to play outside. I don't have to go back to school for another week, but I'm looking forward to it. The days have been empty and dull since Charlie disappeared. I miss the routine of school, the fun of it. I miss my friends. The rain spatters the windows and a car swishes past the house, there one second and gone the next. I take a step into Charlie's room, and another. The carpet feels strange, different from the one on the landing or in my room. It's thicker, springy under my feet. I had forgotten; it's weeks since I have been in here. I know I'm not really supposed to be here at all, but I don't care. If I'm quiet, Mum will never know.

I tiptoe around the room, looking at Charlie's things. The bedroom still smells of him, that boy smell of dirt and socks. It's nice to smell him; I miss him. I settle down on the floor, leaning up against the bed, and lay my dolls out beside me.

I sit and play for a while. I put on a fashion show, walking my favourite Barbie up and down my legs while the others watch. I have forgotten where I am, and when I hear a noise from the doorway, I don't look up at first.

'What do you think you're doing?'

Mum is standing there, looking down at me, and the look on her face is scary. She's white and her eyes are staring. I put my dolls down without looking away from her.

'I'm just playing, Mum.'

'Playing?' She reaches over and grabs a handful of my hair, hauling me to my feet.

I cry out, 'Mum, you're hurting me.'

She shakes me, still holding me by the hair. 'You don't come in here, do you understand? You don't come in here.'

'I know, I'm sorry. I won't do it again.' I'm crying now, but she doesn't seem to notice. She is looking down at the dolls on the floor.

'Pick them up.'

I obey, my eyes blurring with tears.

'Give them to me.'

She has her hand out, waiting. I don't know why she wants them. There's nothing I can do but give them up. With her other hand, she grabs hold of my arm and pulls me out of Charlie's room, shoving me through the door of my bedroom.

'Stay in here until I tell you to come out,' she says, and I am suddenly aware of the sweet-sour smell that means she has been drinking again. She pulls the door closed and I sit down on the edge of my bed and howl, really bawl. I have got to the stage of crying where I think I might be sick when I hear something from outside the house. Coughing, I get up and look out of the window.

Mum is standing by the bins at the kerb. She takes the lid off our bin and wedges my dolls in, head first, among all the rubbish bags. She crams the lid back on and comes back to the house, shutting the front door with a bang. My nose is running and I need to pee, but I can't open the bedroom door; I'm too frightened of what she would do if she found me on the landing, disobeying her again. I can't quite believe that she has put my dolls in the bin. I can't believe that she won't go and get them before the bin men come. But in my heart, I know that they are gone for good.

It's late when I wake up and for a moment I don't know why my throat is sore. There is a weight on the side of the bed. My father is sitting there, with one hand on my back and the other supporting his chin.

'Are you all right, monkey?'

I nod, then remember in a rush what happened. 'My dolls . . . '

'Sorry, Sarah. They're gone.' Dad leans over and kisses my cheek. 'I know you didn't mean to do anything wrong. I'll take you shopping on Saturday. We'll buy you some new dolls, OK? Better dolls.'

I don't want new dolls. I loved the old ones. I imagine them in the bin lorry, all broken and mangled, or lying in the dirt at the dump with muck in their hair, surrounded by rubbish.

Dad is looking at me, worry in his eyes, and I sit up and put my arms around his neck. I let him think that I'm excited about the new dolls. I let him think that he's fixed everything, that I'm not upset any more. I let him be happy to have made me happy.

It's what he wants.

Chapter 8

I didn't allow myself to look behind me more than a couple of times on the way to the library the following day. I had called in sick again, and I couldn't help worrying that someone from school would see me out and about in Elmview town centre, manifestly capable of sitting around in an empty school. It would reopen properly on Monday, Janet had said, which meant that I needed to make the most of today. Normality would reassert itself eventually, though at the moment ordinary everyday existence seemed completely out of reach.

The boards advertising newspapers outside Elmview's newsagents were the most obvious sign that things were not normal – HUNT FOR JENNY'S KILLER read one. STOLEN ANGEL read another, with the usual picture of her. She did look angelic, and Vickers had managed to keep the fact of her pregnancy out of the news so far. There was no sign that interest in her murder was subsiding. It was still a huge story, as the news crews roaming the streets of the town suggested. There were other things too that made me shiver: police notices appealing for information in the windows of almost every shop, and flowers left outside the church where the memorial service had been. People walking past me looked nervous, haunted, and I felt as if everyone I passed was talking about it.

The town was quiet, but that was hardly unusual. The residents of Elmview divided their custom between Guildford and Kingston when it came to proper shopping; the tiny town centre was strictly for the basics. It was dying slowly, small businesses withering away week by week and nothing replacing them. The only surprise was how long the whole process was taking.

The local council wasn't going to give in without a fight, though. The library had been recently refurbished and the tang of fresh paint still hung in the air, making my nose sting. There was a queue of people in front of me, but by the time I reached the librarian's desk, I still hadn't worked out what to say. The librarian was young and had obviously taken great care to differentiate herself from the dowdy-cardigan stereotype: full make-up, poker-straight highlighted hair, a skimpy top and narrow black trousers tucked into wedge-heeled boots. The nametag she wore was too heavy for the fabric of her top, dragging it down to reveal a canyon of bony sternum. I squinted at the nametag, eventually determining that her name was Selina. Almost before I had finished explaining that I wanted to look at the archive of newspaper files, she bounded up from behind her desk.

'We've actually got all the back issues of the local paper archived on CD-ROM, going back to 1932. What are you looking for exactly?'

'Oh – er, local history, basically,' I said, reflecting that

I should have thought up a credible cover story before launching into a conversation about it. 'I'd like to start from . . . let's say 1992.'

'Is that when you moved here or something?' the librarian asked, leading the way to a computer terminal. I followed her, not answering.

'This is really a fantastic system. They did it for the millennium. If you'd been here a few years ago, you would've had to look at the files on microfiche. They were a nightmare – the reader was always breaking down, and it was so noisy,' Selina prattled, making a fair amount of noise herself. She tapped in a password. 'Before that, it was all bound copies of the paper – massive, leather-bound books. They took up so much room. Now, you're looking for 1992 . . . '

I found it ironic that a librarian should find actual books objectionable, but I didn't say that to Selina, who was exploring a filing cabinet that stood beside the terminal. She slid open a drawer, flicking through the contents at lightning speed. The drawer was filled with CDs in plastic sleeves.

'I've got local news for 1992 on this disc and I can give you national as well, if you like.'

'Local and national would be brilliant, thanks. If I want to look at any other years, can I find them myself?'

'Absolutely, as long as you remember to sign them out.' She showed me a clipboard that was kept on top of the filing cabinet. 'Put in the date, the time, your name and the serial number of the CD. And don't try to put them back when you're finished; just bring them over to the desk. I'll file them again. It's not a complicated system, but you'd be surprised how many people don't seem to be able to follow it. I'm not saying that you would get it wrong, but we just have a rule, you see. Oh, and there's a printer under the desk; you can print out anything you like and there's a charge of five pence a page that you pay when you're finished. It's not bad value, really. We don't make a profit from it, or anything. It would cost twice that at an internet café, though I suppose they have to keep an eye on the bottom line.'

She chattered on at full volume and I glanced around, hoping that no one was being disturbed. The other library users seemed to be able to tune her out. I was glad that I'd been a bit cagey about what I was looking for; I could just imagine the details being broadcast to the entire room.

'Just give me a shout if you need any help,' she said, before barrelling off to her desk again. On the basis of her own approach to voice-projection, I thought she might mean it literally.

I sat down and clicked through introductory screens and lists of files. The date of Charlie's disappearance – the second of July – is engraved on my heart. I clicked on the files for that day in 1992 and felt somehow jolted as the screen filled with the front page of the *Elmview Examiner*. The lead story was about the council's plans to replace sewer pipes on the high street and the traffic chaos that would result. There was nothing to hint that anything out of the ordinary would happen that day. The paper had only been published weekly then; I clicked on the following week with a feeling of intense foreboding. Charlie made the headlines.

FEARS GROW FOR MISSING BOY

> Concerns are growing for the safety of the missing Elmview schoolboy, Charlie Barnes. It is a week since the last confirmed sighting of the 12-year-old and police are very keen to trace him. Charlie (pictured below) went missing from his home in the Wilmington Estate on Thursday 2 July. Anyone who may have seen Charlie since, or who knows his current whereabouts, is advised to contact their local police station immediately. Charlie's father, Alan Barnes, said yesterday: 'We are very anxious about our son and dearly want him to come home. All we want to do is see him and tell him how much we love him.'

I flicked through the newspapers, local and national, following the story as the days and weeks passed. The headlines jumped out at me from the facsimile pages. *Sunday Times*, 5 July 1992: SEARCH FOR MISSING BOY CONTINUES. *Daily Mail*, 7 July 1992: WHO TOOK CHARLIE? *Sun*, 9 July 1992: GIVE US BACK OUR BOY.

I stopped to look at the pictures. One had a large image of Mum looking away from the camera, her face thin and lined with tension and worry. Her hand was up at her throat, her other arm wrapped around her body. She looked quite beautiful – distraught, certainly, but still lovely. Smaller images of Charlie and me by the Christmas tree, from a couple of years before, clutching presents; Charlie on his bike; Charlie in school uniform, grinning madly, his shirt open at the neck to show off his stupid necklace, a leather thong with three beads on it. He had insisted on wearing it all the time; he could be stubborn when he wanted to be.

Scraps of articles caught my attention, describing the horrible, futile process by which they failed to find my brother, or the person who took him.

Surrey police have discounted eyewitness accounts of a middle-aged man behaving suspiciously in the Wilmington Estate around the time of Charlie Barnes' disappearance. Extensive investigations have failed to provide the police with any leads in the search for the missing schoolboy. Detective Chief Inspector Charles Gregg, who is leading the investigation, said, 'We know that the public are anxious to help in any way with tracing Charlie. We appreciate the information that we have already received, but unfortunately it hasn't panned out. If anyone remembers anything that may help in the search for Charlie, they shouldn't hesitate to get in touch.'

Surrey Assistant Chief Constable Harold Spark reacted angrily at a press conference yesterday when asked if the police had run out of ideas in the search for Charlie Barnes. A five-mile search area surrounding the schoolboy's home has been extensively canvassed over the past few weeks, but the rewards have been disappointing. No credible sightings have been reported since Charlie's disappearance ten days ago . . .

Police have denied that they are investigating Charlie Barnes' father, Alan, in relation to his son's disappearance. However, locals suggest that the focus of the investigation has shifted to the family, pointing out that Alan Barnes has been re-interviewed recently and asked to account for his movements on the day in question.

I shivered again. As the days had passed with no sign of Charlie, sympathy began to be replaced with suspicion. Statistically, as Blake had said, those most likely to be responsible for harming a child are not strangers but family members. Without a credible suspect, the attention had turned back to us. The tone of the reports started to change as the journalists speculated on the state of my parents' marriage. They began to say what had previously been unprintable.

Laura and Alan Barnes are, they say, the victims of a whispering campaign that is stirring up rumours against them. Almost a month since Charlie was last seen, suspicion is growing that his parents may know something about what happened to him. A neighbour, who didn't want to be named, said, 'You've got to wonder about it. No one knows where this child has gone, and they're there on telly and in the paper, giving interviews as if they're celebrities. You'd almost think they were enjoying the attention.' Another local told me, 'Their story doesn't hang together. This is such a busy area. If someone had come here looking to kidnap a child, I don't see how they wouldn't have been spotted.' The Barnes angrily deny that they are enjoying the media spotlight, claiming instead that they are using the media to try to keep Charlie in the public eye, so that people will recognise him if he is seen. However, the questions are unlikely to die down.

My family was fair game, entertainment for the masses.

Almost against my will, I searched again for my parents' names, swapping discs to see what was reported in 1996. There it was, four years after Charlie's disappearance, a sidebar article with a headline that jumped out at me. CHARLIE PARENTS SPLIT. It was another passage of veiled innuendo and recycled quotes. The article included a bland comment from a relationship counsellor about the effect that stress could have on a marriage, and some dry statistics about marriage breakups in the wake of traumatic events. It didn't begin to convey the horror of it.

I was beginning to feel tired and my eyes were burning from gazing at the screen. I stretched and looked around, realising that I had been reading for longer than I thought. Selina was chatting animatedly on the phone and the library had emptied out. It was coming up to lunchtime, but I wasn't remotely hungry. I changed tack, going back to the discs for the early nineties. Sliding the first one in, I clicked in the search box and typed in 'Wilmington Estate', scanning the results: local events, petty crimes, an increase in burglary rates and car thefts in the area. I was looking for abduction attempts or convictions for paedophilia. I hesitated over a report of child neglect on the other side of the estate, but there was surely no possible connection between a malnourished baby and what had happened to my brother.

I soon found myself on 1992 again. Charlie came up in the first set of results. On the second page, there was: ' . . . fundraising effort for Laura and Alan Barnes by residents on the Wilmington Estate . . . ' That had been early on, before the community had changed their mind about us. I switched discs, looking at 1993, then 1994. Same old, same old – small crimes, graffiti epidemics, vandalism and some attempted arson. The same stories repeated over and over again. I persevered, scrolling through the results doggedly, feeling the first cold stabs of disappointment. The 1996 results were briefly exciting, with a series of reports about a local man who had been convicted of child abuse, but he had only moved to the estate in 1993. Besides, he seemed to be interested in very young girls.

I was sitting with my chin on my hand, mindlessly scrolling through the files as months and years passed by when the name jumped out at me. ' . . . Derek Keane (41) of 7, Curzon Close appeared in court to be charged with the manslaughter . . . ' I knew that name. Derek Keane was Danny's father. I hit the link quickly.

MAN PLEADS NOT GUILTY TO MANSLAUGHTER

Derek Keane (41) of 7, Curzon Close appeared in court to be charged with the manslaughter of his wife, Ada (40). Keane spoke only to give his name and address, and to enter his plea of not guilty. Ada Keane died on Saturday last after falling downstairs at her home on the Wilmington Estate. She leaves two sons, Daniel (18) and Paul (2). Neighbours reported hearing an argument before the incident and police arrested Keane on Monday. The trial was set for October.

In 1998, I was fourteen and completely wrapped up in my own misery. I had also been in Manchester with Aunt Lucy and Uncle Harry for most of that year while Mum was in hospital. It was no wonder that I didn't remember Ada's death. At some stage, I must have been told something though, because I had known she was gone, but not how. I hit print, then went back to the search screen and typed in 'Derek Keane'.

KEANE CONVICTED OF WIFE'S MANSLAUGHTER

The week-long trial of Derek Keane at Kingston Crown Court concluded yesterday with a unanimous verdict of guilty. The court had listened to evidence from forensic experts suggesting that Ada Keane had been involved in a struggle immediately before the fall that killed her. Keane (41) admitted to arguing with his wife but denied hitting her in the course of the argument.

The prosecution alleged that Keane had slapped his 40-year-old wife, leaving a bruise on the side of her face that experts agreed corresponded closely to the size and shape of Derek Keane's hand. Edward Long QC, prosecuting, told the jury, 'You must convict Mr Keane if you believe that his actions led directly to the tragic death of his wife, even though you may not believe that this was his intention.' Keane claimed that his wife's fall was an accident, but the jury believed the prosecution's version of what occurred on the night of 20 June this year. Keane was sentenced to five years in prison.

The picture accompanying the article showed a thickset man with greying hair, his cuffed hands held up to hide his face from the cameras outside court. I squinted, trying to see if there was any resemblance to Danny, but it was hard to see much of his face. I printed it anyway. I barely remembered Mr Keane. Charlie and Danny always played at our house or in the street, never at Danny's house. And Danny's mum – she had been a thin woman, with short hair and a cigarette on the go almost constantly, trembling ash as it balanced on her lower lip. I had thought her much older than forty.

So Danny had been left at eighteen with no mother, a father in prison and a two-year-old brother to look after. Ours wasn't the only tragedy in Curzon Close. It seemed 1998 had been a bad year all round. I went back to the search screen and typed in 'Alan Barnes', knowing what was going to come up, hating to see it there on the screen in black and white. TRAGIC DEATH OF MISSING CHARLIE'S FATHER. My throat closed up and I swallowed, cursor hovering over the link.

I didn't have the first inkling that anyone was looking over my shoulder until a hand came down on top of mine and clicked the mouse for me. As the screen went blank and the disc whirred, I quit the program, hoping to override the instruction to open the file on my father's death. I had recognised the plump, pale hand on top of mine. Ace reporter Carol Shapley, on the trail of a big story.

'I'm finished,' I said, gathering up discs and printouts.

'Oh, don't worry. I'm not in any rush. And you can leave those discs.' There was a humourless smile on her face. 'It looks as if we're interested in the same subject, doesn't it?'

'I have no idea,' I said stiffly, hugging the CDs to my chest. 'I'm afraid the librarian asked me to return the discs to her, though. There's a system.'

Carol shot a look at the librarian's desk. 'Selina? She won't mind if you hand them over to me. She knows I'll look after them.'

I shook my head. 'Sorry. I just don't feel comfortable with that.' I was not going to be bullied by Carol Shapley. I stared straight at her, my face carefully neutral, while she gave me a hard, pebbly look.

Seeing I wasn't going to back down, she gave a little yawn. 'Fine, then. Return them. But it's going to take Selina a while to file those discs. Maybe you can help me in the meantime.'

'I really don't think so.' I picked up my bag, hooking it over my good shoulder, and limped towards the librarian's desk. My hands were shaking, I noted, as I flipped through the pile of printouts to count up how much I owed her.

'Five pages?' Selina said brightly. 'That'll be twenty-five pence, then. Gosh, you didn't print much, did you? You were on there for a while. I thought you'd have tons and tons of stuff.'

'She's very selective,' Carol said, leaning in from behind me before I could say anything. 'She knew what she wanted.'

'Good for you,' Selina said brightly, vacant as ever. I squirmed.

It took forever for Selina to find change for my fifty-pence piece, and then I had to reassure her that I didn't want a reinforced envelope to protect the pages.

'Did you manage to find everything that you were looking for?' She blinked up at me earnestly.

I assured her that I had and thanked her for her help, tucked the folded-over pages into my bag and headed for the door as quickly as I could. Carol was hot on my heels.

'I've been wanting to have a chat with you for a couple of days, actually, Sarah, and I think you know why,' she said, getting to the door first. 'You told me a little white lie the first time we spoke, didn't you?'

'I don't know what you mean,' I said, inwardly cursing my lack of a car. I looked up and down the road for an escape route, but I couldn't see how I was going to get away.

'A little bird told me that you were the one who found

Jenny's body, Sarah,' Carol cooed in my ear. 'That wasn't the impression you gave me, was it?'

'Look, I don't want to talk about it.' My mind was racing. Who the hell had told her I had found Jenny? Not the Shepherds, not Vickers, certainly not Blake – but Valerie Wade was a possibility. She wouldn't be able to resist Carol's flattery. It was irrelevant: what mattered was that Carol knew.

And if she knew that, she might know a lot more, like what was going on with the investigation. I stopped thinking about how to get away from her and started to plan how I might find out what she knew. I needed a new source if I was to know what was going on: Blake had made it quite clear that I should stay out of it, so he wouldn't tell me what was happening. Besides, he and I had other things to think about. Without warning, a series of not entirely welcome images flooded into my mind: Blake moving over me, his face intent. His hands, slow and sure, tanned darker than my skin. A shiver raced over my body. Now was not the time. I closed my eyes for a half-second, then dragged myself back from Blake's bed in time to hear Carol say, 'Come on, Sarah. We'll talk off the record. I won't write about anything you don't want me to cover.'

'And you won't identify me?' I said, trying to look as if I was still considering whether or not to speak with her, hoping to hell she hadn't noticed my attention waver.

'Definitely not. I'll keep you out of it completely.' I could see the anticipation of victory gleaming in Carol's eyes.

'OK then,' I said, affecting to be reluctant, and I followed as she headed for a nearby coffee shop. She ordered sand-wiches for both of us and made a big show of paying for them. She was in control and she wanted me to know it.

The coffee shop was small and dark. Carol led the way to a window table and took out a tape recorder. 'Do you mind?' She checked that it was working. 'I like to be completely accurate.'

I bet, I thought.

'So,' she said as the waitress dumped two china mugs brimming with dark-brown tea on our table. 'Let's start at the beginning. Tell me about Jenny.'

With as little drama and emotion as possible, I described my experience of teaching Jenny, and my overall impres-sion of her. I tried to make what I said as bland and unquotable as possible. 'She was very nice. Very hard-working. She always tried her best.'

Carol leaned in. 'And then – what happened? She wasn't in school, was she?'

I shook my head.

'Did you know she was missing?'

'Not until her father came to the school on Monday morning,' I admitted. 'He was obviously concerned that she hadn't been seen since Saturday, and wanted to speak with her classmates. No one knew anything, though.'

'Right.' Carol was nodding encouragingly. I doubted she'd heard anything new so far. 'And then you went out for a run.'

'Yes.'

'And then you found her,' she supplied.

'Mm.' I looked out of the window.

'Tell me about that,' Carol said after a couple of seconds, when it became clear to her that I wasn't planning to expand on it.

'Well, it's hard to remember exactly what happened. I saw something strange, realised it was a body, and called the police. They came, and the rest you know.'

'So when did you realise you knew her? When did you recognise Jenny?'

'I'm not sure.'

'Did you look closely at the body when you found it?'

I had seen the fading daylight on her pale, cold skin. I had seen the row of dry half-moons her teeth had carved in her lower lip.

'I didn't really get that close,' I said smoothly.

It was time to turn the tables on Carol; she'd had enough from me. 'You must know a lot about what's going on if you found out I was the one who discovered the body.'

'I have my sources.' Carol sipped her tea smugly.

'What's happening now? Have they got a suspect?'

'They're looking at a couple of people, but to be honest, I don't think they know what's going on. They didn't get anything from the body. Nothing usable for forensics. The girl was completely clean.'

That was interesting. 'Did they find out how she died?'

Carol looked at me shrewdly. 'They announced it was drowning, didn't they?'

'Oh, yeah,' I said, realising I had made a mistake.

'Didn't it look like drowning to you? You saw the body. Why does drowning seem weird? Wasn't she near a pond?'

I shrugged. 'I must have forgotten.'

Carol shook her head, annoyed. 'No, you knew there was something odd about it. You're trying to pull a fast one on me, aren't you?'

'Not at all,' I said, injecting a note of outraged innocence into my denial that didn't fool Carol for a second.

'You know very well, Sarah, that the body wasn't near water, was it? But that's because she didn't die there. They were able to tell that she drowned in chemically treated water.'

'What do you mean?' I was genuinely puzzled.

'Tap water. She was drowned in a house. In a bath, or a sink, or something.' Carol's tone was matter of fact. She dumped a spoonful of sugar into her tea and stirred it briskly, the metal clinking against the thick china mug.

I squeezed my hands together under the table, so Carol couldn't see them shaking. Someone had coldly ended Jenny's life, in a bathroom or a kitchen. They had turned somewhere domestic and safe into a slaughterhouse.

'How are the Shepherds coping?' I asked, suddenly aware that a silence had fallen between us.

'Mum's distraught, obviously,' she said through a mouthful of bacon sandwich. 'I haven't had a usable quote from her. She's either zonked on pills or in tears. I doubt the police have been able to get anything either. Dad – well, Dad's another story. He's angry. I've never met anyone wound so tight.'

Fear had burned in his eyes when I had first seen him. The anger had come later. I picked at my food. 'It affects different people in different ways.'

'Well, you'd know that, obviously,' Carol said.

I looked up, suddenly wary. The journalist was staring at me, eyes as flinty as ever.

'I was doing some digging in the files, you see – much like you were back there in the library, I imagine. And what did I find? Another child who went missing, quite a while ago. Fifteen years, is it?'

'Sixteen,' I said, knowing that there was no point in prevaricating.

She smiled without humour. 'That's right. Because you were only a little girl, weren't you? In fact, I was surprised I'd recognised you. But it came to me straight away. Imagine how surprised I was, Sarah, to see your picture in the paper with your poor parents. I wasn't put off by the name change – it was dead easy to check that out. Mother's maiden name, isn't it?'

I didn't say anything. I didn't have to.

'So I was thinking,' Carol said, taking another huge bite of her sandwich and speaking with a wad of white bread, bacon and ketchup muffling the words, 'I'd write a little piece about what it's like for the family in these cases. You know, what happens to the ones who are left behind.'

Involuntarily, I made a little noise indicative of dissent. Carol picked up on it. 'Oh, I'm not asking you to cooperate. I'm telling you. Did you think I didn't notice you getting the inside track on the investigation? Did you think you were going to get away without paying me back for that? I think it could be a fantastic human-interest story, don't you? Two tragedies in one place, and you're the connection. It's almost . . . well, *creepy*, really. And I'm the only one who's put it together, which makes it a very saleable proposition.'

'Look,' I said weakly, 'I really don't want to say anything.'

'No, *you* look. There are two ways we can do this. I can put together a nice little piece with your help that will get the readers snivelling into their morning paper, or I can write something myself that goes through every rumour that there ever was about you and your family and your poor dead dad, because everyone got to thinking that he might know more than he let on, didn't they? And now there's this. I just think there's something weird about you being so involved in this. You're a proper little tragedy junkie, aren't you? Probably miss the attention you used to get. Everyone's forgotten Charlie, haven't they? Do you really think that's fair? Don't you want people to remember him?'

I didn't say anything and she leaned over, her breasts settling and spreading against the greasy Formica tabletop. 'It's up to you, Sarah. You can talk to me or not. I can write it without you. Or . . .' and she smiled, 'I could just go straight to your mother.'

'No, don't,' I said, distressed. 'Leave her out of this.'

'Why should I? She might have valuable insights for me.' Carol sat back in her chair. 'You know how your dad killed himself, Sarah—'

'It was an accident.'

She jumped on it. 'An accident that set you and your mum up for life. Nice little wad of insurance money. Your mum hasn't had to work since.'

It was true, she hadn't, and she was none the better for it. I stood up and grabbed my bag, too angry to speak.

'Before you rush out of here, just have a think about this,' Carol said. 'If you cooperate with me, we can have a nice little chat and I'll make you look like an angel. I won't even give your new name away. You get a chance to set the record straight; I get a nice human-interest piece that should go well in the Sunday papers. I'm thinking the *Sunday Times* would be a good fit for it. Maybe the *Observer*. Something high-end, anyway.'

I hesitated, torn. I didn't trust Carol. On the other hand, I could certainly trust her to make me look bad. 'I've worked hard for my privacy. I don't want to be photographed. I don't want anyone to be able to recognise me from the article.'

'Of course – that won't be a problem. Come on,' she wheedled. 'It's up to you.'

It really wasn't. I knew I should tell her to go to hell. I knew no good would come of talking to her. But I couldn't take the risk.

I sat down on the edge of the chair again, defeated. 'What do you want to know?'

1992

Seven weeks missing

The smell of school on the first day back: chalk dust, fresh paint, disinfectant, new books. At the front of the classroom, my new teacher – new for the class and new to the school – is tall and slim, with very short dark hair and green eyes, and her name is Miss Bright.

As the last of the class file in, I fidget, excited and a little bit nervous. My dad has bought me a schoolbag and matching pencil case with Beauty from *Beauty and the Beast* on them, and I notice Denise Blackwell looking at them as she sits down near me. I turn and smile at her. I've always wanted to be friends with her. Denise has almost-white fair hair and tiny stud earrings that glint in her ears and a dainty, toes-out way of standing.

Instead of smiling back, Denise looks straight at me for a minute, then looks away and starts whispering with Karen Combes – Karen, who has a permanently snotty nose, who wet herself on our first day at school. I can tell the whispering is about me: Karen leans forwards so she can stare at me while Denise is speaking to her. I frown and put my hand up to my head to hide my face.

A figure comes and stands by my desk: Miss Bright. 'Oh dear. Are you bored already? That's not a very good start, is it? You look like you're falling asleep. Come on, sit up straight. Make an effort.'

Everyone in the class laughs, a little too loudly, hoping that Miss Bright will like them. My face is flaming. I stare straight down into my lap, my hair hanging down.

'What's your name, sleepyhead?'

'Sarah Barnes,' I say very quietly.

Miss Bright stands there for a second, not saying anything. Then she pats my arm. 'Don't worry. Just try to pay attention, all right?'

I look up to see her walking away. Her face is red, as if she's embarrassed. I can't think why for a minute, and then I realise. She's been told to be nice to me because of Charlie.

I'm not like the others any more. I'm different.

At breaktime, I ask if I can stay in the classroom. I tell Miss Bright that I don't feel well and she lets me sit with my head on my arms while everyone else goes outside to play. I make clouds on the shiny surface of my desk with my breath. The classroom is silent, apart from the ticking of the clock on the wall. I stay there again at lunchtime. Everyone else goes to the lunchroom to eat, and then outside to play. I can hear them outside, laughing and screaming.

When the bell rings at the end of the day, I get up and join the others who are queuing by the door. I can feel that everyone is looking at me. I look down at my hands, tight on the handle of my new schoolbag, until Miss Bright opens the door.

Mum's late. Other parents are late, too, and all around me children are playing chasing and jumping about, laughing and shouting at the tops of their voices. I keep my eyes fixed on the school gate, where Mum should be. Every time I see a dark head there, my heart lifts, but it's never her. Eventually I wander over to the gate so I can see more of the street, then slip outside. The playground is too noisy: my head hurts.

As soon as I step outside the gate, I realise that I have made a mistake. Kids, including classmates of mine, mill about, unsupervised. Denise comes towards me, Karen in tow. I can't go back into the playground, or run away. It's too late. Denise leans in, too close to me, and says in a low voice, 'You think you're special, don't you?'

I shake my head.

'There was a letter about you from the school. They told us we had to be nice to you.' Denise's face was mean, her eyes narrow. 'Did you cry when your brother ran away?'

I don't know what the right answer is. 'Yes,' I say at last.

'Cry baby,' Denise hisses, and Karen starts to laugh.

'No, I didn't,' I say, feeling desperate. 'I didn't cry. Not really.'

'Don't you care about your brother?' Karen, this time. 'Don't you miss him?'

Tears are stinging at the back of my nose but I won't cry in front of them, I won't.

Denise comes even closer. 'My mum says that your dad knows where he is. My mum says that your mum and dad are covering up what happened to him. They're just pretending he's run away. My dad says he's probably dead.'

There are other children crowding around us now. Someone shoves me in the back, hard, and everyone laughs. I turn around to see who did it. Michael Brooker is nearest. He is bright red with excitement, but his face is expressionless. I know he did it – everyone is looking from him to me and back again.

'You pushed me,' I say at last, and his eyes go wide.

'Me? Me? I didn't, I swear. What do you mean, pushed you? It wasn't me.'

There's a smothered laugh. Someone else jostles me from the other side and I turn, starting to panic, outnumbered. Looking around, I can see nothing but malice in their eyes. Before I can think what to do, a long arm reaches through the crowd of children and grabs hold of me.

'Fuck off, all of you,' a rough voice says, and I recognise Danny, Charlie's best friend. Danny, who goes to the secondary school up the hill – Danny, who is like my guardian angel at that moment. 'Come on, Sarah. I'll walk you home.'

I push through the crowd of my classmates and no one tries to stop me.

'I'm supposed to wait for Mum.'

'Don't worry about that. We'll probably bump into her on the way home.'

I feel a wave of gratitude to Danny, who has always been nice to me, even when Charlie told him to ignore me. 'Thanks for making them leave me alone.'

'Little shits, they are. I was just walking back from school when I saw you.' Danny leans down, his face close to mine. 'Listen, Sarah. If anyone ever tries to give you a hard time about Charlie, just tell them to fuck off. If they won't leave you alone, tell me, and I'll get rid of them for you.' He balls his hands up into fists. 'I'll teach them a lesson. I'll look after you.'

'Until Charlie comes back,' I say, and regret it as Danny's face drops.

'Yeah, until Charlie comes back.' Danny looks

ahead and nudges me. 'There's your mum. Go on, run.'

Before I can say anything else – even goodbye – Danny has gone, crossing the road without looking back. Mum is standing at the corner, frowning. When I reach her, she says, 'You're supposed to wait for me.'

I can smell that she has been drinking again. I shrug. 'I didn't know if you'd come or not.'

I think she is going to say something else – argue with me – but instead she sighs. We walk the rest of the way home in silence, while I think about Danny and what he said about looking after me, and I feel warm inside for the first time in a long time.

Chapter 9

I had to walk home in the end. When Carol was finished, she gathered up her things and hurried out of the café without a backwards glance, and certainly without the offer of a lift. On the way back, my mood worsened as the ache in my knee intensified. I just hoped I hadn't said too much.

Turning in to Curzon Close, I found myself staring at Danny Keane's house. I bit my lip. I was coming to realise that I couldn't avoid him any longer. He was an important link with Charlie. It was time – past time – to talk to him, no matter what had happened between us, even though the thought of it washed colour into my cheeks. I shook my head, as if I could physically dislodge the memory from my mind. I couldn't allow teenage humiliation to stand between me and the truth. Reading about what the Keanes had endured made it easier. We were both survivors. He'd understand what was driving me as no one else could.

The Keanes' house was in a poor state of repair. A car had leaked oil on the paving that covered the front garden, leaving a greasy patch the shape of Australia. Weeds flourished between the slabs. The doorbell had been dismantled and electric wiring spilled down from the disabled fitting in a way that didn't look entirely safe. In a nod to suburban respectability, there were net curtains in all the windows, but they were grey with dirt and torn in places. The house looked deeply unloved, which it had in common with the one I occupied. Both houses looked like lifeless wrecks.

Danny's motorbike wasn't outside, but on the off chance that he might be there I decided to knock on the door anyway. The door was a cheap, acrylic one that made a flat, dull sound as I rapped on it with my knuckles. There was no other way to announce that I was there; the holes left for door furniture had never been filled. Someone had stuffed them with toilet paper to block out draughts. I felt slightly self-conscious on the doorstep, hoping that Mum hadn't spotted me, wondering how long I should wait before knocking again or giving up. After a minute, there was a scuffling sound from behind the door, but it didn't open. I knocked again with the same result, then crouched down to the letterbox.

'Hello . . . it's Sarah. Sarah from across the road. Sorry to bother you. I – I just wanted to talk to Danny, if I could . . . '

At the mention of Danny the door swung open, revealing a hall littered with cardboard boxes and unidentifiable machine parts. It was mildly chaotic and none too clean. From behind the door, a greasy mop of hair and a small, suspicious eye appeared.

'Hello,' I tried again. 'I'm Sarah.'

The mop didn't answer.

'Er . . . are you Paul?'

'Yuss,' the mop said, nodding sanguinely.

'I live across the road,' I said, gesturing behind me at the house. 'I, er, used to know your brother.'

'I know who you are,' Paul said.

About to carry on with my explanation, I stopped, mouth open. There was something about Paul's tone that surprised me. It was flat, uninflected, but somehow loaded with significance. It was not a little unsettling.

'Great,' I said lamely. 'Well. We've never met, have we?'

A shoulder appeared, apparently for the express purpose of delivering a shrug.

'It's nice to meet you, Paul. Is Danny here?'

'He's at work,' Paul said slowly, his voice edged with insolence. Silly me. Of course, it was mid-afternoon. Ordinary people were at work. I wasn't because the school was closed. Which led neatly to my next question.

'Why are you at home at this time on a weekday? Shouldn't you be in school?'

I had slipped into my teacher tone of voice and got a cheeky grin in return.

'Don't go to school no more.'

I must have looked confused, because the boy pulled the door back and shuffled into view. He was obese. Not fat – huge. He was taller than average for his age, but that in no way made him look proportionate. Flesh hung in rolls down his arms, creasing around the joints. His torso was wreathed in soft bulges under a tent-sized T-shirt. He wore stained tracksuit bottoms and his swollen, misshapen feet were bare. His toenails were long and jagged, yellow against the bluish-grey skin, suggesting poor circulation, a body too strained to manage effectively. With difficulty, I looked away from them to meet his gaze again. His face was defiant, but there was a hint of hurt too.

'Got bullied,' he explained. 'Home-schooled now.'

'Oh, right,' I said, understanding. At the same time, I couldn't imagine that studying alone in a house like that would be too easy. 'How do you like it?'

'It's all right.' The boy shrugged. 'Got a high IQ, don't I. School was boring, anyway.'

'Good. That's really great.' I smiled. 'Well, as I said, it was Danny I came to see. Do you know what time he'll be back?'

'Nah. He comes in whenever.'

'Right.' I started to edge away from the door. 'It was nice to meet you, Paul. I'll catch up with Danny some other time. Maybe you could let him know I was asking for him.'

Paul looked disappointed. 'Don't you want to come in?'

I did not want to go into the house. Paul wouldn't know anything about Charlie, which was why I had gone over there, and I didn't know when Danny would get back, or even if I would have the nerve to talk to him when he did. Besides, the house was squalid beyond belief. But I could also tell that Paul was lonely. If he didn't go to school, and Danny was out all day, he probably didn't get to talk to many people. I'd never seen him coming or going – not that that meant much. I kept my head down when I was at home, and I didn't exactly keep sociable hours. But I had a feeling that Paul just didn't spend any time outside his own house. And he was how old – twelve? Too young to be shut in. I would feel guilty if I walked off, I knew. I would be letting him down. We survivors had to stick together.

'Thanks,' I said brightly, stepping across the threshold and just managing not to hold my breath. The house smelled like a locker-room – old socks and damp clothes and sweat. Paul shut the door behind me, then led the way down the hall to the kitchen. The house was a carbon copy of ours, but the hall felt different, darker. Looking around, I saw that the door into the sitting room was closed. The one at home was panelled glass; this one was solid. It made the hall feel smaller. I was glad to get into the kitchen, where the afternoon sunshine picked up every mote of dust that hung in the air. The room was warm and quite comfortable, with a sofa against one wall and a table in the middle that was covered in books and loose sheets of paper, a laptop sitting in the middle of the mess. It seemed to be used as a living room as well as a kitchen, and even though it was strikingly untidy, there was something homely about it. The draining board was piled high with dishes and pans, but they were clean. Storage was limited to a couple of cupboards, the remains of a fitted kitchen that had left marks on the walls where most of it had been ripped out. One door hung off its hinges, revealing row upon row of tinned beans and boxes of cereal, bought in bulk. A battered microwave in the corner looked as if it had seen hard service over the years. In the corner, a giant freezer hummed to itself beside a large, dented fridge. But on top of the fridge was an expensive-looking sound system for an iPod, and a massive TV was mounted on the wall opposite the sofa. Danny seemed to spend his money on home entertainment, if not home comfort.

'Have a seat,' Paul said, gesturing towards the table, and

I went over and pulled out one of the vinyl-seated chairs. It pitched violently to one side as soon as I let go of it, and I saw that it was balancing on three legs.

There was a chuckle from behind me. 'Not that one. The leg's here, look.' Paul was pointing at the kitchen counter, where the chair leg lay, splintered at the top. 'Danny broke it the other day, and–'

He broke off for no reason that I could see, but he looked flustered. Affecting not to notice, I chose another chair and sat down.

'Cup of tea?' Paul padded over to the kettle.

'That would be lovely.' I crossed my fingers that the mug I got would be free of botulism and watched him move about the kitchen, gathering mugs and teabags. He was quick and deft in his movements, in spite of his bulk, though the mild exertion of making tea was causing him to wheeze. There was, underlying everything, a certain confidence in the way he behaved, something that I wouldn't have expected from a boy of his age. I was starting to like my neighbour. He caught me watching him and smiled cheekily; I had the feeling that he was pleased I had agreed to come in, though why he should be, I wasn't sure.

'Milk?' he asked, opening the fridge with a flourish to reveal several two-litre cartons of full-fat milk, a tray of lager, chocolate desserts in pots and packets of cheddar and sliced ham. No vegetables. No fruit.

Paul was waiting for an answer, carton poised over one of the mugs.

'Just a splash,' I said quickly.

'Sugar?'

'No, thanks.'

Paul dropped four heaped teaspoons of sugar into his mug and stirred it in. I winced, suddenly protective of the enamel on my teeth. He pushed some papers aside and put my mug down in front of me, then scuttled sideways to retrieve a packet of chocolate digestive biscuits from a cupboard. I shook my head when he offered them to me. He threw himself into the chair opposite mine and lifted three biscuits out of the packet, dunking them into his mug for a couple of seconds, then forcing them into his mouth in a single sticky wad. I watched, fascinated, as his cheeks bulged like a python's belly full of live prey.

When he could speak, he said, 'Got to get 'em in in one go.'

I nodded. 'Good technique.'

'I've been practising.'

I smiled into my mug. He was a bright kid, just as he had said. A stack of several fat books was on the table in front of him and I turned the pile to read the spines. Programming. Computer language. Theories of computing. Higher maths. The philosophy of technology. I was lost; I could barely understand the titles.

'Do you like computers?' Paul asked, opening the top book on the pile and riffling through the pages. His face had brightened at the very word and for a second I could see the young boy hidden in that shroud of overstretched skin.

'I don't know much about them,' I said apologetically. 'How about you?'

'Love 'em.' He had started reading, eyes glued to the page. 'They're brilliant.'

'Are you . . . good with computers?' I didn't even know what questions to ask.

'Yeah,' Paul said, sounding matter-of-fact rather than boastful. 'Built my own. Got my own operating system – well, it's based on Linux, but I've done my own thing with it. Computers are what I want to do.' He looked up from the book briefly, his eyes shiny with enthusiasm. 'They're what I do now.'

'What do you mean?'

He shrugged. 'It's all internet, yeah? No one knows I'm only twelve. I do a bit of testing for people, try things out. Do websites for people. Work on stuff. I've got a friend in India; he's at university there. We're trying to solve an equation that no one's ever worked out.'

I had been wrong about him being trapped. As long as his broadband worked, he could go anywhere, meet anyone, be himself without being judged.

'Where do you get the books?'

'Off the internet, mainly. You can get them second-hand – they don't cost that much. Sometimes I order books from the library; Danny picks them up for me. I don't like that so much, though. You can't keep them for as long as you like. It's annoying.'

'Is Danny into computers?'

Paul shook his head. 'He doesn't get it. Danny's good with mechanical things – cars and stuff. He likes using computers, but he doesn't *love* them.'

It was fairly transparent that Paul pitied his brother.

I felt similarly uncertain about how computers actually worked – email and online shopping were about as much as I could manage – but I didn't want Paul to lump me in with the semi-skilled users like his brother. It was important to me to gain his trust. I was starting to think I might be able to help Paul. I could rescue him, set him on the right track. All he needed was a little encouragement.

'And so Danny goes out to work, and you stay here, is that right?' I asked gently, careful to keep any criticism out of my voice.

'Yeah. Don't have to go out any more. I do the shopping and stuff online and they deliver it. Danny gets anything else we need. He looks after me.'

There was looking after and looking after. Danny had given his brother a roof over his head and supported him when he dropped out of school. He obviously encouraged the boy in his computer studies. He'd probably been more of a dad to him than his own father. But set against that was the catastrophic weight gain he had done nothing to stop. Paul had been allowed to run away from the problems he'd had in school rather than dealing with them. It wasn't ideal.

As I watched, Paul absorbed two more biscuits and flicked to the index of the book he was holding, completely engrossed. Maybe it wasn't fair to Danny to criticise him. There was something steely running through Paul, disguised though it was by his soft, swollen appearance. If he wanted to eat, was there anything anyone could do to stop him? It wasn't as if I had ever been able to prevent my mother from drinking. Could I expect Danny to do better for his brother?

I had been supporting my chin on my hand, watching Paul read. I must have made some small movement, because my elbow skidded on a loose piece of paper and shot into a pile of books, knocking them to the floor with a clatter. I jumped out of my chair and started to gather them up, smoothing out crumpled pages and stacking them neatly. With some difficulty, Paul bent down to retrieve a couple of sheets of closely written foolscap that had slid under his chair. The effort made him grunt like an old man, and I fiercely regretted whatever had driven him to find comfort in food. It was wrong that a twelve-year-old boy should be almost unable to bend down to pick up a piece of paper.

When I finally straightened up with the stack of books and slid them on to the table, I noticed a copy of the local paper that had been hidden under the pile. Under Carol Shapley's byline, there was an account of Jenny's death beside a large colour picture of the girl. I lifted the paper and laid it to one side, not wanting to put the books down on top of Jenny's photograph. It felt disrespectful, somehow. Paul was gazing at the paper too, an odd expression on his face.

'You were her teacher.'

I was surprised. 'Jenny? That's right. How did you know?'

'I knew her from primary school.' On closer inspection, his eyes weren't piggy as I had assumed, but dark brown and rather beautiful. They were almost lost in twin canyons of flesh that creased to his temples, and as I watched, moisture slid along the folds. He rubbed at them with a grubby paw. 'Do you know what happened?'

I shook my head. 'The police are investigating, though. I'm sure they'll find whoever did this to her.'

He flashed a look at me, then stared down at the paper again. 'I can't believe she's gone.'

'Did you see much of her?' I asked.

He shrugged. 'Now and then. Used to help her with her maths when she needed it. She was lovely. Never said anything nasty about me. She didn't care about . . . about this.' He gestured at his body, his movements suddenly awkward. I bit my lip as his face twisted and he buried his head in his arms, shoulders shaking. I reached across the table and patted his arm, trying to comfort him. After a minute or two, he looked up at me, his face red and shiny with tears.

'I just . . . I just *miss* her.'

'Me too,' I whispered, on the edge of tears myself. 'Me too.'

As I left the house, I told Paul that he needed to do more than sit in front of a computer all day.

'You should think about going back to school.'

'School's boring.'

'School's the best place for you,' I countered. 'There's more to life than computers. When was the last time you read a book that wasn't about maths or machines?'

He rolled his eyes expressively. 'OK, teacher. I'll read something else.'

'Make sure you do.' I waved and headed back across the road, starting to think about novels that he might enjoy – I could borrow them from the school library. He was clearly such a bright boy, but he needed to broaden his horizons. I would talk to Danny about it, I decided. I could follow up by asking about Charlie. Out of all of these shattered lives – Charlie's, mine, Danny's, Mum's even – Paul's might be put back together.

The smell of the Keanes' house stayed on my clothes and in my hair for hours afterwards. Without really analysing why, I found myself cleaning the whole house obsessively – dusting, vacuuming, sweeping, the works. I cleaned the bathroom and my bedroom, but not the living room, where Mum was spending the day watching television, the glass in front of her refilling, as if by magic, every time it got within a swallow of being empty. When I put my head around the door, she gave me a look Medusa would have been proud of. I withdrew.

It was only when I was on my knees cleaning the oven that it occurred to me that I was reacting to the grimy house across the road, where everything I touched had had a film of grease on it and crumbs dusted every surface. I couldn't live with the thought that our house would look like that to an outsider – unkempt, ignored, barren. I watered the plants on the kitchen windowsill, even though they were half dead and wholly unlovely. I made the windows gleam and the floor shine, and I replaced the mustiness of undisturbed air with lemon-scented chemicals and an unseasonably sharp breeze from outside. I even took everything out of the kitchen cupboards and cleaned them, getting right in to the back. Appliances that I barely recognised, let alone knew how to use, stacked up along the counter, straggling plugs that hung off the end of tortured flexes. I doubted that any would pass contemporary safety testing; they looked as if they would burst into flames as soon as you plugged them in. I found blenders, mixers, even what I identified incredulously as a yoghurt-maker. Without a second thought I filled a box with out-of-date kitchenware. We'd had a charity leaflet through the door asking for donations. They were in the area collecting early on Saturday morning and were looking for unwanted household goods. These things definitely counted as unwanted. In all honesty, I couldn't imagine anyone else wanting them either, but surely it was better than just throwing them away. At the back of another cupboard, behind a stack of pink-flowered plates I didn't recognise and couldn't remember ever having seen in use, I found a small plastic plate and cup decorated with a strawberry motif. I sat back on my heels by the open door and turned them over and over. I hadn't seen them for years. These were the only utensils I would consider using until I went to school. There was even a photograph in the album of Mum and me in the garden, when I was about three. I was eating a sandwich off my special plate while she held a toy parasol over my head to shade me from the sun, and laughed at me. It must have been high summer; she wore a striped sundress with spaghetti straps. The memory of sitting on the grass with Mum was sharp and bright. Love, indulgence, care, tenderness – I had known these once. It was just that my luck had run out when Charlie's did.

I blinked back tears. For some reason, it went right to my heart that Mum had kept the plate and cup. Of course, she had obsessively preserved a lot of things in our house, but that was to do with Charlie, with trying to pretend that nothing had changed since the day he disappeared. This was different. This was about me. More than that, it was the kind of thing a normal mother might do. It was one tiny, fragile link with a woman I had never known, something that I might have laughed about with her if things had been different. If things hadn't fallen apart. I put the little plate and cup back in the cupboard with a sigh, and carried on.

It was getting dark by the time I'd finished. I hefted the box of fossilised electrical goods down to the end of the path, where the charity collectors couldn't miss it. I straightened up, hands on hips, and at that moment, a car door slammed. I whipped around, sure as I could be that someone was behind me, my heart thumping. The adrenalin ebbed away at the sight of the empty road, the blank-windowed houses like so many false fronts in a Wild West town. Nothing moved. No one spoke. I peered to left and right, squinting to see if anyone lurked in the shadows, then headed for the house. I felt slightly ridiculous as I scanned the view from the front step before shutting and bolting the door, but after all, I still had the bruises to show for my last display of witless bravado. From now on, I had decided, if I felt threatened, I was going to react accordingly. Ignoring my instincts could have got me killed.

Of course, it doesn't matter how many locks and bolts you have on a door if you open it just because someone rings the bell. I knew this. But in spite of myself, and in spite of the fact that it was after ten and I wasn't expecting anyone to call, I hurried to answer the front door while the air still vibrated. The sound had set my nerves jangling too and my heart was thudding as I opened the door, leaving the chain on, still wary. Through the narrow gap, I could see a huge bunch of lilies and roses wrapped up in shiny cellophane and curling florist's ribbon. The flowers quivered invitingly, hiding the person holding them from my view.

'Yes?' I said, and was somehow not surprised, but still disappointed, when the bouquet was lowered to reveal Geoff's face.

'Not the welcome I was hoping for, but OK.' His eyes were bright with excitement and he was grinning as if we were sharing a joke, just the two of us. 'I wanted to give you these.'

I stared back stonily, not charmed. 'Why?'

'Does there have to be a reason?'

'For you to buy me flowers? I would have thought so, yes.'

Geoff sighed. 'I saw them and I thought they were as beautiful as you, then.' He pushed at the door, and the chain thrummed. He frowned. 'Aren't you going to open the door properly?'

'I think I'll leave it as it is,' I said, resisting the urge to slam the door on his hand.

He gave a somewhat strained laugh. 'Well, the flowers won't fit through that gap, Sarah. Unless you want me to slide them through stem by stem.'

'Please don't. Look, Geoff, I don't want to sound ungrateful, but I don't really need any flowers.'

'No one *needs* flowers, Sarah. People like to have them, though.'

I held on to the latch, trying to sound firm. 'Not me.'

'That's too bad. No flowers for you, then.' Before I could say anything else, he threw the whole bunch over his shoulder. I heard them crash to the ground behind him. I opened my mouth to say something, then shut it again, nonplussed.

Now unencumbered, he leaned against the door frame. Before I had time to react, he had snaked a hand through the gap in the door and ran it down my hip, pulling me towards him. 'Unorthodox, but if you want to play it that way, OK . . . '

I stepped back smartly, out of range. 'I don't want to "play it" any way. What the hell are you doing?'

He pushed against the door again, hard. His face had gone red. 'For God's sake, I'm just being friendly, that's all. Why are you acting as if I'm threatening you?'

'Maybe because I feel threatened?'

'I wanted to give you some flowers,' he went on, as if I hadn't said anything. 'Just a bunch of flowers. There's no need to be such a bitch about it. *You* said you wanted us to be friends. You said it yourself. This isn't very friendly, Sarah.'

'Well, maybe I was wrong about being friends.' I realised with a sinking feeling that I wasn't going to get Geoff to go away and stop bothering me by being nice. I'd tried ignoring him. I'd tried being friendly but firm. It was time to be blunt. 'I'm sorry if I've misled you about how I feel, Geoff. I'm just not interested in you. I don't even really like you, if I'm honest. I think you should just leave me alone.' There wasn't much that he could misinterpret about that.

He bit his lip, then punched the door frame so hard that he must have hurt his hand, but he didn't seem to notice. I retreated to the foot of the stairs and hung on to the newel post, my heart fluttering in my chest.

'It's always about you, isn't it? Never what *I* want.'

'It's *always* what you want! You don't listen. I've never encouraged you to feel anything for me. I would never go out with a colleague. And even if you weren't working at the school, I would never have been interested in you. We have nothing in common.' I shook my head. 'For God's sake, Geoff, you don't even know me.'

'Because every time I try to get near you, you run away.' He sighed. 'Just stop fighting me, Sarah. Why won't you let me get close to you? Is it because you're afraid of being with me? Afraid of actually feeling something for a change?' His voice deepened. 'I know this ice-princess routine is all an act. I could make you happy. I know what women like. I could teach you to love yourself – and your body – the way I do.'

I couldn't help it; I laughed. 'Do you really think I'm frigid just because I don't want to sleep with you?'

'Well, what's the problem, then?' He sounded affronted. He honestly couldn't understand how I wouldn't find him attractive.

'I don't like you. I don't fancy you. And to be honest, I don't trust you.'

'That's lovely, that is. Charming. How do you think

I feel? I go to a lot of trouble to be nice to you, I make every effort to be there for you, and I get nothing in return. I've always liked you, Sarah, even though you can be a stuck-up bitch sometimes, but I've had enough, quite frankly.'

I folded my arms. He might have reached his breaking point at long last. I was happy for him to feel he'd had the last word as long as it was the last word I had to hear on the subject.

'I suppose you think I've behaved like a twat. Well, that's fine. I'm not surprised.' Geoff paced up and down for a few seconds. 'I knew you were upset about that girl's death, and I thought I could help you get through this, Sarah. If you'd just let me help—'

'I don't need your help, Geoff,' I said quietly.

He pointed at me through the gap in the door. 'No, you don't *know* that you need it, but I do. I'm not going to abandon you to get through this on your own, even if you want me to.'

I sat down on the bottom step of the stairs and put my head in my hands. 'Why won't you leave me alone?'

'Because I care about you, Sarah.'

He didn't care about me. He cared about crossing me off his little list. He was competitive and he couldn't stand to fail, and that was all there was to it. I couldn't bear to look at him.

He patted the door. 'You couldn't open this, could you? I'd rather talk to you properly.'

'I don't think so. I'm really tired, Geoff. Maybe you should go home.'

'Oh come on, let me in. What do I have to say to persuade you?'

'It's not that,' I said, wishing that he would just leave. 'I just need some time to myself. You've – er – given me a lot to think about.'

He nodded. 'OK. OK, that's fair.'

'So you're going to go home?'

'Yeah. In a while.'

'In a while?'

He waved behind him. 'I'm just going to hang around here for a bit. Make sure everything is secure. I feel like you need someone to keep an eye on you. I'm glad you've got a good solid chain on this door. There are a lot of weird characters about. You're very vulnerable, Sarah, do you realise that? Living here on your own with your mum?'

I frowned, trying to read his change of mood, wondering if Geoff was trying to frighten me. Even if I didn't show it, I was scared. He was excited by the argument, not put off. I didn't like it and I didn't trust him and once again I had a strong feeling that it could have been him in the driveway two nights earlier. I forced a short laugh. 'I don't feel vulnerable. What I feel is tired. I'm going to go to bed, Geoff. Please don't stay out here for long.'

'Just for a while. I'll see you tomorrow, maybe.'

'OK,' I said, inwardly cursing.

He stepped off the porch and waved at me cheerfully, back to being Mr Nice Guy, before heading back down the path. I shut the door then locked every lock and shot every bolt. He was sitting on the wall at the end of the garden, lighting a cigarette, when I peered out. He looked as if he owned the place.

A noise from behind me made me jump, and I turned to find Mum standing in the living-room doorway.

'Who was that?'

'No one.'

'You talked to him for long enough.' She took a slug from her glass. Her eyes were glittering dangerously. 'Why didn't you ask him in? Are you ashamed of me? Were you afraid your friend would judge you because of me?'

'He's not a friend, Mum,' I said, feeling desperately tired. 'I didn't want him in the house. It had nothing to do with you.' An idea occurred to me, an idea that sharpened into fear. 'Don't talk to him, if you see him. Don't answer the door, OK?'

'I'll answer the door in my own house if I like,' Mum said tightly. 'You don't tell me what to do.'

'Fine.' I held my hands up. 'Let him in if you like. Who cares?'

Seeing the chance of a fight slip away, she lost interest and turned to go upstairs. I watched her slow, staggery progress and felt like crying. I didn't know what to do about Geoff, and there was no one I could talk to. I couldn't tell if I'd overreacted or not. All I had were suspicions. All the evidence was that he liked me, nothing more. The fact that he made my skin crawl would mean nothing to the police.

Well, there was one policeman who might care. If I dared, I could ask Blake to get rid of him. He hadn't liked Geoff when he met him at the church. The two men had circled one another like stiff-legged dogs sizing up their prospects in a fight, and I would have put my money on Blake to win every time.

I wandered into the living room and sat down on the sofa, stifling a yawn. I would decide what to do after a good night's sleep. Geoff was safely outside the house, and we were safely inside it. And in the morning, everything would probably be a lot clearer.

1992

Three months missing

'You're walking on a beautiful beach and the sun is high in the sky,' says the voice behind me, the syllables long and sing-song.

Waaaaaalking. Beee-yoooootiful. I am bored. I have to be very quiet and very still and not open my eyes and I have to listen to the lady, who is still talking about the beach.

'And the sand is pure white fine sand, lovely and warm on your bare feet.'

I think about the last time I was on a beach. I want to tell the lady, Olivia, about it. It was in Cornwall. Charlie made me stand near the sea and dug a moat around me. It was deep and wide, and when the channel he had made reached the surf, the water rushed in and filled it, rising higher with every wave. I wasn't frightened until the island of sand started to wash away from beneath me. Dad had to rescue me. He rolled up his trousers and waded into the water to pick me up and carry me to where

Mummy was waiting. He called Charlie a dangerous idiot.

'Idiot,' I say now, very quietly, not even as loud as a whisper.

Olivia's voice is even slower now. She is listening to herself, concentrating. She doesn't hear me.

'So now I'm going to take you back, Sarah.' I suddenly want to fidget, or laugh, or stamp my feet. 'You're absolutely safe here, Sarah.'

I know I'm safe. I open my eyes a tiny bit and peek at the room. The curtains are drawn, even though it's the middle of the day. The walls are pink. There are books on shelves behind a desk that's covered in papers. It's not very interesting. I close my eyes again.

'So let's go back to the day your brother disappeared,' Olivia coos. 'It's a summer's day. What do you see?'

I know I'm supposed to be remembering Charlie. 'My brother,' I suggest.

'Good, Sarah. And what is he doing?'

'He's playing a game.'

'What sort of game?'

I have told everyone about Charlie playing tennis. She expects me to say tennis. 'Tennis,' I say.

'Is he on his own?'

'No,' I say.

'Who else is there, Sarah?'

'Me.'

'And what are you doing?'

'Lying on the grass,' I say confidently.

'And what happens then?'

'I go to sleep.'

There's a little pause. 'OK, Sarah, you're doing really well. What I want you to do is think back to before you fell asleep. What's happening?'

'Charlie is playing tennis.' I am starting to get irritated. It's hot in the room. The chair I'm sitting on has a shiny plastic seat and my legs are sticking to it.

'And what else happens?'

I don't know what she wants me to say.

'Does someone come, Sarah? Does someone speak to Charlie?'

'I – I don't know,' I say eventually.

'Think, Sarah!' I can hear excitement in Olivia's voice. She's forgetting to be calm.

I have thought. I remember what I remember. There isn't anything else.

'I'm hungry,' I say. 'Can I go?'

From behind me, there is a sigh and the sound of a notebook snapping shut. 'You weren't under at all, were you?' she says, getting up and walking around to face at me. Her face is pink and her lips look dry.

I shrug.

She runs her hands through her hair and sighs again.

In the hallway, Mum and Dad jump up when we come out.

'How was it?' Dad asks, but he's talking to Olivia. She has her hand on the back of my neck.

'Fine. I really think we're making progress,' Olivia says, and I look up at her, surprised. She smiles at my parents. 'Bring her back next week and we'll try another session.'

I can tell they are disappointed. Mum turns away and Dad starts patting his pockets. 'I should pay . . . ' he starts.

'Don't worry,' Olivia says quickly, 'you can settle up after the final session.'

He nods and tries to smile at her. 'Come on, Sarah,' he says then, and holds out his hand. Olivia gives me a little shake before she lets go of my neck. It feels like a warning. Released, I run to Dad's side. Mum is halfway down the corridor already.

On the way home in the car, rain running down the windows and tapping on the roof, I tell my parents I don't want to go back.

'I'm not listening to this,' Mum says. 'You're going back, whether you like it or not.'

'But–'

'If she doesn't want to go back, Laura . . . '

'Why do you always take her side?' Mum's voice is high-pitched, angry. 'You spoil her. You don't care about how much this means to me. You don't even care about your son.'

'Don't be ridiculous,' Dad says.

'It's not ridiculous to want to try everything we can to find him.' She points her thumb into the back of the car, in my direction. 'She is the only link we have with what happened to Charlie. And she can't – or won't – tell us what happened. This is to help her, too.'

It isn't. I know that very well.

'It's been months,' Dad is saying. 'If she'd seen or heard anything useful, we would know by now. You've got to give up on this, Laura. You've got to let us get on with living.'

'How the hell are we supposed to do that?' Mum's voice breaks; she is shaking. She leans around her seat to look at me. 'Sarah, I don't want to hear another word of complaint from you. You will go back and you will talk to Olivia and tell her what happened – tell her what you saw – because if you don't . . . if you don't . . . '

The window beside me has steamed up. I use my sleeve to wipe a patch clear so that I can look out at the world sliding by. I watch the cars and the people and I try not to listen to my mother crying. It's the saddest sound in the world.

Chapter 10

Morning came a lot earlier than I had been expecting. Light pulsed through the curtains and it took a second for me to realise it was a brighter light than the cool blue of dawn – not that dawn was on a regular twice-a-second cycle anyway.

I sat up, leaning on one elbow, and like a shaken kaleidoscope, the diffuse noise outside suddenly resolved into distinguishable elements. In the trees near my window, birds were uttering sharp, staccato alarm calls and peevish chirps at being disturbed. As if in answer, radios crackled and bleeped, and low voices murmured, edged with urgency. Engines were running – more than one car. Even as I listened, another came into the cul-de-sac, high on revs before the brakes bit down and the engine cut out. *Someone in a hurry*, I thought, sitting up properly and pushing my hair back off my face. Then footsteps, even-paced and purposeful, too close to the house for comfort. Kicked gravel skittered along the road and I shivered, suddenly reluctant to find out what was happening. The urge to turn over and draw the duvet over my head was almost irresistible.

I couldn't do it. I was out of bed the next second; two steps took me to the window and I tweaked the curtain to one side to peek out. It was still night, or nearing the end of it. Two police cars were parked on the other side of the road, lights flashing in the syncopated rhythm that had disturbed my sleep. Directly in front of the house was an ambulance. The back doors were open and I could see movement through the semi-opaque windows set along the sides. A small group of policemen stood around at the back of the ambulance, and with a start I recognised one of them as Blake. It was his car I had heard driving into the cul-de-sac; he had abandoned it at an angle to the kerb a few yards down the street and left the door hanging open in his hurry to get out. Vickers was sitting in the passenger seat, eyes hooded against the overhead light. The trenches in his face were darker and deeper, I thought, but whether the change in his appearance was caused by a trick of the light or the early hour or gnawing worry I couldn't tell. Maybe all three.

I let go of the curtain and leaned against the wall. I couldn't make sense of what I had just seen. I couldn't quite believe it, either – if I had pulled back the curtain again and found that the street was completely deserted, I almost wouldn't have been surprised. There was something surreal about finding all of these people on my doorstep – quite literally, I discovered, looking out again and down at the head of a man who was walking out towards the road from our porch. What had he been doing? What was going on? Why were the police there in such force?

The electric milk float from the local dairy was parked up at the end of the road. And there indeed was the milkman, all muffled up against the night air, wearing a high-visibility jacket and talking earnestly to one of the policemen. The uniformed officer was listening patiently, nodding but not taking notes, and had turned his radio towards his mouth as if he was just waiting for the chance to speak. I hoped the milkman wasn't in trouble. He was a nice man who operated in the small hours, between the return of the last night owls and the first early risers, pattering silently through his shadowy world. I couldn't think what he could have done that would arouse the interest of so many police. And there was the ambulance, too.

The window in front of me was fogging up; impatiently, I moved to the other side, and that movement was enough to attract Vickers' attention. He had got out of the car and was leaning on the open door, talking to Blake. As I moved, his eyes met mine. Without appearing to react, he carried on speaking, but didn't look away. Blake flicked a look up at me over his shoulder, so quickly and casually that it felt like an insult, then turned back, nodding. I could tell I wasn't going to be left to watch the scene undisturbed. With an effort, I wrenched myself away from Vickers' pale blue scrutiny and headed to my wardrobe for clothes. I wanted to get downstairs before anyone rang the doorbell and woke Mum up – they had enough problems without her having hysterics about all the police in front of the house.

I dragged a pair of Ugg boots out from the bottom of the wardrobe and put them on, tucking my pyjama bottoms into them, then found a fleece and pulled it over my head without bothering to undo the zip. The men gathered outside had looked cold, rubbing their hands together as they talked, their breath pluming in the light from the car headlights. I needed layers.

It took me an age to unlock the front door: I fumbled with the keys and the bolts were resistant. I swore under my breath as I struggled with it. A familiar silhouette loomed outside and I hoped against hope that Blake would understand that I was trying to get the door open, that there was no need to ring the bell or use the door knocker, that if he did, Mum would be sure to wake up . . . The last bolt thudded back and I pulled open the door. Blake's face changed from set professionalism to amusement for a split-second, as he surveyed my cow-print covered bottom half.

'Nice outfit.'

'I wasn't expecting visitors. What's going on? What's the emergency?'

'We got a call–' he began, but broke off looking irritated when I shushed him. 'What's the problem?'

'I don't want Mum to know you're here.'

With a dark look in my direction, Blake reached in and took the front-door keys from the lock, then grabbed my arm and drew me out of the house, letting the door close behind me. I dragged my feet as I followed him down the path, suddenly self-conscious as I noticed how many people were standing around, watching us. When we got as far as the garden gate, I said, 'This is far enough. And I'd like my keys back, if it isn't too much trouble.'

'OK then.' He dropped them into my hand and I pushed them into my pocket, curling my fingers around them, out of sight. 'I'll tell you why we're here if you tell me what your pal Geoff was doing in this neck of the woods. He doesn't live anywhere close to this estate, and yet this is where we find him in the middle of the night. Anything to do with you, by any chance?'

I was mortified. 'He hasn't been causing trouble, has he? I thought he would just calm down and go home.'

Something flickered in Blake's eyes and his face went very still, with that coolly amused look that I recognised as his poker face. 'So he *was* here to see you.'

I squirmed. 'He came over. I didn't want him to – I mean, I didn't know he was coming, and I didn't let him in.'

Blake waited, saying nothing. I bit my lip.

'He brought flowers. Quite a big bunch. I – I didn't want them.'

'Those flowers, by any chance?'

They were becalmed in the middle of the front garden where Geoff had flung them, an unlovely tangle of broken stems and crushed petals. The plastic wrapper was pebbled with condensation.

'Look, I don't want to get Geoff in trouble,' I said, meaning it, to my own surprise. 'He went a bit over the top last night. I'm sure he didn't mean any harm. He was a bit frustrated that I wasn't – that I didn't—'

'Reciprocate,' Blake suggested.

'Thanks. Yes. And so I left him out here to calm down.'

'OK. What time was this?'

'Half past ten, maybe?' I frowned, trying to remember. 'It was after ten when he rang the bell, and then we talked for a while. I couldn't get rid of him.'

'And you didn't let him into your house.'

'I didn't even take the chain off the door,' I said simply. 'He was in a strange mood.'

'Did he scare you?'

I looked at Blake and suddenly understood that he was angry – furious. But not with me.

'Well – yeah. I don't know if I was right to feel threatened, but the whole situation with Geoff – it was just a bit out of control. He wouldn't take no for an answer.' I found myself blinking back tears and stopped, gathering what was left of my composure. 'You'd better tell me. What did he do?'

At that moment, one of the paramedics jumped out of the back of the ambulance and shut the doors before hurrying around to the front. He turned the ambulance with competent economy of effort and drove out of Curzon Close, lights still whirling, followed by one of the police cars, also lit up. As the sound of the engines faded away towards the main road, I could hear the sirens begin to whoop. I might have been imagining it, but there was compassion on Blake's face. Before he spoke, he looked past me and straightened up, his face neutral. 'Hello, guv. Sarah was just asking about Mr Turnbull.'

I turned. Up close, Vickers looked more than ever like a tortoise, wrinkled and ancient.

'Bad business,' he said. 'Did you hear anything, Sarah? Anything out of the ordinary?'

I shook my head, wrapping my arms around myself, suddenly cold. 'What is it? What should I have heard?'

The policemen exchanged a glance and it was Blake

who spoke at last, Vickers having silently pulled rank. 'A call came in from Harry Jones, the local milkman, about –' he checked his watch 'forty-five minutes ago. He'd found something.'

Instead of explaining any further, Blake put his hand on my arm again and drew me forward, and this time I didn't resist him but stepped through the garden gate onto the pavement. To my left, Geoff's car was parked, two wheels on the pavement, facing away from me. The tyre on the right had been slashed and formed a puddle of tattered rubber on the roadway. The back window was a haze of fractured glass and more glass glinted on the road. My hand had gone to my mouth in shock. I took a few more steps on legs that were slightly unsteady. From that angle, I could see the side windows were dark and empty, the glass smashed to bits, jagged teeth poking up from the window frames.

'But why would Geoff vandalise his own car?' I asked Blake, still not understanding.

'He didn't. Your milkman found him in the front seat. Whoever did the damage to the vehicle did the same to him, I'm afraid.'

'*What?*' My heart thudded in my chest, my throat as tight as if someone was squeezing it. I rounded on the two policemen. 'He's not . . .'

'Not dead, no.' Vickers ground out the words, his voice sounding rusty and worn. 'But he's not in a good way, my dear.'

'Head injuries,' Blake explained. 'It looks as if his attacker laid into him from close range with a blunt object of some

kind, very violently. You can see the damage that was done
to the car.'

I could, and I couldn't imagine how anyone could survive
an attack like that.

As if he had read my mind, Vickers nodded towards
the car. 'Being in there might have saved his life. The frame
would have protected him from the worst of it. Confined
space, you see. No room for a decent swing.' He mimed
striking a blow and my stomach turned over. I swayed,
feeling sweat break out across my back and prickle beneath
my breasts. My hands and feet were like ice and my head
spun. I shut my eyes on the scene, as if I could make it
go away if I didn't look at it. The darkness was so close;
it would be so easy to slip down into it, away from everything. Hands that I knew belonged to Blake held on to
my shoulders and squeezed, hard.

'Easy now. Deep breaths.'

I took in a few good lungfuls of the clean night air,
keeping my eyes closed, dimly aware that he was turning
me away from the car, away from the patch of ground that
was slick with blackish liquid, liquid that I now understood was blood. He manoeuvred me to the garden wall
and pushed me down so I could sit on it, holding on to
me until I was able to wave him away and assure him that
yes, I wouldn't fall.

A long way off, I could hear him explaining to Vickers
that Geoff had been in Curzon Close to see me, but that
I hadn't seen him after ten thirty. A silence fell between
the two detectives. I could almost hear Vickers' mind
working.

'OK,' he said eventually. 'So our lad came here and got sent away with a flea in his ear. But he didn't go far. Why?'

I had recovered enough to speak. 'He said he wanted to hang around for a bit. He said – he said there were weird characters about.'

'Is that the exact phrase he used?' Vickers asked swiftly. I nodded.

'What did he mean by that?' Vickers wondered, mostly to himself. 'Maybe he'd seen something.'

'Maybe he was just looking for an excuse to hang around,' Blake said.

I felt myself blushing. 'That's what I assumed. I thought he just needed to calm down before going back home. He was having a cigarette when I looked out.'

Vickers rubbed his face with his hands, producing a dry, rasping sound from the bristles that were beginning to frost his jawline. 'So the lad is all hot and bothered and doesn't know which way is up, and he decides to cool off out here.'

'I think it was partly to show me he wasn't going to go away just because I asked him to.'

Vickers nodded. 'More than likely. So he's sitting out here, minding his own business as far as we know – you'll check around when it gets to be more knocking-on-doors o'clock, won't you, Blakey? Just ask if anyone heard anything strange in the small hours. Though this is the closest house to where the incident took place.' He looked at me. 'Is that your bedroom up there, right at the front? Well, if you didn't hear anything, I wonder who would have. No new mothers along this road, are there?'

I shook my head, amused in spite of myself, and he looked disappointed. 'Best witnesses in the world, they are. Up at unsociable hours, nothing to do but feed their babies and look out of the window. Nursing mothers and pensioners, they're my two favourite kinds of witness.'

Something was nagging at the back of my mind. I looked at the boxes and bags by the road and frowned.

'What is it?' Blake asked, his eyes watchful.

'Nothing – just that there was supposed to be a charity collection this morning. I thought I heard them earlier, clattering around. I was half asleep – I don't really know what time it was. But it's still too early for them now, isn't it?' I looked at my wrist distractedly, only to realise that I hadn't put my watch on. I looked back up to see Blake and Vickers exchanging meaningful glances. 'You don't think – I didn't *hear* it, did I?'

Neither of them responded, letting me come to my own conclusion. 'Oh, God.'

Blake cleared his throat. 'If you don't mind, sir, I'm going to have a word with the uniforms. We need to sort out retrieval of the vehicle.'

'Can't leave it sitting there,' Vickers said, nodding. 'Get plenty of pictures before they move it though – make sure the SOCOs take this one seriously. It's an attempted murder anyway.'

I looked from him to Andrew Blake, reading in their faces what neither of them was saying out loud. They were planning to treat this as if it was a murder investigation. Which meant there was a good chance that Geoff might die.

Blake crossed the road to where one of the police cars was still parked, and the two occupants levered themselves out to talk to him. I watched them chatting and joking while Vickers continued to speak, dropping words as dry as dust into my ear, more for his benefit than mine.

'So he's sitting there, middle of the night. Maybe he's walked around for a bit to help himself get over the little scene he's had with you. Did he embarrass himself? Thought so. Made a bit of a tit of himself in front of the girl he likes, and now he's getting over it. He drives a Golf. Nice little car, but you don't attack someone to take their car if they drive a Golf. A Merc or a Jag or a BMW maybe, but not a little VW. Plus, you don't attack someone in their car if it's the car you want. Blood and all sorts all over the inside. Who wants to drive around in a mess like that? You drag him out onto the road, give him a few lumps to stop him getting up and causing you problems, then drive off, sweet as you like.'

Vickers sighed, his eyes focused on the rear of the car. I could tell he wasn't seeing the wrecked car that was parked on the road, but the car as it had been hours before, perfect, carefully kept, clean and shiny. 'I come up, ready to do damage,' he said softly. 'I start off with the driver, don't I? Stop him from driving off. I get the door open and I start bashing. He fights back, or maybe he doesn't get the chance, but he slides over towards the passenger seat and I don't have a great angle on him any more. I think I've done enough to take care of the driver, but I'm still angry. I don't feel like I've got satisfaction yet. There's still the car, though. I can work off my feelings on that. So I break the windows on my side of the car and go round to the back to do the rear window. Nice big target, that. Then I get out my knife and I do the tyres. I can't be bothered, for some reason, to come round to the left side of the car. Why is that?'

'Not enough room?' I suggest. The neighbours' hedge needed a trim; leaves boiled out over the footpath. There was barely enough space to walk between the parked car and the overgrown bushes.

Vickers frowned. 'Could be. But it could also be that I don't see the car from that side. I've been looking at it from the right – gazing at it, maybe. It's become the focus for all I'm feeling. I identify it strongly with the person I'm attacking.' He turned to look across the road to the houses that faced us. 'It's as if someone was watching. I wonder if any of your neighbours saw someone funny lurking around.'

I looked in the same direction, suddenly seeing the front gardens as potential hiding places, feeling that prickling sensation that had plagued me for days, the feeling that I was being watched. I wondered if I should say anything to Vickers. I wondered if I was going mad.

Before I could speak, Vickers continued. 'The one thing this crime scene does tell me is that the attacker knew his victim and knew that the car meant a lot to him. So we can ask Mr Turnbull about his associates when he's up to talking to us.' The tone of his voice gave away what he was really thinking. If *he's up to talking to us.*

Geoff had always been fussy about his car. He would

groom it before getting into it, whisking dead leaves and detritus out from under the windscreen wipers, inspecting it front and back for signs of damage. 'The car was in mint condition. You could have guessed he loved it,' I said slowly. 'You wouldn't need to know him for that.'

'But you would need to know him, or know something about him, to attack him like that, do you see?' Vickers countered. 'I've seen a fair bit of violence one way or another, and that scene there is all about raw feeling.' He looked at the car again, hands on his hips, and shook his head. 'I just wish I knew how this fitted in.'

'Fitted in? Fitted in with what?'

Vickers gave me a look. 'You don't think that this is connected with what's happened to poor little Jenny Shepherd? Why else do you think Blake and I are here?'

'But I don't see –' I began. He put his hand on my arm.

'Sarah, look at the facts. We've got a young girl dead. This man, who was known to her, who is one of her teachers, turns up far from home in a street that, as the crow flies, is not far at all from where Jenny lived. He's been half-killed by person or persons unknown. Jenny's suffered a violent death. This is too much of a coincidence for me to ignore it. Anything that happens on this estate – anything – could have something to do with Jenny's murder. I've now got two very violent crimes that are well outside the usual run of criminal activity in this area. If I look at each of them in isolation, I'll make a bit of progress here and there; I might get lucky and run across a witness, or my murderer might just be waiting for a chance to confess. Not very likely, but it does happen. If I keep them separate, I'm waiting for a breakthrough that might never come on both of them. But put them together, and I start seeing all sorts of patterns, do you understand? Points of coincidence. It's like algebra; you need two parts of the problem to get the third.' The DCI's face was bright with enthusiasm for his job; he really loved what he did. I was momentarily sidetracked by the reference to algebra, my mind off chasing a rabbit that was the memory of being told I had no mathematical capabilities, none at all . . .

Vickers went on, 'Now, don't be fooled into thinking I've decided that whoever killed Jenny is also to blame for this. It's a possibility, and it's got to be explored, but I'm not fixated on that, you understand. There are lots of ways these two crimes can be connected, Sarah. Lots of ways.'

I caught a sideways look from those sharp eyes and, like a good pupil, offered a suggestion. 'Revenge?'

'Right you are.' He beamed at me in an avuncular way. 'Our boy Geoff could have been up to his neck in what happened to Jenny, and it doesn't take a genius to spot that. He's a bit of a lad, I've heard. We know Jenny was sleeping with someone, and he certainly had the opportunity to get to know her, to tell her she was special, to get her to do whatever he asked of her. Wouldn't be the first time a teacher took advantage, would it?'

'But that doesn't fit in with what Jenny told Rachel,' I objected. 'Or the photograph she showed her.'

'I don't,' Vickers said carefully, 'believe every word of what Rachel told us. Jenny might have lied to her, to put her off the scent. And Rachel might be lying to us, even now. Someone might be trying to get us to look in the wrong direction. We haven't found the photograph, you know, or anything else that would prove Rachel was telling us the truth.'

I couldn't believe that Geoff had been sleeping with Jenny; he wasn't like that, but I knew that the chief inspector wouldn't listen to me any more than he had listened to Rachel. 'Jenny was pregnant. Can't you check the DNA to find out if he was the father?'

'Don't worry, we will. But it will take a while for the results to come back. Besides, the point just now isn't whether Geoff Turnbull was guilty of abusing Jenny Shepherd, but whether someone might *believe* that he was. Someone puts two and two together. Maybe they have a bit more information than we do. Maybe it's just a hunch. But whatever it is, they feel they have to do something to get justice for Jenny, and they aren't prepared to wait for the Old Bill to get around to it.'

In my mind's eye I saw Michael Shepherd, a man transformed by grief, a man with a dark look in his eyes, and knew that Vickers saw the same thing. I could imagine the explosive power that might be unleashed if that combination of rage, guilt and suspicion acquired a target.

'Andy,' Vickers said, with a nod in Blake's direction, 'will be having a word with interested parties in due course. We can't go waking them up in the middle of the night without any evidence, but it's worth a chat, don't you think?'

I could see how it fitted together neatly, but I was still sceptical. I would never, ever believe that Geoff was capable of abusing a child, and not just because he had been so single-minded about pursuing me. It just didn't fit in with what I knew of him, his enthusiastic interest in women, not girls. I found it hard to conceive that he could have abused her and it was impossible to accept that he might have killed her. Then again, I had seen him agitated a few hours before, and I couldn't shake the doubt that made me feel. I didn't know for certain what Geoff was capable of. I had to assume that he was guilty of *something*, or else why would he have ended up getting his head bashed in?

I was also feeling guilty on my own account. I suspected that Vickers would have liked to know about another violent incident, the attack on me. I didn't have his faith in the power of coincidence, but it would be another part of the picture he was creating. But as I opened my mouth to tell him about it, the words died unspoken. First and foremost, my reasons for not reporting it were still valid. Secondly, he might not understand those reasons. And thirdly, I still didn't think it was relevant. If I had been right all along and Geoff was the one who attacked me, well, he was now well and truly out of the picture. I wouldn't need to worry about him while he was in hospital.

But the main reason why I didn't say anything to Vickers was more fundamental: I didn't trust him. And I was pretty sure that he didn't trust me. Whether it was that he was picking up on the confusion I was feeling about Geoff, or whether he had ideas of his own, there was, for the first time, an edge in what he was saying to me. And with that in mind, it behoved me to be wary. With an effort I dragged myself back to the present, to the reality of cold feet and a terrible urge to yawn, and prepared to match wits with the policeman.

Vickers had wound down to silence, but now he turned to me again with a gleam in his shrewd eyes. 'If you knew anything that might be relevant, given what I've been saying – if you knew there were connections that I should know about, is what I mean – you'd tell me, wouldn't you?'

'Well, you're leaving out the obvious one,' I said stiffly, knowing that Vickers had nudged me in this direction, knowing that to avoid mentioning it would arouse more suspicion than it would allay. 'I knew Jenny too. I taught her. I found her body. And all of this –' I waved towards the car, not wanting to think about what it signified. '– has happened right on my doorstep. So I'm right in the middle of your coincidences, wouldn't you say?'

Vickers smiled thinly and I saw with sadness that I had been right to be suspicious. *But I liked you . . .* I gathered together all of the logic I could muster. 'However, I think there's a flaw in your reasoning.'

He raised his eyebrows.

'This has nothing to do with me. I don't know anything about what happened to either of them.' There was a thin, thready quality to my voice that spoke of exhaustion. 'Sometimes coincidences are just that. Why does there have to be a connection between the two?' *Or even three?* More than ever, I was sure I had been right not to give Vickers that little piece of ammunition.

'There doesn't have to be a connection, but for now I'm going to assume there is. Just because you aren't willing or able to see it doesn't mean you don't know something that would be of interest to me. Two crimes like this

– two violent assaults – and of course I'm going to see a link.'

'I think you're looking for patterns that don't exist because you don't have the first idea what happened to Jenny. Add *that* into your equation.'

'We have various lines of enquiry. We're not at liberty to discuss them with members of the public at present, but this is an active investigation.'

'Well, that's not what it sounds like,' I said waspishly. 'It sounds like you've got no ideas and no proof, and you're trying to make this fit some hypothesis that you've been working on since Jenny's body was discovered. I know what you police do. If you don't have evidence, you start getting creative.' The face of my poor father, interviewed time and time again, came into my head. The cloud of suspicion that had surrounded our family, that could have been dispelled by the investigating officer if he had only cared to. I spoke again, my voice low and passionate. 'You can forget about me implicating myself. I'm not involved in this, and I don't know why circumstances are conspiring to make you think that I am. All I know is that I've done my best to cooperate from the start. I don't know why this has happened to Geoff, or why Jenny was murdered, and if I did I would have told you long ago.'

'We'll see,' Vickers said, his eyes cold. 'We'll see.'

'Are you finished with me?'

'For now. But you can expect us to be in touch.' Vickers started to stroll towards Blake's car. 'Don't go on any long holidays, OK?'

I stalked back to the house. In the hall mirror, my eyes

were bright with anger and my hair was wild. My lips were compressed into a hard line, and it was with an effort that I relaxed them. I knew Vickers had intended to rattle me, and it had worked. But I also felt that I didn't know anything that could be of use to him. The mugging was a red herring, but I couldn't tell him about it now – I'd had every opportunity to mention it, after all. So now I was hiding something from the police, feeling guilty about it, and looking guilty too. If I wasn't careful, this was all going to go very wrong indeed.

The one thing that I didn't want to think about was Geoff, but as soon as I acknowledged that to myself, I couldn't think about anything else. I checked the clock in the kitchen – almost five – and gave up on the idea of going back to bed. As I made a mug of tea, I slowly worked through the facts one by one. Geoff was in hospital. That was bad. Very bad. He had head injuries. My stomach squeezed at the thought. He could die. He could survive, but barely. He could be permanently compromised. He could recover fully. I wanted to believe that the last outcome was the most likely, but I just didn't know. Blake and Vickers had looked grim when they talked about him. I stirred the milk in, no longer sure that I wanted to drink the tea but committed to making it. Were they trying to make me feel guilty so I would tell them everything I knew?

I sat down at the kitchen table and watched the steam curling up from the mug. The ironic thing was, in spite of my shouting at Vickers, I was inclined to agree with him. I did feel guilty. If I had just been a bit nicer to Geoff – if I had acted on the feeling that someone was watching me – if I had got them to investigate who attacked me – then everything might have been different. Although I hadn't tried to put myself there, somehow I was at the centre of everything. It would have been nice to understand why.

1993

Ten months missing

A blackbird is digging in the lawn on a sunny evening in April. I sit on the doorstep and wriggle my toes inside my shoes. The rules are very clear: I have permission to sit there, but not to leave the front garden. If anyone speaks to me, I am to go indoors and call for Mum. Warned away from people, I have become very shy.

The blackbird is beautiful, a glossy bird with round, amber-red eyes that stare at me unblinkingly as he bounces around the lawn, working at the grass to pull up clumps of moss. He is building a nest in the holly bush next door, hauling as much as he can carry to where his brown-feathered mate is organising the construction. She keeps up a steady stream of encouraging song. I am shading my eyes, trying to see her in the branches, when a voice says hello. The blackbird shoots up from the lawn in a whirr of startled wings. I jump to my feet, on the point of running indoors, but the man standing at the end of the drive looks friendly. He's holding a dog on a lead, a red setter, and the dog is prancing about excitedly, tail wagging.

'Nice evening, isn't it?'

'Yes,' I say, almost without making a sound.

'Is this your house?'

I nod.

'We've just moved in down the road. Number seventeen.' He nods towards it. 'I've got a little girl around your age – Emma. She's nine. How old are you?'

'I'm nine too,' I say.

'Great. Well, maybe you can come around and play with her sometime. She's looking for a new friend.'

I nod, beaming. A new friend. Already I am imagining a girl as dark as I am fair, a girl who isn't afraid of heights or spiders, a girl who likes animal stories and ballet and dressing up in old clothes to act out scenes from books.

Behind me, the front door opens so violently that it crashes back against the wall inside the house.

'Get out of here!' My mother's face is contorted, almost unrecognisable. 'Leave my daughter alone!'

The man takes a step back, pulling the dog behind him, stiff with shock. 'I'm sorry – I – I should have thought. It's just – we've just moved in down the street and—'

'He has a daughter,' I say to Mum, wanting her to understand, wanting her to stop looking at him like that.

'Don't you teach her not to talk to strangers? Don't you care about her safety?' Her voice is too loud.

The man apologises quickly and walks away. He doesn't say goodbye. I hope that he will come back with his daughter, that we can still be friends once I've explained about my mother and Charlie and the rule.

Mum waits until the man is out of sight, then grabs my arm, hard. 'Go inside and go to your room! I told you not to talk to anyone.'

'But—' I begin, anxious to defend myself.

'Inside!' She pulls me through the door and flings me towards the stairs, letting go of my arm when I am off balance so I fall, knocking my head against the banister. I begin to cry, wailing for my father, for my mother, for comfort of some kind.

Mum is standing with her back to the front door, leaning against it with her hands to her mouth. Her eyes are round and I can see her skirt vibrating as she shakes. There's a movement to my left. My father is standing in the living-room doorway, eyes not on me but on Mum. I stop screaming, but keep up a steady whimpering to remind Dad that I am there, on the floor, hurt.

'Laura,' he says, in a voice that doesn't sound like his, 'this can't go on. You are hurting people. Hurting Sarah. You've got to stop.'

Mum slides down the door, crumpling into a ball, shoulders shaking. She whispers, so softly I can hardly hear her, 'I can't . . . '

Dad raises his hands to grip his head. 'This can't go on,' he says again. 'I can't live like this.' Then he turns around and slams the living-room door behind him, walking away from both of us.

I pick myself up and go upstairs, leaving Mum in the hall. I go to my parents' bedroom, where my face is red and distraught in the mirror. My eyes are big, glazed with tears. There is a bump already, swelling above my right eye, and five red marks ring my arm, topped with five scarlet half-moons where my mother's nails dug into my flesh. Lodged in my throat, all sharp corners, is the knowledge that she doesn't love me, that I have failed her again. I swallow it down so that it sits, a solid mass, in my stomach. I'm not sure what has happened between my parents, but I know it was my fault. I disobeyed Mum, and let her down. From now on, I'll be good. I'll be better than good. I'll be perfect. And I'll never disappoint her again.

Chapter 11

Even though hospitals never close, it was after eight when I rang St Martin's, where the police had told me Geoff had been taken. The largest hospital in the area, it had been a Victorian foundation, redeveloped in the best brutalist style during the 1960s. It occupied a vast site near a dual carriageway, with a substantial accident and emergency department and countless sprawling buildings housing specialist units. Geoff would have a chance there, however bad his injuries were. I sat at the kitchen table and watched the hands sweep around the face of the kitchen clock, wanting to call and yet somehow afraid to, in case there was bad news, in case he was gone. It wasn't hypocrisy to hope that he lived. I'd never wanted Geoff to die, just to leave me alone.

Whatever the standard of the medical facilities, the switchboard at St Martin's was far from state-of-the-art. By the time I got through to A&E, I was shaking. A woman with a swooping South African accent told me that yes, Geoff Turnbull was a patient and no, he wasn't awake yet. She couldn't tell me anything else about his condition at the moment.

'Oh, please . . .' I said, strung out on too much caffeine and tension.

'I can't because I've just come on shift, hey,' she said, sounding irritated. 'I've told you everything I know myself.'

'OK,' I said meekly. 'Can I come and visit him?'

There was a tiny pause. 'If you *like*,' the voice said, sounding as if that was the most bizarre request she had ever heard. Her accent dragged out the 'i' of 'like', giving the word a full two syllables of incredulity. *If you la-ak.*

I thanked her and hung up, feeling stupidly relieved. As long as Geoff wasn't dead, there was hope. And going to sit beside his bed, even if he didn't wake up straightaway, would give me something to do. It might even make me feel less guilty.

St Martin's was too far away for me to be able to walk there. Rather than getting a taxi or trying to work out the bus routes, I called Jules. It was quicker. Besides, she owed me. On a few occasions, I had picked her up from nights out that had gone wrong. The least she could do was return the favour.

I could tell at once that she wasn't in a good mood as she pulled up outside the house. She didn't smile as I hurried out to the car. No make-up. Matted hair pulled back in a ponytail. Hoodie and tracksuit bottoms. This was off-duty Jules, straight out of bed.

'I really appreciate this,' I said, getting into the passenger seat. She drove a Toyota that had seen better days. Boxes of tissues and loose CDs littered the back seat. The felt above her head was streaked with mascara from her habit of putting on her make-up while stopped at traffic lights; the brush always dragged on the ceiling when she lifted the wand away to separate out her lashes with a fingernail. It looked like she'd been squashing spiders up there.

'You'd better appreciate it. I couldn't believe it when I looked at the time.'

'Sorry,' I said, only half meaning it.

'So what time is your appointment, anyway?'

'Er – nine thirty.' I had told her I had a hospital appointment and my car was in the garage. It had seemed easier than trying to explain why I was going to see Geoff when she knew how I felt about him. At the thought of the conversation that would have ensued, my stress levels had gone up another notch. A lie had seemed like the only viable option. Now that I was with her, though, I found myself wondering if I should confide in Jules. She was my friend, after all. The only trouble was that I couldn't think where to start. I'd never trusted her enough to tell her the truth about my family – the things that had made me who I was – and now was not the time.

'That car of yours is a heap of shit,' Jules said, grinding her gears and swearing. 'You need a new one.'

I needed the spare keys, but Aunt Lucy hadn't posted them yet. She had promised me they would be with me by Monday. In the meantime, I presumed my car was still parked near the Shepherds' house. I didn't feel like going to check.

'Are you nervous?' Jules was looking at me with real if belated concern. I realised that I'd been chewing my lip.

'Not really – it's just a check-up for my back.'

'I had no idea you had back trouble. It's usually the tall ones, you know? I did notice you were limping a bit when you came out of your house just now. How long has it been bothering you?'

'A while,' I said vaguely, looking out the window. We weren't far from the hospital now. Traffic was heavy; people out and about on a bright Saturday morning, heading for the shops. Jules joined the end of a queue of cars and checked the clock on the dashboard.

'Loads of time.'

'Er, yes.'

I didn't say anything else and Jules flicked the radio on, crooning along to a pop song I didn't know. 'Oh, because you lied to me . . . Don't try to deny me . . . '

Eventually we inched forward far enough so she could edge out of the line of cars and into the dedicated turning lane for the hospital. We swung through the gates and ground to a halt facing a signboard with directions to about twenty departments.

'Which way?'

I looked blankly at the signs, reading desperately. Accident and Emergency was to the left.

'Left, please.'

The car didn't move. 'Are you sure?' Jules was frowning. 'I'd have thought it would be out-patient care.'

The sign for out-patient care featured an arrow that hooked round like a question mark and looked as if it would take us a long way from where I needed to go.

'Um, no. The specialist I'm seeing has rooms near A&E,'

I said awkwardly. 'In fact, that's where I'm supposed to go.'

'Really? That's so weird. Usually they keep them totally separate, don't they?'

I nodded, hoping she would stop asking questions and just drive me there.

She looked at me and sighed. 'OK, for you, I'm going to give up the rest of the morning.'

'What?'

'I'll come in with you. You look like hell, Sarah. I don't know if it's nerves or what, but you look like you didn't sleep at all, and you're so quiet.' She patted me on the knee. 'Don't worry, I don't mind. I'll just park the car and we can go in together.'

'No!' I said, starting to panic. 'Please, Jules. I just want to go by myself.'

'Sorry for suggesting it. I thought it would help.' She pulled up at the drop-off point before the ambulance bay, her face thunderous. 'I suppose you'll be OK to get home yourself after your *consultation*.'

'I'll be fine.' I chose to ignore the stress she'd placed on the final word; I had guessed that she didn't believe me. She was a better friend than I deserved. But what mattered at that moment was finding out how Geoff was, and finding out what had happened. I grabbed my bag and opened the door. 'Thanks for the lift.'

'I don't know what all this is about, Sarah,' Jules replied, staring straight ahead of her, 'but I'm not impressed. Whatever it is, get it out of your system before we get back to work, OK?'

I didn't answer her, but I paused on my way in to the hospital to watch her as she drove away, hoping that she'd wave, hoping that she'd be willing to forgive me. And Jules being Jules, she gave me a smile as she went.

Inside, I queued behind would-be patients who were besieging the receptionist with a bewildering assortment of problems, all of which seemed to require sitting down on an orange plastic chair to await attention. Through double doors lay the promised land where medical treatment was dispensed, but although hospital staff were coming and going like worker bees on a sunny day, none of the people in the waiting room ever seemed to be taken through. The chairs were filling up. I felt an overwhelming lack of enthusiasm for sitting there and hoped I wouldn't be made to wait. It was a bigger casualty department than the one at the small-scale medical centre where I usually ended up with Mum, but no more efficient, by the looks of things.

The receptionist brightened behind her protective glass when I finally made it to the desk. Unlike most of the others in the queue, I wasn't covered in blood or raving incomprehensibly. I even had a straightforward request – I just wanted to see Geoff. Nonetheless, she was launching into her well-worn spiel about taking a seat on the plastic chairs to my left when a doctor in wrinkled blue scrubs dashed through the double doors and interrupted her.

'Karen, did you manage to get hold of Geoff Turnbull's next-of-kin?'

'I haven't had a chance,' she said coolly, waving a hand at the queue. 'I'm a little bit busy.'

The doctor ran his fingers through his very untidy hair and sighed. 'We're going to need to let them know if we have to operate.'

It was a gift. 'I may be able to help.'

'Who are you?' The doctor stared down at me. He had a long, pointed nose. I felt like a beetle being inspected by a hungry bird.

'I'm a colleague of Geoff's. I mean – I'm a friend. I could get the number for his parents from the school where we work. If you wanted it.'

The doctor, who had very big bags under his eyes, waved his hand at Karen. 'Oh, don't worry about it. It's her job, if she'd only get around to doing it.'

He earned a venomous look from the receptionist for that but it didn't seem to bother him. 'Give her the number for the school, though,' he said, grinning a little. 'Make it easy for her.'

I scribbled it down on a bit of card the receptionist slid out from under her screen. 'It will go straight through to the school secretary at home if you select that option,' I explained. One of Janet's grievances was that she had to take emergency calls at weekends. This certainly counted as an emergency in my view.

'Thank you.' Karen smiled sweetly when I pushed the paper back under the screen. Then her face snapped back to a scowl that was aimed at the doctor.

He turned back to me.

'Are you here to see Mr Turnbull?'

'Er, yes – if I can.'

The doctor nodded and strode to the double doors,

holding one open without looking around, expecting me to follow him. I ran to join him.

'Got to go to intensive care. I'm Dr Holford, by the way.'

'Sarah Finch,' I said, slightly out of breath. He was tall and lanky and moved fast; it was taking a lot of effort to keep up with him. Corridors led off corridors as we hurried through the accident and emergency department. Arrows on the ground pointed the way to radiology, then haematology. Dr Holford seemed to be taking his own special short cut to intensive care. I would never find my way out. I was starting to regret not bringing Jules. Or a ball of string.

'He's not in great shape. We're keeping an eye on him for the next twenty-four hours. If the swelling in his brain doesn't go down, we'll have to operate.' Dr Holford had an abrupt way of speaking, rattling out the words in short bursts, as if they built up inside him and then blasted out. 'And you're his girlfriend, did you say?'

I hesitated, afraid that if I didn't have a close enough relationship with Geoff, I wouldn't be allowed to see him. 'Er – very close,' I settled on eventually.

'It's iffy. I'm not going to lie to you. The next few hours are critical. He's not going to be sitting up in bed, ready to talk to you.'

I tried to imagine how I would feel if I was emotionally involved with Geoff, if he was my boyfriend, if I was in love with him. Would Dr Holford's brusque manner reassure me? Would I be irritated by it? Would I be in tears?

Dr Holford stopped at a door marked ICU. There was a graphic of a mobile phone with a line through it on the wall by the door and I dug in my bag for mine while the young doctor punched in the code to open the door. As we stepped through the doorway, the noise level seemed to drop immediately. The lights were muted here, unlike the harsh strip lighting that made the rest of the hospital so bleak. Six bays led off a central nurses' station, where two nurses sat, writing on charts. At the sight of Dr Holford, both beamed.

'How are you holding up?' one asked him.

'Not good.' Then, to me, he explained, 'Double shift. I'm nearly at the end of it. Twenty-five minutes' sleep in the last twenty-two hours.'

That explained the red eyes and the end-of-tether manner. I nodded and smiled wanly as I lost interest in Dr Holford, because across the room I had seen a man I recognised, sitting on a chair outside one of the bays, reading a newspaper. The last time I'd seen him was at the church, at Jenny's memorial service. He had been standing beside Blake. A big man with a heavy build and a boxer's nose, he looked desperately uncomfortable, perched as he was on a small chair, with one leg flung out in front of him. Dr Holford stepped over it delicately, looking more and more like a stork.

'This is your guy in here,' he said, ushering me in. I sidled past the policeman without speaking to him, cringing for fear that he might stop me or ask me what I was doing. I didn't make eye contact with him, though I was aware that his gaze followed me into the room. I walked up to the foot of the bed, still expecting to be told to stop and explain myself at any moment. Dr Holford was checking the machines that stood burping to themselves on either side of the bed, and I was free to look at Geoff unobserved. I was glad of a moment or two to compose myself, because what I saw was frightful.

If the doctor hadn't told me it was Geoff lying there, I wouldn't have known him. His face was swollen and shiny with bruising. His eyelids were black, suffused with blood. An oxygen tube ran into his nose, while another tube pulled at the corner of his mouth. His head was heavily bandaged, with just a tuft of matted hair sticking up at the top. It was a horrible contrast to how he looked from the neck down: owing to Geoff's obsession with the body beautiful, he was as healthy and lean as an athlete. His arms lay on top of the covers, palms down, unmoving. He was bare-chested, the blankets covering him up to the armpits.

I must have made a small sound, because Dr Holford looked around at me.

'I warned you. Not looking too good, is he?'

I cleared my throat. 'How is he? Is he . . . improving?'

'No change.' The doctor looked at me, and I saw his face soften. There was kindness in there along with the fierce intelligence. 'Listen, why don't you sit down and spend some time with him. Talk to him if you like.'

'Will that help?'

'It might help you.' He stalked out of the room, mumbling something to the nurses as he went.

The ICU was hot, stifling. I slid my jacket off and put

it over my arm. Somehow, I felt reluctant to sit down on the chair that was placed near the head of the bed. I was an impostor. That chair was there for those who fought the fight along with the doctors and nurses with prayers and whispered promises, bargaining to keep their loved ones from slipping away. This was the first time I had ever volunteered to spend time with Geoff. I couldn't lie; it helped that he was comatose.

I stepped around carefully to the chair and put my bag and jacket down on the floor, watching to see if there was any reaction to the sound. Not a flicker.

I heard one of the nurses scolding the policeman outside. She had a strong West Indian accent. 'No, darling. No mobiles in here. You know the rules.'

I sat down in the chair gingerly. From there I could see the policeman's vast bulk draped over the edge of the nurses' station, where he was leaning in to use the phone, one hand jammed to his ear. The leather of his jacket was puckered across the curve of his back, straining at the seams like a canvas sail in a high wind.

As I watched, the nurse padded into the bay, blocking my view. 'You can hold his hand, sweetheart,' she said. 'Don't be afraid.'

Holding Geoff's hand was approximately the last thing I wanted to do, but I couldn't confess that to the nurse. She waited, smiling encouragement. I reached out tentatively and touched the back of the hand near me, covering it with my own. It was hot and dry, but tacky to the touch. Dirty. I turned his hand palm upwards, very gently, to see black dirt ingrained in the creases of his palm and his fingertips, highlighting the whorls and ridges of his finger-prints. There was dirt and there was dark dried blood. His nails were clotted with it. I shuddered and put his hand down again, feeling queasy.

This had happened outside my house. Perhaps this had happened because of me.

I sat back in the chair and folded my arms, squeezing the hand that had touched Geoff's until my fingernails dug into my flesh, trying to erase the memory of his hot, slightly sticky skin against mine. I could still feel it, like an amputee with a phantom limb, a ghost irritant that was impossible to ignore. I stared at the wall opposite me and wished there was a window. I wondered who had chosen the precise shade of beige that most resembled baby poo to decorate the unit. I wondered why I was there. I wondered if Geoff would recover, if he would ever forgive me, if I would ever forgive myself.

I don't know how long I had been sitting there when I heard Andy Blake's voice – quite a while, but it was hard to keep track of time in the sensory deprivation of the ICU. He was talking to the policeman outside the door, speaking in a low voice so all I could catch was the tone, which was serious. I recognised his voice before I saw him, and when I leaned back to try to catch sight of him, I found the two policemen looking in at me. There was outright hostility on the battered face of the older man. Blake was frowning. Without acknowledging me, he nudged the other policeman and led the way out of the ICU. I felt nettled, childishly irritated, and wanted to run after them, shouting, 'I wasn't listening anyway! I don't care what you have to say about me. I'm not *interested*.'

Beside me, Geoff slept on. Permission had come from his parents to operate, and Dr Holford had been in with the surgeon to assess him. I had removed myself, standing out in the corridor alone. All I could think was that Geoff wouldn't have been lying there if I had handled things differently. If I was better at saying no. If I had let him come in and talk. If he had found someone else to pursue. If I had taught in a different school. If I had never even become a teacher in the first place. The guilt was a physical weight on me. Conversation was impossible. I had leaned against the wall while the nurses pattered about their business without fuss, without troubling me. In the next bay, there was a fall from high up on some unsafe scaffolding; he was hanging between life and death. A massive stroke that had happened at the dinner table was now safely under control on the other side of the unit. Visitors thronged both rooms, ashen with terror or pinkly grateful. There was no one there for Geoff apart from me. I didn't know his friends. His parents were too frail to come to see him, the nurses had said. I didn't know if he had brothers or sisters. I didn't know anything about him at all, except that he had liked me, and wanted to make me like him, and we had both handled it badly. I was beginning to accept that I had overreacted. I played back all of the things he had said to me – all of the things he had done – and saw them in a new light. He had meant well, I thought. He had meant to do no harm.

A soft tap on the door behind me made me jump.

'Sorry to interrupt – can I have a word?' Blake, looking serious.

I stood up slowly, stretching out limbs stiff from sitting. His choice of words annoyed me straightaway. What did he think he was interrupting? And what did he want with me anyway? I could feel bad temper starting to build inside me like a thundercloud as I followed him through the unit to a door labelled 'Relatives' Room'. Someone had added the apostrophe in Tippex. The glass panel let into the door was carefully covered with a dull green curtain to allow for privacy. The room was small and overcrowded with furniture, but at least had a window, although the view was of the incinerator chimney, currently wheezing dark grey smoke into the clear blue day.

Blake waited by the door, shutting it firmly behind me. I stepped carefully through the chairs, around a coffee table, heading for the window so I could look out.

'Bit of a surprise to see you here.'

I didn't turn around. 'Why are you surprised?'

'I didn't think you liked him,' he said easily.

'I don't.'

'Do you mind turning around, please?'

It might have been couched as a question, but it was definitely an order. I turned, leaning against the windowsill. Blake was sitting down on one side of the coffee table. I suddenly realised that the furniture had been rearranged to make an impromptu interview space. That was why the chairs were jostling for space and the layout in the room was so confused.

'Come and sit down,' Blake said, indicating the chair opposite him.

Mulishly, I resisted. 'I'd rather stand. I've been sitting for a while.'

'Is that right?'

'Yes,' I said stiffly. 'I wanted to come and see how Geoff was doing. He – he doesn't have anyone else.'

Blake leaned back in the low chair and put his hands behind his head. 'Oh, I see. He's someone else you can take responsibility for now, isn't he? No wonder you're here doing the Florence Nightingale bit.'

'What do you mean?' I was glad my back was to the light; the blood had rushed to my face.

'This is your pattern, isn't it? Something bad happens to someone you know, and you have to make it better.'

I frowned at Blake. 'Like what?'

'Like the little business with your brother?' He reached under the chair and pulled out the newspaper his colleague had been reading. It was a tabloid with thick black headlines. From where I was standing, I could read the banner that ran across a double-page spread: TRAGIC TEACHER: I FOUND JENNY BUT I COULDN'T FIND MY BROTHER. And a picture underneath, a close-up of me outside the school, looking away from the camera, my brow furrowed.

'When were you going to tell us about that?' Blake asked, holding it out to me.

I came away from the window and went across the room to pick up the paper without consciously ordering my limbs to move. Fucking Carol Shapley. She must have worked very fast indeed to go from our interview to the printed page so quickly. So much for a sympathetic story.

> Sad Sarah Finch choked as she talked to me about finding her favourite student's body. Touched by tragedy herself, she knows all about loss. 'I know how Jenny's family must feel,' she wept. 'But at least they have a body to bury.'

'I didn't say that,' I muttered, mostly to myself, skimming through the paragraphs at top speed. It was all there: Charlie's disappearance, Mum's nervous breakdown, Dad's death, Jenny's death – but the story was almost unrecognisable, slickly told, broken into easily digestible chunks for a greedy readership. I read on to a third page where the story trailed off into speculation about what might have happened to Jenny, and what Carol alleged were my pious hopes for the future for Jenny's parents. ('I hope they stay together and support each other. They'll get through it but they'll never forget.') After reading the last lines, I closed my eyes for a second. I didn't need to read it again – I could probably have recited it line by line – but I flicked back to the start and looked at it without seeing the words. I was hugely reluctant to put the paper down and meet the steady gaze I knew was trained on me.

'I'm sorry I didn't say anything about my brother, but I didn't think it was relevant,' I said at last, sitting down and wrapping my hands around my knees for comfort.

His eyebrows shot up. 'Really? I would have liked to

know about it before the media. How did they find out about it, anyway?'

In a dull voice, I told him about Carol and her perseverance. I explained that I hadn't felt I had any choice but to cooperate with her.

'She lied to me,' I said, flicking the open newspaper with my nail. 'She told me they wouldn't use my new surname, or anything that would enable anyone to recognise me. That's why there isn't a posed photograph. I don't know when they took that one. Probably that day when they were all lined up outside the school – the day after Jenny was found.'

'The day after *you* found her,' Blake said pointedly.

I looked up. 'So what?'

He didn't answer me directly, just looked past me, an exasperated expression on his face.

'Listen,' I said, getting heated again, 'don't be fooled into thinking that there's anything more than a coincidence at work here. I didn't tell anyone about Charlie. I don't speak about him, ever. It's not the kind of thing that's easy to work into a conversation, is it? And I can't expect other people to care about the fact that my brother disappeared and I've never been able to get over it. It happened. I had to live with it growing up, I have to live with it now, but the difference is that most people don't remember or care. So at least I can feel what I feel in private.' And I was so used to keeping it suppressed that I didn't even know how to start being open about it. Hiding things came naturally to me now.

He shrugged. 'So why stick around? It must be horrible, living in the same house.'

'Mum,' I said simply, and explained her need to stay in the place where we had always lived, just in case Charlie miraculously reappeared.

He shook his head. 'This is what I'm talking about, Sarah. If she won't move, fine. Leave her to it. Why do you have to live there with her? She's a grown-up. Just because she's ruined her own life, that doesn't mean that you have to ruin yours.'

'I can't abandon her.' I ran the edge of my nail along the seam of my jeans repeatedly, mindlessly. 'Everyone else did. I can't do that to her.'

'Just like you can't leave Geoff lying in a coma on his own,' Blake said heavily. 'I can't say I was surprised to find you here.' He leaned forward. 'You do realise that if things had been different, if you'd told me about how he was behaving, he might have been in line for a charge of harassment?'

I didn't look up.

'This isn't someone who you should feel bad about,' Blake said, sounding half irritated, half compassionate. 'You might even say he got what was coming to him.'

'You don't really think that.'

Blake sighed. 'He was a cocky little shit, Sarah, who wouldn't take no for an answer. You get taken advantage of, left, right and centre. You've got to start standing up for yourself.'

As I tried to sniff back the tears that were stinging the back of my nose, Blake reached over and grabbed a box of tissues from a side table, handing it to me.

'Is that your professional opinion?' I didn't bother to keep the sarcasm out of my voice.

'I apologise,' he said stiffly. 'I seem to find it hard to be professional when I'm talking to you.'

There was a brief, awkward silence as we both thought about the last time he had been completely unprofessional in my presence. I didn't dare look at him.

'I promised myself I wouldn't do this,' Blake said, almost to himself, 'but the fact is, I just don't get you. I don't know where you got that limp, or that bruise on your face – I saw it this morning, so there's no point in trying to hide it now. I don't understand how this –' and he waved a hand at the room '– fits in with you turning up at my flat the other night.'

I blew my nose before I answered, choosing to deal with the second part first. 'I'm sorry about that. I shouldn't have done it. It was just – I needed to do something impulsive. Feel something, for a change. That night, I felt as if I was sinking in quicksand. You were something to hold on to.' I risked a look at him. 'I didn't think you'd mind.'

He shrugged. 'Well, I didn't. But that's not the point.'

'Look, what happened the other night – it was great. But it's not my life. My life is going into school day after day, hoping that I'm doing a good enough job. I go home in the evenings and I never know what I'm going to find. On a good night, I stay in and mark papers while Mum drinks until she passes out. On a bad night – well, I do much the same. I might not like it, but that's how it is. Just for a moment a couple of nights ago, I felt like having a break from all that, and I was brave enough and stupid enough to do it. And I should probably have found someone who wasn't involved in the case to sleep with, but I just—' I broke off. I couldn't say the next two words in that bland, dead little room. *Wanted you.* It was too much.

'As I said, I didn't mind.' Blake sounded as if his mind was on something else.

I sat back in my chair. 'You should probably just leave me to it.' I meant *don't try to understand me. Don't try to fix me. I'm far too broken.*

He clearly thought I was talking about Geoff. 'You aren't going back in there to do the fainting maiden bit, are you?' He looked disgusted. 'I thought more of you, Sarah. You've got all the nurses thinking this is some big tragedy for you, and really you're just loving the attention.'

'I am not,' I said, outraged. 'I just wanted—'

'You just want another reason to avoid living your life. And if he recovers, will you become his chief carer? Follow him around and let him decide how you run your life, like he wanted all along? Will he take over from your mum, bossing you around?'

'I make my own choices,' I said, furious, standing up. 'You might not understand them, but they are my decisions. No one makes me be this way. This is who I am. And this is the right thing to do.'

He stood up too and stepped around the table, moving fast, stopping so close to me that his face was inches away from mine. 'You just keep lying to me, and to yourself, and maybe one day you'll convince yourself that you're happy. But sooner or later, you're going to regret it.'

'That's my problem, not yours.'

His eyes were dark. I felt dizzy, as if I was falling. 'What happened the other night,' he said flatly, 'that's real. That's how you should be living. With this,' and his fingertips grazed my chest, just over my heart.

I was irritated with him, and furious with myself, but at his touch I forgot everything, pressing against him, needing to feel him, turning my face up to his mouth. There was no warmth in him when we kissed, just frustration and anger. I didn't care. It didn't matter. Nothing mattered.

The next second there was a perfunctory knock on the door as it opened. The two of us leaped apart at the same time, knowing that we'd been spotted already and it was too late.

'Sorry to disturb,' said the West Indian nurse, sounding deeply sarcastic. 'Your boss is on the phone.'

Blake swore quietly and grabbed his pile of papers, including the newspaper, before hurrying out past the nurse without another word to her or me. I looked at her, acutely aware of the colour in my face, and didn't say anything either.

'Mm-hmm,' she said, with great and deliberate meaning, and walked away.

There was no way I could stay at Geoff's bedside after that. I crept back to his room to get my things. As I slid out, I muttered an apology to him. Whatever Blake said, I couldn't help thinking I would have to add Geoff to my list of obligations; I had a responsibility to him, whether I liked it or not. It wasn't unreasonable. Blake was wrong. And so typical of him that he thought he knew what was best for me. As well as being embarrassed at being caught by the nurse in his arms, I was annoyed that I'd thrown myself at him again, that I had so little self-respect. Even now, my body was humming with excitement and frustration, traitor that it was.

I went wrong once or twice on my way out of the hospital, confused without the gawky doctor's guidance. When I at last found a door that led to the outside world, I shot through it with a feeling of release, glad to be back in the fresh air. It was a lovely day, bright and warm. I shaded my eyes, dazzled by the sunlight reflecting off car windscreens in the hospital car park, wondering which way to go, and didn't notice at first when a car drew up alongside me.

'Sarah,' said a cheerful voice from the driver's seat. 'Where are you off to?'

I bent down to see DCI Vickers looking at me. Between us sat Blake, who was staring out through the windscreen, pointedly not looking at me.

'Er – I'm just going home,' I said hesitantly.

'We're going back to your neck of the woods, so let me give you a lift,' Vickers said. 'Hop in.'

I couldn't really see how to refuse. It was a couple of miles back along the dual carriageway, not a nice country stroll. Vickers would never believe me if I said I'd prefer to walk.

'Thanks,' I said eventually, and got into the back seat behind Vickers. Blake's ears were tinged with red and he didn't look around at me. I met Vickers' eyes in the rear-view mirror. I recognised the calculating look he'd had when we'd spoken in the early hours of that morning.

'So I should have told you about my brother,' I said levelly.

The wrinkles around his eyes creased and I realised he was smiling. 'That's right. But I'm sure you had your reasons.'

'I didn't mean to hide anything. I just didn't think you needed to know about it.'

'As a matter of fact, I knew already,' Vickers said, then coughed extravagantly for at least twenty seconds. 'Sorry,' he managed at last. 'Smoking. Never do it, my dear.'

It was clearly my day for getting free advice from the police. I smiled politely, my mind racing. 'So – you knew?'

'I've done a few of these inquiries,' Vickers said, flicking an ironic look at me in the rear-view mirror again. 'I checked up on you after you gave your witness statement. It wasn't hard to find out all about it. Very sad case.'

'And – and you don't mind that I didn't mention it?' I didn't want to talk about Blake, not with him sitting there, but he had made enough of a big deal out of it, hadn't he? Why didn't Vickers care? And why hadn't he bothered to tell his team about it?

The chief inspector croaked, 'One of the things I've learned over the years, Sarah, is that everyone has a secret or two they don't want to share with the police. Some of them are worth knowing, some of them aren't. It's experience that tells you which ones are important. Not everything matters, and I try to pick out what my team needs to know and what they don't. I judged that your brother's case wasn't relevant to this inquiry.'

'That's what I thought too,' I said, monumentally relieved.

'You would tell us, though,' Vickers said, pulling on to the main road, 'if there was anything else you'd been holding back. No more secrets, OK?'

I met his eyes again in the mirror, and this time, I looked away first. I hadn't been wrong that morning. For all the warmth and superficial friendliness, there was no trust in those cold blue eyes. Vickers suspected something, and I had no idea what it could be. I didn't answer him, and for the remainder of the journey, the car was silent. It was one of the loudest silences I'd ever heard.

1994

One year and eight months missing

'Mrs Barnes! Mrs Barnes!'

I know the voice behind us; it's my teacher, Mrs Hunt. I look up at Mum, wondering if she's heard her, and if she has, whether she'll stop. Reluctantly, she turns her head.

'Yes?'

Mrs Hunt is out of breath. 'Could I just . . . ask you to come back . . . and have a quick chat with me . . . for a second?' She looks at me, one hand to her chest. 'You too, Sarah.'

Mum turns to follow her across the playground and I trudge after them, keeping my eyes on Mum's feet. Left, right, left, right. I know what Mrs Hunt is going to say. Grey-haired and plump, Mrs Hunt has been my teacher now for a few months, long enough to get the measure of me. I've been warned a couple of times. I won't think about it, I decide, and make my mind go blank. It's a trick I've taught myself. I can just switch off when I feel like I've had enough. I do it a lot.

Back in the classroom, in Mrs Hunt's domain, she pulls up a chair for Mum and motions me to the front row. I sit down slowly, folding myself into Eleanor Price's seat. I imagine that I am Eleanor, with her thick glasses and bright red hair. Eleanor is a teacher's pet. She likes sitting at the front, close enough to show Mrs Hunt what page we are on in our history book, close enough to volunteer to carry a message to another teacher.

'Mrs Barnes, I wanted to speak to you about Sarah, because I am quite concerned about her current performance. I've spoken to those of my colleagues who have taught her and we all feel that she's just not trying. She doesn't do her homework, Mrs Barnes. She daydreams in class. She can be very rude to her fellow students and she is often offhand with me.'

That's what annoys her, I think with some satisfaction. Mrs Hunt is a favourite teacher in the school, warm and cheerful, everyone's friend. I don't confide in her. I don't ask for help. I slide out of the classroom before she can get a chance to talk to me.

Mum is making an effort to engage with her. 'That's very worrying. I'm sure she'll try harder now, though. Won't you, Sarah?'

I stare into space. I am Eleanor Price. This has nothing to do with me.

'She just seems so withdrawn,' Mrs Hunt

whispers, her eyes greedily scanning Mum's face. 'Are there any problems at home that I should know about?'

Tell her, I want to shout. Tell her about the drinking and the arguments about it.

Artlessly, Mum lifts a hand to brush her hair off her forehead. As her sleeve slips back, Mrs Hunt's face is a picture of shock and curiosity. Mum's forearm is blue-black with bruising. There are other bruises, I know, other marks. She is a clumsy drinker. Often, she falls.

I am waiting for her to explain this, but before Mum speaks, the teacher leans forward. 'There are places you can go, you know. Shelters. I can give you an address—'

'That won't be necessary,' Mum says.

'But if there's violence in the home – if your husband—'

'Please,' Mum says, a hand up to halt her. 'Not in front of Sarah.'

I am paying attention now, properly. She can't let Mrs Hunt think that Dad is responsible for her injuries. She couldn't.

'There are things I have to put up with, but I keep them from her,' Mum is saying, her voice low. 'She has no idea—'

'Oh, but she must!' Mrs Hunt says, her fingers sinking into her face as if her cheeks are made of dough. 'How could you keep it from her?'

Mum shakes her head. 'We're working things

out, Mrs Hunt. We'll get there in the end. Things are improving between us, really, they are. And Sarah will improve too. Thank you for taking the time to speak to me about her.' She is standing up, picking up her bag. 'I assure you, Sarah is our top priority.'

Mrs Hunt nods, her eyes moist. 'If there's ever anything I can do for you—'

'I'll let you know.' Mum turns to me with a brave little smile. 'Come on, Sarah. Let's go home.'

I don't say anything until we've left the school building and walked back out to the road, away from the crowds by the gate.

'Why didn't you tell Mrs Hunt the truth?'

'It's none of her business,' Mum says shortly.

'But she'll think that Dad – I mean, she sort of said she thought he'd done that to you.'

'So?' Mum whirls around and looks at me. 'You know, your father isn't perfect, whatever you might think.'

'He didn't do that,' I say, pointing at her arm. 'You did that to yourself.'

'One day,' Mum says softly, 'you'll understand that your father has done plenty of damage to me, even if you can't see the bruises.'

'I don't believe you.'

'Think what you like. It's true.'

My eyes have filled with tears, and my heart is thudding. 'I wish you were dead,' I say, and mean it.

Mum pulls back for a second, then laughs. 'If there's one thing you should know, Sarah dear, it's that wishes don't work.'

And I do know it. She's right about that, even if she's wrong about absolutely everything else.

Chapter 12

For the second time that day, Curzon Close was full of police cars when we pulled into it, and I exclaimed in surprise.

Without turning his head, Blake said flatly, 'We've got a warrant to execute.'

'A warrant? I thought you usually did that sort of thing at five in the morning.'

'Only when we think we might catch someone napping,' Vickers said over his shoulder, pulling in by the side of the road. 'We're pretty sure the house is empty this time.'

I had a nasty feeling I knew which house he was talking about.

'The officers didn't get an answer when they started knocking around, asking about what happened last night,' Vickers continued. 'Not that we got much help from anyone else, to be honest. Sound sleepers on this road, but they did do their best to answer our questions. It's part of our protocol to do a check on all the locals to see if there's anyone who might be – of interest, shall we say. And who popped up but your neighbour across the road, one Daniel Keane. Know him?'

I started to shake my head, then stopped. 'Sort of,' I said in the end. 'I haven't spoken to him in years. No, I don't really know him. I used to.' I was babbling. I stopped talking and bit my lip.

Vickers and Blake were both looking at me. The matching expressions on their faces suggested they were interested.

I sighed. 'Look, he was a friend of Charlie's, OK? After Charlie disappeared, I wasn't allowed to talk to him any more. We grew up. I didn't speak to him. I see him from time to time, but I can't honestly say I know him.'

Vickers looked satisfied. 'Right, well, in that case you may not know about Mr Keane's past. A few years ago, he was in all sorts of trouble. Convictions for assault, which amounted to getting into fights outside pubs, pretty much – a bit of theft, driving offences, that sort of thing. Small-time bad behaviour. He got picked up after a very nasty GBH where some poor laddie got a fractured skull, but they never had enough to charge him with it. Then, magic. No more offences. He stopped getting in trouble, got a job, and we stopped watching what he was up to. Until now. We've called the garage where he works, and he hasn't been seen there today – he was expected to show up as usual this morning, and he hasn't been in touch. Incidentally, they have no complaints about him. Never even been late for work before.'

Blake moved restlessly in the front seat. 'We'd better get a move on. The lads are waiting.'

I became aware that I was holding them up. In confusion, I gathered up my bag and jacket and mumbled thanks to Vickers for the lift. I didn't look at Blake as I hurried towards my front door, vaguely aware of the men beginning to organise themselves outside Danny's house. As I slid the key into the lock, I suddenly thought of Paul. Even if he had been there, I was pretty sure he wouldn't have answered the door to the police. He would have been terrified. He was probably in there at that very moment. I turned back, then hesitated, wondering if I should say anything. If Danny had gone, as the police seemed to think, wouldn't he have taken his brother too?

While I wavered on the doorstep, events were moving fast across the road. At a nod from Vickers, the small team of uniformed officers lined up outside the front door. The one at the front shouted, 'Police! Open the door!', and then, without waiting for a response, swung a red battering ram at the door. It bent and bowed under the assault as the policeman hit it repeatedly, aiming for the hinges. At last it gave way and the first policeman pulled back, allowing the men who had been waiting behind him to charge in, yelling 'Police!' at the tops of their voices.

I wandered back down the path towards my front gate, wrapping my arms around myself, shivering a little despite the bright sunshine. Vickers and Blake stood outside, waiting. From inside the house, there were sounds of running feet and shouted orders, of doors crashing open. Then there was a pause. Someone rattled at one of the windows at the front, pushing it open, and called, 'We're having a bit of trouble getting one of the doors open, Sarge.'

'Give it some welly,' Blake called back.

More banging ensued. I dithered, then made up my mind and set off with decision across the road, heading for Vickers.

'Inspector, there's something you should know,' I said, coming up behind him. 'Danny has a younger brother –'

As I spoke, there was a shout from inside the house. 'Someone get an ambulance!'

'Wait here,' Vickers said, and sprinted for the door, following Blake. I stood there, shifting from foot to foot, watching the front of the house to see if there were any clues to what was wrong. *If anything has happened to Paul . . .* I thought, and couldn't finish the sentence.

It seemed an eternity before the ambulance crew arrived and rushed past me, directed by one of the policemen who had come to the door at the sound of the siren. As they went in, Blake shouldered his way out past them and came straight for me.

'You knew about the brother, did you? Could you identify him?'

'What's happened?' I whispered, fear closing my throat. 'He's not . . . '

'Dead? No. Not yet, anyway. What does he look like?'

I swallowed, thinking. 'Dark hair, brown eyes. He's twelve, but he looks older.'

'Build?' Blake asked impatiently.

'He's big. Well, he's obese.' I felt bad for saying it.

He sighed. 'That sounds about right, then. Twelve? Jesus. How do you get yourself in that kind of state in twelve years? That takes real dedication.'

'He's had a lot to deal with,' I snapped, feeling protective of him. 'I don't think he likes himself very much.'

'That's pretty obvious. He's tried to kill himself.'

'How?' I managed to ask.

One of the uniformed men who happened to be passing took it upon himself to answer. 'Hanged himself off the door. Poor fucker. No wonder we couldn't open it.' He looked at Blake. 'Here, we worked out why it didn't work. He only stretched the washing line, didn't he? It was one of those plastic-coated ones, and the knot he tied in it slipped. He was too heavy for it, so the rope was too long and his feet ended up touching the ground. Too fat to swing. My God, I think I've seen everything.'

'Is he going to be OK?' I asked, hating the policeman for the casual way he was talking about Paul.

The man shrugged. 'Maybe. They're working on him. He was out cold when we found him.'

There was a series of bumps from inside the house, and Blake said, 'They're bringing him out.'

'Keep your end up, mate,' one of the paramedics said as they edged out through the front door. Two policemen were helping them with the stretcher. With Paul. His face was covered with an oxygen mask, but there was no mistaking the bulk of his stomach, or the mop of hair at the top of the stretcher. One plump hand lolled down lifelessly from under the blanket.

'Make an effort,' came from behind me, where the policeman who'd spoken to me was leaning against his car, grinning.

'Give us a hand,' said one of the stretcher-bearers.

'With my back? Not on your life. Do myself a permanent injury.'

'He's not a joke,' I said quite fiercely to Blake, wanting

him to tell them to shut up. 'He's not an animal, or some-thing. That's a child on that stretcher.'

Blake ignored me and I squeezed my hands into fists, frustrated.

The ambulance crew had got the stretcher down onto the path and let the wheels down. They hurried past where I was standing. Up close, Paul looked terrible. His skin was blue-tinged, and I wondered how long he had been there – and how long he would have been there if the police hadn't broken in. What had Danny been thinking to leave him like that?

Blake went after them and leaned into the ambulance once they'd transferred him. He came back to me looking grim, but what he said was reassuring.

'They say he's been talking to them. He's coming and going at the moment. They think he'll be OK but they're not hanging around here.'

As he spoke, the ambulance took off, lights and siren going.

Blake turned back to me. 'So you don't know Danny, but you do know Paul.'

I winced at his tone of voice. 'Not well. I just spoke to him once. Anyway, you didn't ask me about Paul.'

'I didn't know about Paul,' Blake said softly.

I shrugged. 'I met him yesterday for the first time, OK? I went over there –' I hesitated, then went on, explaining about why I had wanted to talk to Danny, explaining that I'd thought he could tell me about Charlie. 'Paul's a lovely kid. Sweet-natured. And don't underestimate him because he's fat. He's very bright. He knows more about computers and technology than either of us, I bet.' It was important to me that Blake should realise Paul was a human being, not just a blob.

Blake was looking at me expressionlessly. 'So you've never been in the house before yesterday.'

'No.'

'You just took it into your head to find out what happened to your brother.'

I nodded. 'I suppose this whole thing with Jenny just stirred it all up again. I found myself thinking about what happened to him and wondering about it. You don't think about it usually – day to day. You just live with the consequences, most of the time.'

Blake looked past me and I turned to see Vickers shambling out of the house, looking even more grey and dispirited than usual. He held up something in his right hand, something silver with tassels, and more than ever I felt as if I was dreaming, because what he was holding made no sense at all.

'That's my bag!'

It was the bag I had been carrying three nights before – the bag I had lost to the mystery mugger. I went straight over to Vickers and reached out for it. He held it away from me, and I was aware of Blake coming up behind me.

'That's mine,' I repeated. 'Where did you get it?'

Vickers looked tired. 'It was in the lounge, Sarah. Where you left it.'

I shook my head. 'No. You don't understand, I lost this bag. I mean, I didn't lose it. It was taken.'

'Not another story,' Blake said. 'There's always an answer for everything, isn't there?'

'It's the truth,' I said with dignity, addressing Vickers only. 'Someone mugged me on Tuesday night. They pushed me over and took my bag. That's why I haven't been using my car – I didn't have the keys. You've seen me walking around; you just gave me a lift. Why wouldn't I drive to the hospital if I could?'

Vickers unzipped it and peered inside. I was overcome with a massively inappropriate urge to giggle. There was something incongruous about the grey man in the grey suit rooting through a silver leather handbag as if it was his own.

'No keys,' he announced finally, and suddenly I didn't feel like laughing any more.

'What? They must be in there. Did you check the inside pocket?'

Vickers looked at me reproachfully. 'I tried there first. It's where my wife keeps her keys too.'

'May I check for myself?'

He handed the bag over without saying anything else and I riffled through it, uncomfortably aware that both men were watching me. I ran my hand through the little bits of paper and receipts that had accumulated at the bottom of my handbag, trawling for the keys. I found an eye pencil and a stick of lip balm, a biro that had long since ceased to work and some paper clips, but no keys, and not much else. In the end, I had to admit defeat. 'OK, but the keys were in there when it was stolen. There were other things too – my diary, some pictures.' I was trying to think what else I had lost.

'Come on,' Vickers said, and stood back. 'Come and have a look yourself.' Blake started forward, moving to intercept me. 'Guv, forensics, we can't –'

'She's admitted being in the house already,' Vickers said mildly. 'I don't think forensics will prove anything one way or another. But we won't let her touch anything, just in case.'

Blake bit his lip, but he didn't say anything else. He moved back to allow me through.

I stepped past him into the hallway, and looked around.

Nothing had changed since the previous day except for the damage the police had done in breaking down the door. Flakes of paint littered the worn carpet where the door had thudded against the wall. I smelled again the sweaty-socks odour I had noticed before, and something else, something sharper than that. Fear.

Unlike before, the door to the living room was ajar. 'Is this where you found the bag?' I asked. 'Can I go in and look for myself?'

'Go ahead,' Vickers said. 'It won't take you long.'

I understood what he meant as soon as I pushed open the door. The smell of bodies that pervaded the house was stronger in here, rancid, and I gagged a little, trying to breathe shallowly through my mouth. The room was dim, with cheap blinds pulled down over the front window. Until Vickers hit the switch by the door, the only light was the sunshine leaking in around the edges of the flimsy blinds. I blinked at the sudden harshness of the bare bulb in the ceiling, before taking in the squalor that it revealed.

The room was practically empty. A double bed covered

in a stained, dirty fitted sheet had its head against the opposite wall. The headboard was covered in grubby pale-green velour and looked as if it dated from the seventies. On one side of the bed a box of tissues stood on the floor, used tissues littered around it. There was a little pile of well-thumbed magazines on the other side – pornography, I realised, repelled. A thin, lumpy duvet had been thrown across the foot of the bed and dragged on the floor, which was carpeted in dark brown acrylic pile that glinted in the light and squeaked a little under my feet. The walls were covered in off-cream paper with a raised pearlescent pattern in it, a prim and proper wallpaper at odds with the room it decorated. A long dirty mark on one wall suggested that at one time something large had stood there, maybe a sofa.

I turned to Vickers. 'But this is a three-bedroom house. Why were they using this as a bedroom when there were only two of them living here?'

Vickers didn't respond directly, but guided me further into the room, so I could see what the door had previously blocked from view. A small, battered bookcase was the only other piece of furniture in the room, if you didn't count a video camera mounted on a tripod as furniture. I looked at the camera, puzzled, and turned to Vickers for an explanation. Instead, he pointed at the bookcase.

'Your bag was there, on the bottom shelf. See anything else you recognise?'

I stepped gingerly across the carpet, not wanting to think about what might be living in it or when it might last have been vacuumed. A chill ran through me at the sight of what was on top of the bookcase.

'Those are my pictures. They were in my bag.'

Someone had arranged them against the wall, propping them up. They were small pictures, passport-photo sized. It seemed wrong to see them there. The two detectives came and looked over my shoulder as I pointed at them in turn. 'Charlie. Charlie and me. Dad and me. Mum and Dad.'

My diary was lying face down, splayed open, and I reached out to pick it up, tutting at the crumpled pages. Blake put out a hand to stop me. 'Don't touch anything yet,' he said quietly.

'OK, well, that's my diary.' I looked closer. 'And that's my pen – oh!'

'What?' Vickers asked quickly.

'Well, it's just strange, that's all. I thought I'd lost it. It must have been in my bag all along.'

'When did you lose it?'

'Months ago. I looked for it everywhere. It was my dad's.' The pen was silver, with his initials engraved along the barrel and a distinctive crosshatched pattern chased in the metal. 'I thought I'd lost it in school. I tore the place apart looking for it. I can't believe it was in my bag all along.'

The policemen didn't make any comment, and I scanned the rest of the shelves, looking through a miscellany of random things – a stone with a hole in it; a worn leather thong with three beads threaded on it; the skull of a tiny animal, maybe a shrew. There were odd coins and other bits of rubbish too. I looked through the mess methodically, trying to see what else was hidden there without touching anything. The end of the fob on my keyring was sticking out from behind a propped-up postcard from Scotland, and I pointed it out to Vickers, who edged the postcard away with the tip of his pen and nodded when he'd seen the keys for himself. On one of the lower shelves I spotted a hairclip that I knew I hadn't seen for at least six weeks and a cheap bracelet I'd worn to school and taken off halfway through the day, annoyed by the rattle and drag of it as I wrote on the board. 'I definitely last had this bracelet in school,' I said, turning to Vickers. 'There's no way it was in my bag. I left it on my desk in my class-room. How the hell did it end up here?'

'That's what we'd like to know,' Vickers said quietly. 'There seem to be a lot of things belonging to you here, considering you haven't been in contact with the inhabit-ants of this house until yesterday, by your own account.'

'I can't explain it,' I said, totally confused. 'I don't get it. What *is* this room?'

Blake beckoned me over to the video camera and pointed to the viewfinder. 'Don't touch anything, but have a look through there and tell me what you see.'

'It's focused on the bed.' As the words left my mouth, something clicked in my mind. 'Oh . . . do you mean that they were making videos here? Home-made porn? How gross.' I was suddenly glad I hadn't been allowed to touch anything. 'And Paul must have been here while they were making them. Poor kid. I hope Danny didn't let him see anything.' I looked at Vickers. 'But why is all my stuff in here? What's going on?'

He sighed. 'Sarah, we're going to have to assume that you were involved in this to some extent.'

'What?' I couldn't believe what he'd just said. 'I told you, my bag was stolen! These are my things but I didn't leave them here – I don't know how they got here.'

Blake had gone to the door, where he had been having a muttered conversation with one of the policemen who were searching the house. He turned back. 'Sir, can I have a word?'

'Don't touch *anything*,' Vickers reiterated forcefully, and waited until I nodded before following Blake out of the room. A uniformed officer came and stood in the doorway, watching me. He didn't speak and I didn't either. I just stood there and looked at the spare, bleak room, feeling ill.

When they finally came back, I said, 'What's going on?'

The two men looked even grimmer than they had before. Vickers leaned against the wall, looking like his legs were too weak to hold him up, and let Blake do the talking.

'We've just been upstairs, where the officers have discovered a large amount of home-made child pornography. In one of the bedrooms upstairs, there's an advanced set-up – computers, high-speed broadband, customised video software, stacks of DVDs.' He pointed at the camera. 'That thing records straight onto disc. They'd film down here, then go upstairs and upload it onto a host site. These things are pretty hard to trace. The people who run them are good at faking IP addresses, hacking into other people's computers to use their details, so it's hard for us to track back and find out who's putting this shit out there.'

'But why?' I was starting to shake.

'Money,' Blake said briefly. 'There's a lot of cash in this business. If you're coming up with good product, you can charge what you like. The same videos and images get swapped around all the time. The paedos get sick of seeing the same old kids and the same old rape and torture. Plenty of punters out there willing to pay to see fresh child abuse. The good suppliers will create it to order. You can commission them to make your fantasy come true. If you pay enough, you can even get the child to scream your name. Makes you feel like you're actually there, not just watching on your computer.'

I flinched, hating the brutal tone he was using.

'This is a professional set-up.' Blake waved a hand at the room. 'There's nothing here to identify where the filming is taking place. This room has been cleaned out – nothing personal appears on camera. There's just the bed and a blank bit of wall. Nothing for the police to go on if we do find these videos or images on the net. This room could be anywhere, pretty much. All we can do is pick up the customers, the idiots who use their own credit cards to pay for it.'

'I can't believe it,' I said, shaking my head. 'Here? In this house? In the middle of a quiet little suburban cul-de-sac?'

Vickers spoke then, his voice quiet and flat, unemotional. 'These things *can* go on without anyone knowing. It's amazing what people don't see if they don't know what they're supposed to be looking for. Look at Fred and Rose West. No one on Cromwell Street had the least idea what the Wests were doing, because they couldn't even imagine that people could be so evil. Good people don't think of these things. Evil people can't think of anything else.'

He spoke of good and evil with all the force and severity of an Old Testament prophet, and I saw that he believed in evil, good old-fashioned evil, not the psychologist's excuses of upbringing and circumstance.

'It's almost creative,' he said, mostly to himself. 'It's their art, you could say. Think of all the effort this takes, all the organisation.'

Revolted, I turned back to Blake.

'We've had a quick look at the images upstairs – stills and a couple of bits of the DVDs. It'll take us a while to go through everything, but at this stage it looks like they had a bit of a theme for their work.'

'What do you mean?' I whispered.

'One victim, a few different abusers.'

'Not Paul?' I said, my heart breaking for him as I began to understand what had made him the way he was. No wonder he couldn't live with his secret being found out.

Vickers shook his head. 'No. Not Paul. Jenny Shepherd.'

I looked at the two men with complete incomprehension. '*Jenny?* But how? What was she doing in this house?'

'That's what we'd like to know,' Blake said, and I felt like Alice falling down and down the rabbit hole, the ground giving way beneath me. Nothing made sense any more, except that I could finally understand how the childish, underdeveloped girl who'd sat in my English classes could have been four months pregnant.

'What about Paul?' I said eventually. 'You can't think he was involved.'

Vickers looked troubled. 'I know he's a child, Sarah, and he's not well, but the sad thing is that we do believe he played an active part.'

'You said it yourself, he has the computer knowledge,' Blake pointed out. 'From the looks of it, he's the one who runs the technological side. The computers were all in his bedroom.'

Vickers sighed. 'If you possess any information that would either exonerate or implicate the boy, I'll be glad to hear it, now or at the station.'

I stared into the middle distance, saying nothing. I couldn't think what to say. I had a feeling that Paul wouldn't have volunteered to be part of anything sordid and evil, but the evidence was stacking up against him.

'I don't know,' I said eventually. 'All I can tell you is that he seemed like a nice person.'

Blake stirred. 'Lots of people seem nice. Lots of people seem innocent. Sometimes it's hard for us to pick out the ones who are guilty at first, but we usually get there in the end.' He gestured at the pile of things I had identified as mine. 'Don't you think you have some explaining to do?'

'*Me?* Are you crazy? I didn't have anything to do with this. I don't know anything about it.' Even to my ears, I sounded as if I was lying. I looked from one to the other. 'You have to believe me.'

'You knew the girl,' Vickers said. 'You live in the same street. Your things are here. You are the link. As ever, Sarah, you are the link.'

'You can't seriously think I'm involved.' There was nothing in their faces to suggest they believed me, though:

Vickers' eyes were cold, arctic blue and Blake's expression was grim. A jolt of pure panic ran through me and I fought it down. They were playing some kind of game – I just didn't know the rules.

'It would be better if you told us what happened, Sarah, before this goes any further.'

'There's nothing to tell. I can't help you. And it's been a long day already, and I'm tired.' I sounded petulant; I didn't care. 'I'm going home. Why don't you go and find out what really happened here, and when you do, let me know. Because *I* wasn't involved, so I'm as much in the dark as you.'

It was all right, as exit lines go, and I turned to leave without waiting for a reply. I hadn't got more than two steps towards the door when I felt a hand grab my arm and pull me back to where I had been standing.

'Let go of me!' I glared at Blake.

'No chance.'

Vickers looked at me tiredly. 'If you won't talk to us, Sarah, we only have one option remaining to us.'

'I don't understand what you mean.'

'I mean that we have to compel you to come and talk to us.'

Vickers slipped out of the room then, pushing past me, leaving me to think about what he'd said. I heard him talking in an undertone in the hall to someone I couldn't see.

'You can't really think I'm involved.' I was trying to read Blake's face, waiting for him to admit that it was all a big joke, that they didn't mean it really.

'I don't know what to think,' he said, and his voice sounded strange, harsh. I looked up at him and didn't know him.

Before I could respond, Vickers came back with another man. He was balding and overweight, in his forties. Even if he hadn't been standing beside Vickers, I think I would have known he was a cop immediately. There was something about his eyes, a deep-seated disillusionment and distrust that suggested he had heard too many lies. He began to speak in a flat, droning voice without inflection, running the words together as he ran through a recitation he had performed countless times before.

'Sarah Finch, I'm arresting you on suspicion of the murder of Jenny Shepherd. You do not have to say anything but it may harm your defence if you fail to mention when questioned something that you later rely on in court. Anything you say can be used in evidence. Do you understand?'

My mouth popped open involuntarily: the classic re-action to shock. I looked at Vickers, to see his reaction, but he had the thousand-yard stare firmly in place. Blake looked down at his feet, refusing to meet my eye.

'You can't do this,' I said, not really believing that it was happening. 'You can't think this is right.'

Vickers said, as if I hadn't spoken, 'DC Smith, can I leave it to yourself and DC Freeman to take Miss Finch to the station? No need for cuffs, I'd have said. We'll see you there.'

Smith nodded and beckoned to me. 'Better get a move on.'

'Aren't you taking me in yourselves?' I asked Blake and Vickers, and I didn't try to keep the bitterness out of my voice.

Vickers shook his head. 'You won't be dealing with us directly from now on. We know you, you see. It could cause us disclosure problems if this gets to trial.' Blake turned away sharply, and I wondered if Vickers had picked up on something between us, or if it was really just routine. The chief inspector ignored his sergeant and finished, 'Best to let other members of the team take it from here.'

'Best for whom?' I asked, but there was no response.

DC Smith put a meaty hand on my arm and pulled me into the hall, where we had to wait for a stream of policemen to pass by, carrying boxes and bags of evidence to the cars that were waiting outside. Computer hard drives, CDs, DVD cases and a webcam were visible through the heavy-duty clear plastic bags. One of the officers carried something long and heavy, wrapped in brown paper – a golf club? A poker? I couldn't tell. He gave Vickers a meaningful look as he passed, and the chief inspector nodded soberly without speaking. Then there were more bags, personal stuff – clothes, toys that had to belong to Paul, photographs in frames, documents of various sorts. The whole house was being torn apart; there would be nothing left by the time they were finished.

And they were probably planning to do the same to me. I slid a look sideways at Vickers, noting the hard lines of his face and the resolute set of his mouth. There was no gentleness there. I couldn't blame him. What had happened in that house didn't bear thinking about. I literally couldn't think about it.

I stood there like a zombie as the police worked around me, barely listening to their hurried conversations. To give them their due, no one seemed excited by the discoveries they were making. Troubled, if anything. It was hard, knowing that a child had suffered terribly in that very house, and no one had helped her.

For myself, I felt numb. I had abdicated responsibility. There didn't seem to be any point in arguing any more. I couldn't make sense of what had just happened. Even leaving aside the fact that I was apparently in serious trouble with the police, there was the question of why my possessions were in the house. OK, so Danny had been the one who attacked me and took my bag. That explained who had mugged me, but not why. And the other things – things I knew I hadn't had in my bag, things I had missed over the previous weeks and months. How had they come to be there?

Blake had gone outside, and when he came back, he nodded to Vickers. 'No press yet. I wouldn't hang around, though – it won't take them long to work out what they're missing.'

What they were missing. A bitter taste flooded my mouth. What they were missing was an arrest. A real live suspect being taken in for questioning. And I was just starting to appreciate that I was almost certainly standing in the house where Jenny died.

Smith turned to me. 'Come on. Let's get a move on.'

I walked out of the dim, dank hall into the midday

sunshine without looking back to see if Blake and Vickers were following, and the light dazzled me for a second. There was a beat, and then a strange susurration began, like wind in the trees. The sound built in volume, becoming characteristically human. Around the end of the road stood most of the neighbours – little kids with their mothers holding on to their shoulders protectively, elderly retirees who made thrice-daily trips to the local shops for some human contact, middle-aged women with sour, speculative expressions on their faces. I refused to make eye contact with any of them, even though I could feel them staring at me with bovine interest. The irritation prickled up and down my spine. They had missed out on the first sensational incident of the day because poor Geoff had been discovered at such an antisocial hour. They weren't going to miss anything now. And neither was anyone else. In the absence of the media, the burden of capturing what was taking place had fallen on my neighbours, who were taking their responsibilities seriously. At first glance, I hadn't understood why three or four of them held their arms in the air, but I soon realised that they were filming, using their mobile phones to capture the moment as I walked out of the house, Smith in front of me, another officer behind me, heading for the car. Without really thinking about it, I straightened my back. I wasn't wearing handcuffs. I was not going to shuffle to the car trying to hide my face, like a guilty person. I would walk with my head held high, and no one would know I was under arrest. I had no reason to hide. But the colour beat in my face as I went down that path.

Smith opened the back door of the unmarked car that had drawn up on the road. He stood beside it, waiting for me to get in, a parody of a chauffeur. I didn't look at him as I sat into it. The door slammed, and for the first time I felt like a prisoner. The driver was young, with red hair and a narrow fox's face. DC Freeman, I assumed, and didn't speak to him, even though he was openly assessing me. Waiting for Smith to get into the passenger seat, I stared past the young officer, towards my house. There were no signs of life over there, no hint from the outside of how my mother and I lived. I thought about asking them to let me tell her where I was being taken, but looking across at the house brooding in the sunshine, my heart sank. It was more than likely she had no idea what was going on. Then again, I couldn't exactly criticise her for that. Neither of us seemed to have noticed much. How had I missed the abuse that had been visited on a vulnerable child yards from my front door?

I had an urge to jump out of the car, run up to the front door and bang on it until Mum answered, then hold on to her and not let go. She could defend me from the police and stand up for me, like a good mother should. God knows what would actually have happened if I'd tried, assuming she even bothered to open the door. I blinked away tears angrily. I was homesick for a place that didn't exist, lonely for a mother I didn't know at all. I was on my own.

As Smith shut his door with enough force to rock the car on its axles, Freeman turned to him.

'She's not what I was expecting.'

'She doesn't look the part,' Smith agreed. 'Doesn't mean she didn't do it.'

My face burned. 'As it happens, I didn't. This is a mistake.'

'That's what they all say.' Smith clapped his colleague on the shoulder. 'Let's get a move on.'

The engine started and I sat back in my seat. I wasn't actually surprised that the officers didn't believe me. I couldn't expect them to, when I had failed to convince Vickers and Blake, who knew me a whole lot better than they did.

'You've got it wrong,' I said as we turned on to the main road, for the sake of having the last word. But in spite of my bravado, I couldn't deny that I was frightened. All I had to defend myself now was my innocence, and I had an awful feeling it wasn't going to be enough.

1996

Four years missing

'All right, decision time. What kind of ice cream would you like?'

I pretend to think. 'Hmm. I think perhaps . . . chocolate?'

'Chocolate? How unusual,' Dad says. 'It's unorthodox, but I think – yes, I'll have the same. What a good idea.'

Both of us always have chocolate ice cream. It's sort of the rule. Even if I wanted to have something else, I wouldn't, because Dad would be so disappointed.

He gets the ice cream and we walk down to the seafront. It's a bright, hot day in the middle of summer and the pier is packed with daytrippers like us. I spot a bench in the distance and run to sit on it before anyone else can nab it. Dad follows more slowly, licking his ice cream methodically, smoothing it into a point.

'Hurry up,' I call to him, nervous that someone will try to share the bench if I'm the only one

sitting on it. If anything, it makes him slow
down. He's properly dawdling now and I look
away, irritated. Sometimes it shocks me that
Dad can be so childish at his age. Immature,
that's the word. It's as if I'm the adult and he's
the kid.

'Well done,' Dad says, sitting down beside me
at last. 'This is perfect.'

It is. The sea is silver-blue, the pebbly beach
white in the sunshine. Overhead, gulls wheel
and shriek. People are all around us, but on
our bench, with Dad's arm around me, I feel as
if we're inside a bubble. No one can touch us.
I lick my ice cream and feel happy again, nestling
against Dad's side. I love these trips that we
take, just the two of us. I'd never say it to Dad,
but I'm glad that Mum doesn't come with us.
She'd ruin it. She certainly wouldn't sit on a
bench eating ice cream and laughing at two fat,
wet dogs playing in the surf.

We've been sitting there for a few minutes
and I am eating the wafer part of my ice-cream
cone when Dad shifts his arm from around my
shoulders to the back of the bench and says,
'Monkey . . . there's something I've got to tell
you.'

'What?' I'm expecting it to be a stupid joke or
something.

Dad sighs and rubs his hand over his face
before he goes on. 'Your mother and I – well,

we haven't been getting on for a while. And we've decided that the best thing to do is to split up.'

I stare at him. 'Split up?'

'We're getting a divorce, Sarah.'

'A divorce?' I have to stop saying the last two words of his sentences, I think irrelevantly. But I can't think what else to say.

'It will be all right – really, it will. I'll see you lots and lots. We can still have days out like this – I'll come every weekend if I can. And you can come and see me. I've got a new job, in Bristol. It's a great city. We'll have loads of fun.'

'When are you leaving?'

'In two weeks.'

Two weeks is too soon. 'You've known about this for ages,' I say accusingly.

'We wanted to make sure we had worked everything out before we told you.' Dad's forehead is creased into about a hundred lines. He looks stressed out.

I'm processing all of this information as fast as I can, trying to understand. 'So why can't I come with you?'

Dad looks blank. 'Well, there's school for one thing.'

'There are schools in Bristol.'

'Wouldn't you miss all your friends?'

I shrug. The answer to that is no, but I don't want to upset Dad. He's always asking me about my friends. I give him the impression that I'm popular enough, never admitting that I spend most lunchtimes in the school library, reading quietly. I'm not exactly unpopular – just off the radar. Where I prefer to be.

'I could start somewhere new in September. It would be a good time to change.'

'I see that, Sarah, but – well, I think it would be better for you to stay with your mother.'

'You know what she's like. How would it be better to stay with her?'

'Sarah—'

'You're leaving me behind with her, aren't you? You get to leave, and I have to stay.'

'She needs you, Sarah. You might not see it, but she loves you very much. If you left with me – I just don't think she'd make it. I don't want to abandon her like that. It wouldn't be fair.'

'So why are you going?' I ask, and I'm starting to cry and my nose is running and I can hardly see my father through the tears. 'If you're so worried about her, why are you leaving?'

'Because I have to,' he says quietly, looking miserable. 'Sarah, it's not up to me. It's not my idea to go.'

'Stand up to her! Tell her if you don't want to leave us. Don't just go,' I shout, and people are looking around, they're nudging one another, but I don't care. 'Why do you do everything she says, Dad? Why do you let her walk all over you?'

He doesn't have an answer, and I am crying too hard to ask the last question, the one I really want to ask.

Why don't you care enough about me to say no?

Chapter 13

Freeman took a roundabout route to the police station, heading down residential side streets and narrow lanes until we arrived at the back gate. Neither policeman said a word to me until the car sat idling at the barrier, waiting for the pole to go up. Smith cleared his throat.

'If you're wondering why the yard is so busy, it's gone out over the radio that you're coming in. Everyone wants to have a look. You're going to be quite the celebrity.'

I hadn't realised that the yard was crowded, but peering between the front seats, I could see that uniformed officers were standing around in little groups, their eyes on the car. There was a uniform expression on their faces too: disgust, principally, mixed with open curiosity and a hint of satisfaction. The job had been done. They'd got one. Mixed in with the uniforms were civilian workers who looked just as self-righteous. Marie Antoinette couldn't have faced a tougher crowd on her last public appearance.

Freeman swore softly, and I could tell that he was nervous about driving into the yard with such a big audience. He revved the engine and swung into a space by the back of the station, hitting the brakes just a fraction too hard.

'Steady,' Smith growled, and turned to me. 'All right back there? Ready for your close-up?'

I was failing to warm to the detective. Something about

the fact that he was arresting me for something I hadn't done – hadn't dreamed of doing – stuck in my throat. I didn't answer him; I just twisted my hands in my lap. I was cold and somehow detached, as if all of this was happening to someone else.

Freeman pointed. 'Through that door is the custody sergeant. All you have to do is follow DC Smith and stand where he tells you to stand.'

I nodded mutely, and when Smith opened the door, I climbed out of the car as instructed and followed him up a ramp, through a door marked 'Custody'. I didn't dare look left or right, just fixed my eyes on his wide back and tried to match his pace. A whistle came from somewhere behind me, shrill and unexpected, and I jumped. It was like a signal to the near-silent crowd in the yard, and the door closed behind me on a swell of jeers and comments. I caught sight of my reflection in a glass inner door as we passed through it and felt vague pity for the young woman in a jaunty striped T-shirt and faded jeans, the young woman with a fall of blonde curls down her back that looked too heavy for her small head, and a frozen expression on her pale face, her eyes wide and dark with fear.

The first thing I noticed was the smell. The sweetish stink of vomit was overlaid by the scent of pine disinfectant. The floor was very slightly tacky and my sandals pulled against my feet as I walked. I was so nervous, I could hardly feel my legs. My stomach was in knots.

A large desk took up most of the space in the hallway we had reached. DC Smith swaggered up to it. A female sergeant stood behind it, a motherly type with a scrubbed, fresh complexion. She looked at me, then back at Smith. In a resigned tone of voice, she asked, 'What have we got?'

'All right, skip,' Smith said with a nod, and stood up slightly straighter, like a child about to recite his catechism. 'I'm DC Thomas Smith, the arresting officer, and this is Sarah Finch. She was arrested at 12.25 this afternoon at 7, Curzon Close on suspicion of the murder of Jennifer Shepherd, on the instructions of DCI Vickers.'

There was a scuffling sound from behind me and Vickers suddenly appeared at my elbow. I looked past him to see Blake standing against the wall, hands in his pockets, staring into space. Something told me that he knew very well that I was looking at him, and no power on earth would induce him to look back. I turned my attention to Vickers, who had been confirming the circumstances of the arrest. Of *my* arrest.

The custody sergeant leaned across the desk. 'Just a few questions for you, madam.' Her voice was matter-of-fact, businesslike.

The questions were all to do with my welfare, and my replies when I answered were only just audible. No, I didn't consider myself to be a vulnerable person. No, I didn't have any special needs. No, I wasn't on any medication, and I didn't feel that I needed to see a doctor.

'And do you want to see a lawyer?' the sergeant said, with the air of someone getting to the end of a well-worn spiel.

I hesitated, then shook my head. Lawyers were for guilty people with something to hide. I hadn't done anything wrong. I could explain my way out of this more easily – and more quickly, probably – if I didn't have to deal with a lawyer.

'That's a no, then,' she said, marking it on the form. 'Initial the custody record for me, and sign in the box.'

I took the pen she handed me and signed where she had pointed. All done in accordance with the rules and regulations.

They emptied my pockets there and then, collecting an old faded receipt, some change and a button I had meant to sew on a shirt. My bag and my belt also disappeared. I had no shoelaces and nothing else that I could use to harm myself. Somehow, being stripped of my belongings was the worst moment of all. It was humiliating and degrading. I stood in front of them, my face burning, and wanted to cry.

The custody sergeant produced a bunch of keys and came out from behind her desk, humming to herself distractedly. 'This way, please.'

I followed her through a battered door that led to a line of cells, some apparently occupied, some with the heavy doors standing open. The stench was unbearable – stale urine, vomit, and overlying all of it the heavy smell of human excrement. At the very end of the hallway, the sergeant stopped.

'This is you,' she said, pointing.

I looked through the open door at a completely bare cell, containing only a concrete block the size and shape of a bed and a toilet in the corner that I didn't want to look at, let alone use. I walked in and stopped in the middle of the cell, looking around. Bare floor. Cream walls. High window. A whole lot of nothing. Behind me, the door thudded shut. The metallic sound of the key turning in the lock scraped across my overstretched nerves. I looked around to see the custody sergeant's eyes peering through the wicket in the cell door. Evidently she was satisfied with whatever she saw, because without further comment she snapped the wicket shut, leaving me alone.

When they came back, hours later, I had made myself as comfortable as it was possible to be on a bare concrete slab, sitting against the wall with my knees drawn up to my chest. It had taken me a while to overcome my reluctance to touch anything in the cell. Even though it was superficially clean and smelled as if it had been thoroughly disinfected, I couldn't help thinking about all of the previous inhabitants. There were no bodily functions, I suspected, that hadn't occurred in that cell, with the possible exception of childbirth.

It had been a long wait. Every time the custody sergeant jangled her keys in the passage, my heart jumped painfully, and every time the fear and anticipation drained away slowly. With the exception of the offer of a cup of tea (declined) or a glass of water (accepted), I had been left alone since I was locked in my cell. The water had been tepid and slightly viscous, and came in a small paper cup. There hadn't been anything like enough of it, but I didn't dare ask for more.

As I sat there, trying not to panic, I started to plan what I would say in my interview. Vickers knew me. I could appeal to him, or even to Blake. I was a nice person, a good person, and they had made a terrible mistake. Surely I would be able to convince them?

I hadn't yet got as far as counting the bricks in the walls or pacing up and down, but I was seriously tired of being locked up by the time the key slotted into the lock and my cell door swung open. The custody sergeant was there, along with a man I'd never seen before. He was small-framed and stood very straight. He had a dark, saturnine face, and wore an immaculate navy suit with a silver tie.

'This is DS Grange,' the custody sergeant said. 'He's going to take you down for an interview. Come on, up you get. Don't keep us waiting.'

I got down off the bench slowly, adrenalin surging through my veins and my blood thudding in my ears. Up close, DS Grange proved to have streaks of silver in his dark hair and I placed him in his forties. His immaculate posture made him seem taller than he was; I was used to being shorter than absolutely everyone I met, but he had less of a height advantage than most men. The custody sergeant had a good two inches on him.

'This way,' Grange said briefly, and I followed him through the door at the end of the dank, cell-lined corridor. Another dingy passageway appeared, and he walked quickly along it, checking to make sure I was following him, and holding a fire door open for me to pass through. His manner was courteous without being warm, and I was feeling quite unsettled by the time we got to a door marked 'Interview Room 1'. He held it open and I slipped through.

I recognised the set-up straightaway from every police drama or crime documentary I had ever seen. A table took up the centre of the room with two chairs on either side of it. One end abutted the wall, and an outsized tape recorder stood there, attached to both the table and the wall with steel clips, presumably to prevent irate interviewees from throwing it at their interrogators. There were two video cameras mounted by the ceiling, in opposite corners of the room, pointing at the table. The different angles would give a complete picture of what went on in the room. Another man was bending over the tape recorder, fiddling with it. He looked up as I came in, assessing me in one practised glance. He was younger than Grange, thirty-ish, about a head taller and three stone heavier. He looked like a rugby player to me. His shirt strained over muscled shoulders, the collar digging into his neck as he turned his head, leaving a blanched mark in his suntanned skin.

'This is DC Cooper,' Grange said, and pointed to one side of the table. 'Take a seat, Sarah.'

I hesitated. 'Wait a minute – who are you? Where's DCI Vickers? Or DS Blake? Or the men who arrested me?' I had forgotten their names already.

Grange sat down in one of the chairs. He busied himself with arranging his notepad and pens before answering me.

'We've been brought in to interview you. We're specialist interviewers, part of the team on this enquiry. DCI Vickers has briefed us.' He looked up for a moment, then returned to lining up his pens with mathematical precision. 'Don't worry. We know all about you.'

Not in the least reassured, I sank into the chair he had indicated for me. Cooper finished whatever he had been doing with the tape recorder and sat down beside the older detective, knocking one leg of the table as he did so. The whole thing juddered and he mumbled an apology as Grange's pens slid out of alignment. The older policeman's lips tightened with disapproval, but he nodded to Cooper, who switched on the tape recorder and began to speak. His voice was gravelly and deep, but he also had a completely incongruous lisp. Glad of the distraction, I worked out that his two front teeth were chipped. They trapped his tongue on the sibilants as he ran through an introductory spiel for the benefit of the tape – the time, the date, the room in which we sat, the police station in which the interview was being conducted, their names and ranks. As he reached the end of his preface, he looked at me. 'This interview is being recorded on tape and on video, OK?'

I cleared my throat. 'Yes.'

'Could you please state your name and date of birth.'

'Sarah Anne Finch. The seventeenth of February, 1984.'

Cooper shuffled through the papers in front of him, looking for something. 'OK,' he said. 'I'm now going to caution you again.'

He read the caution from the page in front of him, stopping to explain what each clause meant. I was finding it hard to concentrate. I wanted to get on to the interview proper, so I could explain that I was completely innocent and get the hell out of there. There was no way that this was going to end up in court. I couldn't possibly be put on trial for something I hadn't done. It was unthinkable. I barely listened, and was caught out when Cooper asked me a question.

'Sorry, what did you say?'

'You've declined the right to legal advice. Can you explain why?'

I shrugged, and then blushed as he pointed to the tape recorder. 'Er, I didn't feel that I needed legal representation.'

'Do you feel well enough to be interviewed?'

I felt nervous, tired, a little bit sick and thirsty, but I wasn't inclined to delay proceedings any further. 'Yes.'

'Now I just want to confirm the circumstances of your arrest. You were arrested, weren't you, today, that's the tenth of May, at 7, Curzon Close, for the murder of Jennifer Shepherd.'

'Yes.'

'And you were cautioned there, and you didn't say anything at that time.'

'That's correct.' I was trying to appear calm, and I lifted my chin and looked the detective in the eye as I answered.

As Cooper scribbled something on a form, Grange leaned forward.

'Do you know why you were arrested, Sarah?' He spoke quietly, with deliberation, and I felt frightened of him without knowing why.

'I believe a mistake has been made. I had nothing to do with Jenny's death. I had nothing to do with whatever took place at that house. I had only been inside the house on one occasion, and that was two days ago.'

Grange nodded, but I didn't get the feeling that he was agreeing with me – more that I had said what he expected to hear. 'So you can't see why we would be interested in speaking with you.'

'Not really. I knew Jenny – I taught her. And I did find her body. But I spoke to the police about that. I spoke to Chief Inspector Vickers. I explained all of that. And I know there were things of mine in the house, but I don't know how they got there. I certainly didn't *leave* them there.' My voice was getting higher and faster and I stopped short, dismayed that I sounded so flustered.

Grange raised a hand. 'We'll talk about that in a moment, Sarah, if we can. First, I'd like to make a few suggestions to you about how *we* see your involvement in the case, and you can tell me what you think.'

'I think your first mistake is to think I have any involvement in the case at all,' I said steadily.

Grange flipped over a page in his notebook without acknowledging what I'd said. He was reading and I guessed he was reminding himself of the case against me. I stared at him, hot with anger, impatient to hear how they could possibly tie me into Jenny's death. Grange wasn't giving anything away and I turned to look at the other policeman. Cooper's round, slightly protuberant eyes were fixed on me, and his pen was poised above his notebook, ready to note any reaction I gave to what they had to say. I settled back in my chair and folded my arms. I felt hostile, and I wanted them to know it.

'The investigative team has been suspicious of you from the start,' Grange began at last, and I felt a physical shock at what he said. The investigative team included the chief inspector, Valerie Wade and Andy Blake. They couldn't have thought I was involved. *He* couldn't.

'There is often a question mark over the person who

discovers the body in a murder investigation, particularly if they have a connection to the victim. It suggests knowledge on the part of the discoverer as to the location of the body, especially if there has been a search to locate it, and it provides a ready explanation for there to be forensic evidence of the person in question at the scene: trace evidence, fingerprints, shoeprints – that sort of thing. That muddies the waters for us. Your presence at the scene in the woods contaminated it for us, so we can't prove that you were there at a different time – as, for instance, when dumping the body.'

I interrupted. 'I'm five foot two and I would guess that I weigh about fifteen pounds more than Jenny did. It wouldn't have been possible for me to carry her to the place where she was found. It's an isolated spot – difficult terrain. I physically couldn't have done it.'

'Not alone, no. We believe you were helped in that task by someone else, and that you took the responsibility for cleaning up after that person, knowing that any traces *you* left could be explained away.'

'What other person?'

'I'll come to that, if I may,' Grange said with a reproving look in my direction. He had a script that he was planning to follow, and I was trying to jump ahead. I subsided. I genuinely wanted to hear what they thought I'd done.

'From the time that the body was discovered, you kept coming to the attention of the police. You made every effort to involve yourself in the investigation, taking it on yourself to speak to Jennifer's friends before the team interviewed them. Your curiosity was noted and the team's suspicion increased. It is our belief that you were feeding information about the investigation back to your conspirator, so that when it became clear that he was in danger of being arrested, he was able to get away.'

'Danny,' I said in a whisper.

'Daniel Keane, yes,' he said with some satisfaction. 'However, you needn't worry about him. We've got good intel on him. We'll pick him up.'

'I hope you do. He can tell you that this is a complete fabrication. I haven't spoken to him in years, never mind conspired with him, or whatever you're suggesting.'

'It must have come as a shock to you, all the same,' Grange said, leaning across the table, 'when you realised that you weren't just getting a lift home from the police. It meant you had no time to send a quick text to Danny or Paul to let them know that the police were about to execute a warrant. No time to wipe the files, clear the hard drives, destroy the evidence. No time to get your personal possessions out of the house.'

'I don't know how those things got there,' I said lamely. 'I told you that. And I told DCI Vickers.'

'He said it was an Oscar-worthy performance,' Cooper commented. 'But it didn't convince anyone.'

Grange took over again. 'Then you were defending Paul, telling the officers that they shouldn't interview him, that he was vulnerable. It was clear to everyone that you were afraid Paul would forget the story you'd agreed with him when you went to the house two days ago. Paul's only a kid. You couldn't count on him to cover for you.'

'That's ridiculous –'

'Is it?' Grange was like a predatory shark closing in on his target. 'Because it doesn't seem ridiculous to us. You're too good to be true, Sarah. You live with your mother, teaching day in, day out at that posh school, looking at all the things you can't have. It's all so easy for those girls and they don't even know it. We've searched your house – spoken to your mother. Pretty grim sort of life for a young woman, isn't it? Pretty dull. Not much joy in it.'

I was struggling to take in the fact that they'd searched the house – searched my room, my things. My face burned at the thought of strangers' hands turning over my clothes, going through my letters and books. Judging me. And worse than that, what if the hands hadn't belonged to strangers? An image of Blake sitting on the edge of my bed came into my mind, and the look on his face was contempt mingled with pity. And pity was the last thing I wanted from him.

I pulled myself back to the small, airless room. 'If you spoke to Mum, she'll have told you I couldn't have been involved. I was with her when Jenny disappeared.'

Grange didn't blink. 'She wasn't able to be that helpful, I'm afraid. If you were relying on her for an alibi, you'll have to look somewhere else.'

I sat back, stymied. Of course she hadn't been helpful. She'd be useless as a character witness – hostile to the police and vague about dates and times. Why had I thought that might be the way out of this nightmare?

Grange was back on the hunt. 'You and Danny Keane – you're the leftovers. Both of you, you've had to survive all your lives. That's the sort of thing that would bring two

people together. Bonnie and Clyde, you know the thing –
except robbing banks isn't in fashion these days, and it's a
lot easier to procure a little girl, turn her head with flattery and false friendship, and abuse her on camera.'

I shrank back in my chair, intimidated in spite of myself.
Grange looked at his notebook, then leaned forward again.
'We believe that you and Daniel Keane engaged in a
conspiracy, first of all to abuse Jennifer Shepherd, then to
get rid of her when you discovered that she was pregnant.'

I shook my head. 'No. No way.'

'Yes,' Grange insisted. 'You saw her in school and realised
that she was vulnerable. She was an only child. She trusted
adults, didn't she? She was used to being around them all
the time, so it was easy to get her on her own and make
friends with her. She didn't live far away from you, so she
could make excuses to come over in the evenings and at
weekends. She lied to her parents – you helped her to come
up with stories, didn't you? And Daniel Keane charmed her
until she didn't know right from wrong and before she knew
it, she was being used by strangers, over and over again, for
your financial gain, and thanking you for the privilege.'

He turned and without being asked Cooper handed him
a folder that Grange flipped through before looking at me
again.

'We've recovered these images from the computers in
the house. There may be more once we've completed our
examination of the computers, but these are sufficient
evidence to bring charges against those involved in abusing
this girl.'

He opened the folder and flicked through the contents

again, then selected something. 'Did you know that we have a system for grading images containing paedophile material? It runs from level one to level five, level one being the least offensive. This is a level one image.'

He slid the photograph across the table and I looked down to see Jenny smiling at the camera, looking over her shoulder. She was wearing underwear, a vest and pants dotted with pink flowers, kneeling down with one hand on her hip. The material of the vest clung to her chest, showing that it was completely flat and undeveloped. There was a flowery barrette in her hair and she looked very young and very innocent.

'Level one is sexualised posing,' Grange said, giving each syllable full weight. 'Not necessarily nude. Nothing else going on. Titillating, you might say.'

I swallowed, completely repelled. The thought that someone might find the image erotic was beyond me.

'Level two.' Grange slid another photograph across the table, the shiny paper screaming on the laminated surface. 'Solo masturbation. Or non-penetrative sexual activity between children. But in this case, solo masturbation.'

I looked down at the picture for a split second, then looked away, feeling the tears starting in my eyes. 'Stop,' I managed to say. I didn't want to see it. I didn't want to know that these things existed.

'Level three.' Another photograph slid across the table. 'Non-penetrative sexual activity between children and adults.'

I had closed my eyes and turned away, sobbing hard now.

'The face of the man is pixellated,' Grange mused, 'but I think we can tell that's Daniel Keane. He has a tattoo on his right arm, doesn't he? One like that? A Celtic design?'

'I have no idea,' I said, still not looking at the image. There were things I didn't need to see, things I could never forget if I did look at them. My nose was running and I sniffed hopelessly. 'Could I have a tissue?'

'Then there's level four,' Grange said, ignoring me. 'Penetrative sexual activity of all sorts – children with children, children with adults. That includes oral sex, as you can see.'

Two more photographs skimmed across the table and one slid over the edge, landing on the floor at the edge of my vision. I saw it before I could stop myself from looking and my reaction was instant and visceral. I bent down, turned my head to one side, and was comprehensively sick all over the floor. Grange pushed his chair back with a smothered exclamation and jumped out of range, not quite quickly enough. Splashes of vomit spattered his immaculate trousers and shoes, though I was too miserable to care.

'Stop the tape, Chris,' Grange snapped, and Cooper muttered a quick 'Interview suspended at 6.25 p.m.' before he did so.

I was vaguely aware of Grange leaving the room and a female police officer in uniform coming in. Between them, Cooper and the other officer guided me into a different interview room and gave me a cup of water. I rinsed my mouth out, feeling lousy. My head was throbbing and my throat was raw from retching. I hadn't eaten for hours, so what I had thrown up was almost pure stomach acid.

They waited twenty minutes or so before restarting the interview. I couldn't help looking at Grange's trouser cuffs when he came into the room, noting the damp patches where someone had tried to sponge the material. His jaw was tight with tension, but he was civil enough when he spoke to me.

'Do you feel able to continue with this interview?'

'Yes.' My voice was husky and I cleared my throat, wincing as I did so.

'Would you like another glass of water?' Cooper asked.

'I'm OK,' I whispered.

Grange sat back in his chair. 'Right, well, we'll pick up where we stopped.'

'No more photographs,' I said quickly. 'You've made your point.'

'There's still level five. Don't you want to know about level five?'

I clenched my hands into fists, trying to keep myself under control. The detective clearly suffered from small-man syndrome. Shouting at him – challenging his authority – would achieve nothing. I had to try civility. 'Please don't show me any more images.'

'Right. We don't want to have to change interview rooms again,' he said, with an attempt at humour. Cooper laughed loudly. I couldn't quite manage a smile.

'Let's get back to you and Daniel Keane,' Grange said, the good humour evaporating. 'I'm prepared to believe that you weren't involved with the abuse directly. I'm prepared to believe that you hadn't seen photographs of that sort before. But I am still quite sure that you were integral to the plot to abuse Jennifer Shepherd for your personal gain.'

'Absolutely not,' I said with as much force as I could muster.

Grange's eyes narrowed. 'It must have been a disaster when you realised that Jennifer was pregnant. Maybe you didn't know that she had started her periods. She still looked like a child, but in fact she had been menstruating for a number of months. You knew the whole thing would come out once her parents knew about her pregnancy, and you knew that you would face prosecution. You would receive a very serious sentence for procuring a girl for purposes of abuse, making money off that abuse, and on your eventual release from prison – which would not have been a pleasant experience, as I'm sure you can imagine – you would be prohibited from working with children again. You would have been fairly unemployable, in fact. The stakes were very high for you. High enough for you to feel that a girl who was coming to the end of her usefulness anyway – a girl who you had treated as a commodity to be exploited for your financial gain – was eminently disposable.'

'No,' I said, shaking my head. 'None of that is true.'

'No? And it's not true that you and Daniel Keane had agreed that if you got away with the murder of Jennifer Shepherd undetected, you would look for another victim once the dust had settled? It was a nice moneyspinner for the pair of you, too lucrative to abandon it completely, especially when you had the whole process set up and customers demanding new material.'

'That's absolutely ridiculous.'

'So that isn't the reason it was necessary for Daniel Keane to attack Geoff Turnbull?' Grange's eyes were sharp, watching for a reaction from me at the mention of Geoff's name. 'Because Geoff was hanging around, wasn't he? And you had people who wanted to be able to come and go, if you'll pardon the expression, regulars for the little club that you had set up. We've found images of four different men engaging in the abuse so far, most of them older than you and Daniel Keane by some way, as it happens, so we aren't sure where he recruited them – maybe you'd be able to help us with that? No? They would have been very unhappy about a teacher turning up at all hours of the day and night, someone who might be able to work out what was going on, who might recognise the victim as she arrived at or left the property.'

'What makes you think Danny attacked Geoff?' I asked, stuck on the first part of what Grange had said.

'We found an iron bar in the property when it was searched, shoved under one of the beds in a black bin bag. It was stained with blood and other matter. There were hairs on it that we have visually matched to Geoff Turnbull, though they will be doing DNA testing to confirm it. We're very confident that this is the weapon that was used to attack Mr Turnbull.'

I sat back, bemused. Geoff would have been in the way if Danny was up to no good across the road from my house. But it was a fairly extreme way of getting rid of him. And, as Vickers had said, it looked personal. I filed it away under 'to be thought about later' and concentrated on what Grange was saying. The tone of his voice had softened.

'Look, Sarah, we understand that you've had a lot of bad experiences in your life, with your brother's disappearance and your father's death. We understand why you might be drawn to Daniel Keane – he's one of the only people in the world who might understand what it was like for you, growing up. Maybe all of this was his idea. Maybe he took advantage of you too. You might have thought things would work out differently. You might not have understood what you were getting yourself into until it was too late.'

Grange was looking sincere. I didn't believe him for a second.

'You're in a lot of trouble at the moment, but we can help you if you help us. If you can tell us what really happened with Jennifer – if you can fill in the blanks for us – we can do a deal for you. Come up with a lesser charge. Make sure you do less time in prison – maybe make it possible for you to go to an open prison.'

I wasn't stupid enough to believe what Grange was saying, but I could work out what it meant. They had a lot of ideas, but no real evidence. They needed me to implicate myself and help to tie up the case against Danny at the same time. I had no problem with Danny going to prison for a long time – for ever, preferably – after seeing the images of Jenny being abused. But I had to make them understand that far from being the brains behind the outfit, I hadn't even noticed what was going on right across the road.

'What this comes down to,' I said, choosing my words with care, 'is a combination of coincidence and circumstance. I can understand why you were suspicious of me. It was strange that I kept coming to your attention; I can see that now. But the only reason I involved myself in the investigation was because I thought I could help. No one helped when my brother disappeared. I wanted whoever did this to be caught, and I hope you do catch Danny Keane, I really do. But I didn't have anything to do with the abuse. I didn't even know that Jenny knew Danny.'

I paused for a second, working through what I needed to say. 'You say that my things were in the house. That's correct. But as I told DCI Vickers, I was the victim of a mugging this week. I now believe it was Danny Keane who attacked me.'

I stood and turned so my back was to the policemen, then pulled my T-shirt up. The bruising across my shoulder had gone from black to yellow-green over the previous days, but it was still there. I turned to face them again, rolling the leg of my jeans up far enough to show them my knee. It was puffy and discoloured, and I heard Cooper give a little sympathetic hiss.

'My bag was stolen. That's why I haven't been driving – I didn't have my keys.' I sat down. 'If I had had access to the house, I would certainly have wanted my car keys. DS Blake saw me at the memorial service for Jenny. He can confirm that I had to walk there, even though it was a very wet evening, and that I needed a lift home afterwards.

'I don't know how Jenny came to Danny's attention as

a potential victim, but I do know that she and Paul Keane were in primary school together. I don't know why Geoff was attacked. I don't know why I was mugged. I think those are questions that only Danny can answer. I promise you, I haven't spoken to him since I was a teenager.'

Grange stirred. 'That just isn't credible, I'm afraid. You live yards from him.'

'It's true. We had a falling out.' I could remember the circumstances very clearly; I hoped to God the policemen wouldn't ask me to explain what had happened. 'I went to his house this week so I could ask him about what happened to my brother, and that's how I met Paul. I'd forgotten he even existed, to be honest with you. I hadn't seen him for years.'

'Why ask him about your brother now?'

I moved restlessly in the chair, trying to think how I could explain it. 'What happened with Jenny . . . it just brought it all back. I started to think about how the Shepherds must be feeling, and then I thought about my parents – about my dad in particular. No one cares about Charlie any more – no one except my mum, and it's broken her. I spent years trying to pretend that Charlie had never existed. I tried to run away from what happened to my family, but I couldn't go on ignoring it for ever. I thought I might find something. I thought that maybe no one had asked the right questions, or spoken to the right people. I thought – I thought I could make everything right again.' It sounded stupid once I'd said it out loud and I sat and looked at my hands, not wanting to see the detectives' faces.

There was a muffled knock at the door and Cooper stopped the tape as Grange went to answer it. He went into the corridor and closed the door behind him. I sat in silence, not attempting to engage with Cooper while I waited for Grange to return. I had done all I could. I had said all I had to say. There was nothing to do but wait, so that's what I did.

1997

Five years missing

The phone is ringing. I am lying on the sofa, cutting my split ends with nail scissors, and I make no attempt to answer it, even though it is just a few feet away.

Mum comes out of the kitchen and I can hear she is annoyed when she lifts the receiver; her voice is sharp.

Her side of the conversation is brief, barely polite. After a minute, she leans in from the hall. 'Sarah, it's your father on the phone. Come and speak to him, please.'

I don't move immediately. I am concentrating on one last curl, angling the scissors carefully to trim a single hair with three separate ends that spiral away from the main shaft like spurs.

'That's disgusting,' Mum says. 'Stop that immediately. Your father is waiting for you.'

I get off the sofa and go to where she is standing, taking the phone from her without speaking to her or even looking at her.

'Hello.'

'Hi, monkey. How are you?'

'OK.'

Dad sounds cheerful – too cheerful.

'How's school?'

'OK.'

'Are you working hard?'

Instead of answering, I sigh into the phone. I wish he could see the expression on my face. It's hard to convey 'I don't give a shit' over the phone without saying the words, and I don't quite dare to.

'Listen, Sarah, I know things are hard, but you have to try, sweetheart. School is important.'

'Right,' I say, kicking the skirting board slowly, deliberately. I have heavy boots on, black Caterpillar boots with thick soles and steel toecaps that I persuaded Dad to buy me. I can't even feel the impact as my toe connects with the wall.

'Stop that,' Mum says from behind me. She is standing in the kitchen doorway, listening in. I turn away from her more, tucking the phone between my shoulder and my ear, hunching over. 'Dad, when can I come to see you?'

'Soon. The flat is nearly ready. I've just been painting the second bedroom, actually. As soon as I get it set up, you can come and stay.'

'It's been ages,' I mutter into the phone.

'I know. But I'm trying, Sarah. You have to be patient.'

'I have been patient,' I say. 'I'm tired of being patient.' I give the skirting board another vicious kick and some paint flakes off it. 'Dad, I have to go.'

'Oh, OK.' He sounds surprised, a little deflated. 'Have you got plans?'

'No. I just don't really have anything else to say to you.' It feels good to be mean to him. It feels like what he deserves.

There's a little pause. 'Right, then.'

'Bye,' I say, and I put the phone down quickly, so I can't hear him reply.

When I turn around, Mum is still standing there, her arms folded, a half-smile on her face. I can tell that she is pleased with me, and I feel glad for a second, before the guilt kicks in, and the resentment. I don't even care what she thinks.

As I go into the living room and flop back down on the sofa, I wish that I'd been nicer to Dad on the phone, but it's too late now. He's gone.

Chapter 14

They left me sitting in the interview room for quite some time. Grange returned to collect Cooper, but didn't speak to me. A female officer in uniform slipped in and stood by the door in silence, apparently oblivious to my presence. I followed her example, staring into space instead with my arms folded around my knees. I expected that they would take me back to the cells eventually. I had the distinct impression that the interview was over.

When the door opened again, I was surprised to see Vickers standing there. He got rid of the uniformed officer with a jerk of his head and came in himself, pulling Cooper's chair around from the other side of the table so that he could sit facing me, without having the table in the way. He eased himself into the chair slowly, as if his back was aching, and sighed before he spoke.

'How are you doing?'

I gave him a one-shouldered shrug. *How do you think?*

'You'll be glad to hear that we've been talking to young Paul Keane at the hospital, and he's categorically denied that you were involved in a conspiracy. He's corroborated everything you've been telling us. For the time being, no other evidence of your involvement coming to light, I'm satisfied that you weren't in fact connected with the plot to abuse or murder Jennifer Shepherd.'

It wasn't a ringing endorsement of my innocence, but I took it for what it was: an apology of sorts and reassurance that they weren't going to interrogate me any further.

'You won't find any more evidence. I told you, I wasn't involved.'

'So it seems,' Vickers said, clasping his hands in front of him and examining his knuckles as if they were a source of some fascination to him. He didn't say anything else, and I wondered what he was waiting for.

'May I go?'

'Mmm. Well, of course you can, if you want. I'd understand that, if you wanted to go home. You're probably tired, and a bit upset.'

'Just a bit,' I said drily.

'Yes. Well. I'd understand, as I say, if you wanted to head off.'

There was a little pause. I knew he wanted something else. I wondered if it would be too rude to say no before I heard what it was. 'But?'

'But – well, when I say that we've been talking to Paul, we haven't been getting very far.' He rubbed his neck with one wrinkled hand. I knew he was playing up the tired-old-man thing to gain my sympathy, and waited for him to get to the point, unmoved.

'The thing is, he won't tell us much, Sarah. All that we've been able to get him to say is that you weren't involved. He's been no comment this, no comment that – we couldn't even get him to confirm his name and age at first. It was only when we started to ask him about you that he talked. You made a big impression on him. He said you were kind to him.'

I felt tremendously sorry for Paul. All I had done was talk to him – treat him as a fellow human being. How could that have made such a big impression on him that he'd break his silence to defend me? It must have taken great courage. Bad as it had been for me to be locked up, then interviewed – interrogated – at least I was an adult and had some idea of my rights. And I knew I was innocent.

'You shouldn't be interviewing him at all. Of course I'm grateful to him for confirming what I've been telling you. But he is a child. He's immensely vulnerable. He's just tried to kill himself, for God's sake. And if you're right about the part he played in Jenny's abuse – and I'm not saying you are; you were wrong about me, after all – I imagine he's desperately ashamed to have been found out.'

'You've got a point there,' Vickers said, trying to look shame-faced. The apparent unease did not sit well with what I knew of him – he was pure steel underneath – and I stared him down, refusing to respond.

Vickers crossed one skinny leg over the other and spent some time smoothing the material of his trousers over the uppermost kneecap. Eventually he looked up at me. 'I don't think it's fair to ask you to help us, Sarah, given what we've put you through, but I'm in a difficult situation. We've got no chance to build a good relationship with the boy. There's no trust there at all. He's had no support from any reliable adult for a good many years, so he doesn't respond very well to us or to his old teachers, and there's no other family. We had a social worker sitting in, and I know they do good work, but this one was about as much use as a piece of damp string to a man with diarrhoea, if you'll pardon the expression. I'm going to have to appeal to your good nature, and your desire to see justice done.'

'What do you want me to do?'

'Come to the hospital with me. Now.' Vickers had dropped the quavery old-man voice and I noticed again how penetrating his cold blue eyes could be. 'He trusts you. He likes you. We've asked him if he'd talk to anyone and yours was the only name that got a good reaction. He thinks you're some sort of angel.'

'I don't believe this,' I said, struggling to take it in. 'How can you go from accusing me of murder one minute to asking me for help the next?'

'We had grounds to suspect your involvement in some aspect of the crime,' Vickers said reprovingly. 'Following our investigation, we are now satisfied that you weren't involved. But arresting you was the correct course of action, legally, and it has cleared your name.'

'So I should be grateful?' I was shaking with anger.

'I didn't say that.' Vickers softened slightly. 'I know it was hard, Sarah. And if I had any alternative, I'd let you go home and recover from this in your own time. But I don't have a lot of choice. I need to know what Paul knows, and I don't have time to waste making friends with him. I've got Jennifer Shepherd's parents on the phone asking if there's any news, I've got the press asking all sorts of questions, I'm trying to coordinate the manhunt for Daniel Keane under huge pressure from the bosses and all I need is to be able to say to all of them: yes, we're on the right track. We might not have him yet, but it's only a matter of time, and he's definitely the one we're after.'

'I don't want to be part of this,' I said, shaking my head. 'I don't want to be involved in badgering that poor child for information that will incriminate his brother.'

'Please, Sarah. You know what it's like – not knowing. For the sake of the parents, won't you help us?'

That was it. He'd got me. Vickers always found the right angle in the end. I might not want to help the police, but I hadn't the heart to make the Shepherds wait for the truth.

To give him his due, the inspector managed to avoid sounding triumphant as he led me out of the interview room and down the corridor towards the front of the police station. He prattled on about the rooms we were passing – 'and that's where we spoke to you, you'll remember, the night that Jennifer's body was found, that's my office in there'. I tuned most of it out, smarting from the looks I was receiving from Vickers' colleagues. It was evidently taking a while for the news of my release to filter through. Barely disguised hostility seemed to be the common re-action as Vickers ushered me down the hall.

We came into the reception area of the police station, the part that was open to the public, to discover a one-man riot in progress. Vickers and I stopped as one, side by side, stunned. A tall, broad-shouldered man was strug-gling with two uniformed PCs and a woman. The woman was clinging to his arm for dear life, and as he tried to shake her off she turned her head and I recognised Valerie. The man was shouting at the top of his voice, spitting invective at the civilian receptionist. She looked petrified behind her scratched and yellowed plexiglass screen, and I didn't blame her. The man's anger was colossal. I had recognised him too, with a chill. Michael Shepherd was at the very limits of his self-control and it was impossible to predict what he might do. And if he knew that I had been arrested – if he knew that the police had suspected me of anything at all to do with his daughter's death – then I absolutely didn't want to be in a room with him, surrounded by police or not.

'I want to speak to the inspector, and I want to speak to him *now!*' he demanded, his voice raw with sharp-cornered rage.

'If you'd just calm down for a second—' Valerie puffed and I reflected that those words, and the exact manner in which she delivered them, were likely to provoke the precisely opposite effect.

'Shut the fuck up,' Shepherd barked. 'What the fuck do you know?'

I hadn't noticed Vickers moving, but suddenly he was standing to one side of the little group. At the sight of him Shepherd gave a great sigh and stopped struggling.

'There's no need for an argument, Mr Shepherd. Sorry I wasn't available before. I've been tied up, I'm afraid.'

'They said on the news that someone had been arrested. Is that true?' The words came out of Michael Shepherd in a rush.

'We're pursuing a definite line of enquiry.'

I flinched as Shepherd's fist crashed down on the counter in front of him.

'That's what you keep saying, but you don't tell me anything. I don't know what's going on. I just don't – I don't . . .'

Shepherd was shaking his head, bewildered, anger turning to confusion and despair. Vickers couldn't resist a glance in my direction. I could see he was pleased I had seen Jenny's father in that state. He had realised it would persuade me – as nothing else could – to carry out what he needed me to do. I hated him for it, but he was right.

Vickers hadn't calculated how quickly Michael Shepherd would recover, and how alert he was to what was going on around him. Noticing that he'd lost Vickers' attention for a second, he whipped around to see what the policeman was looking at. I shrank back as his coal-black eyes found me and his brows drew together.

'You,' he said, on a ragged breath, and started towards me. 'You're in this, aren't you? You're the one they've arrested.'

The two uniformed officers ran to intercept him at Vickers' panicky command and dragged him to a stop a couple of feet away from me. I held my ground and Michael Shepherd's gaze. The heat of it was scorching.

'I was just about to tell you about Miss Finch,' Vickers said, catching up and inserting himself between us in an act that was unlikely to be effective, should Michael Shepherd break free. I appreciated his chivalry, all the same. 'We're satisfied that she played no part in the murder of your daughter, Mr Shepherd. In fact, she has been helping us to find out more about what happened to Jenny before she died, and she is continuing to provide us with every assistance.'

Shepherd's eyes still bored into mine and I knew he would kill me if he had the chance, believing that I had harmed his daughter.

'Are you sure?' he asked harshly.

'Positive. She had nothing to do with the abuse of your daughter, and nothing to do with her death.' Vickers was sounding a lot more certain about that than he had in the interrogation room earlier, but he needed to convince Shepherd, and quickly.

What he said made Shepherd turn his head, but it didn't calm him – quite the opposite. 'The *abuse?*'

Just for a second, a flicker of uncertainty passed across Vickers' lined face. 'You were told about that, I believe. DC Wade spoke to you and your wife about it this afternoon.'

'She told us lies,' Michael Shepherd hissed. 'It's not true. None of it is true. If you tell anyone, I'll sue.'

Vickers put his hand out and patted the air vaguely, as if that might soothe the man in front of him. 'I know it's hard to take in, but you needed to know what happened. We think the – er, molestation – led directly to Jennifer's death, Mr Shepherd. It is true, sadly, and there is plenty of evidence of it that we are going to use in prosecuting those responsible. That means that some of it will be in the public domain and there's no way we can keep it out of the media. Now, we aren't planning to make the images and videos public, I can assure you of that, but some of them will be shown in court and they will be reported on, but not in any detail.'

'Images,' Michael Shepherd repeated, not seeming to take in what Vickers was saying. He turned back to me. 'Have you seen them? Have you seen my Jenny?'

I didn't have to speak or even nod for him to know that I had. I wanted to tell him that I hadn't wanted to look, that I would do my best to forget what I had seen, if I ever could, but before I could speak he whipped back to Vickers.

'You told her? You showed her? How many other people have seen these images? Everyone, I suppose. All laughing and joking about them. Mocking my daughter. My little girl, and she's nothing but a slag to you, is she? A little whore who deserved what she got.' His face was working, his chin quivering. Valerie volunteered a 'hush now' that was ignored.

'Everyone's going to know. Everyone's going to know about it and there's nothing I can do.' He fell to his knees and raised his hands to his face as raw sobs tore their way out of him. The rest of us stood around in silent horror, mesmerised by the big man's total collapse.

'Val, take him through and give him a cup of tea or something, for God's sake,' Vickers said, the strain showing in his voice. 'There's whisky in my drawer. Dig it out and pour him a double, then take him home. Make sure the press don't see him like this.'

He grabbed me by the arm and hustled me out past the little group. 'Nothing we can do here, but plenty you can do at the hospital,' he said, tugging impatiently when I hesitated. 'Now do you see why it's important? That man's going to destroy himself if we don't finish this soon.'

Fundamentally I liked Vickers and I understood what drove him. I didn't want to suggest to him that finding Jenny's killer might not be enough to save her father, but I thought it.

We left the police station by a side door that led into the car park. I had lost track of time in the cells and it was a surprise to find that the sun was setting. I stopped for a second just outside the door and took a long, deep breath; no air had ever tasted sweeter. Deliberately, I let Vickers get fifty yards ahead of me, wanting a moment to myself. As I started to follow him to his car, there was a sudden flash. I looked around, disorientated, to see a single photographer standing to my right, hunched over a little, holding a huge camera. The instant I turned around and gave him the angle he wanted, he snatched six or seven pictures in quick succession, the flash as bright and remorseless as strobe lighting. I threw up my arm to shield myself from the camera, peripherally aware of Vickers turning and running back towards us. I couldn't understand what had happened – how the photographer had known who I was, for starters – but I knew with bitter clarity that I had lost something I'd fought for. One picture would be enough to ensure I was never anonymous again. The police might have grudgingly admitted I was innocent, but innocence didn't make a story. Suspicion and speculation, as I knew only too well, did.

I didn't have to spend too long wondering who was

responsible. As Vickers tackled the photographer, a figure stepped out from behind a car.

'Sarah, do you want to tell me about the arrest? Why did the police take you in for questioning? How are you involved in Jenny's death?'

I had to hand it to her. She might have been a grafting reporter on a small-time local newspaper, but Carol Shapley had an instinct for finding a story that the national papers couldn't hope to match.

'Who told you to come here?' Vickers said roughly, over his shoulder. He'd pushed the photographer against the wall, pressing his face into the brickwork, and I noticed that he was wheezing a little. The inspector was stronger than he looked, though, and even though the man was struggling, I didn't think he had any chance of getting free.

Carol smiled. 'I've got sources everywhere, Chief Inspector Vickers. They keep me informed.'

'Well, your sources misled you. There's no story here. And you're on police property. You shouldn't even be standing there.'

She ignored him. Her eyes were like searchlights as they swept over me, missing nothing. I felt totally exposed. 'Sarah, we can do a follow-up to the last story, explaining what's happened to you today. We can completely clear your name.'

'I don't think so.'

'Don't you want people to know you're innocent?'

What I wanted was to stay far, far away from her. I looked away without speaking, knowing that anything I said would be used to make a better story.

The door behind me banged as a couple of uniformed officers came out, laughing a little, oblivious at first to what was going on.

'Over here, lads,' Vickers ground out, and the pair responded like well-trained dogs to a whistle, no questions asked. I felt slightly sorry for the photographer as his arms were twisted behind him and he was dragged to the ground with main force. Vickers stepped back and wiped his mouth on the back of his hand. From the other hand, he swung the photographer's camera by the strap.

'Better make sure this hasn't been damaged. Wouldn't it be terrible if it was broken?' As he spoke, he opened his hand and let the camera fall to the ground. 'Oh dear. Silly me.'

The photographer kicked at the officers who were holding him, earning himself a knee in the ribs. Vickers ignored him, picking up the camera and switching it on.

'It still works,' he said pleasantly. 'Isn't that wonderful? Modern technology at its finest.' He crouched down beside the photographer. 'Can I look at the pictures you took just now?'

The man was swearing, his voice low and bitter.

'Less of that, or you'll find yourself under arrest.'

'You can't arrest me for swearing,' the man said, outraged.

'Section five of the Public Order Act says I can,' Vickers said, scrolling. 'Swear again and find out if I mean it. What does this button do? Delete, is it?'

Carol had moved to stand beside Vickers. 'You can't do this. I'll report this – this censorship. Police brutality. Abuse of powers. I'll make sure you get in so much trouble, you never work as a police officer again.'

'Oh no, my dear, you've got it wrong. I can make sure you never write another word for the *Elmview Examiner*. Eddie Briggs is a good friend of mine, and he's no fan of yours, Mrs Shapley, even if he is your boss. Then there's your car – I'm sure if I go and look at it, I can find some very pressing reasons why it needs to be impounded – for your own safety, you understand.' He smiled at her. 'Bit of advice for you: don't pick a fight with the police. We will win.'

'Are you threatening me?'

'Yes,' Vickers said simply. 'And if you know what's good for you, you'll forget you ever saw this. Miss Finch is absolutely innocent; I'm quite satisfied of that. She was brought in to speak to us at the police station for operational reasons. She's been very helpful and very understanding, and what she deserves is a little bit of respect, and her privacy.'

'Why are you doing this?' Carol's lips were thin and I thought she was trying not to cry. 'Why are you standing up for her?'

He leaned in so his face was inches away from hers. 'Because I don't like bullies, Mrs Shapley, and I don't like the way you work. And I'm watching you. No passing on the information anonymously. If I read one word about Miss Finch in the papers, or hear a single syllable about her on any news programmes, I will hold you personally responsible. I'll make sure you never get another story from Surrey Police. I'll call in every favour I can to make your life a misery. Believe me, Mrs Shapley, I mean every word I say.' He thrust the camera at her. 'Now, do we have an understanding?'

She nodded sulkily.

'Let him up, boys.'

The uniformed officers sat back and let the man scramble to his feet. His clothes were dishevelled and dirty, and his eyes were full of loathing.

'Give me my camera.'

Carol handed it over and he checked it, running his hands over it, rubbing at a scuff mark. 'This is an expensive bit of kit. If it's damaged—'

'If it's damaged, send the bill to Carol. Now hop it. I'm tired of looking at the pair of you.' There was something in Vickers' demeanour that suggested he wasn't in the mood for further discussions. Wisely, in my view, the pair of them walked off without another word. Carol took the time to glare at me and I stared back, unflinching, even though the cold hatred on her face was chilling.

Vickers nodded to the two uniformed officers. 'Thanks, lads.'

'No problem,' one of them said, his voice so deep it rumbled. 'Anytime. Anything else we can do for you?'

'Not at present. You can get on your way.'

The two officers headed across the car park, as unruffled as if what had just happened was all in a day's work – but then, for them, it was. I was mildly surprised by how effective Vickers had been at manhandling the photographer, but I really shouldn't have been. He would have done his time on the street in uniform too, even if it had been decades before.

He turned back to me. 'Are you all right?'

I realised that I was shivering and my hands were clammy. 'Yes. I suppose so. Thank you for that.'

Vickers laughed. 'For nothing. That was my pleasure. She's an evil cow, that Shapley woman, and you've had enough trouble from her for one lifetime.' He gave me a sidelong look. 'Besides, I like to think that it might make up for what happened today.'

'It wouldn't have happened at all if you hadn't arrested me in the first place,' I pointed out.

'How right you are. Ah, well, I still owe you a favour, then, for agreeing to help us with Paul. Don't worry, I won't forget.'

'Don't worry. Neither will I.' But I was smiling as I said it. I couldn't imagine how Vickers would be able to repay me, but that wasn't the point. What he was telling me was that I was back on his side, on the side of the angels, and it felt like a good place to be.

I was going to end the day where I had started it, I realised, as I tracked Vickers through the corridors towards the paediatric unit at St Martin's, where Paul was recovering under the watchful gaze of DS Blake. Blake leaped to his feet when Vickers pushed open the door. I moved from behind Vickers to look at the bed where Paul was lying curled up on his side, his eyes closed.

'Thanks for coming in, Sarah,' Blake said, digging his hands into his pockets.

I ignored him, my attention on Paul. His breathing was hoarse, his cheeks were flushed and sweat had slicked his hair to his forehead.

'Is he OK?' I asked, keeping my voice low.

'He's been in and out all day. The doctors are happy

with him – say he's recovering well, all things considered. They won't let us talk to him for very long when he is awake, and we can't wake him up, I'm afraid, even though you're here.'

'I wouldn't let you,' I said, surprised and not a little irritated. 'I don't mind waiting. I have Paul's interests at heart.' I didn't say *even if you don't*, but the words hung in the air as if I had.

Vickers jumped in before Blake had a chance to reply. 'Speaking of Paul's interests, this is Audrey Jones, Paul's social worker.' He gestured to the corner of the room, where a middle-aged woman was sitting, arms folded under her big, cushiony bosom. 'Motherly' was the word that came to mind – whatever that meant. Neither Paul nor I had experience of that sort of mother. In fact, Paul probably didn't remember his own mother at all, as he had been so young when she died. Audrey nodded at me pleasantly enough, and went on sitting. Dynamic she wasn't, and not particularly interested in the latest visitor either. I could see why she hadn't been much use to Vickers, all in all.

There were only two chairs in the room and Audrey was occupying one. Blake had stepped away from the other, but I didn't feel I could claim it. I was so tired I felt lightheaded. I needed to sit down and I needed caffeine in large quantities.

'Do you think he'll be asleep for much longer?'

'Probably another half hour,' Blake said, checking his watch. 'He comes and goes, but he's due some food in a while, and that should wake him up.'

'Do you mind if I go and get a cup of coffee?' I said,

turning to Vickers. I knew I wasn't a prisoner any more, but I still didn't feel I could walk out of the room without his permission.

The chief inspector hesitated for a fraction of a second, but assented. 'Why don't you take Andy with you?' he suggested as I reached the door, almost as if it was an afterthought. 'I can mind young Paul, and you could do with a cuppa, couldn't you Andy? The canteen's in the basement, I believe.'

Without waiting for me to answer, Blake was striding towards the door. I clearly wasn't getting a choice. I gave Vickers a look that I hoped would convey *I know your game*, and got the limpid baby blues in return. He could have had a dazzling career as a criminal if he'd taken another path in life, I reflected. No one on earth would have believed him capable of wrongdoing of any kind. At least, not at first glance.

'We really are grateful to you, you know,' Blake began as soon as the heavy door closed behind us. 'Especially with what happened today.'

'Being accused of being a paedophile and a murderer? Oh, forget it. Happens all the time.'

'Look, I never thought it was true.'

I stopped at that, looked at him for a beat, then stalked on, shaking my head. It was a shame that Blake's legs were so much longer than mine. He had an unfair advantage in the keeping-up stakes.

'We had to arrest you, you know. We couldn't do it any other way. Not once you said you weren't going to cooperate any more.'

'And search my house? Go through my things? Talk to my mother? You couldn't have done that without arresting me, could you?'

A muscle jumped in his jaw. 'That wasn't fun.'

So he had been there. I turned away, wanting to hide my face, afraid that my mortification was easy for him to read.

'I didn't believe it, Sarah. But what was I supposed to say? "She can't possibly be guilty because I've slept with her"? I don't even know you – not properly. I didn't have anything concrete I could use to contradict the evidence. Instinct isn't enough.' He'd been speaking at full volume and I frowned at him. Belatedly, he recalled where he was and looked up and down the corridor, checking to see if anyone had overheard.

'I don't think this is the time or the place to talk about it.' I stabbed the button to call the lift, imagining it was Andy Blake's eye.

He leaned against the wall and folded his arms. 'I don't want you to think that I wasn't doing my best to get you out of there today. I stood up for you.'

I laughed. 'You're not getting it, are you? I don't care. Whether you believed I was guilty or not doesn't matter to me in the slightest. I don't care what you thought, or what you think now. I'm not here for your sake, and I'm not here because Vickers asked me so nicely. I just want to help Paul, help the Shepherds and get out of here.'

'Fine,' Blake said, his jaw clenched. 'Let's just drop it, OK?'

I didn't respond. The lift was empty when it arrived and I stood with my back against the wall on one side, as far away from Blake as I could get. He pressed the button for the basement and leaned back against the other side, watching the indicator change as the lift sank down.

Something else was bothering me.

'What is it?' he said, without looking at me, as if I had spoken.

'Did you have to say that in there?'

'Say what?'

'About Paul waking up for food. If he heard you, do you have any idea how hurt he would be?'

'Christ, I didn't mean – I wasn't even talking about Paul.' Blake sighed. 'Every two hours the catering staff come around with the trolley. They practically batter the fucking door down with it. It sounds like the end of the world, and if he could sleep through that I'd be very surprised.'

'Oh,' I said, in a small voice, and couldn't think of another thing to say until we had queued up for polystyrene cups filled with steaming liquid. Blake had something greyish that purported to be tea, while I had opted for coffee. It moved like tar and I hoped it was as strong as it looked. He led the way to a table that was far enough away from the other users of the canteen to allow us a little privacy. We were in the original hospital building and the room was cavernous, Victorian architecture at its most lugubrious. The walls were white-painted brick, reinforced with arches that contained heavy cast-iron radiators on full blast in spite of the mild weather. Half-moon windows ran around the top of the room just above ground level, and let in a paltry amount of natural light. All of the lighting at that time of the evening was artificial, however, and the canteen was bathed in the harsh glare of energy-efficient bulbs in great glass shades. Small round laminated tables and stackable plastic chairs filled the room, looking flimsy against the heavy-duty background of Victorian engineering competence. The canteen wasn't busy – just a few tables were occupied, some with staff, some with dressing-gowned patients sitting with their families or on their own. The hot food had looked villainous when we walked past the counter, belching steam under heat lamps, and I could hardly believe that it was worth the effort to get out of bed and come to the canteen for dinner.

Across the table, Blake stirred his tea with intense concentration, ignoring me. Maybe Vickers hadn't sent him to make sure I didn't escape. Maybe he had really thought his subordinate needed a break. The unforgiving lights gave a bleak, greyish cast to Blake's skin. He looked exhausted.

'Are you OK?' I asked, suddenly needing to know.

'I'm all right. Tired.'

'At least you're getting somewhere.'

He winced. 'When we aren't arresting people who have nothing to do with the case.'

'Seriously, forget about it. I'll get over it.'

He took a sip of tea and his face contorted. 'Jesus. How's the coffee?'

'Hot,' I said, watching the steam curl up from the cup in front of me. I couldn't stop thinking about something that Grange had said to me. 'Andy – there was one thing I wanted to know. They said – they said that the team was suspicious of me from the start.'

He shifted in his chair. 'That's just routine, Sarah.'

'Is it? Because I was thinking . . . when you came and took me out to lunch, that was part of it, wasn't it? You were trying to find out more about me. Vickers probably sent you, didn't he?'

Blake had the grace to look embarrassed. 'It wasn't the worst job I've been told to do, believe me.'

I had really tried, over the previous few days, not to assume anything about Andrew Blake. I had been careful to have no expectations. I certainly hadn't imagined a future for us. But it wasn't until that moment that I knew for certain that nothing was ever going to happen between us. I managed a brittle laugh. 'I thought you liked me.'

'I did – I do. Look, Sarah, everything that's happened since then has nothing to do with the job. I met you – what, six days ago? And in the beginning, my only interest was in finding out more about you. But then, things changed.' He leaned across the table. 'You seem to think I don't care about what happened between us, but I could lose my job if that came out. It was risky, Sarah, and stupid, and I don't regret it for a second.'

And the risk was probably part of the thrill, I thought miserably. 'It must happen to you a lot – women throwing themselves at you.'

'Because I'm such a catch,' Blake said, his voice laden with sarcasm. 'Look, it does happen now and then – of course it does.'

I thought of the policewoman at the station glaring at me, of Valerie Wade's frantic determination to keep me and Blake apart, and I reckoned it happened more than occasionally.

'It doesn't mean I act on it,' Blake went on. 'I never do, if it's connected with work. Until you came along.'

'How flattering,' I said thinly, defences still up. 'But you still arrested me. You didn't even question me yourself.' The hurt rang through my voice in spite of my best efforts to suppress it.

'Routine,' Blake said quickly. 'Don't believe what you see on TV – it's never the investigating officers that do it. Grange and Cooper are trained for it. They're good at what they do.'

'I believe you.' I hadn't exactly appreciated their techniques, all the same.

'Sarah, I did know you weren't involved, even if you don't believe me.'

'What if I had been? Like you said, you don't know me. What if they'd proved that I was part of it? Would you have cared then?'

'Well – probably not.' He sat back and shrugged. 'If you commit a crime like that, you've got to take what's coming to you. Once you step over the line, that's it.'

'And there's no way back?'

'Not as far as I'm concerned. That's why I do this job – because there are some people who don't belong in society. The way they choose to live hurts other people, and my job is to stop them. Simple as that.'

'What about Paul?'

'What about him?'

'He's just a kid. He's probably been coerced into taking part in all of this. I'm not really comfortable with asking him questions about it. I don't want to be the one to trick him into implicating himself. I mean, what's going to happen to him?'

'It's up to the courts to decide, not you.' Blake looked at me and frowned. 'You have to appreciate that he's done something very bad indeed, Sarah. He's committed a serious crime, and whatever the circumstances, he deserves to be punished. Criminals – no matter who they are – have to take responsibility for what they've done. It kills me when you get them to court, the things they come out with. It's never their fault. They always have some excuse, even when they're pleading guilty. But there's no excuse for something like this. He's old enough to know the difference between right and wrong, and if there are extenuating circumstances, the courts will take them into account.'

'It's all black and white, isn't it?'

'As far as I'm concerned, yes.' All business again, he pulled a folded sheet of paper out of the back pocket of his jeans. 'I've got this for you – it's a list of questions we'd like you to ask him. There are a few things we really need to know before we talk to his brother.'

'If you catch him.'

'We'll catch him.' He sounded very sure of himself. But then, they had seemed very confident when they arrested me. I found myself wondering if Vickers and his team really knew what they were doing.

'Have a read through that,' Blake said, nodding at the paper. It was lying in front of me, still folded over. 'It's just to give you somewhere to start. You don't have to stick to those exact questions in that order, but try to make sure you get the answers we need.'

'I'll do my best,' I said, suddenly nervous on my own account. He noticed and smiled.

'You'll do OK. Just take your time and try not to get flustered. We'll be there, but we won't interrupt unless you're really in difficulties.'

'It's just a conversation.'

'You'd be surprised how easy it is to forget the most important questions when you're in there,' Blake warned. 'It all seems pretty easy, sitting here, but when you're listening to the answers and asking follow-up questions, you can get sidetracked and never get back on course.'

'I understand.'

'Here.' He handed me a pen. 'You can make some notes if you need to.'

I pulled the cap off the pen and unfolded the paper. The list was shorter than I'd expected. How Paul knew Jenny. How they got the idea to abuse her. Who came up with the plan. How Paul was involved. Why he didn't do anything to stop it.

'I don't think it's fair to ask him that,' I said, pointing to the last question. 'He's just a kid, and he's totally dependent on his brother. What would you expect him to do? Call the police?'

Blake sighed. 'Look, if he tells you he was too scared to say anything, or that he was threatened, that could help him. You're right, he probably didn't have any choice but to help, but we need to know that before we talk to his brother.'

'All right.'

'If you get the chance, we also want to know how they

convinced Jennifer to go along with it and keep it a secret. Did they threaten her? Bribe her with presents? We didn't find anything out of the ordinary when we searched the Shepherds' house – no electronics that the parents hadn't bought themselves, no jewellery. She tested negative for drugs, too.' I must have looked surprised, because Blake explained, 'Get them hooked on drugs and they'll do pretty much anything for a fix.'

In spite of the stuffy atmosphere in the canteen, I shivered. 'Maybe they used something you didn't test for.'

'Unlikely,' Blake said shortly. 'Anyway, there had to have been something that kept her coming back and kept her quiet. We need to know what it was.' He stirred his tea. 'We also want you to ask about the other abusers – we need to ID them as soon as possible, and so far we haven't found anyone who recognises them. The computer experts are trying to undo the pixellation on their faces. In the meantime, we're circulating some of the non-sexual images that feature them, to see if any coppers in other stations spot a familiar tattoo or birthmark, but there isn't much to go on.'

I nodded. That was something I didn't feel any reluctance about. The men who'd abused Jenny deserved everything they got.

Blake must have read something in my face, because he reached across the table and touched the back of my hand. 'Hey – don't get too caught up in all this. I know it's hard.'

'I'm fine,' I said, and tried to mean it.

'Yeah, well, you might think that. But we've got you

doing something that you're not trained to do, and it's a big responsibility. I told the boss I thought this was a bad idea.'

'Why? Don't you think I'm capable of asking a few questions?'

He shook his head. 'It's dealing with the answers that might cause you problems, Sarah. You've got to be prepared to hear some unpleasant things.'

'I've seen and heard quite a bit today, thanks,' I said levelly, thinking without wanting to of the glossy photographs that Grange had taken such pleasure in showing me.

'Yeah, but you haven't had to keep your composure. You haven't had to pace the questions. You haven't done an interview that didn't go anywhere.' He leaned back in the chair and stretched. 'I know you think you're going to go in there and he's going to tell you everything that happened, up to and including how his brother killed Jennifer Shepherd, but I've got to tell you, more than likely you'll get nothing from this. He has no real reason to trust you. He's got a hell of a lot to lose if he's honest with you. You aren't exactly in-timidating – and there's no point in looking at me like that; I'm not quaking in my boots over here. Don't take it personally. You just might not hear what you're expect-ing to hear.'

I knew he was right, but it was still irritating to be told that I was going to fail. 'Should we get back?'

Blake checked his watch. 'Yeah. Finish your coffee.'

I eyed the half-cup I had left. Now that it had gone cold, it was even less appetising than it had been when freshly brewed, if that was the word for what they'd done to it. 'No thanks.'

'I don't blame you.'

We didn't talk on the way back. When the lift arrived on the fourth floor, Blake strode back to the paediatric wing while I wandered along behind him, reading through the questions, feeling the tingle of nerves down my spine and in my fingertips. The words seemed to dance on the page and I found myself slowing down, dragging my feet. Outside the door to Paul's room, I ground to a halt, trying to pace my breathing. Blake looked around.

'Come on. Sooner you go in, the sooner it'll be over.'

'I'm just . . . preparing.'

'Get in there,' he said gently, and pushed the door open. I took one more deep breath, as if I was diving into deep water, and went in.

1998

Five years, seven months missing

My father is late. Very late. I lie in bed and cuddle my toy pig, frowning at the clock on my bedside table. It's nearly eleven o'clock and he hasn't called. It's not like him to be so late. Every time a car drives past our house, which isn't often, I get up and look to see if it's him. I don't know why I care. Every two weeks, he comes, and every two weeks it's exactly the same. He drives from Bristol on Friday night and comes to the house to say hello to me. He waits outside in his car, because Mum won't let him come in. He spends that night and the Saturday night in a Travelodge, and on the Saturday we go out together and do something that's supposed to be fun, like a walk in the country, or a trip to a stately home or safari park – something boring, something I would never choose to do if it wasn't for Dad.

He shows me pictures of the flat in Bristol, of the room that he says is for me, and the cupboard I can fill with clothes. I've never been there. Mum won't let me go. So Dad comes every two weeks instead, with this look on his face like a pleading dog, like he knows it's not enough but he hopes I don't mind.

I mind. And I'm old enough now to show it.

Lately, I've been wondering if I should tell him not to bother coming every two weeks – once a month would be enough for me. But I know it means a lot to him.

Or does it? I lie on my back and look at the shapes the trees make on the bedroom ceiling. I'll have to draw the curtains before I can go to sleep. He isn't coming. Maybe he's fed up with driving all that way for two nights in a shitty hotel, even though this is supposed to be my birthday weekend. Maybe he just doesn't care about me any more.

I let the tears slide down the sides of my face into my hair. After a while, I get distracted by the tears themselves. I'm trying to get them to fall equally on both sides. For some reason, my right eye is much more teary than the other one. I forget why I'm crying for a second, and then it all comes back. It's stupid, anyway. I don't even care.

Two seconds later I prove I've been lying to myself, as a car stops outside the house and I leap off the bed to look out the window. But it isn't Dad's crappy Rover. It's a police car. And

I stand by the window, unable to move, watching the policemen get out and put on their caps, then come slowly up the drive. They aren't hurrying, and that worries me.

As the policemen disappear under the porch, I pad out to sit at the top of the stairs, out of sight but within earshot.

Mum answers the door and the first thing she says is, 'Charlie!'

Stupid. They aren't here about Charlie. Even I know that.

Mumble mumble mumble. Mrs Barnes. Mumble mumble. Mr Barnes was driving on the motorway. Very dark. Mumble mumble. Lorry driver couldn't avoid him . . .

'He didn't have time to get himself out of trouble,' I hear suddenly, clearly, from one of the officers.

I can't help putting it all together. I don't want to know what they're saying. I can't avoid it though. This isn't what I want. This isn't how I want it to be. My feet are bare and they have got very cold from being out of bed on a February night, especially when the front door is wide open. I hold on to my feet as tightly as I can and I clench my toes and I wish the police officers out of the house, back down the drive, into their car, as if I can rewind them and the rest of the day. I rewind and rewind to the last time Dad was here, to the time before that, to the time before he left. None of it has happened. None of it is real.

There's still time to change everything so it all works out. There's still time for everything to be OK after all.

Chapter 15

This time, the television was on in the hospital room, and Paul was sitting up in bed, propped against the pillows, flicking through the channels at high speed. He didn't look away from the screen as Blake followed me in. I stopped by the foot of the bed and looked a question at Vickers, who was slumped in one of the chairs with the general demeanour of someone who had reached the end of his reserves of patience.

'We've had some food,' he announced, with a nod to indicate he was talking about Paul. 'We haven't felt much like talking, though.'

Paul's eyelids flickered, but he kept gazing at the TV. There were only five channels on the hospital service, and absolutely nothing to watch on any of them, but that didn't seem to be putting him off. One of the channels was showing a news bulletin, and I flinched as the high street appeared behind yet another reporter updating the nation on the latest developments in the hunt for Jenny's murderer. Paul didn't seem to react, just carried on. I guessed that the TV was a delaying tactic, that he wasn't really seeing it. The Paul I had met on Friday – had it really been just a day ago? – was very far from mindless. The inane channel-hopping was a smokescreen.

His eyes were red, with blue puffy shadows under them,

and now that he was sitting up I could see the mark on his neck – a raw, livid line that tracked across under his jaw and up to his ear. No cry for help; that had been the real deal. If he'd used a different kind of rope . . . if the police had been a little bit slower . . . it didn't bear thinking about.

I felt a nudge in the small of my back: Blake, who frowned at me meaningfully.

'OK, OK,' I mouthed, glaring back. I walked slowly around the bed so I was standing between Paul and the TV.

'Hi. It's good to see you again, Paul. How are you feeling?'

He looked at me for a moment, then dropped his gaze.

'There really aren't enough chairs to go around, so do you mind if I sit on the bed? And can I turn the TV off so we can talk?'

He shrugged and I sat down, then took the remote control out of his hands and hit standby. The room was very quiet once the TV was off. I sat for a moment, listening to the air whistling in and out of Paul's lungs. His throat had to be very sore if the bruising on his neck was anything to go by.

'Do you want a drink?'

'Yes please,' he croaked, and I poured him a glass of water from the pitcher on the nightstand by the bed. He took a sip, then fumbled the glass back down.

'Paul, the police have asked me to talk to you because they think you'll answer me if I ask you some questions.'

He looked up, then returned to staring at his hands without speaking.

'I know you think you're in trouble, but everything is going to be OK,' I said, sounding confident, fairly sure that I was lying to him. 'We just need to know what happened. Please, Paul, just tell me the truth if you can. If there's anything you don't want to answer, just say and I'll move on, OK?'

I felt rather than heard Blake react to that, but Vickers raised one hand reprovingly and nodded to me when I glanced at him. I would ask the questions, but I wouldn't browbeat Paul. And I knew as well as Vickers did that the questions he *didn't* answer would give the game away.

Paul hadn't said anything and I leaned in closer. 'Is that OK?'

He nodded.

'Right.' I didn't need to consult the sheet of paper in my hand to recall the first question. 'How did you and your brother get to know Jenny?'

'I told you that already.' Paul spoke distinctly, slowly, biting off the end of each word. Colour washed up into his face and I knew he was annoyed.

'I know you did,' I said soothingly. '*I* remember, but these policemen don't know about it. Just tell me for their sake.'

'School,' Paul said finally, having glared at me for a moment.

'Primary school,' I clarified.

'Yeah. She was my friend in school. I helped her with her maths and she – she was nice to me.'

'And you stayed in touch when she went to a different school?'

He shrugged. 'She knew where I lived – we'd talked about it, cos we were the only ones in our class who lived on the estate. One day there was a knock at the door and it was her. She'd been having trouble with geometry – she just didn't get it – and she asked if I'd give her a hand.'

'And you did,' I said.

'Yeah.' His voice was gruff and low. Even allowing for the hoarseness, he sounded upset.

'So, Paul, you and Jenny were spending time together at your house. And her parents didn't know about it.'

'Her dad didn't like me. He called me a fat freak.' Paul's eyes swam in tears for a second and he blinked them away, sniffing.

'How did she get to spend time at your house, then?'

'She told them she was with her friends. There was some girl who lived nearby, and she'd cycle off to see her, supposedly. She had a mobile – her dad made her have one so they could track her down – and she'd tell them she was places she wasn't.' Paul laughed a little, remembering. 'She'd ask if they wanted to speak to her friends' mums when they rang her up and I'd be sitting there, shitting myself. She was like that – always laughing, always playing games.'

I nodded, and looked down at my list of questions. It was hard to make myself say the words, but I couldn't avoid it for ever.

'Paul, you know that the police found . . . things at your house. Images. Video. Pictures of Jenny, doing things. Did you – I mean, were you – did you think of it in the first place?'

He looked wounded and shook his head, cheeks quivering. 'No. It was all them – him and her.'

'Him?'

'Danny. I told him it wasn't right. He shouldn't have gone near her, no matter what she said. He's too old for her.' Paul was struggling to sit up, lashing out with his legs, distressed. I stood up quickly to avoid getting kicked.

'It's OK, Paul. Just calm down. Have some more water.'

The boy took a few deep, quivering breaths, then drank obediently. The water gurgled as he swallowed it; there wasn't a sound from anyone else in the room. I could feel the policemen willing me to stop pussyfooting around.

'At some stage, something must have happened,' I said quietly, sitting down again, 'because she got involved with your brother, didn't she?'

'Dunno,' Paul said. His face was very red.

'Was she frightened by him?' I tried to keep my voice as gentle as possible. 'Was that why she kept coming back? Did he threaten her?'

'No way,' Paul said. 'It wasn't like that. She – she liked him.'

'So as far as she was concerned, they were boyfriend and girlfriend.'

'I guess. Stupid, really, cos he's loads older than her.' Paul sighed. 'Danny wasn't interested in her. Not really. She just – she loved spending time with him. She'd do anything for him.'

That 'anything' meant a world of degradation. My mouth had gone dry and I swallowed, trying to concentrate on the job I had to do. Blake had thought I wouldn't be able to handle this. I didn't want him to be right. I took a few seconds to breathe, letting the images fade away, then started again.

'Was it your idea to use the internet to sell the videos and pictures of her?'

Paul shook his head again, then shrugged. 'Sort of. Danny thought of it, but it was me who had to work out how to do it – hide our IP, find sites to host the images, build the websites.' In spite of everything, he sounded proud of what he had achieved. 'We were making real money. People from all over the world were buying our stuff.'

I couldn't stand it any longer. 'But Jenny suffered so that you could make those images.'

'Whatever,' Paul said, and his nose wrinkled.

'No, not "whatever". You're talking about this like it was a legitimate business, but Jenny was being abused, Paul. Don't tell me you didn't know about it.'

He wriggled. 'I didn't really know about a lot of the stuff that was going on. Danny made me stay in my room whenever they were – you know.'

I could guess.

'Did you meet the other men who came to the house?'

'No. I had to stay upstairs.'

'Do you know what they were doing at your house?'

'Having a party, sounded like.' He was definitely looking uncomfortable. I wondered what he had heard. I wondered how hard it had been for Danny to persuade his 'girlfriend' to put herself at the disposal of those men. I wondered if she had screamed, now and then.

'So you didn't see anything when the pictures and videos

were being made. Did you look at the pictures or watch the videos afterwards?'

'No.' That was an outright lie; his ears were flaming scarlet but his eyes never left mine. 'Danny told me he'd stop the whole thing if he caught me looking. He told me he'd batter the living daylights out of me. I was just supposed to set everything up and let him upload it.'

'Does he ever hit you?' Grotesquely, I was hoping he would say yes. An abused Paul had a reason for going along with the plan.

'Nah. All talk, that's all he is. I'll skin you alive, I'll smash his skull in, I'll rip her head off, fucking this and fucking that . . . ' Paul laughed. 'He's always having a rant about something. I just ignore him, mostly.'

'You said he told you he'd stop if you looked at the images – didn't you want him to stop?'

'No way. It was really good, you know. Jenny was always round at ours. She was really happy, most of the time – blubbed now and then, but girls do, don't they? And Danny was happy that we weren't skint any more. And I was able to help. That was good – bringing in some cash. I wanted to do it, for Danny.'

I cleared my throat. 'And was Jenny paid for her part in it?'

He looked vague. 'I don't think so. I don't think she wanted anything. She would have had to hide it from her parents and it was all a bit too much hassle, I think. She just wanted to be with Danny.'

Poor, stupid Jenny, infatuated with a man who was prepared to use her to subsidise his lifestyle. Bad luck that she encountered someone like that at such a young age. Worse luck that Danny was a pretty boy, with the kind of doe eyes and fine features that appealed to teenage girls. And worst of all was the fact that he'd been prepared to kill her once he was finished with her.

'So tell me about how she died.' My voice was neutral, as if the question wasn't really that important, but my palms were sweating. I wiped them surreptitiously on the bedclothes, aware that Vickers and Blake were leaning in, hardly breathing, waiting for Paul to speak.

He frowned. 'I don't know anything about it. Really. I told you that already, when you were at the house.'

I nodded; he had said that. As far as I could tell, he had meant it, too. So Danny had managed to kill Jenny and get rid of the body behind Paul's back. I supposed there were things that even Danny felt Paul shouldn't know about.

'When did you last see her?'

He thought for a second. 'Middle of last week, after school. She shut herself in the living room with Danny, but not for very long. She ran off – never even said goodbye to me. She was all upset about something, but Danny didn't know what it was.'

I was absolutely sure that Danny Keane knew exactly what it was. I could just imagine it. Jenny, confused and scared, going to the man she loved to tell him she was pregnant, and Danny panicking. He couldn't let her tell her parents about him. Maybe she'd refused to have an abortion. Maybe he hadn't even suggested it. The easiest thing of all was to end two lives in one go, and get rid of the whole problem once and for all. But he hadn't made the problem go away. He'd brought it right to his door, and mine.

'And how has Danny been behaving since then – since the middle of last week?'

'Up and down. He was well shocked when he heard about Jenny being – you know. He came in, swearing and that, stuck the TV on *Sky News* and watched it for hours. He couldn't believe she was gone.'

Or he felt guilty about what he'd done. Or he was reliving the excitement of killing her through the exhaustive reports on the rolling news programmes. Or he was watching to see if there was any hint that the police were on to him.

Paul was carrying on, childishly candid. 'He was gutted – crying, a bit, whenever her picture came up. I thought he was going to go mental when he watched the first report. He kicked the leg right off that chair – you know, the one I showed you.'

I remembered the chair. I could imagine Danny sitting at the table, jumping up in anger and fear: anger that she had been found, fear that he would be caught. It hadn't gone to plan and he had lashed out.

I don't know what showed on my face, but Paul looked at me worriedly. 'You believe me, don't you? He was really upset. It was the end of everything. Everything he'd worked for.'

'Everything he'd worked for was illegal. Everything he'd worked for, he got as a result of the suffering of your friend.'

'She was OK,' Paul said sulkily. 'She wanted to help. It was her choice to be there.'

'I find that very hard to believe,' I countered, not caring that I sounded angry. 'Anyway, if it was such a good job, I'm sure you wouldn't have had any trouble in finding a new girl to take over from her. Danny could have recruited someone, I'm sure.'

'Yeah, but she was perfect, Jenny – she looked right and she knew you. He'd never have got that lucky again.'

I started. 'What do you mean? Why would it matter that she knew me?'

'Danny is, like, obsessed with you.' Paul laughed. 'He made Jenny leave her hair down because that's how you used to have yours when you were her age. He made her dress like you too. Things he remembered you wearing – tops and stuff. He'd go shopping for clothes for Jenny, surprise her with presents to wear at our house. She couldn't take them home in case her parents saw them. She never knew it was because of you. But he was always on at Jenny to tell him stuff about you – what you'd said in school, what sort of mood you'd been in. He couldn't get enough of it. It used to piss her off.'

'Why,' I said, with some difficulty, 'did your brother care about me? We haven't even spoken to one another in years. He doesn't even know me.'

'He knows loads,' Paul said confidently. 'He used to keep an eye on you – you know, watch you coming and going, make sure you were OK. He wanted to know anything to do with you. Basically –' and he started to blush '– he says he's in love with you.' The last sentence was delivered in a low, gruff voice, and I thought for a second I had misheard. I looked over to the two policemen. Vickers nodded at me, encouraging me to go on. Blake raised his eyebrows. They'd heard it too, then.

'He can't be,' I said flatly, returning to Paul. 'You can't love someone you don't know.'

'He does.' Paul sounded certain. 'He just does. He's been in love with you for years.'

An image flashed into my mind. 'In the front room, there are shelves, aren't there. And they've got all sorts of stuff on them – random things, like keys, a pen, old postcards – bits and pieces of junk, really. Things you wouldn't usually put on a shelf.'

Paul was nodding. 'Danny calls it his trophy cabinet. It's all the things that are really important to him. He keeps them in there because I'm not allowed to go in and he thinks I'd break them or something. But I look at them when he's out at work, and I've never broken anything.'

'Paul, quite a few things on the shelves belong to me. Do you know how they got there?'

'Jenny got them for him.' He sounded totally matter-of-fact. 'She got whatever she could off your desk or out of your bag while she was in school. She used to try to get to class before everyone else, and while she was in there on her own, she'd look for things for Danny.'

I remembered walking into my classroom at lunchtime and finding Jenny in there, half an hour early for her English class. I'd made a joke out of it, I recalled, a bitter taste filling my mouth. I'd thought she was so keen on English, so willing to learn. I'd thought she liked my classes. Another thing I'd got wrong.

When I didn't say anything, Paul sighed. 'It's all fucked up, isn't it? We were all trying to do things for other people. Jenny made the videos and nicked stuff because she wanted to impress Danny. I went along with it because it meant I got to see her all the time.' He looked at me pleadingly. 'She might not have come round if it was just me. I didn't think she'd bother if it wasn't for Danny. Even if she wasn't there to see me, it sort of didn't matter.'

'So she was there for Danny, and you helped because of her.'

'She'd do anything for him. And I'd do anything for her. And I know you don't get it, but Danny – Danny would do whatever he had to, just to get closer to you. All the money we made – he was saving it up so he could buy a house. Get himself a decent car. He was going to ask you out. You were all he talked about.'

No one said anything. It became clear, suddenly, why Paul had been so desperate to help me, why he had trusted me enough to talk about what he and his brother had done. Danny would have wanted to protect me – *again*, I thought with a shiver, forcing an unwanted memory back into the darkest recesses of my mind. Paul was just doing his best for his brother, as ever. I wondered why hospitals always had to be so hot. The air in the room was thick and soupy, and suddenly intolerable.

Just then, there was a quiet knock at the door. Blake hurried over and opened it, leaning through the gap to have a whispered conversation. I caught a glimpse of a bullish head; my old friend from outside Geoff's room. I felt slightly guilty at the thought of Geoff. I had pretty much forgotten him all day. Of course, I'd had troubles of my own to deal with.

Paul was leaning back against the pillows, looking out the window. Vickers had stood up and was easing the waistband of his trousers slowly, mindlessly. I knew his complete attention was focused on the conversation that was taking place at the door, that he had probably forgotten that I was there at all. The social worker continued to sit, the same benign expression on her face. It was as if she'd heard none of Paul's confession. How, I wondered, could you sit and listen to that easy recitation of the bleak and sordid details of the brothers' crimes without feeling something? In fairness, outrage wasn't an ideal reaction in a social worker. Some sort of glimmer of awareness would have been nice, though.

Blake let the door swing closed and spoke to Vickers as if no one else was in the room. 'We're on.'

Vickers made a low sound in his throat: satisfaction, a big cat's purr at having brought down its prey. He turned to Paul. 'We'll leave you in peace, young man. You concentrate on getting better, and don't worry about all of this.'

The words were meant and said kindly, but Paul looked totally unimpressed. He closed his eyes, shutting the rest of us out. I couldn't help but feel that Vickers was wrong – Paul had every reason to be worried. I wondered how they were going to handle his case – if he was going to be prosecuted, or if they would take into consideration his age and his cooperation and just take him into care. There was no one else to look after him. For good or bad, he was on his own.

Seeing that I was about to be left behind, I jumped up and followed Vickers as he headed out of the room, hard on Blake's heels.

The three policemen had gone into a little huddle outside in the corridor by the time I got there. I let the heavy door close gently behind me and waited for them to finish. Bull-neck was receiving instructions, nodding intently as Vickers spoke in a voice too soft for me to overhear. After a couple of minutes, the stocky policeman detached himself from the group, muttering 'excuse me' as he edged past me into Paul's room. The changing of the guard, I guessed, which meant that Vickers and Blake had somewhere better to be.

'Did you find him?'

They turned, looking startled, and Blake glanced at Vickers for permission to tell me what was going on. The older man nodded.

'They picked up Daniel Keane an hour ago at Victoria Coach Station. He was boarding a coach to Amsterdam when they spotted him. He's being transferred back here as we speak, so we're heading back to the station.'

'That's brilliant,' I said, meaning it. 'Give him my best if you get the chance, won't you.'

'Oh, we'll be asking him about you, don't worry. He has a lot of explaining to do.'

Vickers was looking restless. 'We should get going, Andy. Sorry, Sarah, but I think we need to head off.'

'Fine. I understand.'

'Are you OK to get home from here?' Blake asked. 'Reception will give you the number for a taxi company.'

'Don't worry about me. I'll probably check in on Geoff again before I go.'

The two men went very still. I looked from one to the other, seeing the same expression on their faces. 'What?'

'Sarah—' Blake began, but Vickers spoke over him.

'I'm sorry, but he's gone.'

'Gone?' I repeated stupidly, hoping I had misunderstood.

'He died just after two o'clock this afternoon.' The inspector's voice was gentle. 'He never regained consciousness, I'm afraid.'

'But – but they weren't even really worried about him earlier.' I was struggling to take it in.

'He had a massive bleed in his brain, caused by the head injuries he sustained in the attack.' Blake, lapsing into notebook-speak. 'There was nothing they could do. I'm sorry.'

'That makes two,' I whispered.

'Two?'

'Jenny and Geoff. Two people who should be here. Two people who didn't deserve what happened to them.' My voice sounded strange in my ears – lifeless, hard. 'Don't let him get away with it.'

'We won't,' Blake said with conviction.

'Why don't you go and have a little sit down,' Vickers suggested. 'Take a few minutes, then go home and get some rest. Is there anyone you'd like us to call for you?'

I shook my head.

He took out a fat brown leather wallet, shiny as a conker from years of use, and extracted a business card. 'If you need anything, my number is on there.' He pointed. 'You call me if you need to.'

'Thank you.'

'I mean it.' He reached out and patted my shoulder.

'Right.' I occupied myself with putting the card in my handbag. 'Please, don't worry about me. I'll be OK.'

'That's the girl,' Vickers said. 'We'll be in touch, anyway. We'll let you know what he says.'

I nodded and managed a half-smile that seemed enough to reassure them. They headed off in the direction of the lifts, walking fast. I stood in the centre of the corridor, threading the handle of my bag through my fingers over and over again, until a small pyjama-clad girl asked me to get out of her way. I jumped to one side and watched as she forged past, dragging a drip on a stand that was much taller than she was. She had such a sense of purpose, wherever she was going. I leaned against the wall, drained of energy, and wondered what that would be like. I had never felt so useless in my entire life.

The corridor was not an ideal place to stand, and after moving for a third time to get out of someone's way, I drifted towards a door marked 'exit'. Pushing it open, I discovered a flight of stairs, and trudged down as far as the ground floor, forcing myself to put one foot in front of the other, holding on to the banister. There I found a door that someone had propped open, and wandered out onto a paved area with a few garden benches scattered around it. It seemed to be the smoking area for those patients who were mobile enough to get outside for a cigarette now and then. Metal containers were nailed to the ends of the benches, each one piled with cigarette butts, and the acrid smell of scorched tobacco hung in the air.

The area was deserted now, the night air being a degree or two below what was comfortable. I sat down on the bench furthest from the door and folded my arms, shivering deep within myself in a way that had nothing to do with the air temperature.

It was all too much. That was the phrase that kept repeating in my mind. Too much. Too much suffering. Too many secrets. I couldn't begin to make sense of what I felt about the news that Geoff had died. Just because he wouldn't take no for an answer, Geoff had put himself in the path of a whirlwind. Geoff's ego had led him into a collision with a man who harboured a true obsession, who wouldn't let anything stand between him and what he wanted. And what Danny Keane wanted, it was apparent, was me.

I pulled my knees up to my chest and wrapped my arms around them, squeezing tightly, leaning my forehead on my kneecaps. None of this was my fault. None of this was because of anything I had done. I wasn't special, or remarkable. Danny had projected something on to me that I wasn't, had assumed that I was exceptional in a way that I wouldn't dream of claiming for myself. I was just ordinary. The only thing that was different about me was the guilt that had trapped me in my tedious life like a moth on a collector's pinboard. But because of me, Danny Keane had left bloody fingerprints all over people's lives – the Shepherds, Geoff's family, poor fat Paul. I dug my nails into my upper arms. I was a victim, like the others whose little trophies appeared on Danny Keane's shelves. This wasn't something I had wanted.

'I hope they beat you black and blue,' I said aloud, picturing Danny's face, his brilliant eyes, the high cheek-bones that few teenage girls could resist. But even as I said the words, I was distracted. Something had snagged below the surface of my mind. I concentrated, groping for whatever it was, running back over the thoughts that had been jostling for attention. What was it? Something that was important . . . something I had seen and not understood.

Trophies.

The realisation came in a rush and I gripped the edge of the bench, mouth open, heart pounding in my chest. With shaking hands I pawed through my bag, fumbling for the phone, shuffling scraps of paper in the search for Vickers' bloody card – where was it? Not that . . . why did I carry so much shit around? Receipts . . . shopping list . . . Maybe I had left it upstairs on the paediatric ward . . . Or not.

Holding the card as if it was a precious, fragile thing, I dialled the mobile number, double-checking the digits, forcing myself to slow down. Inevitably, it was switched to voicemail. I didn't bother to leave a message, dialling the station number instead.

The receptionist sounded as if she was at the end of a very long shift.

'He's not available at the moment; can I put you through to his voicemail?'

'He'll be available for me,' I said, trying to get a note of command into my voice, thinking it would have been more effective if I had been able to control the shake in it. 'Tell him there's something he needs to know urgently before they talk to Danny Keane. Tell him it's vital that he speaks to me.'

With a muffled sound of irritation, she put me on hold and I waited, tapping my feet impatiently, an instrumental version of 'Islands In The Stream' whining in my ear, off the note. I would not have put money on getting through, life-or-death dramatics notwithstanding, and I was almost startled to hear Vickers at the other end.

'Hello, yes?'

'You need to ask him about the necklace,' I said without preamble. 'The one on the bookshelves. Leather, with beads on it. A leather thong.'

'Hold on,' Vickers said brusquely. There was a sound of shuffling and I pictured him leafing through the file. 'I've got a photo of it, yes. On the top shelf. What's the significance of it? Did it belong to Jenny?'

'No, it did not,' I said grimly. 'It belonged to my brother. And there's no way that Danny Keane should have it. The summer he disappeared, Charlie never took it off. Not even in the bath. He was wearing it the last time I saw him, and I was the last person to see him before he went missing.

'Are you sure?' Vickers asked.

'Without a doubt,' I said. 'Will you call me and let me know what he says?'

'Without a doubt,' Vickers echoed, and put down the receiver.

I sat and listened to the silence, fiddling with my phone. Things never worked out the way I thought they would. I had assumed for years that my mother had been wrong to think I could unlock the mystery of what happened to Charlie. I had resented her for being unreasonable; it had burned through our relationship and salted the earth it stood on so nothing else could grow. And now, it was starting to look as if she'd been right, much though I hated to admit it.

I felt totally drained, but I had to muster the energy to move. It was time to go home.

1999

Seven years missing

The park is different at night. It's dark under the trees, where the streetlights don't shine, and all I can see is the red glow from the end of Mark's cigarette. The cherry, he calls it. It flares and fades as he draws on it and I can see the side of his face, the line of his cheek, his eyelashes sweeping low. I think he likes me, sometimes, and other times I'm not so sure. He's three years older than me. He's just passed his driving test at the first time of trying. And he's good-looking enough to turn heads as he swaggers down the high street. All the girls in my school are obsessed with him.

There's a scuffling sound: Stu changing position beside Mark. I move over, trying to take up less space. A light rain has started to fall, and the little group of us crowd closer together. Annette's elbow is in my side and when everyone laughs at a joke Stu's cracked, she jabs me, hard. It's deliberate. She doesn't like me.

'Let's play spin the bottle,' she says, holding up the vodka bottle and shaking it so the mouthful of liquid left inside sloshes about. I lean into Mark's side, hoping that he'll say no. I feel sick. I just want him to put his arm around my shoulders and talk to me in that funny, quiet way he has. It's not what he says, exactly. It's the way he makes me feel.

'It's too dark,' another girl says, and someone else – Dave – takes out a bike light and puts it on. Around the circle, faces are sloppy with drink, all drooping eyelids and wet mouths. I haven't had as much as everyone else, and I don't want to play spin the bottle, not with these people, not now. It's late, and I'm tired, and I keep checking that my keys are in my pocket, so I can get back in quietly, before Mum realises I've gone out.

Abruptly, I come to a decision. I get to my feet and Annette laughs loudly. 'Don't fancy it, Sarah?'

'I'm going home.' I pick my way over legs, bending to clear the branches as I step out into the open air. Behind me, there's a scuffle, and Mark follows, shrugging off the jeers of his mates. He puts his arm around me and I feel warm, cared for, thinking that he's going to walk me home – but he guides me away from the path, towards the groundsman's hut, a couple of hundred yards away from the group.

'Don't go,' he murmurs into my hair. 'Don't leave.'

'I want to, though.' I'm pulling away from him a bit, half laughing, and his hand tightens on my arm. 'Ow. That hurts.'

'Shut up. Just shut up,' he says, and pulls me after him into the shelter provided by the wall of the hut.

'Mark,' I say, protesting, and he shoves me hard into the wall so my head bangs against it. Then his hands are on me, grabbing, feeling, probing, and I gasp from shock and pain and he laughs under his breath. He goes on and on, mauling me, and then there's a noise nearby and I look and it's Stu, with Dave coming up beside him. Their eyes are wide, curious. They are there to stop me from running away. They are there to watch.

'You love it, don't you,' Mark says, and his hands go to my shoulders and push, so that I fall to my knees in front of him and I know then, I know what he wants me to do. He is fumbling at his jeans, his breath coming fast, and I close my eyes, tears prickling the inside of my lids. I want to go home. I'm afraid to do what he wants, and I'm afraid to say no.

'Open your mouth,' he says, and cuffs the side of my head to make me look at him, to make me see what he's holding. 'Come on, you bitch. If you don't want to, there's plenty of girls who will.'

I don't see what happens, but suddenly there's a bright light that's red through my eyelids and I hear Dave swear, his voice high and frightened. The two boys run, their feet slipping on the grass, and before Mark can react there's a hollow sound and he buckles, falling sideways, his legs kicking. I jump up, my eyes screwed up against the light that I now see is a narrow beam from a torch, and whoever is holding it turns away from me, playing the light over Mark's body, over his lower half, his trousers and underwear bunched around his ankles.

'You cunt,' the person holding the torch says, and at first I think he's talking to me. 'Couldn't you find someone your own age? Taking advantage.'

He steps forward and kicks at Mark, connecting hard with his thigh, and Mark groans. The torch wheels around and for a moment I see a face I know: Danny Keane, Charlie's friend. I don't understand. I step back, and the torch stabs the shadows, finding me, running over my top. It's ripped at the front, I realise, fumbling at the tattered edges, trying to draw it together.

There's silence for a second as Danny stares at me and I look back, eyes screwed up against the light of the torch.

'Go home, Sarah,' Danny says, and his voice is dead. 'Go home and don't do this again. You're just a kid. Be a kid, for God's sake. This isn't for you. Just go home.'

I turn and run, haring across the grass as if I'm being chased, and behind me I hear a thud, and another, and I have to look, to see what's happening. Danny is crouching on top of Mark, and slowly, methodically, he's knocking out his front teeth with the heavy torch, while Mark screams and screams.

As I run, I know two things. Mark will never speak to me again. And I will never be able to look Danny Keane in the eye again for as long as I live.

Chapter 16

Not for the first time, I sat beside my mother on the sofa and had no idea what she was thinking. She seemed to be concentrating on the television, watching a quiz show I had never seen before and couldn't get a handle on at all. The bright colours of the set and the audience's shouts and cheers jarred; I would have preferred to sit in silence. My mouth was dry, and the urge to fidget was almost irresistible; nothing could ease the restlessness that I was feeling. The plush fabric on the arm of our ancient sofa had come in for some surreptitious gouging. It wasn't doing the material any good, but it went some way towards relieving my feelings. I had tucked my feet up under me to stop myself from tapping them compulsively in time to the quickened beat of my heart, and now they were tingling, threatening pins and needles. My stomach twisted. I hadn't eaten for hours – couldn't think of eating. The only thought I had, running around and around in my head remorselessly, was *what did he say?*

The phone call had come twenty minutes earlier, after a long day of waiting. Vickers, asking very properly if my mother was there, if he might come around and talk to us both, as he had information he thought we would be interested to hear. *Tell me now*, I had nearly begged, but I knew he wouldn't. There was nothing but professional courtesy in his voice. Deliberately or not, he had shut me out again. I was back on the wrong side of the partition between the police and the civilian world.

I'd warned Mum as soon as I got off the phone with Vickers. I'd told her that the police were coming to the house for the second day in a row, that it was something to do with Charlie's disappearance. She hadn't seemed surprised. No hand to her chest, no widening of the eyes, no uptick in blood pressure. She had waited a long time for this. I could only guess that she had lived this moment in her mind more times than I could imagine, so there was nothing to surprise her. She sat beside me, as remote and unfathomable as the stars, and I couldn't find the words to ask her how she was feeling. She hadn't even spoken to me about the search the police had conducted the previous day, the questions they'd asked her. I'd stood in my room and stared at it for a long time when I got back from the hospital, trying to see it through Blake's eyes, trying to see what had been opened and what had been moved. It felt strange – altered, somehow – and I had turned to leave it with a feeling of claustrophobia that overlaid the shame that had stayed with me since I'd heard about the search.

And now I was waiting for the police to come again, this time impatiently. In the end, I wasn't even in the sitting room when they came to the door. I was in the kitchen, boiling the kettle to make tea that neither of us particularly wanted to drink. Out of sight of Mum, I could pace and fidget to my heart's content. The long-drawn-out hiss of the kettle coming to the boil effectively blocked out sounds from the rest of the house, and as it clicked off, I froze, hearing voices from the hall. Forgetting about the tea, I shot out of the kitchen, my heart pounding.

'Hello, Sarah,' Vickers said, looking past my mother, who had opened the front door. A pretty female officer that I recognised from the station stood beside Vickers. No Blake. Well, that didn't matter.

'Please,' I said, gesturing to the sitting room. 'Sit down. Would you like a cup of tea? I've just boiled the kettle.' After all that impatience, I was stalling. Now that they were here, I didn't want to hear what they had to say. I couldn't imagine how Mum was going to deal with it either.

'We're all right for tea at the moment,' Vickers said, leading the way into the sitting room. 'But don't let me keep you from having one yourself.'

I shook my head wordlessly, and sank down on a hard chair by the door. Mum settled herself with dignity in Dad's old armchair. The police had taken the sofa. The female officer perched on the edge uncomfortably. Vickers leaned forwards, his elbows braced on his knees, and ran the fingertips of his right hand over the knuckles on his left, over and over. He didn't say anything at first, just looked from Mum to me and back again. I couldn't read his expression for a moment – was there no news? Maybe I had been wrong about the necklace. Maybe Danny had stalled them. Maybe he had refused to answer any questions. I rubbed my hands down my jeans and wondered how to begin.

'How can we help you, Chief Inspector?'

The words had come from Mum and I blinked at her, surprised. She was sitting there as calmly as a queen, in complete control. I started a rough calculation of how much she had had to drink during the day, then gave up. Enough to stiffen her backbone, not so much that she couldn't deal with this visit like a lady. Her hands were folded in her lap; the telltale quiver wasn't apparent.

'Mrs Barnes, as you are probably aware, we've been investigating the murder of a young girl in this area that occurred a few days ago. During that investigation, some things have come to light about the disappearance of your son. We have reason to believe, Mrs Barnes, that Charlie was murdered very soon after he disappeared in 1992, and we know who was responsible.'

Mum waited, her composure holding. I couldn't breathe.

'Charlie was friends with a boy named Daniel Keane – Danny – who lived at 7, Curzon Close with his mother and father, Ada and Derek. Charlie spent a lot of time with Danny, and indeed he was interviewed following Charlie's disappearance. At the time, he denied any knowledge of Charlie's whereabouts and there was no reason to believe he was lying. He has come to our attention in connection with the murder of Jennifer Shepherd – the young girl I mentioned just now. Having him in custody, we raised the issue of Charlie's disappearance, and found that he was more helpful on this occasion. He told us a number of things we didn't know before.'

Vickers' voice dropped slightly. A wind that wasn't there lifted the hairs along my arms. I could barely breathe.

'What we didn't know at the time of Charlie's disappearance was that Derek Keane was a prolific and determined sexual predator. He operated in this area, attacking women over a period of fifteen to twenty years. At the same time, he engaged in physical and sexual abuse of his son and a number of other children.'

'Not Charlie,' Mum said, shaking her head.

'Not initially,' Vickers said heavily, regretfully. 'Daniel Keane claims that he went to some trouble to ensure that his father was never alone with Charlie, and managed to hide the abuse he was experiencing from your son. Derek Keane preyed on young girls and boys from poor backgrounds – children who had been taken into care, mainly, who he met through the youth club that used to operate on this estate. I don't believe that he ever did an honest day's work in his life, but he used to act as a general handyman at the club. It was the perfect place for him to meet and gain the trust of vulnerable youngsters, and he took full advantage.'

The youth club had closed down ten or twelve years before. The building, essentially a red-brick shed with high, barred windows that had been adapted into a club in the 1950s, had eventually been demolished. I had never gone there – too young before Charlie's disappearance, too over-protected afterwards. To my childish imagination, the club had seemed like a wonderland, a place where children ruled and adults were present by grace and favour. I had longed to be allowed to go, yearned to look inside. The high windows, so tantalising at the time, took on a distinctly sinister cast in retrospect. They had hidden more than innocent fun. I swallowed convulsively, willing myself to listen to what Vickers was saying.

'Derek was violent in and out of the home and regularly

spent short spells in prison. According to Danny, his family lived in fear of Derek, and his moods dictated the pace of their lives. When he was happy, they had learned to be happy along with him. When he was angry, withdrawn or drunk, they tried to stay out of his way.

'In the summer of 1992, things had been pretty quiet and stable in the Keane household for a couple of months. Derek was preoccupied with some scheme to make money – some sort of motor-insurance fraud. He spent a lot of time away with his gang of pals, driving to different parts of the country to stage accidents. By his own account, Danny relaxed. When Derek wasn't there, Charlie was free to come and spend time at the Keanes' house. They preferred to meet there rather than here because they didn't have to involve Sarah in their games.' Vickers looked at me apologetically before he went on, but I wasn't upset; it rang true.

'On the second of July, young Charlie left here at some time in the late afternoon. There was no record of anyone he knew seeing or speaking to him again after the point that Sarah saw him, as you are aware. We now know that he didn't go far. He went straight across the road to see his best friend.'

Mum was leaning forward, white bone shining through the thin skin stretched over her knuckles. If her hands hadn't been clenched in her lap, I wouldn't have known she was upset by the policeman's calm recitation of the facts.

'Unfortunately, Danny wasn't at home. He'd gone to the supermarket with his mother, in part because he didn't want to remain in the house alone with his father. Derek had come back from a long trip and was catching up on some sleep. Danny didn't want to run the risk of waking him accidentally.

'We believe that Derek answered the door when Charlie knocked on it. Rather than telling him to shove off, Derek asked him to come into the house. He could be pleasant when he wanted to be, and of course Danny had always hidden his abuse from Charlie. There was no reason for Charlie to be afraid.'

Vickers paused and cleared his throat. He'd been talking without a break for a while, but I recognised it as a stalling tactic. This was the hard part. *Get it over with*, I willed him silently. *Just say it*.

'We aren't sure what happened in the house, but we believe, based on what Derek told his son, that while they were alone together, something happened to Charlie. We can assume, given his past behaviour, that Derek took the opportunity afforded him by an empty house to abuse Charlie. However, Charlie was not like his usual victims. He was brave and intelligent and he had a close relationship with his parents. He knew what had happened was wrong. He wouldn't be comforted, or frightened into silence. Derek must have panicked, knowing that he would be in serious trouble when Charlie went home and complained to his parents. By the time Danny and his mother came back to the house, Charlie was dead.'

The last word fell with a thud into the absolute silence in the room. Mum leaned back in her chair, one hand to her chest. She looked drained. Even though I had been expecting it – even though I had known it for years – the shock of having it confirmed shuddered through me.

'Derek wasn't what you might call clever, but he had cunning and an instinct for self-preservation,' Vickers went on after a short, respectful pause. 'He knew that you and your husband, Mrs Barnes, would be quick to sound the alarm when Charlie failed to return home. He hid Charlie's body in the boot of the car – which, incidentally, would have been the riskiest part of his plan, as the car was parked on the driveway in front of the house. No garage with these houses, so no privacy. But he was lucky and no one spotted him. When Danny and his mother came home, the only sign that anything had happened was Derek's strange mood. He was irritable and absorbed in his own thoughts. He sent Ada out to spend the evening at her friend's house, telling her not to think of coming home before he sent for her. She tried to take Danny with her, but Derek forbade it, saying that he needed his son's help. If Ada suspected later that her husband was responsible for Charlie's disappearance, she never spoke of it to Danny or to anyone else, as far as we can tell.'

Mum was nodding, her eyes unfocused. 'But she must have guessed. I remember, you see, she gave me flowers,' she murmured, mostly to herself. 'Pink carnations. She couldn't even speak to me. Pink carnations.'

Knowing that Mum was capable of going on like that indefinitely, I spoke over her. 'But Danny stayed at home. When did he realise what had happened?'

'When his father showed him Charlie's body,' Vickers

said grimly. 'Derek waited for nightfall, which must have been pretty stressful as sunset would have been late enough at that time of year. Then he made Danny get into the car with him. They drove a couple of miles towards Dorking, to a place in the middle of nowhere, where there's an alleyway that ran behind a little development of houses. There was an access point there for railway workers that led down to the train tracks. Derek had a friend who was a British Rail maintenance worker, who'd told him about it. It wasn't overlooked by houses – the embankment is heavily planted with trees and bushes at that point. The railway was a branch line that wasn't in use at the time. It was a great place to dispose of a body.' Vickers sighed. 'I don't think Danny has ever got over the shock of opening the boot of his dad's Cavalier to see his best friend's body lying there. Derek didn't give him any warning, just told him to help carry the torch and the shovel while he carried Charlie onto the embankment.'

I couldn't bring myself to feel the pity that Vickers obviously expected. I was sure it had been traumatic for Danny. He'd had a horrendous childhood. Fair enough. He had still let my parents live in agonising ignorance of what had happened to their son. He had kept his father's secret, well into adulthood. He had told the truth only when he was backed into a corner. If I hadn't seen Charlie's necklace, Vickers wouldn't have known there was anything to ask him and Mum could have gone on hoping against hope, dying a little bit more every day. And then there was Jenny. He had absorbed the lessons his father taught him. The abused boy turned into an abuser. The murderer's son turned into a murderer. I couldn't feel anything for him but loathing.

Mum stirred in her chair. 'How did Charlie die? You didn't say – how did he kill my boy?'

Vickers looked uneasy. 'We don't know, I'm afraid. We won't know until we find the body and do a post-mortem, and even then, after all this time, we will only find skeletonised remains. Bones,' he clarified, misinterpreting the look of horror on my face. I understood the term, all right; I just couldn't understand why he would say it in front of my mother.

But instead of disintegrating as I had expected she would, Mum was nodding. At that sight, I had, if not exactly a light-bulb moment, a slowly dawning suspicion. It was just the faintest inkling that the woman I had thought I knew wasn't what I had believed her to be. There was strength there, strength and steadfastness, even if I hadn't seen or recognised it before.

Vickers was continuing to speak, drawing back a curtain that had fallen sixteen years before. 'It took a long time to dig the grave. Danny guesses that it was over two hours before his father was finished. The ground would have been hard and full of roots; it wouldn't have been easy to get down to any sort of depth. But he must have been determined, because he did a good job. Most graves of that sort stand out a mile. Animals get into them. They smell the decomposition, dig up the bodies – or parts of them – and give us a clue that there's something to investigate. Or you can see the excavated earth piled up on top of the body and you can tell something's been stuck in the ground there; a burial mound is pretty much unmistakable. I'll say this for Derek Keane: he found a good spot where not many people went and he dug a deep enough hole, and that's probably why we never found Charlie.

'There was also the fact that his wife and child were too frightened of him to think of telling anyone that he had been involved. There again he was clever, because he'd involved Danny in disposing of the body. Ada wouldn't have wanted her son to get in trouble, however convenient it might have been to find a way of locking her husband up for ever. He did keep her out of the house while he was dealing with Charlie's body, so she might not have been sure. Even if she had her suspicions, she didn't take it any further. And Derek had Danny frightened of his own shadow. The boy never said a word to anyone. He was convinced he'd be slung in jail too. His father made out to him that what he'd done would actually be seen as worse, because while Derek had acted on the spur of the moment, Danny had helped him to bury the body in cold blood.'

'Poor child,' Mum said and I looked at her, surprised and not a little shocked, before realising that she didn't know about what he had done to Jenny. I thought Danny was evil, pure evil, and I wasn't really interested in why he had turned out that way.

'Why did he tell you all this now?'

Vickers shifted a little on the edge of the sofa. I gazed at him imploringly. I didn't want Mum to know I had been involved. The thought of explaining it all to her made me feel faint.

'Ah . . . we got some new information that led us to

make enquiries with Mr Keane. I think he'd been waiting to be asked, to be honest with you, Mrs Barnes. Pretty much as soon as our interrogators mentioned Charlie's name, he told us everything. We were talking to him about another matter as well, and I think it's fair to say he wasn't as forthcoming there.' He shot a meaningful look in my direction and I suppressed a sigh. Of course Danny wouldn't own up to Jenny's murder – not when there was no one else to blame.

'How can you be sure he isn't making it all up?' Mum's voice was steady, but her eyes looked strained.

'We believe that he's telling us the truth, Mrs Barnes, or I wouldn't be here,' Vickers said gently. 'He doesn't have any reason to lie to us about Charlie.'

I cleared my throat and the three of them turned to look at me. The policewoman started, as if she'd forgotten I was even in the room. 'What happened to Danny's mother? Derek killed her too, didn't he, a few years after Charlie?'

Vickers sighed. 'There was a lot of local gossip about the younger boy, Paul. People were saying that he wasn't Derek's son at all, that he had been conceived while Derek was in prison in 1995. The dates didn't match up, and there's no way Ada would have dared to be unfaithful to her husband, even if he was tucked away in Pentonville. But the rumours were enough to send Derek off the deep end. Ada ended up at the bottom of the stairs with a broken neck and there was a ton of evidence she'd been roughed up. They should have charged him with murder, but they reckoned they'd get a conviction for manslaughter.' Vickers shook his head. 'Juries can be funny about domestic murders. You never know which way they'll jump. It only takes one loudmouth with suspicions about his own wife to start sticking up for the defendant and you can lose the lot. They're like sheep – where one leads, the others follow, even if it's against all common sense. He got five years; he was out in three. And not long after that, his luck ran out.' There was a definite note of satisfaction in Vickers' voice. 'He wasn't back more than a couple of months before he met his maker. He fell down the stairs in his house late one night, after coming back from the pub, and cracked his skull. Never woke up.'

Vickers couldn't have missed the coincidence. That was how Ada had died. I wondered, unease prickling up and down my spine, if that had been Danny's first murder. But from what I had heard that evening, Derek had deserved it, and more. No one would have mourned Derek Keane's passing.

'So there's just the two boys left. Danny was eighteen when his mother died, and he pretty much brought up Paul on his own. They looked at taking Paul into care, but Danny managed to convince them to leave him where he was. For better or for worse, there was a trend at the time to keep families together.' Vickers shrugged. 'You might think he would have done better in a foster family, or if he'd been adopted. With a heritage like that, he's never really had much of a chance.'

We sat for a moment in silence, contemplating the fate of the Keane family. Then Mum stirred. 'What happens now?'

I glanced at her, then looked again, really stared. Her face had smoothed, somehow – lost that clenched look I hated so much. Just for a moment, I could see the woman I only knew from photographs taken before Charlie disappeared, and she was beautiful.

'Now we find Charlie,' Vickers said levelly. 'We've arranged to search the area Danny described to us, starting tomorrow morning at seven. We're bringing him along so he can show us where he remembers his father digging. The pair of them walked some way from the access gate. I'm hoping that he'll recognise the place when he sees it, so he can help us to narrow the search area. Otherwise we'll be there for weeks.'

'Don't you have high-tech searching equipment, like on TV?' I asked.

'That stuff never works. In my experience, you either get inside information or trip over the body. But we've got Danny, and he's cooperating. We'll find Charlie. Don't you worry.'

He stood up, joints protesting with a volley of cracks that sounded like small-arms fire, and extended a hand to my mother. 'I know this must be a terrible shock for you, Mrs Barnes. Can I suggest that you let my colleague here make you a cup of tea?'

'I don't—' Mum began, but he cut her off smoothly.

'I want to have a word with Sarah, if that's all right, before we go.'

The policewoman was standing at Mum's elbow, and helped her to her feet at Vickers' nod. I was braced for Mum to argue with them, and it was a surprise when she meekly followed the woman to the door. When she got there, however, she stopped, one hand on the door frame for support, or effect, or both.

'I must thank you, Chief Inspector Vickers.'

'No need. No need at all.' Vickers shoved his hands in his pockets and ducked his head. 'If you have any questions or want any reassurance, do call me. Sarah has my number. And we'll let you know as soon as we find anything.'

Once Mum was safely installed in the kitchen behind a closed door, Vickers headed out to the front of the house and I followed.

'He didn't confess to Jenny's murder, in case you didn't guess.'

'Why am I not surprised?' I folded my arms tightly, hugging myself against the cold. It was starting to rain again, coin-sized drops of water falling like hammer blows around us.

'The sex was all her idea. He went along with it because he wanted to make some money – his job doesn't pay enough.' Vickers' tone was cutting. 'He recruited abusers from his dad's old mates. That was something they had in common, apparently – an interest in kids.'

'I don't think I want to hear any more,' I said, and my teeth were starting to chatter.

'What he told us confirmed what Paul said – he did it all for you.'

'God . . .'

'He never thought he was worthy of you, apparently. He's got you up on quite a pedestal. So he went on living out his fantasies with young Jenny, who didn't know any better.

He's immature. Inadequate. Afraid of women. Kids are easier to handle.'

'I understand,' I managed. 'Thank you for explaining.'

Vickers nodded. 'I know you'd have preferred it if I hadn't told you, but it's for the best. Get it out in the open. It'll be reported, when it comes to court – you need to prepare yourself for the publicity.'

'Will I be a witness?' I couldn't think of anything worse than standing in court, accusing Danny, looking him in the eye . . .

'Up to the CPS and the barristers, but I can't think why. You don't actually have anything relevant to say, do you? Not now Danny's confessed. It's not as if you witnessed anything strange going on over there.' Vickers jerked his head in the direction of number 7 as he spoke.

'No,' I said numbly. 'I didn't notice anything.' I'd been lost in my own tragedy, blind to the new one that was unfolding across the street. I'd kept my head down, my face turned away. I'd missed all the clues.

Vickers leaned past me and called, 'Anna!'

The kitchen door opened and his PC hurried out, looking relieved. Vickers turned and went down the path towards his car. I followed him again, drawing the cuffs of my jumper down over my hands.

'Inspector, I just wanted to say – thank you for not saying anything about Danny and me in front of Mum.'

'She's a real lady, isn't she? Dignified.'

'She can be,' I said, thinking of the many occasions when she had been quite the opposite. It was true, though, she hadn't let me down in front of the police.

Vickers had turned away from me and was folding himself into his car. I went over to stand by the door.

'Inspector . . . tomorrow, could I come along?'

He stopped dead. 'To the dig, you mean? Why?'

I gave a one-shouldered shrug. 'I just feel that someone from the family should be there.'

'You do know that Daniel Keane is going to be there too.'

I nodded. 'I'll stay well away from him, I promise. I really don't want to talk to him.'

Vickers lifted his right leg into the car and reached past me to grab the door handle. I hopped out of the way. 'You can be very persuasive when you choose to be. But I don't want any scenes. This is not your opportunity to get your revenge.'

'I wouldn't dream of it. I just – I'd like to come along. To be there for Charlie.'

He sighed. 'We do try to respect the wishes of the family on these occasions. Against my better judgement, I'll send Blake around to collect you tomorrow morning. Be ready at 6.30.'

I beamed. 'Thanks.'

'Don't thank me. And wear wellingtons, if you've got them. Have you heard the forecast? We'll be needing an ark if it doesn't let up soon.' Shaking his head, Vickers slammed the car door. I watched him drive away, strangely glad that he had been the one to tell us about Charlie. I couldn't tell how Mum would react once the news had sunk in, but at least she had heard it with composure, and believed it.

The rain was beginning to be more organised, gathering strength. Even so, before I went inside, I forced myself to look across the street, at number 7. The windows were dark, the curtains drawn. The house had an abandoned look, and all of the little defects I had noticed before looked worse, as if it was starting to corrupt and decay before my eyes. 'I hope you fall down,' I said aloud, hating it, hating what it represented. All those years of waiting. All that pain.

I still saw Danny Keane as a monster, not a victim. He'd chosen to follow in his father's footsteps, even though he knew better than anyone else how much damage that could do. It was hard to accept that across the road, not fifty yards from my front door, there had been such a catastrophic failure of imagination, of self-awareness, of simple humanity. Knowing it had happened didn't make it any easier to understand.

Mum was holding a glass when I got back to the sitting room, which didn't surprise me. But the difference I had marked in her appearance was still there. She looked up when I came in.

'Have they gone?'

I nodded.

'Were you surprised by what he had to say?'

I didn't really know how to answer her. Did she mean about Danny? Or that Charlie was dead? 'I didn't know that Derek Keane was so evil,' I said in the end, lamely.

'I never liked him,' Mum said and took a long swallow from her glass. Whisky, by the looks of it. 'I never liked Charlie playing with Danny. Your father —' I stiffened, ready to leap to his defence '—always thought I was a snob, because the Keanes weren't well off and Danny always looked – well, dirty. But I didn't like Derek. He came over here, just after we moved in, and asked if I needed any jobs done around the place – you know, DIY. There were lots of things to do, actually – the house was very run-down. About as bad as it is now,' she said with a little laugh, looking around in some surprise as if she hadn't actually seen it for a decade or so. 'But there was some-thing about him. His eyes. They were . . . greedy. And I was on my own in the house, just with you. You were only a baby. I said no, we were fine, and I shut the door straight after that; I didn't even say goodbye. It was rude, really. I wouldn't have done it ordinarily. But there was something about him that frightened me.' She sighed. 'I'm glad to know, you know. About Charlie.'

'It's better to know.' It was the first thing we'd agreed on in years.

She drained the glass and set it down. 'I'm going to bed.'

'I might be gone in the morning, when you get up. I'm going out – early.'

'To where they're going to dig?'

I spun twelve different lies around in my head, then gave up. 'Yes.'

'I'd do the same if I were you.'

I gaped. I was poised to give her all the reasons why I should go, all the arguments that would persuade her it was the right thing to do. Not needing them was distinctly weird.

She stood up and came over to me. With just a second's hesitation, she put her arms around me and squeezed. 'You're a good daughter, Sarah,' she whispered, then went past me and up the stairs before I could muster a response. And the good daughter sat down on the sofa and cried her heart out, for her mother, for her father, for Charlie and Jenny and all of them, all the victims, for longer than I care to admit.

2002

Ten years missing

The bedroom is small, overheated and full of people I don't know, and I sit on the floor, my knees pulled up to my chest. The stereo is pumping out a bass-heavy dance track. It's so loud that the beat vibrates in my chest. Two girls are kissing uninhibitedly in the corner, while a group of boys heckle them from the bed, half entertained, half awed. I am holding a coffee cup filled with blackcurrant vodka, as sticky as cough syrup and about as inviting.

The room is dim, lit only by a desk lamp that has been twisted to shine up the wall. I don't know whose room this is, or how they managed to decorate it in the space of two days with cushions and posters and a rug for the floor, so that it doesn't have the bland, institutional austerity of my own room down the corridor. People are dancing, shouting conversations, making friends. I try to decide what to do with my face, settling on a frozen half-smile. I am petrified. I am never going to fit in. I have made a mistake by choosing this university, this course, this hall of residence.

A tall, athletic guy pushes through the crowd and sees me. He's a second-year student who I met earlier in the day at an induction session. To me, he seems terrifyingly grown-up and accomplished. He reaches out and grabs my hand, hauling me to my feet.

'Come with me,' he bawls in my ear.

'Where to?' I ask, but he doesn't hear. He draws me out of the room and down the corridor to the stairwell, where there's a little group of people. I don't recognise most of them, but one or two are on my course. The stairwell is cool and quiet. A girl with a nose piercing and a distant expression has opened the window, and is smoking, against all regulations. She tries half-heartedly to waft the smoke out through the window with her hand, but most of it blows back, swirling around us. I would like a cigarette, I think. I would like to have something to do.

I slip the cup of vodka through the banisters onto an unoccupied step and sit down where the others have made space for me. The second-year sits beside me and puts an arm around my shoulders. I can't remember his name. I can't possibly ask what it is. He introduces me to everyone. They are talking about people I don't know, about parties they went to last year and work they have to do for the following week, while the other first-years swap stories and ask questions. The others seem so bright, so funny. The occasional question comes my way and I answer briefly, smiling until my face hurts. Some of them are very drunk. Others are very drunk indeed. No one except me is sober, and I feel bored and boring.

I don't know who starts it, but suddenly the conversation is all about families.

One of the boys I haven't met before turns to look at me. 'How about you? Any little sisters I should know about?'

Everyone laughs; he has a well-earned reputation for sleeping with visiting younger sisters, I gather.

'Neither little sisters nor big sisters. Sorry.'

The girl by the window lights another cigarette. 'How about brothers?'

It's just a casual question. She doesn't mean anything. Before I've even thought about it, I hear myself say: 'No. No brothers either.'

That's it. That's all I have to say. No one asks any further questions. No one suspects a thing. It's so easy to lie, so easy to be an only child, one without a past, someone to take at face value, someone to like. Just like that, I've left the last ten years behind. I feel something click in my mind, something that I think is freedom. It's only later, much later, that I identify it as loss.

Chapter 17

I was ready to go long before Blake's car drew up outside the house. I had passed another restless night, waking up finally at half past four to the sound of soft, relentless drumming on the roof. I pulled back the curtain to see the rain, hypnotised by the sheer volume of water that was swirling in the gutters and coursing down the road. The ground was already saturated; the neighbours' lawns looked boggy and bloated. I watched for a few seconds before realising with a jolt that if the weather stayed like that, the dig might not go ahead. After all these years, where was the urgency for anyone except Mum and me? I bit my lip; I didn't think that we could wait any longer.

It was a distinct relief to see Blake's car when he turned up. He was better than on time: five minutes early. I had showered and dressed quietly, without disturbing Mum, pulling on an old pair of jeans that were, it transpired, too big for me, sitting low on my hips. I looked in the mirror. My stomach was concave, my ribs sketchily visible under lifeless skin. When was the last time I'd sat down and eaten a proper meal? I couldn't recall. There was precisely no chance that I would manage a sit-down breakfast that morning; my throat closed up at the prospect of food. I found a belt instead, and covered the join with a long T-shirt and a hooded anorak. High fashion it wasn't, but it would do.

Before Blake had time to turn the engine off, I ran out to the car, hood up.

'Nice morning for it,' he said and peered into the footwell, frowning. 'Did you remember your boots? Those trainers won't last long.'

'Why is everyone obsessed with what I'm wearing on my feet?' I waggled the plastic bag I was holding. 'My boots are in here.'

'Where we're going is basically a bog at the moment. The embankment is held together with luck and a few tree roots. Give it another couple of hours of this weather and the whole thing will slide down onto the tracks.'

'Not really,' I said, nervous again.

He laughed. 'Not as far as I know. But we went out and had a quick look yesterday to see what sort of equipment we'd need, and the conditions were horrible. Vickers wrecked his shoes. Poor bloke, he only has two pairs.'

I smiled, too tense to laugh. I was feeling a strange mixture of emotions – excitement and dread all jumbled together, overlaid with a sense that it was important not to get too excited, that they might not find anything, that Danny Keane might have been lying.

'How's your mum?'

'Surprisingly OK. She took the news well, actually. I was expecting – well, I wasn't expecting her to be calm.'

He shot a glance in my direction. 'The boss was very taken with her. Not like that usually, is she?'

'No,' I said candidly. 'She can be difficult. It's not much fun sometimes, being around her.'

'That's what I thought.' Of course, Blake had met her when he searched the house. I squirmed.

'So what happens now?' He was watching the road and I couldn't see enough of his face to be able to read his expression.

'What do you mean?'

'I mean—' He broke off, then tried again. 'Correct me if I'm wrong, but I get the impression that you've stayed with your mother to make up for what happened when Charlie disappeared. Now, assuming we find him today, that's all over. This is the end. You've got to start thinking about where you go next, what you do. You don't strike me as the most committed teacher in the world.'

'Is it that obvious?'

'It's no way to live, Sarah. You've got to do what's right for you, not for anyone else. You're young enough to change your life, however you want to. You just have to decide what you want to do.'

'It's not that easy.'

'No, it *is* that easy. It's exactly that easy.' The car purred to a stop at traffic lights and he turned to look at me. 'It's not something to be scared of, you know. You'll be happier.'

'Maybe.' I couldn't imagine it. Mum's problems had started with Charlie's disappearance, but that didn't mean they would evaporate once he was found. She might need me more, not less, now that she knew what had happened. We would go on for as long as we had to. It was all I knew how to do.

The windscreen wipers hissed back and forth eight or nine times before I spoke again. 'Is Danny going to be here this morning?'

Blake's eyelids flickered as he registered the change of subject. 'Yes, and stay away from him. He'll be cuffed and escorted by police officers, under our control, but I still don't want you near him.' Without looking at me, he said, 'He's totally obsessed with you, you know.'

'It seems so strange. He doesn't even know me.'

'That's even worse. He's in love with the idea of you. He can make you into anything he wants,' Blake said soberly. 'And don't be fooled – he is dangerous.'

The word clicked in my mind like a key turning in a lock. 'Has he confessed yet? To Jenny's murder?'

'Not to hers, no. We got a confession from him about Geoff Turnbull, though, in the middle of the night. They pushed him pretty hard and eventually he admitted it. The physical evidence was overwhelming. That iron bar we found at the house was the weapon. He said he was watching Geoff, he'd seen him coming and going and didn't like the way he was behaving towards you. On the night in question, Danny just snapped.' Blake frowned a little, concentrating on the road. 'I don't know exactly what happened that night, but whatever Danny saw from across the road, he decided to intervene. Geoff was a sitting target. Danny couldn't even claim it was a fair fight, not that that's any kind of defence. Basically, his only excuse is that he wanted to protect you.' Blake looked at me swiftly. 'But don't take that to mean it was your fault, do you hear me? It's not like you asked him to do it.'

But I had wished Geoff gone, and I hadn't cared, not really, when I found out he was in hospital, and I couldn't go back and relive it so I needn't feel ashamed. That would stay with me, whatever Blake said.

'We can't shift him on Jenny. He's not going to go for it, for whatever reason. He's happy to talk about everything else – proud, nearly; you can't shut him up once he gets going on how clever he was to make money off it. But when it comes to how she died, he clams up. Denies everything. We haven't made any progress yet, but we will.'

'Good,' I said with feeling. I wanted him to confess to everything – to own up to all of his crimes. He'd had to help his father to dispose of Charlie's body, and I could see why he had attacked Geoff, even if I deplored it. It was his treatment of Jenny that made me feel he was truly evil. To use her like that and throw her away when he was finished with her . . . I turned my head away from Blake and swallowed, fighting for composure.

The car turned into a narrow lane lined with buddleias that had found footholds in neglected yards and outhouses. Their leathery leaves swept the flank of the car as Blake crept past parked cars on the right.

'Is this it?' I asked, feeling my palms becoming clammy. 'I wouldn't even have known this was here.' I had had no clear picture in my mind of the place Vickers had described and it surprised me to see it and realise how close it was to where I lived.

'It's the sort of place you only know about if you're from around here or you work on the railways. There aren't usually cars parked here; this is all to do with us.'

So it was a big operation, I realised, and felt a prickling rush of embarrassment. This had been my private sorrow for so long, it seemed selfish to have dragged all of these people – thirty, maybe? – into a bleak back alley. 'Thank you for this,' I said, in the end.

Blake grunted. 'No need for that. This is the job.'

'Mm. But thank you for everything else, too.'

That earned me a sidelong look before he turned back to concentrate on the narrow lane ahead of us. A young officer was moving cones, allowing Blake's car through so he could park near the end of the alley. I recognised Vickers' car and Blake pulled in behind it. He turned the engine off and we sat for a second, the only sound the rain rattling on the roof of the car.

'When this is over –' he started.

'I was wondering –' I said at the same time, then laughed. 'You go first.'

'I was just thinking, we've done this backwards, haven't we? When this is all over, I'd like to get to know you, Sarah. Find out what you're really like.'

The rain was sliding down the windscreen in rivulets. I watched the shadows move across his face and felt so happy that it almost hurt. 'I'd like that,' I said eventually.

Blake leaned across, drawing me towards him. I kissed him with commitment and gratitude, almost forgetting why we were there for a few breathless moments, aware only of him, feeling, for once, completely safe. His mouth curved against mine and I pulled away to see him grinning at me.

'Right, then. Glad we've got that sorted. Now get your boots on.'

As he got out of the car, swearing at the rain, I slid my feet into my wellies and shuddered at the dank chill that struck up through my soles. With legs that didn't feel like my own, I got out of the car and waited, hood up, for Blake to finish getting ready. The air was thick with the scent of saturated grass and leaves. From where I stood, I could see steps leading down to a tall metal gate, and behind it, trees.

'This way,' Blake said, motioning towards the gate. Half of me wanted to run away. The other half wanted to rush through it without waiting for Blake, who was fussing with his mobile phone. He came eventually, guiding me through the gate with, 'Watch your step.'

Thick nettles had grown up around the gate, but someone had trodden them down, making a narrow path through the trees. The nettles were slick with rain and slippery underfoot and I followed along in Blake's footsteps, focusing on the ground. The path led to the right, parallel to the railway line that was just visible through the trees. To my left, the ground fell away sharply, and I struggled to keep my footing in places, keeping my balance by grabbing on to convenient tree trunks. After a couple of hundred yards, Blake turned left and began to work his way down the slope, looking back to check I was following. I edged down carefully, afraid of falling and slithering to the bottom of the embankment in a flurry of wet leaves and mud. I could hear voices up ahead, and as we rounded a stand of juvenile beech trees the dig came into view. It was well under way, with a white canvas tent pitched over the spot where the officers were working, shovelling earth and sifting carefully through it, watched by, among others, DCI Vickers.

Blake had stopped at the edge of the clearing. Now he turned to me. 'Do you want to get a bit closer?'

'I'm all right here.' There was a heavy, rich smell of turned earth in the air and, in the distance, the mournful two-note hoot of a train's whistle sounded. It was a peaceful place, but lonely, and I didn't feel at ease.

'Why do you think he left Jenny in the woods?'

'What, Danny?' Blake shrugged. 'Who knows.'

'This would have been a better place, wouldn't it? And he remembered it well enough; he should have thought of it. She'd never have been found if he'd left her here. Like Charlie. And he'd have got away with it.'

'Lucky for us that he didn't, then.' Blake touched my arm. 'Are you OK?'

I was seeing the clearing in the woods again. 'He didn't even bury her. He didn't even try to hide her – not really. The way she was laid out – it was as if he wanted someone to find her.'

'Maybe he was proud of what he'd done.'

'Maybe.'

Vickers had spotted us and was making his way across to us. 'Morning. Everything OK?'

I nodded. 'Have they found anything yet?'

'Not yet,' the chief inspector said briskly, 'but that's just because they're taking their time. We're pretty sure we're digging in the right place. Danny's indicated the place that he remembers the burial taking place, though he wasn't altogether sure if it was here or one other spot. The forensic team have done some probes and they think he's there,' he said, gesturing over his shoulder to the dig in progress, 'and the cadaver dog went for that spot too.'

'Cadaver dog?'

'They're trained to sniff out bodies. You can train a dog to look for anything – drugs, food, explosives, money, anything that gives off an odour they can identify,' Blake explained.

'But surely after all these years there'd be no trace of a smell.'

Vickers smiled. 'Not to us, maybe, but dogs are a lot more sensitive to smell than we are. And this one is quite sure there's something worth investigating back there, between those trees. We're just taking it slowly so as not to damage the body. We want to get him out in one piece.'

'How long do you think it will take?' I asked, but someone in the tent called Vickers and he left without answering me.

'It might be a while,' Blake said. 'Are you OK here or do you want to wait up there?'

He pointed past me to where a big blue tarpaulin was stretched between a few trees, some way up the slope. A couple of people were standing under the makeshift shelter, watching the proceedings, including the dog handler and his liver-and-white spaniel. It looked appealing. Being under the trees should have provided some protection from the rain, but the leaves were overloaded, dumping great gouts of water onto the ground now and then. My anorak was heavy and cold across my shoulders as the rain soaked into it rather than running off. I turned back to Blake.

'I'll go up there. Let me know if anything happens.'

'You'll know. There's always quite a fuss when they find what they're looking for. But I'll keep in touch.'

He headed off to join the group under the white tent and I trudged up the embankment, my feet slipping inside my boots. They were heavy with mud by now and dragged as I walked. Arriving at the blue tarpaulin, I felt self-conscious as the others made room for me. I pushed back my hood and crouched by the spaniel. He was sitting bolt upright, alert to every sound and movement around him, his chocolate-brown eyes alight with interest.

'Is it OK if I stroke him?' I asked his handler, who assented, and I ran my hand over the dog's sloping skull, stroking his ears gently. He stuck his nose in the air, enjoying the attention. It was easy to forget the grim job he did.

I didn't look up as a few more people crowded in under the tarpaulin, just moved over a bit, making space. There was some conversation but I wasn't listening; my mind was down the slope, under the white canvas, and when a voice said, 'Hello, Sarah,' I turned without thinking to look up at Danny Keane.

He was two feet away, no more than that, and I froze where I was crouching, unable to move. His eyes were fixed on me, unblinking, and all I could do was think of the expression that had been on Blake's face in the car when he'd spoken about him. *He's totally obsessed with you . . . don't be fooled, he is dangerous . . .*

It was a couple of seconds before I realised that Danny was flanked by two policemen, that there were more around us and down the slope within earshot if I screamed, that Danny, for all that I knew of him and all that he had done, was not actually a threat to me at that moment. I stood up, moving slowly, and stepped back a little. His clothes were soaking wet and clung to his body, which was whippet-thin and lean like a long-distance runner's. His hair was plastered down over his forehead and as I watched he raised both hands to push it back. His wrists, I saw, were joined with handcuffs. He was holding a cigarette, and he dragged on it greedily as he watched me straighten up.

'Are you OK?'

I stared at him. 'What did you say?'

'Just – this must be really weird for you.' He motioned towards the dig. 'After all this time, to be here, looking for Charlie.'

'Yeah, it's . . . strange.' Not as strange as talking to a man who I knew to be a violent, unprincipled murderer, but strange nonetheless. I was starting to wonder if Danny Keane wasn't nervous. He passed his tongue over his lips, as if they were dry, and he kept his head turned slightly away from me, looking at me sideways. It was unnerving.

What I should have done was leave the sheltering tarpaulin and head back down the hill, away from Danny. But as I stood there, I started to think. He owed me an explanation. He had done all of these things, supposedly for me. This was my one chance to hear his reasons. If I was going to get him to talk to me, he'd have to believe that I didn't hate him.

'Thank you for telling them where to look. For Charlie, I mean.' I tried to keep my voice level, smiling a little. It felt totally fake to me, but he responded with a smile of his own.

'That's OK. It was the least I could do.'

I cleared my throat. 'Um – how did you remember where he was buried?'

'It's not the sort of thing you forget.' Then he leaned towards me, half whispering, 'I'd have thought you'd be frightened of me.'

'Because of what you've done? Or because you attacked me?' I could hear the quiver in my voice, but perhaps he couldn't.

'I never.' He shook his head. 'You've got that all wrong.'

'You attacked me,' I insisted. 'You had all of those things of mine in your house, and you got a big thrill out of terrifying me.'

'I didn't. I didn't mean to scare you. That wasn't what I was trying to do.' His face softened. 'That night, when I held you – I could feel your heart beating, like a little bird's.' His voice was gentle. 'Where were you anyway? I waited for hours.'

I ignored the question. I was coldly furious, trembling, but still outwardly composed. 'If you weren't trying to frighten me, what exactly were you trying to do?'

He turned away from me and rolled his head from one shoulder to the other before answering, affecting to be relaxed, but I knew he was playing for time. Eventually he said, 'Look, I just needed a way to get close to you, OK? I thought I could give you your stuff back and that would give us a chance to start talking. With Jenny gone, I didn't know how I was going to keep in touch with you.'

Keep in touch? He had no idea that spying on someone – stealing from them – wasn't a proper relationship. I could almost have felt sorry for him. Almost.

'We weren't in touch. You don't know me. You don't have any idea what I'm like.'

'I've known you my whole life,' he said simply. 'And – and I've loved you that long too. Whatever you've done, I've loved you. I just wanted to be there for you. Protect you.'

'Is that why you attacked Geoff?'

'That wanker,' he said, and laughed. 'He got what was coming to him.'

'And Jenny? What did she deserve?'

Before he could answer, a shout went up from down the hill. The dog skittered towards the white tent, tail whirling with excitement as his handler ran alongside, and Danny turned to stare after it. I saw the side of his face properly for the first time and drew breath sharply. The dull light of a wet morning couldn't hide that the bruise on his cheek was a proper pearler, swollen and bluish, darkening to beetroot in the centre. They hadn't handled him gently, that was quite obvious.

Even though I knew what the sounds from down the hill signified, I found that I didn't care. I was focused on Danny, waiting for him to reply.

'Jenny?' His eyes were vacant. 'What do you mean?'

'Do you think she deserved to die?' My voice was shaking and I swallowed hard.

'Course not.' He looked at me as if I was mad. 'She was only a kid.'

'So you're upset. That she's dead, I mean.'

'Yeah. I'm going to miss her. Well –' He stopped for a second, then smiled. 'I wouldn't miss her as much if you and me could be friends. Or whatever.'

My skin crawled. 'If you miss her so much, why did you kill her?'

He looked stung. 'How can you ask me that? You of all people. I didn't. You have to believe me, I really didn't.'

'So who did? One of those men who you brought to your home to abuse her?'

'No way,' Danny said confidently, turning to flick his cigarette away. It hit a tree some way down the slope with a shower of sparks. 'No way. They never knew who she was. I looked after her, you know. I was watching over her all the time, in case they did harm to her.'

Harm . . . he had no concept of what that word meant. Sickened, I turned away, almost crashing into Blake who was breathing hard, as if he'd just run up the slope. He grabbed my arm and I stumbled as he pulled me behind him, away from Danny.

'What do you think you're playing at, Milesy?' He glared at the young policeman who had been charge of Danny, who came stumbling forward, looking worried. 'I thought I told you to keep him well out of the way.'

Danny's eyes flicked from Blake to me and back again, and a slight frown creased his forehead. I wondered what he had seen in Blake's face. Before he could say anything – before I could hear Milesy's stammered explanation that they had had to take shelter because of the weather and there was nowhere else to go – I took Blake's hand off my arm and slipped down the slope, heading away from the little group without caring where I was going. I concentrated on picking my path through the trees, stepping with precision between roots. I didn't bother to put my hood up. The raindrops fell onto my head and slid down through my hair. The ground was glistening, the tree trunks glazed with moisture, and fat drops fell off leaves all around me. One plopped down between my collar and my neck. I could feel it trickling down my back, soaking into my T-shirt.

Sounds came from behind me: rustling leaves and cracking twigs. Someone was in a hurry, and I wasn't surprised when Blake swung me round to face him, his face taut with anger.

'Are you happy now? Have you got what you wanted?'

'I didn't plan that. How could I? You told me he wouldn't be anywhere near me.'

'And I told you to keep your distance from him too. What happened to that?'

'I was going to get away from him—'

'But you thought you'd have a quick crack at asking him questions first.'

'I thought he might tell me what he wouldn't tell you,' I said flatly. 'I thought he might want to tell me the truth, given that he apparently has feelings for me.'

'Well, if we'd wanted you to do that, I think we would have asked. And I think we would have found a better place to have that conversation than a railway embankment where any confession wouldn't be recorded and wouldn't necessarily be verifiable.' Blake walked away a couple of paces and stopped, shaking his head. Then he turned back to me. 'There are ways of doing this sort of thing, Sarah. Just asking questions at random won't make a case.'

'You're right,' I said, anger surging inside me. 'So why aren't you making a case, if you're such an expert? Why haven't you got him to confess to Jenny's murder? There must be some evidence. Forensics. DNA. You've got to have some way of making it impossible for him to get away with it. The Shepherds won't give a shit about Geoff's murder. They want justice for their daughter.'

'Well, they're going to have to wait. The CPS don't want to charge him yet. They say it's too circumstantial. Any decent defence barrister would have a field day in court with what we've got. We need more, and believe me, we're looking. We have him for Geoff, for raping Jenny, and for the making and distribution of child pornography. He'll be dealt with by the courts. It may take a while – they aren't quick – but they won't make any mistake about him. He's not going to get away with this, Sarah.'

I turned away, frustrated. 'It's not enough.'

'At the moment, it's all we've got.' Blake paused for a second, and when he spoke again, his voice was more gentle. 'Anyway, that's not why we're here. You might have worked it out already, but I came up to tell you that they've found some human remains.'

So there it was. I'd known it as soon as I heard the commotion, but the shock was still physical.

'Are they sure it's Charlie?' I managed, swaying slightly.

'The forensic anthropologist has had a look and says the bones look right, in terms of the age of the victim and how long they've probably been in the ground. But you never get a straight answer from a scientist. They're taking them back to examine them at the lab. They'll confirm it with dental records and DNA samples in a few days. So far, everything corresponds to what Danny has told us. The way the body was positioned, the location, everything. If it isn't Charlie, it's one hell of a coincidence.'

'Thank you for telling me,' I said, meaning it, but my voice was flat.

'Do you want to have a look?'

'No. I don't – I don't want to see the bones. Can you take me home?'

'Of course.' There was a slight hesitation before he spoke – a certain reluctance – but his tone was courteous. He dug in his pocket for his keys and held them out to me. 'Look, I have to let Vickers know where we're going. Can you make your own way back to the car?'

I took them wordlessly and began to trudge back, keeping the railway line on my right. I didn't think much about what I was doing, just concentrated on putting one foot in front of the other, occasionally looking up to see if the gate was in sight. I found it without too much difficulty, guided in part by the crackling static from the radio of the PC who was guarding it. I went past him without speaking and dragged myself up the steps like an old, old woman. When I got to the car, I realised that my hand had been clenched tightly around the keys, leaving a livid red mark on my palm. I sat in the passenger seat and waited, not thinking about anything, running my fingertips over the indentation again and again and again.

The journey seemed much shorter on the way back. Blake was driving fast, braking hard at traffic lights and swearing under his breath at other road-users. The Monday morning traffic was heavy now. He was keen to get back to the dig, in case they found anything else. They were searching, he told me, for other people who had disappeared over the preceding twenty-five years, during the period they knew Derek Keane was engaged in criminal activity. It was too good a body dump to use just once, Blake said. They thought there would be more to find. I couldn't share in his excitement. I was beginning to feel claustrophobic, as if something was muffling my mouth and nose. The evil of Derek Keane seemed to have no end. He had polluted our lives with his perversion, and his legacy lived on with his damaged, dangerous son.

At the house, I said a quick goodbye to Blake. He was all business, his mind on his job. As I walked up the drive, he opened down his window and called after me, 'I'll let you know what the pathologist says in a couple of days.'

I waved in acknowledgement, but I knew what the outcome would be. Danny had no reason to lie. What had happened to Charlie was clear enough. His last moments would have been terrifying; he would have been frightened, hurt and angry. So much sentiment had been varnished over the picture I had of my brother that I couldn't now imagine what he might have done. The paper hero in my mind, the effortlessly clever and resourceful big brother, would have fought back. But the child in a desperately frightening situation might have cried for his mother instead. And that, I reckoned, closing the front door behind me softly and setting my muddy boots down on the mat, was what had affected Mum the most over the years. No matter how much she'd loved him – and she'd loved him more than anything – she hadn't been able to save him.

The house was quiet. I scooped up the post from the mat, separating out a padded envelope with Aunt Lucy's writing on it. My spare car keys, at long last. I would go and get my car, or at least call the AA, as soon as I was finished at home. The post was spotted with raindrops and damp to the touch and I left the lot on the hall table, unable to face opening the envelopes yet. Instead, I went to the kitchen. The kitchen clock was tapping out the seconds like a deathwatch beetle, the sound mingling with the rain pattering on the windows. I stared at the clock uncomprehendingly. It was only nine o'clock. I had expected it to be at least lunchtime.

At the thought of lunch, my stomach turned over. I was hungry, I told myself, peeling off my soaked anorak and hanging it on the back of a kitchen chair. The manufacturer's definition of waterproof did not accord with mine. The shoulders of my T-shirt were dark with rainwater and cold on my skin.

In the fridge, I found a packet of bacon and some slightly out-of-date eggs that I was prepared to risk. I got a frying pan and set about making the greasiest and most unhealthy breakfast that I could imagine, the fried eggs melding with the curling strips of bacon in a puddle of hissing oil. It was exactly what I needed. I made tea and toast, too, and set the table, laying a place for Mum in case she smelled the food and felt hungry. The cooking bacon filled the air with a heavenly smell; it might have tempted her to eat. I moved the frying pan off the heat and left it on the cooker, ready to use if she made an appearance.

Breakfast turned out to be pretty good. The eggs oozed rich yellow goo all over the toast, while the bacon had twisted into salty ribbons dotted here and there with white flecks of pure fat. I ate methodically, warmed by the hot food and strong tea. I would have to tell Mum that Charlie had been found, but I didn't allow myself to think about it while I was eating. I wasn't ready yet. She loved Charlie so intensely, so fiercely, and she had often told me that I wouldn't understand it until I had children of my own. The thought made me shiver. If that was what love was, I didn't want any part in it.

There was still no sound from upstairs as I scraped the last vestiges of yolk off the plate and went to stack my dishes in the sink. I would have to go up and wake her. I poured the last of the tea into a clean mug. It was as dark as gravy after standing in the pot for so long, but I didn't think she would mind. I took a detour to collect the envelopes from the hall table, sorting through them quickly. Bills and junk mail, the usual. Nothing exciting. I stuck them under my arm and went carefully up the stairs, carrying the mug with two hands. The door to her room was firmly shut, as it had been when I left. Everything looked completely normal. There was no reason why I should have hesitated, no reason why my voice should have quavered as I called, 'Mum?'

Silence from within. I tapped again, eyes fixed on the tea that threatened to slop over the edge of the mug every time I moved. 'Can I come in?'

I knew it was wrong as soon as I opened the door. I knew what had happened without taking a step into the room. Mum was more organised than Paul; she hadn't made any mistake. A neat row of medicine bottles stood on the bedside table, caps off, empty. On the floor, a bottle of whisky with a glass or two left in it; beside it, an empty bottle on its side. In the bed, covered neatly with bedclothes, the small shape that was my mother. She lay on her back, arms by her sides, her face waxy in the half-light from curtains that were slightly ajar. There was a sour smell in the room that I traced to the stain down her neck and shoulder and on the mattress; she had been sick at some stage, but not sick enough to save her. Without thinking, I had moved forward to stand beside her. I reached down and touched the back of her hand very gently. Cold. There was no need to check for a pulse. She was gone. She had heard enough to know that Charlie wasn't coming back, then slipped away while I wasn't watching.

I looked, calmly at first, for the note that I had assumed would be there. Nothing on the bedside table. Nothing on the floor. Nothing in her hands, nor in the bedclothes. Nothing on the chest of drawers. Nothing in the pockets of the clothes she had been wearing. Nothing. Nothing. Nothing. She'd left me, and she hadn't cared to say goodbye.

The truth of it – she was gone, like all of them – hit

me then and I cannoned out of the room into the bathroom, all that good food churning inside me. I made it to the lavatory before it came rushing up my throat. I threw up everything that I had eaten that day, threw up until there was only the burning taste of bile in my mouth as my stomach did its best to turn itself inside out. Once it was over, I fell back against the bathroom wall and drew my knees up, balancing my elbows on top of them. I pressed the heels of my hands into my eye sockets as bright lights whirled and swung behind my eyelids.

After a time, I got to my feet and bent over the sink, rinsing my mouth out with cold water. My hands were trembling, I noticed with detachment. In the bathroom mirror, I looked strained, my cheeks hollow, my skin pale. Suddenly I saw how I would look when I was old.

From the hall, I looked through the open door of Mum's bedroom. I could see the lump her feet made under the bedclothes. She would never move again. Never. Never. I couldn't take it in. It was as if my brain was refusing to deal with what had happened. Maybe it was the shock, but I could only think two steps ahead.

There were people I should tell, I knew. There were things that needed to be done. But instead of doing them, I went to where I had dropped the pile of envelopes in the doorway and fished out the small fat one that contained my keys. I needed someone to put their arms around me and tell me everything was going to be all right. I needed someone to talk for me, someone to explain reasonably and rationally what had happened to my family. The only person I could think of who might be able to do that – the only person I could face telling, because he would know what to do – was Blake.

I would get my car, like I'd planned to, and I would go to him, and he would make everything OK.

People die in fires because they refuse to change their plans. People will walk into danger with their eyes wide open because they're afraid of the unknown.

My life was burning down around me, and all I could do was wonder if my car would still be where I'd left it.

2005

Thirteen years missing

I'm going home to get the last few things I want, and that will be an end to it. Everything else is sorted. Ben's found a house for us in Manchester, sharing with four other friends from university. I've got a job with a travel agency. The pay isn't great, but the perks are fantastic – cheap flights and accommodation way above what we could afford otherwise. Ben and I have already planned where we're going to go next year: Morocco, Italy, Phuket for Christmas. Everything's coming together.

All I have to do is tell Mum, grab my stuff, and get the hell out.

It makes me feel sick, thinking about it. I rock with the motion of the train, watching fields slip by. Everything in me is screaming that I shouldn't contemplate going home again after graduating, that I've made the right decision. That part of my life is over. I don't even think that Mum wants me to go back. But I haven't said it to her yet. I haven't told her about Ben, my boyfriend of two years, who knows that he'll probably never get to meet my mother, but not why. And I haven't told Ben about Charlie or Dad or any of the things that have made me who I am. Too many secrets. Too much held back. There will have to be a grand coming-clean one of these days, so he can find out exactly who he's in love with. But not yet.

Mum comes first.

The house looks empty when I walk up the road, lugging my bag; the windows are dark. Mum is never out, but there's no point in ringing the bell. I find my keys and let myself in, aware of a strange smell that might be rotting food, and something else.

When I put on the lights, I see her straight away, lying awkwardly at the foot of the stairs. I'm not aware of moving, of dropping my bag, but suddenly I'm beside her, and I'm saying, 'Mum! Can you hear me? Mummy?'

I haven't called her that for years.

She makes a small sound, and relief makes me gasp, but she's cold and her colour is dreadful. Her leg is bent under her at an angle and I know it's broken; I also know she's been there for a long time. There's a dark stain on the carpet underneath her and the smell is stronger here, ammoniac.

'I'm going to call an ambulance,' I say clearly,

and move away towards the phone that was just inches out of her reach all along. A hand closes around my ankle with surprising strength and I half-scream. She's trying to speak, her eyes fluttering.

I bend over her, trying not to react to the smell of her body, her breath, feeling horror and compassion and shame. It takes her a few seconds to speak again.

'Don't . . . leave me.'

I swallow hard, trying to clear the lump that's blocking my throat. 'I won't, Mum. I promise.'

I call for the ambulance and sit by her bed, and speak to the doctors and clear up the mess at home. I call Ben and tell him I've changed my mind. I let him think that I never really cared for him. I let him think I lied. I stop answering my mobile and ignore texts from my friends. I burn all the bridges. I cut myself off.

And it never occurs to me – not once – that I'm getting it wrong, that I've failed to understand my mother once again.

Don't leave me?

Not quite.

Don't. Leave me.

That makes a lot more sense.

Chapter 18

The policeman outside the Shepherds' house looked bored. He had taken shelter under a cherry tree in the front garden, but the rain was still running in rivulets down his high-visibility jacket and off the peak of his cap. The press had mostly moved on to more interesting stories. Here and there someone sat in a car with steamed-up windows, watching.

In daylight, I could see details I hadn't noticed on my previous visit – the lawn was rutted and gouged by the feet of many visitors. I paused for a second to look over the gate before turning away, towards my car.

'Sarah!'

I knew who it was straightaway, even before I looked back to see Valerie Wade standing in the doorway of the Shepherds' house, peering out through the rain. *Oh great.* I had completely forgotten that she would be there. All I needed was for her to call Vickers and let him know I was at the Shepherds' house. I had a feeling that he would not approve.

'I thought that was you,' she said triumphantly. 'I was just looking out the window and I saw you standing there. Did you want something?'

I wanted to run away from her, get into my car and drive out of Elmview for ever, but that wasn't practical, especially since my car still needed the attention of the AA to get it moving. And my reluctance to explain what I had been doing in the Shepherds' road – and why my car had been outside their house for so long – was even stronger now. I would have to bluff it out. Besides, there was something I wanted to say to the Shepherds. I would never have a better chance. It was as if it was meant to be.

I went through the gate and walked up the path, aware of the policeman watching me from under the branches.

'I was wondering, would it be possible to speak to the Shepherds? I never really got a chance to talk to them about what happened with Jenny, and – well, I'd just really like to.'

Someone moved in the house behind Valerie, and I heard a rumble that was too low-pitched for me to be able to distinguish the words from where I was standing. Valerie stepped back.

'OK. Come on in, Sarah.'

In the hall, I felt suddenly self-conscious and busied myself with finding somewhere for my dripping umbrella to stand and taking off my jacket. The hall reeked of the dense, heady scent of lilies, but an undertone of pond-water suggested they were past their best. I traced the smell to an elaborate arrangement by the telephone. The fat white blooms were tinged with brown, on the point of disintegration, the petals splayed out. No one had bothered to take off the florist's cellophane before ramming the stems into a vase.

'Would you like a cup of tea?' Valerie asked, heading

for the kitchen when I nodded, leaving me unsure where to go. I turned to look around and froze as I faced the stairs. On the second-to-last step, Michael Shepherd was sitting, forearms resting on his knees. He turned his big hands over to look at his palms, studied them for a few seconds, then let them drop. When he looked up at me I was struck again by his coal-black eyes. They still burned with ferocious intensity, but now it was the last blaze of a fire that had nearly burned out. He looked exhausted without being in the least diminished; the self-confidence and power I had noticed previously had been distilled into pure determination to endure. I found myself thinking again of my own father, wondering if he had been as strong, or as undone as the man before me.

'What do you want?' His voice was gravelly, as if he hadn't used it much recently.

'I wanted to talk to you and Mrs Shepherd,' I managed, trying to appear calm and composed. 'I – well, I probably understand better than most people what you're going through. And there's something I wanted to tell you. Something I thought you should know.'

'Really?' His tone was incurious, insultingly so, laden with sarcasm. It whipped blood into my cheeks and I bit my lip. He sighed, but got to his feet. 'Come and talk to us, then.'

I followed him into the sitting room, seeing everywhere the signs of a safe, upwardly mobile life disrupted cruelly and irrevocably. Photographs of Jenny stood in frames on most of the surfaces and hung on the walls, photographs featuring ponies and tutus and bikinis, all the accoutrements of the middle-class child who doesn't know what it is to want for anything. They had given her every possible advantage, every possible opportunity that her friends from wealthier backgrounds might have had. I looked at the pictures, at Jenny's smile, and I thought that none of us had known her. For all that I'd found out about her secret life, I hadn't gained any kind of insight into her. I knew what she had done, but I couldn't begin to understand why, and nor, I suspected, could anyone else. All that we had to go on now were Danny Keane's lies.

The house might have stood in a fairly modest estate, but here too the urge to improve had been given free rein. It had been extended at some stage and the ground floor appeared to be almost twice the size of the house I'd lived in all my life. Glass double doors separated the living room from a dining room. Matching doors led from there into the garden where I could see a patio with high-end garden furniture and a built-in barbecue. The kitchen, visible through an open door, was expensively fitted, all cream units and black marble worktops. A huge TV dominated the living room, its screen so big that the picture was distorted. The sound was off and a Sky newsreader was overenunciating earnestly, her face contorted with the effort of looking serious and engaged with what she was reading off the autocue. A large sofa faced the TV, and Mrs Shepherd sat on it, arms wrapped around her body, gazing at the screen unseeingly. She didn't look up when I walked in, and I had time to notice the extreme change in her too. Her skin was blotchy and raw around her nose and eyes. As before, her hair was lank and stringy. She wore a sweatshirt, jeans and trainers, and the glamorous image she had once projected was long gone; it was functional clothing and it hung on her frame. Where Michael Shepherd burned with rage, his wife seemed frozen by grief.

'Sit down,' Shepherd said brusquely to me, pointing to an armchair at an angle to the sofa. He sat beside his wife and took her hand, squeezing it so hard his knuckles bleached white. It wrung a short cry of protest from her, but succeeded in breaking into her reverie.

'Diane, this is . . . one of Jenny's teachers.' He looked at me blankly and passed a hand over his forehead. 'I'm sorry, I don't remember your name.'

'Sarah Finch. I was Jenny's English teacher.'

'And what is it that you wanted to share with us?' He sounded wary, resentful almost. Diane Shepherd was staring at me hopelessly. I sat up straight, squeezing my hands together.

'I've just come to talk to you because – well, because of that.' I pointed at the TV screen, where a reporter was speaking against a backdrop of trees. The red tickertape running along the bottom of the screen screamed, 'Surrey police discover body on railway embankment – sources say it may be that of schoolboy Charlie Barnes, missing since 1992.' The live image faded, replaced by the standard picture of Charlie that all the media outlets used; the school photograph where he grinned engagingly at the camera, his eyes full of life. I turned back to the Shepherds, who were looking at the screen uncomprehendingly.

'Charlie is – was, I mean – my brother. I was eight when he went missing. The police found his body this morning.'

'Sorry for your loss.' Michael Shepherd's jaw was clenched so hard, the words barely got out between his teeth.

'The thing is, he was killed by Danny Keane's father.' I knew the name would jolt them into attention. This was the hard part. 'When Jenny disappeared, it brought everything back for me. I was – I was sort of involved from the start. I found Jenny, actually, in the woods – you might know that already.'

The two of them were staring at me. Diane looked dazed, her mouth a little bit open. Her husband was frowning and I couldn't tell why. 'Of course I remember. You kept cropping up,' he said finally.

'Tea!' Valerie clattered in from the kitchen with a tray loaded with mugs. 'I didn't know if you'd want sugar, Sarah, so it's on the tray and there's milk too; you can add your own. I know how you two like your tea,' and she gave an awkward little giggle as she bent down to let the Shepherds take their mugs. There were two left on the tray and I realised with a sinking feeling that Valerie intended to join us. Michael Shepherd had noticed too and before she could sit down, he intervened.

'I think we'd like to keep this conversation between the three of us, Val. Can you give us a few minutes?'

'Of course.' The colour rushed into her cheeks. 'I'll be in the kitchen if you need me, though.' She stumped back out, carrying her mug, head held high. I didn't like her at all, not one little bit, but I felt a twinge of pity for her;

what was she supposed to achieve here, apart from making endless cups of tea? They were waiting for news of a confession, I knew, and it could come at any time, but all the same, the Shepherds struck me as being in dire need of time alone.

'You were saying?' Michael Shepherd prompted me. I really didn't want to go on.

'The thing is . . . my parents suffered a lot after Charlie disappeared. They couldn't live with what happened, and they couldn't live with one another, and in the end it destroyed them both. I don't want the same thing to happen to you. No one deserves to go through what they did. If nothing else, I'd like something good to come out of what they endured.' I took a deep breath. 'And there's something else.'

'Yes?'

'Danny Keane . . . the things he did were dreadful. Terrible. But you should understand *why* he did them.' I was getting ready to tell them that it was my fault, that they shouldn't blame themselves. What did it matter if they blamed me?

Michael Shepherd stirred. 'Has he confessed, then? Keane?'

'Not as far as I know,' I had to admit.

'I thought you might have heard before we did. You seem to be well in with the police.'

His tone was unpleasant and I blushed again. 'I've got to know them, that's all. As you said, I kept cropping up.' I pretended to sip my tea, playing for time. It was far too hot to drink. I looked around for a place to put my mug, not liking to put it on the highly polished table at my elbow without a coaster. In the end, I reached down and set it on the floor.

'Look, what I really came here to tell you was –'

There was a clatter of claws on tiling. A small, dirty West Highland terrier shot into the living room from the kitchen and pranced up to me, panting engagingly, head on one side.

'That bloody dog!' Michael Shepherd jumped up from the sofa, towering over the dog that was crouching by my feet with his tail wagging tentatively.

Diane stirred. 'Just leave it. He's not doing any harm.'

'I should have got rid of him,' Michael said over his shoulder to his wife, reaching down to drag the dog by the collar towards the kitchen. He handled him roughly and the little dog whimpered, cringing away from him. I found myself holding the arms of my chair, wanting to intervene but knowing I couldn't. As he disappeared through the open door, I could hear him telling Valerie off. 'I've told you before, he doesn't come into the house any more. The place for him is outside.'

'He just ran in when I opened the door.'

'I'm not interested, Valerie. You've got to be more careful.'

I looked at Diane, whose eyes were closed. Her lips were moving, as if she was praying. Her mouth looked dry, covered with tattered flecks of dead skin, and her eyelids were raw. They flickered as I watched and she met my gaze.

'Is that Jenny's dog?'

It was a moment or two before she responded. 'Archie. Mike can't stand the sight of him.'

That much was obvious from the way he'd handled him. 'I suppose it reminds him. It must have been awful when Archie turned up here without her.'

She started shivering so violently that I could see it from across the room, and I felt sorry at once for reminding her. Her eyes were unfocused and I felt that she was miles away, that she'd forgotten I was there at all. When she spoke, I had to strain to hear her.

'Turned up here? But Archie was here all along . . .' As her voice trailed away, it was as if she came to her senses. She sat up a little straighter and cleared her throat. 'I mean, yes. It was a shock. We didn't expect Archie to be outside the front door at all, because he should have been with Jenny.'

But that wasn't what she'd said.

I sat in my chair as if nailed there, frozen with horror. I felt as if everything I'd previously known and understood had suddenly shifted through fifteen degrees, forming a new and wholly horrible reality. I had to be mistaken, I told myself. I was still in shock because of what had happened with Mum, with Charlie's body. I saw death and violence everywhere, in everything, and what I was imagining was impossible. It was unthinkable.

That didn't mean it wasn't true.

She had turned her head, listening intently to the sounds from the back of the house. The voices were receding, as if Valerie and Michael had gone out to the back garden.

There was time, I thought – not much, but some. Maybe enough.

'Diane,' I said carefully, keeping my voice low and level, 'if things didn't happen exactly the way you told the police, that's OK. But if there's anything – anything at all – that you think they should know about what happened to Jenny, I think now would be a good time to tell them.'

She dropped her head and stared at her hands, which were knotted in her lap. Tension was vibrating through her. I could see her struggling, wanting to speak. I waited, hardly daring to blink.

'He'll kill me.' It was a ghost of a sentence, slipping from her on an outward breath, and I flinched at the fear in her eyes when she looked up at me.

'They'll protect you. They can help you.' I needed to press her, and knowing what I was doing, hating myself for it, I said, 'Don't you want to tell the truth, Diane? For Jenny?'

'Everything we did was for her.' Her eyes were on a picture on the table beside her, a holiday picture of a younger Jenny in a swimsuit, blue sky behind her, laughing down at the camera. Silence settled on the room and I almost jumped when Diane spoke again. 'There's no point, is there? There's no point in any of it. I thought there was. I don't know why.'

'I understand that you're afraid, Diane, but if you just—'

'I *was* afraid,' she interrupted, her voice stronger now. 'I was afraid, so I did what he wanted. But I'm not going to lie for him any more. He thinks what he did was right, but how could it have been? And I couldn't stop him. There was nothing I could do to save her, because everything has to be perfect for Michael. He can't stand it if things aren't just . . . perfect.'

'Even Jenny?'

'*Especially* Jenny. She knew he wouldn't stand for her being disobedient. She should have known it was dangerous.'

I was remembering Michael Shepherd at the police station, the scene he had made when he realised that his daughter's abuse would be common knowledge. At the time, I had seen it as wanting to protect her, even in death. I had got it wrong. He'd wanted to protect her reputation. He'd wanted to protect himself.

Diane's voice had dropped again, so quiet that I could only just make out the words. 'He was devastated about the baby.'

'I can imagine.'

'No. No, you can't. Do you know what he made me do? He made me leave her there. My baby. In the dark, and the cold, and the rain, with nothing to protect her, until someone – you – came along and found her. And I let him do it.'

Tears were sliding down her cheeks. She rubbed them away violently, wiping her nose on her sleeve. I didn't need to push for more; the story came tumbling out of her in a torrent that I couldn't have stopped if I'd tried. It was as if she'd been waiting for a chance to tell someone what her husband had done.

'He found out, you see, about her boyfriend. Oh, he

didn't know the whole story. We had no idea that there were those . . . others. We assumed that she had gone behind our backs to be with Danny because she knew we wouldn't approve. Michael had told her she couldn't have a boyfriend until she was eighteen, you see, so even if Danny had been the same age as her, we still wouldn't have allowed them to see each other.' She blinked, sniffing a little. 'I wondered if that was why she went with him. Because she was supposed to be perfect – Daddy's little girl – and it was hard for her to live up to it. But then, maybe it was just that she was used to doing what she was told. Maybe that's how that man convinced her to do those things. She looked so young, didn't she? She was only a baby, really, and when she told me she was pregnant, I just couldn't believe it.' Now Diane looked at me, anguish in her eyes. 'I shouldn't have said anything. I should have helped her to get rid of it. We could have forgotten the whole thing. She would have been so grateful to me, because she was worried, she knew she was too young to have a baby, and she knew her father would be upset. But I reassured her. I said it would be all right. I said we'd take care of her, like we always did. I didn't know . . . I didn't know . . .'

She almost screamed the last few words, then pressed the back of her hand against her mouth, her chest heaving as she fought for control.

I knew that grief could affect people in strange ways. I knew that hysteria could produce vivid hallucinations; that lack of sleep and mental turmoil could make people confuse fantasy and fact. I knew that guilt was the most destructive emotion of all, that any parent would feel responsible for the failure to protect their child. But I couldn't help but believe every word Jenny's mother was saying. I looked out through the glass doors of the dining room, to where Shepherd was standing in the back garden. It had stopped raining, though the clouds were low and steely grey. He had lit a small cigar. Tendrils of blue smoke swirled away from him, spiralling through the air. I had to find out more. But I had to be quick.

'How did he kill her?'

She shook her head, eyes closed, and said again, 'I didn't know.'

'I understand, Diane. You couldn't have known.' I tried again. 'What happened?'

'When we told him, he *hit* her.' The shock of it was audible in her voice. 'He couldn't stand that she'd lied to him. Then he told her she was dirty. She had to have a bath. He asked me to help her get into the bath. I made her undress . . . I thought it was something that would help. I thought he would calm down while she was out of sight. I didn't think he'd blame her, anyway . . .'

'And then?'

Her eyelids fluttered and she frowned. 'I stayed in the bathroom, you see. Jenny was upset – so upset – and she didn't want me to leave her. So when he came in, he was terribly angry that I was there. He called me a slut, too, and the mother of a whore, and he told me that I could watch, if I liked. And then he put his hands on her shoulders, here–' She gestured to her collarbones, where I had seen the bruises on Jenny's skin. 'He pushed her down so her head was under the water, and he held her there until she stopped fighting. It didn't take long. He's very strong. I tried to stop him, but I couldn't. He's so very strong.

'Then he took her, and he left her in the woods. He didn't even cover her up. I begged him to wrap her up, but he wouldn't. She had nothing to keep her warm . . .'

'Diane, you have to tell the police what happened.'

Her eyes went wide. 'No. He'd kill me. You have to believe me. He'd kill me in a second.' She looked truly terrified.

I pulled my mobile phone out of my bag and started scrolling through the contacts. 'Let me call DCI Vickers. He'll understand, really he will. He'll help.'

My hands were shaking, my fingertips numb. I was trying to sound confident for Diane's sake, but I could barely make the phone work. A noise from the kitchen made my heart jump into my throat.

'Is everything OK?'

Valerie was standing in the doorway. I had never been so pleased to see her. I jumped out of my chair and ran over to her, pushing her into the kitchen. I wanted to get her away from Diane so I could speak freely. I had to make her understand what Michael Shepherd had done. She would know what to do.

She didn't struggle, stepping backwards obediently, but once we were out of range of Diane she stopped dead, like a mule.

'What's going on? We only left you alone for a few minutes.'

'Just listen, Valerie, I've got to tell you –'

'If you've upset Diane—'

'For God's sake, shut up!'

We glared at one another, irritation on both sides, and I allowed myself the luxury of a second spent wishing that any other member of the police was standing in front of me. I took a deep breath. 'I'm sorry, Valerie. This is really important. Just – just listen.'

I started to tell her what Diane had told me, stumbling over the words, getting ahead of myself and having to go back to explain. Her face went pale as soon as she understood what I was saying.

'Oh my God. We have to tell someone.'

'I was going to call DCI Vickers,' I began, but Valerie's pale blue china-doll eyes tracked over my shoulder and widened in horror. I felt fear prickle along my spine even before I whipped around, and when I saw what Valerie had seen, a scream forced its way out of my throat before I could stop it. Michael Shepherd stood in the doorway, holding his wife by the back of the neck. In his other hand, he held a vicious-looking black crossbow, about eighteen inches from tip to tip, pointing directly at us. One bolt was already fitted, ready to fire, and he had another stuck through his belt.

'Don't make another sound, either of you.'

I moved away from Valerie instinctively, making a bigger target area. Fear made my movements awkward. I had been too slow. I had wasted time with Valerie. I shouldn't have bothered explaining things to her; I should have run away. I had left it too late, as usual. My anger was like a red-hot wire cutting through the cold fog of terror and I held on to it for dear life, knowing that it would keep me focused, that it would stop me from giving up. Still edging backwards, I came up against the edge of the kitchen worktop and stopped, reaching behind me with one hand, trying to remember if there had been anything on the counter that I could use as a weapon. Shepherd was looking at Valerie and his face was black with rage.

'Hands,' he spat, and raised the crossbow. 'In the air, now.'

'Hold on, Michael, just hold on,' Valerie said, trying to smile. 'I know you're upset, but this is no way to deal with the situation. Just put the weapon down, let Diane go, and we'll talk about this.'

'There *is* no way to deal with the situation. This bitch –,' and he shook Diane violently '– couldn't keep her mouth shut. And now *you* know about it, and *you* know about it.' He pointed with the crossbow. When it swung around to me, I felt my stomach pull back against my spine. *Oh Jesus.* I lifted my hands so they were level with my shoulders, and was vaguely aware that they were shaking uncontrollably.

'This isn't going to sort anything out, Michael. You're just getting yourself into more trouble, not solving anything. We can talk about what happened to Jenny. We can work something out,' Valerie said.

I had precisely zero confidence that Valerie's nannyish tone would have any impact on Michael Shepherd's behaviour. Just a few feet away there was a policeman; just beyond him, reporters from the world's media. And unless someone did something, we were going to die in that kitchen without any of them knowing anything about it. Valerie was making things worse. Diane was like a broken doll, her head lolling to one side. I doubted she was even aware what was going on. That only left me. I lowered my hands and pushed them into my pockets, trying to look relaxed.

'Look, Michael, I'm sorry for asking too many questions. I think – I think I confused Diane. She was just trying to talk things out with me. It was just talk. I don't think anyone would take it seriously.' *If you weren't pointing a crossbow at me, that might be more credible . . .*

Michael Shepherd laughed, a horrible sound without humour. 'Nice try. Don't try to kid me that you don't believe it.'

'I don't believe you have to shoot any of us,' I said calmly, drawing on the reserves of composure I'd built up over years of handling Mum when she was in a dangerous mood. I was terrified, but I knew better than to show it. 'That's not going to help you or us. I mean, what are you going to do? Shoot everyone who comes to the house to find out where we are? It's not really a plan, is it?'

His eyes glittered. 'There's a plan, all right. It involves getting rid of people who annoy me, like you, you prissy little bitch, coming here, preaching to us.'

'I thought it would be helpful, but I got it wrong. I'm sorry.'

'It's not that easy. My wife talked to you about things she shouldn't have. She showed that she couldn't be trusted. She was disloyal. As soon as she had the chance to betray me, she took it. Not. Acceptable.' He squeezed her neck hard as he said the last two words, and Diane made a tiny noise that was born of pure fear. There was a drizzling sound and I looked down to see a spreading pool of urine at her feet. Shepherd noticed it too. 'You disgust me, cunt,' he whispered in her ear. 'Can't keep control, can you? Pathetic. Just like your daughter. She got it from you, didn't she? Didn't she?'

Diane was sobbing openly now, her eyes still tightly closed, her face twisted with pain and terror so it was almost unrecognisable. I could taste the tension in the room; it was metallic, like blood. He was going to kill her. I could see it in his face.

'Where did you get the crossbow?' I blurted, trying desperately to draw his attention back to me. 'I can't imagine you had one lying around.'

He flicked a glance in my direction that contained nothing but loathing, but after a second he answered. 'Mate of mine from my gym had it. He bought it off the internet – he's into that kind of thing. I asked him if I could borrow it. We had tabloid reporters and paparazzi climbing into the garden, coming up to the windows, bothering us day in, day out. I told him I needed it to scare them off. Don't worry, Val, it's legal. Nice, isn't it?' He tilted it to show me, and I looked at the lethal mechanism of wires and metal and felt decidedly ill. From that range, even if he wasn't a good shot, we didn't stand a chance.

While Shepherd and I had been talking, Valerie had taken the opportunity to edge towards the back door. Now, two steps away from it, she made her move, whirling around and grabbing for the handle, fumbling desperately. I didn't see Michael Shepherd aim and I didn't hear him fire, but suddenly a narrow black rod protruded from between Valerie's shoulder blades and she pitched forward, falling through the door she had managed to open. From where I stood, I could only see her feet. She had fallen awkwardly, the toes of one foot pressed against the ground so her shoe had almost come off, the other foot twisted at an odd angle. I waited in an agony of suspense for her to move, for the shoe to fall off completely. Surely no one could bear to lie like that. But there was no movement at all.

I looked back to Michael Shepherd, who was staring at Valerie, a strange expression on his face. It was half pride, half awe at what he had achieved. 'One shot,' he said, and he let go of his wife, drawing the second bolt out of his belt and fitting it carefully into the crossbow.

'Mike, please.' Diane was crying so hard the words were distorted. 'Don't do this. You have to stop.'

It was as if he relaxed once he saw how easy it was to fire the bow – how easy it was to kill. He moved without haste but with complete focus. I don't think he even heard what she said to him. I felt panic start to build within me and tried to fight it back; it wouldn't help, whatever happened next.

Diane was trying again. 'You're only making things worse. Please, just stop.'

He looked up at that. 'Worse? How could I make things worse? How could they be worse than you and your daughter making a fool out of me? How could it be worse than you deliberately putting the blame on me for what happened? That would suit you, wouldn't it? If I went to prison, you'd be free, wouldn't you? You could go off and start a new life somewhere, and forget all about this.' He jabbed the bow in her direction. 'Well, it's not going to happen. I've told you that before. I said I'd kill you before I let you go, and I will. The only difference is that I'm going to enjoy it, because let me tell you, Diane, you're getting exactly what you deserve.'

She was hysterical now, shaking her head, far beyond words. I thought with desperation that the policeman outside had to hear her, but there was no sound of anyone coming through the front door. The world had shrunk to one room, a room that stank of hatred and misery and blood, and we might as well have been the last people on earth.

Having finished reloading, he drew her towards him and kissed the side of her head, burying his face in her hair. His eyes were closed and I wondered for a split second if now was my chance, if now was the only chance I would get, but I couldn't move. I slipped one hand behind me, sweeping over the counter in ever-wider circles, hoping for a miracle. My fingertips grazed something, pushing it further away and I reached after it, whatever it was, almost sobbing. He hadn't thought twice about ending Valerie's life. He would do the same to me.

Just wait, I told myself. *Wait it out.*

I reached again, my muscles straining, and my fingers touched cold metal.

'Oh my darling,' Michael Shepherd said, his words

muffled. 'I loved you so, so much. I would have died for you. And you threw it all away.' He gave Diane a little push, so she staggered a couple of paces in front of him. As soon as she'd got her balance, she turned slowly, dully, to face him. There was no fight left in her. Standing behind her, I couldn't see her face, but I could see Michael Shepherd's. Just for a moment, he looked stricken with sorrow and I thought, *He can't do it.*

He was a man of principle, though, a man capable of ending his own daughter's life because he was disappointed in her, a man who demanded total respect, and he could do it, and he did. I heard a thud this time, and Diane crumpled where she stood, without making a sound. Even as she was falling I was reaching behind my back again, stretching the last inch I needed to get hold of whatever was on the counter, and before her head finally hit the tiled floor I had shoved it into my back pocket. I had given myself an edge that Michael Shepherd didn't know about, but if I got it wrong, I would make things so much worse. I couldn't let myself think about that. The truth about what would happen to me was lying at my feet.

He had aimed for her face, and the bolt had gone through her right eye. It looked grotesque. Evil. I tore my eyes away after one appalled second and pressed a hand to my mouth, sure I would be sick, sure that I was next. The kitchen counter was digging into my back, and I was glad of the pain. It focused me. I was on my own now. No one was coming to the rescue. It was all up to me.

Michael Shepherd had been gazing down at his wife. Now he lifted the crossbow again and looked at it dispassionately before laying it to one side. 'No more bolts. I'll have to think of something else for you.'

'Why?' *Keep him talking, Sarah, spin it out . . .*

His brow furrowed. 'What do you mean? I can't have you going to the police and telling them everything.'

'The police know everything,' I said, my voice very calm. Weakness made him feel powerful. It was time to see how he coped with someone who wasn't afraid, even if I was shaking with terror. I hoped he couldn't tell. 'They've just been waiting for you to incriminate yourself. Two dead bodies in your kitchen – I'd say you've done enough to get yourself arrested.'

'They think Danny Keane murdered Jenny. You said so yourself.'

I laughed, looking around me. 'I think you've sort of proved that they were off track with that one. How are you going to pass this off as someone else's work?'

He shrugged. 'So what? Who cares? I'm not going to stick around for them to arrest me. I'm going to take care of you, and then I'm out of here.'

'I don't care if you escape or not. The only reason I came here was because I felt bad about Danny Keane – I felt responsible for what he did because he did it to impress me. Now that I know he didn't kill Jenny, I don't give a shit what happens. You don't need to kill me, Michael. You didn't really need to kill her.' I pointed down at his wife's body.

'She deserved everything she had coming to her.'

'Did Valerie?'

'She annoyed me,' he replied simply.

'Me too.' *Forgive me, Valerie, I don't mean it, but I have to stay alive somehow.* 'I probably wouldn't have killed her for it, though.'

Michael Shepherd looked at me and laughed, properly laughed. 'You are a cool customer, aren't you?'

'I've seen it all. Nothing can surprise me now.' I smiled at him and it felt like a grimace.

'Is that a fact?' He stretched and yawned, not bothering to cover his mouth, showing me a pink tongue and ice-white teeth. His neck bulged, the veins and tendons standing out on it like an anatomy drawing. He was hugely powerful and twice my size. I had to keep talking. I slid my hands into the back pockets of my jeans, trying to look relaxed, curling my hand around what I had hidden there.

'Look, I understand why you did it.'

'Really?' He looked at me narrowly, sceptical.

'Of course. Jenny really let you down. She had so many advantages.' I looked around admiringly. 'I mean, look at this place. You'd given her everything and she behaved as if it was nothing.'

He made a noise deep in his throat that sounded like agreement. I was feeling my way cautiously, trying to imagine how he could have justified what he'd done. The lies he'd told himself floated into my mind. Diane had given me the clues to how he thought. All I had to do was follow them. But it was a dangerous path.

'*I* understand,' I ploughed on, 'but a jury might not. You've got to get out of here before the police find out what you've done. You can get away – go into hiding or abroad or whatever – if you leave now. I'm on your side, Michael. I don't want you to have to suffer for other people's mistakes. They all deserved what they got, but you don't deserve prison. I'll stay here and pretend that everything is OK for a few hours – that should give you enough time to disappear.' Even as I said the words, anger rose up in my chest, solidifying into a hard, hot stone behind my breastbone that constricted my breathing.

He frowned. 'Why would you help me?'

'Let's just say I've seen a lot of unfair things in my life. Why shouldn't I help you? You're not like Danny Keane. You had good reasons to do what you did. In your position, I hope I'd have the courage to do the same.'

For a second I thought I'd gone too far, that he wouldn't begin to believe me, but I had been right to think that Michael Shepherd believed in his own infallibility. He nodded. 'OK. I'm ready to go. Just shut up for a second. I've got to think.'

I was thinking too. I was thinking that it would never occur to him that he'd made his daughter what she was. He'd robbed her of her self-esteem. He'd bullied her into submission. He'd created a hunger in her for love and approval that Danny had seen and used. It was Michael Shepherd's fault, all of it, and the knowledge was bitter in my mouth.

'I could tie you up and leave you here. I don't trust you not to call for help, but you can't do much if you're tied up, can you?'

I shook my head.

'I need something to tie you up with. And a gag.' He

half turned away from me, one hand rubbing his head, and in that split second that he wasn't thinking about me, I pushed off the counter towards him. In the same moment, I brought up the scissors I had palmed off the counter, and plunged the blades into the side of his throat, twisting them before I pulled them out. I don't think he saw me move, or knew what had happened until the spray of hot, red blood exploded from him, and one hand went to his throat. It was catastrophic, what I had done to him, and the blood pulsed out of him in fat gouts, saturating his shirt so that it went from khaki to shiny black. I had stepped back smartly, not fast enough to stay out of range of the initial spurt, but quickly enough that he hadn't had time to grab me. Not that he wanted to. All of his attention was focused on himself. He was trying to hold the blood in, pushing his hands against his neck as he moaned, but red seeped through his fingers and coursed down his arms, spattering on the white tiles. He sagged back against the cupboards and slid down onto one knee, his eyes wide, appalled. The blood started to pool around him and spread across the floor, running through the channels between the tiles. It was extraordinary how much of it there was, I thought, and found the echo for it almost immediately. *Yet who would have thought the old man to have had so much blood in him?* I had done what was right. It couldn't be undone any more than Jenny could be brought back to life.

'Please . . .'

I stepped back again, still holding the scissors, blood slick and sticky on my arm and in my hair. I looked into his eyes and I thought of all the different ways he had betrayed his family, and I thought of my own father and realised that in his own way he had betrayed me too, and my mother, who had taken so much with so little respect for me, and I was glad, glad that I had the chance to take it out on someone, glad that someone could suffer for all of the wrongs that had been done to me and around me, glad that it was him. Jenny had been a victim twice over. She could have expected him to defend her, not kill her.

At that moment, I hated them all, all the men who thought other people existed only to fulfil their needs. I hated Danny Keane and his evil father; I hated the faceless men who queued up to abuse innocent children. And I hated the man in front of me, the one who could stand in for all the rest, the only one I could reach. I stared into his eyes and I waited for him die and I didn't lift a finger to help him. It took just over a minute. Not long. It seemed long.

It was only when he slid down the last few inches to lie on the floor and his eyes went dull that I moved, setting the scissors down on the counter, leaving red smears on everything I touched. I turned on the kitchen tap and let the water run into my mouth, swishing it around and spitting it out, the taste of metal making me gag. *Here's the smell of the blood still . . .* I washed my hands, lathering up the soap, turning the suds pink with Michael Shepherd's blood. There was blood under my nails and I worked diligently to get it out. Once my hands were clean, I sat down at the kitchen table, suddenly exhausted. I took out my phone and stared at it. I needed to call Vickers. I needed to tell him what had happened, because I had to get myself out of this now. Before I called anyone – before anyone saw what I had done – I needed a story.

The next second, all thoughts of saving myself fled away. There was a noise from behind me and I knew without looking that I'd miscalculated badly.

When I turned around, Valerie was looking straight at me. She had managed to get into a sitting position, leaning up against one of the cupboards. The crossbow bolt was still sticking out of her back, but she was alive.

I stood up and went towards her and her eyes flared. I realised she was afraid – of me – so I stopped a couple of paces away from her.

'Jesus, Valerie. I thought you were dead. Are you OK?'

'I heard . . .' Valerie said, wheezing a little, ' . . . everything. You didn't have to kill him. He was going to . . . let you . . . go.'

'You don't know that.' I was starting to shake.

'I heard him.' Her eyes were cold. 'I'm going to . . . tell them . . . what you did. You . . . murdered . . . him.'

I looked down at her and I hated her, really hated her.

'So what? Do you really think anyone will care? Do you really think he didn't deserve to die? I did the world a favour, you stupid cow.'

Instead of answering, she lifted her hand to show me the mobile phone she was holding. Her own. And the screen was lit up. 'Did you hear that, sir? . . . At the Shepherds' house. Yes . . . An ambulance, yes. I'll be . . . I'll be OK.'

She disconnected and let the phone fall to the floor

with a clatter, as if it was too heavy for her. 'Even if he did . . . deserve it . . . it wasn't up to you . . . to decide.'

I turned away from her then, and I sat at the table, hands flat in front of me, and didn't speak to her again. I was learning something now that I should have known already. I hadn't ever dreamed that I could get exactly what I wanted, and see it crumble to dust in my hands.

There were noises from the front of the house, the policeman's radio chattering as he pounded on the front door, then shouldered his way in. I was peripherally aware of other uniformed officers filling the kitchen, bending over the bodies, of the paramedics who were working on Valerie and stopped briefly to ask if I was injured too. I shook my head. I just wanted to be left alone. The room was dark with people and filled with noise and I wished they would all go away.

When Blake came, I heard his voice before I saw him, and looked up to see him pushing past another officer, his eyes on me, his face distraught. He crouched beside me and brushed my hair back from my face. 'I thought I'd lost you. I thought you were gone too. Are you OK? Did he hurt you?'

I sat there, frozen, unable to speak as he held me in his arms. He seemed to be oblivious to the curious looks we were getting from the police and paramedics around us.

'What happened? Whatever it is, you can tell me. It's OK, Sarah. Everything's going to be all right.'

He wouldn't want me, once he knew. That was the choice I had made. That was what I was going to have to live with.

Over his shoulder, I saw Vickers. He took in the scene at a glance and stepped around Diane Shepherd's body, then bent down to speak to Valerie. They had got her on to a stretcher by now, and were about to carry her out to the ambulance. I couldn't hear their conversation, but when Vickers straightened up, his face was grim.

'Andy,' he said, touching Blake's shoulder. 'Go and make sure Val is all right, please. Find out which hospital they're going to. I want to have a word with Sarah.'

I could see that Blake wanted to say no and I managed to smile at him a little, and whisper, 'Go on.'

He went at that, and I watched him walk out, and felt that my heart would break, knowing that she would tell him, knowing what he would think.

After a second, I looked up at Vickers. 'He wasn't with you, then. He didn't hear what you heard.'

The inspector shook his head. 'I called him and told him to meet me here. He'll find out, though.'

I looked away. 'Right.'

'Sarah, listen to me,' Vickers said, pulling out a chair and sitting down. He leaned over and grabbed my hands, speaking to me in a voice too low for anyone else to hear. 'Just listen. You're a vulnerable young woman.'

I laughed. 'Tell that to Michael Shepherd.'

He squeezed my hands hard and I looked at him, surprised. His face was serious and there was an urgent note in his voice. 'You're half the size of Michael Shepherd. He'd shot Valerie, killed his wife in front of you, and confessed to killing his daughter. Isn't that right?'

'Yes.'

'You were afraid for your life.'

'Yes.'

'He threatened to kill you.'

'Yes.'

'Then he attacked you.'

I looked at Vickers, and I knew he wanted me to lie.

'You had no choice but to fight back. You managed to get hold of a pair of scissors and you struck out blindly.'

I nodded.

'When he fell back, you didn't know what to do. You were in shock and confused. He died before you had a chance to think of getting help. You washed your hands. While that was happening, Valerie recovered enough to call me. I sent units over here to make sure that you were safe, and they found you in a state of shock. It was only when I arrived that you felt safe enough to tell me what happened. Will you remember all of that?'

'Valerie –'

'Forget about her,' Vickers said heavily. 'She'll do as I ask.'

'It doesn't matter,' I said, and the despair in my voice shocked even me. '*He*'ll know. And he'll never forgive me.'

'Andy? What makes you say that? He'll understand, Sarah. Of all people, Andy will understand. He'd have done it himself if you'd come to any harm.' He spoke even more quietly, and the words were like a silver thread running through the darkness that threatened to engulf me. 'Live your life, Sarah. Walk away from this, and live your life.'

I wanted to believe it was possible, I really did, but I

knew better. 'It doesn't work that way, Inspector. There's always a price to pay.'

But I couldn't help hoping that I was wrong. I couldn't help thinking, even as I said it, that I'd paid enough. Surely by now I'd paid enough.

The house is empty. The furniture is gone: sold, given to charity, taken to the dump. The carpets have been ripped out; only floorboards remain. The walls are bare, with shadowy outlines where pictures once hung. I walk around one last time, checking that nothing has been forgotten. The rooms seem bigger, the ceilings higher. There's nothing to disturb the stillness. There are no ghosts in my house – not anymore.

I walk down the stairs, one hand on the banister. My steps echo. In the kitchen, the silence is absolute. The dripping tap has been fixed at last. The clock is gone. The fridge has been switched off.

There's a noise from the front of the house and I go back to the empty hall. He is standing there, looking at the cardboard box in the middle of the floor.

'Is this everything?'

I nod. 'That's it.'

He crouches down and lifts up the flaps to look inside it. A few photographs. Some books. A child's cup and a plate with a strawberry motif.

'You travel light, don't you?'

I smile at him, thinking that I'm bringing plenty with me, one way or another, and he sees me smile, and he knows exactly why.

'Come here,' he says, and I go, fitting into his arms as if I was made to be there. He kisses the top of my head. 'I'll carry the box out to the car. Let me know when you're ready.'

I watch him leave, then wander into the empty living room and out again. I don't know what I'm looking for. I have everything I need.

I go outside, and I shut the door behind me for the last time. I walk away and I don't look back.

Acknowledgements

I owe thanks to many people who helped, knowingly or unknowingly, in the writing of this book.

Frank Casey, Alison Casey, Philippa Charles and Kerry Holland were always encouraging; without them progress would have been much, much slower. I owe them all a great deal. *Go raibh míle maith agaibh go léir.*

Anne Marie Ryan is a wonderfully gifted editor and friend, and was razor sharp in seeing what needed to be cut from the first draft.

Rachel Petty not only found a hole in the plot but suggested the perfect solution immediately, thereby heading off a nervous breakdown on my part.

My wonderful agent, Simon Trewin, has made all the difference; he is indefatigable and always entertaining. His assistant Ariella Feiner is equally brilliant, and her enthusiasm set me on this path; I will always be grateful. I am also tremendously grateful to Jessica Craig and Lettie Ransley, and everyone at United Agents for their hard work on my behalf.

Gillian Green is the perfect editor – understanding, helpful and encouraging – and has brought this book to life. She and Justine Taylor have done a superb job of picking up the mistakes, infelicities and inconsistencies that I managed to introduce; any that remain are my fault entirely. I feel very lucky to be published by Ebury Press and would like to thank all of those who have brought their dedication and professionalism to the task of publishing my book.

Lastly, I would like to thank my partners in crime, my cat Fred and my husband James. Fred has been my constant companion in the writing of this book. He never quite managed to delete the entire novel on one of his frequent forays across the keyboard, but he has typed some entertaining comments now and then.

Without James none of this would be possible; I can't begin to list the many ways in which he contributed. He has my thanks, and my heart.

Ebury Press Fiction Footnotes

An interview with Jane Casey

What was the inspiration for *The Missing*?

I was interested by the idea of exploring what happens to a family in the aftermath of a terrible crime, particularly when there's no proper resolution. I've always felt that the uncertainty, the strain of wondering about what has happened to a loved one, would be infinitely worse than knowing the truth. Also, I'm fascinated by the fact that very dark secrets can be hidden behind outwardly civilised facades. From that starting point, I found myself wondering what would happen if someone who had been damaged by such a traumatic childhood – someone like Sarah – was caught up in a murder investigation. What would happen if you put someone like that under tremendous pressure? How would they act? The plot came together from there.

The Missing is a brilliant novel of psychological suspense with lots of unexpected twists. Did you know how it would all end when you started out? Are you a planner when it comes to your writing?

From the very start I knew what was going to happen at the end, and how Sarah was going to act in the final scene – everything else in the plot was focused on building up to that point. I did plan it out in some detail, but there were definitely a few surprises once I started writing! Not everything went according to the original plan . . .

The book is set mostly on a housing estate and in a school in Surrey – are either based on real places?
They aren't specific places – I've played fast and loose with the geography of Surrey, in fact, as anyone who knows it will spot immediately! It's a very beautiful part of England with a great wealth of woodland and open spaces. The commuter towns tend to have fragmented communities where people don't necessarily know their neighbours well – the perfect place for crimes to be hidden away.

You're married to a criminal barrister. Does his job come in useful for your research?
It's extremely useful to have an expert in the criminal justice system at my beck and call, though I sometimes wonder what people make of the conversations we have in restaurants! As a lawyer, he wants everything to be accurate; as a writer, I want everything to be dramatic. We generally manage to agree in the end.

Which classic novel have you always meant to read and never got round to it?
I've come to terms with the fact that I may never read Proust. I sort of feel I should, but the motivation is lacking. And I was utterly defeated by *The Scarlet Letter* by Nathaniel Hawthorne. It isn't even particularly long . . .

What are your top five books of all time?
Bleak House by Charles Dickens, *The Secret History* by Donna Tartt, *Gaudy Night* by Dorothy L. Sayers, *Madame,*

Will You Talk? by Mary Stewart and the *Pax Britannica* trilogy by Jan Morris.

What book are you currently reading?
The Moonstone by Wilkie Collins, a phenomenal mystery with one of the first great detective characters to appear in fiction, Sergeant Cuff.

Do you have a favourite time of day to write? A favourite place?
I write in the mornings when it's quiet – usually between six and eight o'clock – and I often end up writing at the kitchen table. But I have written at all times of the day and night and in lots of strange places: trains, airports, cafes, in the garden, in bed, on the sofa while trying to find somewhere for the cat to sit that isn't actually on my laptop . . . anywhere and everywhere.

Which fictional character would you most like to meet?
Captain Wentworth from *Persuasion* by Jane Austen.

Who, in your opinion, is the greatest writer of all time?
For the combination of intricate plotting, unforgettable characters, superb descriptions and his ability to define the era in which he was writing, I have to choose Dickens.

Other than writing, what other jobs or professions have you undertaken or considered?
I never seriously wanted to do anything but write or work with books, and I've been lucky enough to do both. I did

consider being a lawyer, a diplomat or a psychologist at various times, but publishing won out in the end. My worst ever job was being a sales assistant in the Christmas-tree section of a big Dublin department store. The Christmas music started in September, the customers were grumpy, and I was always covered in glitter by the end of the day, which got me some very odd looks on the bus. It took me a long time to recover my love for the festive season.

What are you working on at the moment?
Currently, I'm working on my second crime novel, this time featuring a serial killer. I'm juggling two first-person narratives in this one – it's a lot of fun!

THE BURNING
JANE CASEY

A serial killer who wants to watch you burn . . .

The media call him The Burning Man, a brutal murderer who has beaten four young women to death, before setting their bodies ablaze in secluded areas of London's parks. And now the fifth victim has been found . . .

Maeve Kerrigan is an ambitious detective constable, keen to make her mark on the murder task force. Her male colleagues believe Maeve's empathy makes her weak, but the more she learns about the latest victim, Rebecca Haworth, from her grieving friends and family, the more determined Maeve becomes to bring her murderer to justice.

But how do you catch a killer no one has seen? And when so much of the evidence they leave behind has gone up in smoke?

**Introducing Maeve Kerrigan, Jane's new
Anglo-Irish detective:**

'The number of convincing police officers in crime fiction is a tiny squad but Maeve has the potential to be one of the few female members' *Daily Telegraph*

'Astute, complex, layered – and very twisted. You'll remember this one for a long time' *Lee Child*

THE RECKONING
Jane Casey

To the public, he's a hero: a killer who targets convicted paedophiles. Two men are dead already – tortured to death.

Even the police don't regard the cases as a priority. Most feel that two dead paedophiles is a step in the right direction.

But to DC Maeve Kerrigan, no one should be allowed to take the law into their own hands. Young and inexperienced, Kerrigan wants to believe that murder is murder no matter what the sins of the victim. Only, as the killer's violence begins to escalate, she is forced to confront exactly how far she's prepared to go to ensure justice is served . . .

Shortlisted for the *Irish Crime Novel of the Year*

'Stands out from the pack as both a twisty, well-crafted mystery and as a humanistic portrait of an ambitious professional with a strong moral centre. The series could almost be subtitled "Jane Tennison: The Early Years' *Irish Times*

'Compulsive, menacing and moving – a very satisfying psychological thriller' *Sophie Hannah*